FEATHERED
SERPENT

FEATHERED SERPENT

A NOVEL OF THE MEXICAN CONQUEST

COLIN FALCONER

THREE RIVERS PRESS

NEW YORK

Published by Three Rivers Press, New York, New York.
Member of the Crown Publishing Group, a division of Random House, Inc.
www.randomhouse.com

THREE RIVERS PRESS and the Tugboat design are registered trademarks of Random House, Inc.

Originally published in hardcover in the United States by Crown Publishers, a division of Random House, Inc., in 2002, and simultaneously in Great Britain by Hodder & Stoughton, London.

Printed in the United States of America

Design by Lauren Dong

Library of Congress Cataloging-in-Publication Data
Falconer, Colin, 1953–
Feathered serpent: a novel of the Mexican conquest / by Colin Falconer.—1st ed.
1. Mexico—History—Conquest, 1519–1540—Fiction.
2. Spaniards—Mexico—Fiction. 3. Toltecs—Fiction. I. Title.
PR6056.A537 F35 2002
823'.914—dc21   2002024711

ISBN 1-4000-4957-1

10 9 8 7 6 5 4 3 2 1

First Paperback Edition

For Helen, who was my guide and lover.

Acknowledgments

MY THANKS TO Angela Volknant in Munich, who first edited this project and gave it life; to Miriam Martinez and Beatriz Bustamante in Mexico City, for their kindness and hospitality and their enthusiasm for my Malinali; and special thanks to Diana Mackay at Curtis Brown in London, who twisted my arm and persuaded me I should write this. Your foresight has found me readers all over the world. Thank you. Thanks also to Kate Cooper, at the same agency, for her endless enthusiasm and assistance for my work. My gratitude also to Jane Gelfman at Gelfman Schneider, who decided that the States was ready for me and found Aztec its home in New York. You are wonderful. Thanks to Tim Curnow, my agent in Australia, the best mate a writer could ever have. And, finally, a thank you to Rachel Kahan, my editor in New York, who said she might like to take a look at the manuscript and then bought it. What more could a man ask for?

Preface

THE STRANGEST PART of this story is that it is not a work of fiction. I have not strayed from the actual historical facts of the Mexican conquest; I have merely interpreted the motivations and characters of the participants.

I have tried to keep faith with the known characters of those *conquistadores* such as Cortés and Alvarado and others who took part in the enterprise. The woman Malinali did exist, and her actions and motivations are still a matter of passionate debate in Mexico. However, almost nothing is known about the personal history of this most extraordinary woman before the Spanish insurgency.

At the time of the Spanish conquest, the ruling tribe of the Mexican valley called themselves the Culhua-Mexica. The term *Aztec* did not come into common usage until the nineteenth century.

MEXICO CITY, OCTOBER 2000

FEATHERED
SERPENT

MALINALI

I AM AN old, old woman, dressed in the rags of an Indian, and I will walk the streets of the city tonight, crying for my lost children: the dirty streets, the ancient streets, the streets of the homeless and the dispossessed. I stumble across the great square, near the ruins of the temple, shouting at the ghosts who haunt me.

See me shuffle along the arcades of the plaza, keeping close to the shadows, where the great cathedral leans like a drunken Indian, its old stones sinking into the lake that lies beneath our feet. Hear me crying at night among the stranded ruins of the *Templo Mayor,* now the gringos with their Nikons and video cameras are gone.

On República de Cuba, it is dark, and the tourists are shut away in their expensive hotels on the *paseo* and do not venture to these dark lanes and courts. A frightened Indian hears me weeping, and making the sign of the cross, he hurries home across the plaza with an eye cast fearfully over his shoulder for me, *La Llorona,* the weeping woman of Mexico.

I have reason to weep for what I have done, and what was done to me. And if you venture with me a little way, into this darkened Catholic doorway that smells of age and piss, if you can bear to sit this close to an old Indian woman, wrinkled like a monkey and smelling of death, I will tell you my story, the only story Mexico has.

PART I

FEATHERED
SERPENT

When the time has come, I will return into

your midst, by the eastern sea,

together with white and bearded men. . . .

—PROCLAMATION TO THE TOLTEC PEOPLE
BY THEIR GOD-KING, FEATHERED SERPENT,
CIRCA A.D. 1000

MALINALI

Painali, Tabasco, 1513

I STARE INTO the darkness, listening to the sounds of my own funeral.

It is the Eighth Watch of the Night, when ghosts walk and headless demons pursue lonely travelers on the roads. I am trussed on the floor of my mother's food store. Wicker baskets of vanilla pods are stacked against the adobe walls, and the room is filled with their sweet, cloying smell.

A screech owl twists its great head and watches me from its perch on the carved cedar beam above my head. Its yellow eyes blink slowly. An omen: the owl is envoy from the Lord of Darkness, Mictlantecuhtli, *come to lead me into the underworld.*

And my mother is to send me from this world without even my fare through the Narrow Passage.

I try again to wriggle free, but the thongs around my wrists and ankles bite deeper into my skin. I am weeping now, and my body shakes uncontrollably.

My mother wants me dead.

I close my eyes and listen to the dirge sounds, the bass boom of the conches, the hollow thrum of the huehuetl *drums, the shriek of whistles. I can hear someone shouting my name, then the crackle of flames: another is blackening and shriveling on the pyre in my place.*

The moan of the East Wind to console me. At this moment of my great danger, Feathered Serpent, Lord of Wisdom, is watching over me.

I hear whispers and footsteps outside the hut. My eyes blink open and search the shadows.

There is the sudden flare of a pine torch as they enter. I know them: slave merchants from Xicallanco. They have visited Painali many times; my father had always treated them with disdain. One of them is without an eye, and the flesh is smeared pink around the old scar like cold grease.

The torches throw their faces into shadow. "Here she is," the one-eyed man says.

The gag is making me choke. One of the men laughs at my struggles, but One Eye hisses at him to be quiet. But there is no need for stealth. They could all be drunk and screaming on peyotl *juice, but no one would hear them over the sound of the funeral drums.*

They lift me easily between them and carry me out of the hut into the darkness. The wind moans again, Feathered Serpent growling in anger.

I must not be frightened. This is not the end my father prophesied for me. I am Ce Malinali, One Grass of Penance; I will find my destiny in disaster; I am the drum that beats the sunset for Motecuhzoma; my future is with the gods.

My future is with Feathered Serpent.

1

Tenochtitlán

One Reed on the Ancient Aztec Calendar, The Year of Our Lord 1519

THE OWL MAN staggered, white froth on his lips, laughing at the shadows hiding in the corners of the Dark House of the Cord. His hair, which reached almost to his waist, was matted with dried blood, and the black mantle around his shoulders gave him the appearance of a hunched and malevolent crow.

Motecuhzoma, the Angry Lord, Revered Speaker of the Mexica, watched, the turquoise plugs in the piercings of his ears and lips reflecting the glow of the pine torches. He whispered his questions to Woman Snake at his elbow.

Woman Snake repeated the questions carefully. "Owl Bringer, can you see through the mists to the future of the Mexica?"

The owl man lay on his back on the floor, laughing hysterically, helpless to the grip of the peyote liquor. "Tenochtitlán is in flames!" he shouted.

Motecuhzoma shifted uneasily on the low, carved throne.

The owl man sat up, pointing with crazed eyes toward the stone wall. "A wooden tower that walks to the temple of Yopico!"

"A tower cannot walk," Motecuhzoma hissed.

"The gods have fled . . . to the forest."

Motecuhzoma wrung his hands in his lap. He whispered another question to Woman Snake. "What do you see of Motecuhzoma?"

"I see the Angry Lord burning and no one to mourn him. The Mexica spit on his body!"

Woman Snake stiffened at this heresy. Even under the intoxication of *peyotl*, the obscenity echoed around the cavernous room like thunder. "What other portents?" he asked.

"There are great temples on the lake...marching toward Tenochtitlán!"

"A temple cannot march."

"The Feathered Serpent returns!" The owl man was breathing fast now, his chest heaving, gasping out words between paroxysms of laughter. "There will be a Tenochtitlán no longer!"

Motecuhzoma rose to his feet, his face contorted into a grimace. "Our cities are destroyed...our bodies are piled in heaps..." Woman Snake saw the emperor put both hands to his face.

"Soon we will see the portents in the sky!"

The owl man was on his hands and knees, crawling toward the throne. He collapsed. There was saliva smeared on his cheek. His eyes were like obsidian. "Turn and see what is about to befall the Mexica!"

Motecuhzoma was silent a long time, his face still hidden in his hands. When he removed them, Woman Snake dared a surreptitious glance at his emperor and saw that he was weeping.

"Wait until the effects of the *peyotl* have worn off," Motecuhzoma growled, "then skin him."

He strode from the chamber. Owl Bringer lay on the floor, ignorant of his fate, lost to his wild and fevered dreams, laughing at shadows.

Near the Grijalva River

Hernán Cortés steadied himself on the rail of the *Santa María de la Concepción*, sailing close-hauled, the coast of Yucatán no more than a grease-green border on the port horizon. He sniffed at the taint of tropic vegetation on the salt air. The canvas cracked like grapeshot in the yards above his head, his personal banner whipping from the mast: a red cross on black velvet, below it a Latin inscription in royal blue, the same words that had once graced Constantine's own ensign:

BROTHERS, LET US FOLLOW THE CROSS,
AND BY OUR FAITH SHALL WE CONQUER!

A long way, all this, from the flat and melancholy horizons of Extremadura. And was this not what he had always dreamed of? Here, sailing toward an alien land in uncharted waters, and yet it was as if he were coming home. This wind was his wind, carrying him to his destiny. He knew it as surely as there was a God in heaven.

He looked down at the main deck, at Benítez and Jaramillo hunched in conversation: poor *hidalgos* like himself, men with education and breeding but no inheritance. They had come to the Indies, as he had, to find their fortunes and escape the boredom and poverty of Castile and Extremadura, to free themselves from the petty tyrannies of the grandees and the harping of the priests. They had all rushed to join him in Cuba, these soldiers of fortune, these bored planters, these failed gold miners, looking for plunder and for profit. And he would give it to them, and more besides. It would be an adventure in the old style, with fame and riches and service to the Lord.

This was his hour, and a good day to be alive.

☀   ☀

Gonzalo Norte wanted only to die.

He retched again, spitting green bile into the ocean. Who would believe he had spent eleven of his thirty-three years as a sailor? The last time he had stood on the heaving deck of a ship was eight years ago, in another lifetime. He had forgotten this pitching misery, these stinking holds, this rolling sea.

But it was not the oily pitching of the *nao* that made him wish for death. It was a sickness of another kind, a sickness of the soul. He dared a glance and saw his new companions watching him with their vicious eyes. They feared and hated him, of course. He was a plague carrier, incubus of a contagion worse than any black-blistered pestilence known on this fever coast. A few of them spat in his direction as they passed him on the deck.

I am alone, he thought. I will be alone for the rest of my life.

He felt an arm go around his shoulders. Aguilar! His one friend on this boat, and the pity of it was, he did not have the strength to throttle the bastard.

"Is it not good to be among Christians again, Gonzalo?" Aguilar used the Chontal Maya tongue, for Norte had forgotten all but a few words of his native Castilian.

"Good? For you, perhaps, Jerónimo."

Aguilar had donned the brown habit of a deacon. Only his shaved head and tobacco-dark skin betrayed the fact that a few days ago he was the slave of a Mayan *cacique*. He clutched his crumbling Book of Hours, the anthology of prayers that had been his constant companion through his captivity in Yucatán. "You must leave that other life behind," Aguilar said. "Pray for forgiveness and it shall be given you. You succumbed to the Devil, but you may still be saved."

By Satan's hairy ass, Norte thought. If this constant retching had not robbed me of the power in my arms, I would pitch him over the side and let God enjoy his company in heaven with the other saints. Does he not understand that I have no soul left to save? They have wrenched it from me, like a priest tearing out a heart. Why doesn't he just leave me alone?

"It is not a sin that my faith is stronger," Aguilar went on. "Our Lord is boundless in mercy. Confess your sins and you may start your life anew."

"Just leave me alone," Norte said. "For pity's sake, just leave me alone."

And he retched again.

✳　✳

Julián Benítez felt his stomach rebel as he watched the two men. Only Norte truly disgusted him; Aguilar was merely insufferable, like most churchmen. The two men—Norte was a crew member, Aguilar a passenger, a deacon who had just taken minor orders— had been shipwrecked on the way from Darién to Española eight years ago. They and seventeen others escaped the wreck in a longboat, but most died of thirst long before they reached the coast of Yucatán. Perhaps they were the lucky ones. The survivors were captured by the Mayan Indians, and the captain, Valdivia, and several others were murdered. Only Aguilar and Norte had escaped.

After a few days they were captured again, by a Mayan *cacique* who proved a little more amenable than their first captor. He had even offered Aguilar his own daughter as a wife. As Aguilar told the story, he spent a whole night lying naked beside her in a village hut but had saved himself from the sins of the flesh by taking refuge in his tattered copy of the Book of Hours.

Norte had not proved as resilient, and thus far Benítez was in sympathy with him. He understood Norte's carnality far better than Aguilar's self-imposed chastity. What he did not understand was Norte's later actions: how he could marry a heathen woman and have two children by her, how he could have his ears and lower lip pierced and his face and hands tattooed like a *natural*. In doing so, he had deserted his faith and his birthright and had joined them in their savagery. The man was no better than a dog.

When Jaramillo and the rest of the landing party found Norte on Cozumel Island, he had even tried to run away. Jaramillo would have murdered him with the rest of the *naturales* if it had not been for Aguilar's timely intervention. It was the deacon who had persuaded them that Norte was a Spaniard like themselves.

A Spaniard perhaps, Benítez thought. But not like any of us.

Jaramillo followed the direction of Benítez's gaze. "Cortés should have hanged him," he muttered.

"They could roast me over a small fire, I would never allow myself to be so humiliated."

"When I found him, he had stone plugs through his nose. And look at how his earlobes are torn. Aguilar said that such things are part of the devil worship in their temples."

"Have you noticed?" Benítez said. "He even stinks like an Indian."

"I should have slit his throat on the beach and to hell with it."

"Still, Cortés says we need him and Aguilar to help us talk with the *naturales*."

"Aguilar perhaps, but not him. How do we know what he will say to them?" Jaramillo spat into the sea. "Aguilar says they sacrifice children in their temples. Afterward they eat the flesh."

Benítez shook his head. "I am no lover of priests, but pray God we can bring salvation to these dark lands."

Jaramillo grinned. "Pray God also that we are well rewarded for doing Him such service."

※ ※

Alaminos, the pilot, turned the fleet toward the river mouth. The previous year he had been with Grijalva when they had beached in this spot, and the natives, who called themselves Tabascans, had shown themselves friendly. It was why Cortés planned to make this his first port of call. The men gathered at the rails and watched the coastline resolve into a flat horizon of palms and sand dunes. A New World waiting, with dreams of gold and women and glory.

 2

Potonchán, on the Grijalva River

A CLUSTER OF adobe huts, thatched with palm leaves, surrounded by a timber stockade.

The villagers had gathered on the riverbank, waving spears and arrows, many dressed in quilted cotton armor. Some jumped into war canoes and paddled out to midstream to block the way ahead. From inside the stockade, they heard the beating of war drums and the strident clamor of horns.

Benítez watched Cortés. He wondered what sort of commander he would prove to be. Beneath the beard his lips were thin as a blade. He saw no fear on that proud face, only contempt.

"They do not seem disposed to treat as kindly with us as they did with Grijalva," Benítez said.

Cortés grunted. "We come here in peace. And they shall be like-wise peaceful. Even if I have to kill them to persuade them to it." He broke suddenly from his stillness. Two small guns, falconets, had been drawn up to the starboard side, facing the settlement. "Prepare your powder!" he shouted. "Ordaz, get ready to lower the boats! Aguilar, Norte, come with me!"

Ululating war cries echoed along the river. Benítez shuddered. Unlike some of the others, he was no soldier. He had come to the Indies to build a plantation. He hoped his own body would not beat him to the earth.

✳ ✳

They stood in the longboats, swords drawn, while the clerk Diego Godoy, dressed in elegant black suit and silver-buckled shoes, read the people of the Tabasco River the *Requerimiento* in its original Latin, Aguilar translating. Benítez fidgeted, sweating in his armor: a mail shirt, breastplate, and gorget. If it came to a battle, it would be his first. He prayed he would not show himself to be a coward. Fear of a painful death, fear of a wound, fear of showing fear itself—all these concerns competed for his attention while he tried to concentrate on the words that the royal notary was reading from the scroll.

Aguilar could not make his translation heard above the drums and the war cries.

The Indians had now approached to within a few yards in their war canoes, brandishing spears and leather shields, their bodies smeared with black-and-white grease.

Benítez silently recited a prayer to the Virgin.

"They are painted for war," Jaramillo said.

Cortés seemed utterly calm, one hand on his hip, the other resting on the hilt of his sword. Benítez felt a surge of admiration for him. "You said the *naturales* on this river greeted you with friendship when you last came here," he was saying to Jaramillo.

"They played flutes and danced for us on the beach. Something has apparently aggravated them since then."

Godoy had stopped reading, deciding his efforts were futile.

"Continue with it," Cortés snapped.

Godoy did as he was commanded.

The *Requerimiento* was a document prepared by the Church to be read in all new lands before their possession in the name of the pope and the king of Spain. It began with a short history of Christendom up to the moment God gave Saint Peter the care of all mankind. It then stated that Peter's designated successor was the pope and explained that the pope had granted the islands and continents of the ocean to the king of Spain. The inhabitants of these lands should therefore submit to Cortés, as the legal representative of Charles V. If they submitted, they would be treated well and reap the benefits of Christianity; if not, they would be considered to be in rebellion and would suffer the consequences.

"This is foolish," Norte said in Castilian.

A pulse swelled in Cortés's temple. "Ah, so our renegade has rediscovered the language of civilized men. You think God's law is foolish, Norte?"

"These people do not understand a word of what you are telling them. They have never heard of the pope. It is ludicrous."

"I rejoice in the fact that you have learned to speak like a Spanish gentleman once more. But it is also a pity that you use our great language only to spout heresy."

"Is it heresy to argue for what is reasonable and just? But I suppose this elaborate charade is a sop to your conscience."

"Perhaps one day soon I will see you hanging from a tree, Norte, and my conscience will still be clear."

Godoy finished the *Requerimiento*. The noise of the drums and the ululations of the Indians were deafening now. Two arrows were fired at their longboat from the bank, falling short in the water. Aguilar turned and looked to Cortés for further instructions.

He looked utterly composed, as if the Indians who swarmed around them were no more than a cloud of bothersome mosquitoes. His armor glinted in the sun. The plume that surmounted his steel helmet danced in the breeze.

Benítez tried to imitate his stance, fighting down his terror. Keep still, he told himself. Do not let your companions see you are afraid.

"Tell them that we come as friends," Cortés said, "and that we are only interested in obtaining food and water and establishing cordial relations with them once more."

Aguilar began translating at once, adding his shouts to the din around them.

"Tell them that we have no wish to cause them harm and that as Castilians we are here to do only good," Cortés added.

Another volley of arrows sang from the bank and landed in the river just short of their boat. "By my conscience, if they persist with this violence, the fault for what follows is theirs! Tell them, Aguilar, that they must become peaceable or commend their souls to God!"

"We cannot battle so many," Norte said.

"What does a sailor and a renegade know about military matters?"

"There are thousands of them and just a handful of us."

"If the handful of men are Spaniards, then the odds are always in their favor."

A hissing in the air, and a barrage of stones rained down, launched with slingshots from the bank. Some splashed harmlessly into the water; others clattered onto raised shields and steel armor. But a few found their mark. Benítez heard a man screaming in one of the other longboats.

"Enough!" Cortés shouted. There was a rasp of steel as he unsheathed his sword and raised it toward the brigantine, his signal to fire the cannons.

The falconets were discharged together, the heavy shot hissing across the river to explode with a crack among the mangroves. Leaves and tree limbs rained on the twitching bodies of those Indians unfortunate enough to be caught in the path of destruction. The effect was dramatic. A thousand voices cried out in terror and dismay, and the Indians fled in waves from the riverbank.

Cortés leaped into the muddy and thigh-deep water. *"¡Santiago y cierra España!"*

The soldiers splashed into the water, following him toward the bank. Benítez joined them, carried along in the moment.

✳ ✳

He remembered little afterward of that first battle in the river. Fear made him light-headed; he rushed toward a clutch of brown and painted bodies, almost deafened by the war cries of these *naturales,* the booming of their drums, the shrieking of their whistles.

The Indians, recovered now from their initial fright, had begun swarming back to the river. There were just too many of them. It was impossible to think they could win against such a horde.

I'm going to die here in this muddy brown river.

He was scarcely aware of what he was doing. He slashed wildly with his sword, and an Indian screamed and fell at his feet. The water already churned with fallen bodies and was stained to the color of rust.

Benítez flailed again at another brown body, leaving his guard open. He gasped as he saw a spear thrust toward his chest. But the obsidian blade shattered on his steel breastplate.

He thrust his sword toward his attacker, stumbled on a body underfoot, and fell. He scrambled desperately in the mud, choking on the river water as he tried to regain his feet. He looked up and saw one of the Tabascans standing over him, holding a stone ax. His steel helmet was gone, lost in the water, and there was nothing he could do to protect himself.

But instead of delivering the coup, the warrior grabbed his hair and began dragging him toward the bank. Benítez tried to shift his sword to his left hand and thrust upward. Before he could make the stroke, he saw Cortés splashing toward him, saw him pierce his captor's body with his blade. The man screamed and released him, staggered sideways, clutching at the split in his belly.

Cortés dragged Benítez to his feet.

"*¡Santiago!*" he shouted.

Indeed. Saint James must be with me today, Benítez thought. I should be dead by now. Why did the *natural* not kill me when he had his chance?

 3

BENÍTEZ LEANED ON his sword, dragging breath into fiery lungs, sweat and watery blood from a head wound stinging his eyes. He had survived his first battle. He took comfort in his own performance: he had shown no particular valor, he was sure, but he had proved himself a man. Yet he took no satisfaction in the slaughter;

there was no great pleasure to be had from killing another man, even a heathen. If this was soldiering, then he had no love for it.

He sank to his knees, clutching the hilt of his sword, and said a whispered prayer of thanks to the Virgin. When he closed his eyes, he could see the big Indian standing over him in the river, the stone ax raised above his head. He swallowed back the vomit in his throat.

✳ ✳

Cortés strode toward the ceiba tree that stood in the center of the village. He held his helmet under his left arm, his long, dark hair falling loose around his shoulders. His face was flushed from the battle, but his eyes glittered with excitement. He sensed the same enthusiasm in the men around him. This rabble like nothing better than a scrap, he thought, as long as losses are light.

He made three broad slashes in the bark of the tree with his sword and shouted, "I take possession of this town in the name of His Majesty King Charles of Spain."

Diego Godoy faithfully recorded the moment.

A handful of captured Indians were prodded forward by their guards, their hands roped behind their backs. During the battle Benítez had glimpsed only a blur of feathered headdresses, half-naked bodies, and painted faces. Now he had the opportunity to study his enemy a little more closely. They were mostly bow-legged, and all sported neat loin- and hipcloths. Several others had richly embroidered cloaks, knotted at the shoulder. Many had red tattoos on their faces and bodies, and the flesh of their earlobes had been mutilated.

Like Norte.

"Tell them they have nothing to fear," Cortés announced to Aguilar, who relayed this to the Indians. They received this information stoically and, it seemed to Benítez, with little enthusiasm.

"Inform them that we have been sent by a great king from across the ocean and we have many interesting things to tell their chiefs. Assure them also that we mean them no harm and want only to take on fresh water and provisions for our journey."

Aguilar relayed this to the captives, who exchanged puzzled looks among themselves but said nothing. Alvarado led them away, and Cortés turned to Benítez.

"Post guards around the town. We will camp here tonight and wait for the *naturales* to return. Now we have given them a taste of our steel, they may be in a mood to parley with us."

There was an uneasy silence as the import of Cortés's words sank home. It was León who finally spoke. "My uncle gave strict orders that we were not to sleep ashore."

Benítez saw the look Cortés gave him. It struck him then for the first time: We think we know this man who calls himself our commander, but I wonder if we know him at all.

"Who is the commander here?" Cortés said.

León, a large man with a great black beard and thundering voice, would not be intimidated. "We are under the governor's instruction."

"And under my command!" Cortés shouted. He thrust his sword into the dirt, where it trembled. "If any man wants to challenge my authority, we shall see to it now!"

By Satan's ass, Benítez thought. He means it.

No one spoke. They had left Cuba under the governor's orders. But they were a long way from Cuba now. Cortés looked around, wondered if any of them would challenge him. Not this time, apparently.

"It is settled, then," he said. "We camp here." He sheathed his sword and strode away.

✹   ✹

"There's nothing here," Jaramillo said. He spat in the dirt. "No gold, no silver. Not even a woman."

As they walked through the dusty streets, a few hairless dogs yapped at their heels. Jaramillo and several others amused themselves by skewering them on their swords.

The village was deserted. Benítez wandered into several of the houses. They were simple affairs, the walls made of adobe, the roofs of thatch built low against the sun and rain. There were no doors in the entranceways, and none of the houses had furniture; the beds were just bundles of dry sticks and grass covered with cotton mats. Each dwelling boasted a small shrine in one of the dark corners housing a crude statuette surrounded by small offerings of food.

He looked closer. Demons, shaped out of pieces of red clay. He shuddered.

But they were nothing compared to what they found on top of the pyramid.

✳ ✳

The pyramid was immense, perhaps as high as the courthouse in Sevilla, by Benítez's estimation. It had been constructed of massive stone blocks and towered over the mud-brick houses of the village. Stone dragons and serpents stood sentinel in the courtyard, and strange glyphs had been carved in the stones. It was evidence of a culture far more sophisticated than the one they had imagined.

"Have we found China?" Benítez murmured.

Jaramillo shrugged his shoulders, as bewildered as he.

They followed Cortés up to the summit. It was a steep ascent, and they rested for a moment at the top to catch their breath before stepping into the shrine. Like the houses in the village, it, too, had been constructed of adobe and thatch.

It was dank inside and smelled of the jungle and of death. For a moment they were blind as they waited for their eyes to grow accustomed to the darkness.

Then Benítez heard Jaramillo's voice. "Holy Mary, Mother of God."

A snake was draped across the altar, its length coiled around a marble jaguar. Behind it a stone monster with great goggle eyes and fangs watched them from its nest. The *naturales* had painted it blue.

"It is *Tlaloc,* the Rain Maker," Norte whispered. He sounded almost reverent.

"It is the Devil," Cortés said. He slashed with his sword at the snake on the altar, deftly removing its head with one blow and flicking the body into the musty darkness. He stepped closer to examine the stone jaguar. A bowl had been carved onto its back, and there was a viscous liquid pooled at the bottom. He dipped his fingers into the bowl, sniffed them. Suddenly he hurled the idol onto the floor as if it were ordure. He rounded on Norte.

"What is this?" He was trembling with rage.

Norte was silent.

Jaramillo had meanwhile discovered new offerings on the stone flags below *Tlaloc*'s grinning mask: a small fig tree, some embroidered cloth, the skulls and bones of four dead *naturales*.

"It is human sacrifice," Aguilar said, his voice hoarse. "They believe it will make the rains come and nourish the fields."

Cortés kept his eyes on Norte. He held up his fingers, still wet with blood from the stone receptacle. "The Devil's works," he said, and dried his fingers on Norte's shirt.

"Thanks be to God we are here to lead them to the true faith," Aguilar said.

"How are these infernal sacrifices made?" Cortés demanded.

Aguilar hesitated. "They cut out their victims' hearts while they are yet alive," he whispered, "and offer the blood to their gods. Then they feast on the limbs. It is the fate of all prisoners of war. It should have been our fate, if we had not prevailed."

Some of the soldiers had followed them inside, and they now stood silently at the entrance, staring at the pile of rotting bones. The euphoria of their victory dissipated as they contemplated what had almost been their fate: what might still be their destiny.

Alvarado broke the moment, bursting in from outside. He was panting hard from his ascent of the temple steps. "There is nothing in this whole town worth my spit! They have taken everything!" He stopped, looked around. "What in God's name is this?"

"We have stumbled on a nest of cannibals," Cortés said.

"God's blood." Alvarado turned to Norte. "These savages are your former comrades?"

Norte met Alvarado's stare. Benítez wondered what was going on inside the man's head. Had he participated in any of these rites? Had he eaten human flesh with his adopted tribe? Jaramillo was right, they should have finished him on the beach. Let him die unshriven. It would have been a just fate for such a man.

Aguilar broke the tension. "Let us pray we can lead these people to the one and true faith," he said, and he fell to his knees. Cortés did the same.

Benítez, Alvarado, and Jaramillo could not do otherwise. The soldiers followed suit and allowed Aguilar to lead them in prayer.

The moment they had finished, Benítez rushed outside to the sunlight and scampered back down the steps of that infernal temple, his gorge rising in his throat.

MALINALI

Acalán

SISTER MOON is dismembered, dark in her grave. Witches prowl the night, searching for lonely travelers. The night is clamorous with the ululations of the women, the pulsing of the drums and whistles, a keening hymn for the dead.

I sit, cross-legged, staring at my dead husband. He has been prepared for cremation in the traditional way, sitting upright, bound in a broad cloak of embroidered cloth. His brothers have replaced his entrails as best they could, and I myself have placed a piece of jade in his mouth to pay his fare across the Narrow Passage to the Yellow Beast.

I lean closer to my dead lord, Tiger Lip Plug, so that my lips are just inches from his face. "When you are a butterfly in the Rain Bringer's heaven, I hope you give more pleasure to the flowers than you gave to me."

They have told me my lord died well. He had almost claimed one of the white gods as his prisoner, dragging him by the hair through the shallows of the river, but then another of the Lords of Thunder had incomprehensibly interfered in the duel and struck him with his sword. Two of Tiger Lip Plug's own brothers had carried him back here to Acalán, where he has waited two days and nights in silent agony to kiss the earth. It was the sort of death Tiger Lip Plug would have chosen for himself, I believe. The gods had squeezed every drop of the divine liquor from him before accepting him into the ranks of dead warriors. Even now he resides in the green heaven of *Tlaloc*, the butterfly paradise where fountains bubble eternally and emerald birds skim the surface of the lakes.

I will not miss him.

The doorway to the street is closed off by a tapestry sewn with tiny gold bells. The bells murmur now as Rain Flower appears and kneels down on the mat beside me.

"What is happening, Little Sister?" I ask her.

"The *caciques* cannot decide if these Thunder Men are Persons or are gods. Our warriors claim that they must be gods, for their skin shines like the sun and is so hard, it makes their swords shatter in their hands. They say their canoes can conjure thunder from a clear sky."

"Of course, they are gods. They come from the east and capture the wind in the giant cloaks they hold above their canoes. They are the harbingers of Feathered Serpent returning to us."

"You cannot believe that foolish tale! These Thunder Men came here last year. At Champotón the people killed twenty of them. There they say they are men just as our warriors are men."

"Feathered Serpent is served by moles and dwarfs, as mortal as you or I. Any number of them may die, but Feathered Serpent himself is indestructible. This is his year, the year of his legend."

A pine torch burning on the wall throws my friend's face in shadow. She cannot accept what is so plain to me. I fear for her.

"They are just a few hundred ordinary men against thousands," she whispers, "and tomorrow their hearts will roast in the temple."

Let Rain Flower believe what she wishes. In my heart I know the truth. I have dreamed of this day since I was a child. I still remember my father's promise, that *Quetzalcóatl*, Feathered Serpent, would return on a raft from the east and rescue us from the Mexica. He had whispered another, even more vital secret: he saw through future mist and divined that I, Ce Malinali Tenepal, would be harbinger of these golden days.

My destiny is camped at Potonchán tonight.

Painali, 1506

I remember when my father first told me the legend of Feathered Serpent.

Painali is silent, deserted except for a few slaves sweeping the courts and priests glimpsed occasionally at the shrine of one of the pyramid temples.

The plaza only comes alive on market days or holy days; no one lives in the sacred heart of our town. The noblemen, even priests like my father, use their town houses only when there is a need.

My father drops a lump of copal incense into a burner and starts to pray, facing east, toward the wind, toward Feathered Serpent.

His god was Feathered Serpent, the East God, God of the Wind. His temple was rounded, unlike our pyramids, so that sharp angles could not impede the wind's progress and the wind would flow around them.

After he finishes his prayers, my father sets to work divining the future, the very reason we have come here today.

The secrets of prophecy and divination owe as much to astronomy as to the visions conjured by peyotl *juice. With his almanacs and bright-colored calendar wheels, my father can predict the movement of the stars and sun; the secrets of time itself can be unlocked by mathematical calculation. The future and the past exist on a circle, a wheel: all that has happened before will happen exactly that way again.*

As he makes his calculations, long columns of dots and markings in a codex that I find incomprehensible, he starts to tell me the story of Feathered Serpent.

"Quetzalcóatl is not the greatest or most powerful of the gods, but he is the most beautiful and said to be almost human. He is tall with fair skin, and he has a beard. In his last incarnation, he was the priest-king of a city called Tollán, the capital of an ancient race

called the Toltecs. They were a people of great learning and culture, and Feathered Serpent was their greatest lord. He was very wise and so gentle he would not kill any living creature or even pick a flower from the ground. He taught his people the art of healing and how to watch the stars move around the sky. Raw cotton grew in all colors in their fields, and they harvested ears of corn so fat a man could not fit his arms around them. The people spent all their time playing music and listening to birds.

"But Feathered Serpent had a rival, Tezcatlipoca, the god they call Smoking Mirror. He was jealous of Feathered Serpent's popularity. So one night he tricked him into getting drunk and fornicating with his own sister. The next morning Feathered Serpent was filled with remorse. He went to the shores of the eastern sea and threw himself on a fire. The ashes rose like a flock of white birds, carrying his heart to Serpent Skirt, Mother of All the Gods. Then he stepped whole from the fire, wove a raft from a thousand snakes, and sailed into the dawn. He promised that one day he would return to bring back the paradise that vanished with his departure.

"These Mexica who come here and call themselves our lords sit on the throne of the Toltecs; they live on their land and have taken their temples for themselves. They want us to believe they are from the Toltecs, but they are impostors, and the whole world knows it."

"Feathered Serpent's capital, this Tollán. Where is it now?"

"It lies to the north of Tenochtitlán, they say. But it is just a ruin. Cholula is Feathered Serpent's city now."

"Cholula?"

"It is a holy city, consecrated to Feathered Serpent. Tens of thousands make the pilgrimage there every year. I have been there many times."

"I would like to see Feathered Serpent when he returns," I say, and I see from the look on his face that he finds my child's excitement neither ridiculous nor blasphemous.

"You will see him, Malinali," he says. "You will be right there at his side."

4

Potonchán, 1519

CORTÉS HAD THE bodies of the dead Indians burned and the stone image of Rain Bringer removed from the temple. It took a dozen men to drag it to the edge of the pyramid. They used their pikes and lances as levers and toppled it over the side of the platform and down the steps, sent it crashing into the courtyard below, where it shattered into pieces. In its place Fray Olmedo erected a wooden cross and nailed a picture of Cortés's own icon, *Nuestra Señora de los Remedios,* to the adobe walls.

Cortés set up his headquarters inside the shrine and waited for an answer from the *naturales* to his offers of peace.

✳ ✳

Bright sun, intense heat, the buzzing of flies. Cortés ducked his head as he entered the temple. A wooden table had been transported from the *Santa María de la Concepción,* and he took his place behind it, settling himself into the heavy mahogany chair he had brought with him from Cuba.

His officers clustered around the table, eager for his decision. Cortés sensed the tension among them. They were afraid. They did not yet trust him enough, did not have faith in their divine mission, as he had faith.

He looked around: there was Puertocarrero, golden-haired and aristocratic, but no fighter; the impetuous Alvarado, with his red hair and russet, arrow-shaped beard, gold chain glinting against his black quilted doublet; dour young Sandoval, the horseman; the old warhorse Ordaz; the fiery young León, a *Velazquista* like Ordaz and a troublemaker; Jaramillo, with his vicious hawk's face and pock-marked skin; and finally Benítez, with his ugly, lopsided features and scrap of beard.

Sweat glistened on all their faces.

Cortés solemnly spread the ink-drawn map of the coast on the table in front of them. It had been made by Grijalva the previous year. "Gentlemen, as yet we have received no word from the *natu-rales* as to their intentions, so let us examine our choices. We can return to our ships and explore further the coast to the north. However, it is my opinion that if we are seen to be running away from the Indians, as Grijalva did last year at Champotón, we will only make them bolder, and it will be doubly hard to enforce our will the next time we land. We could wait here for the Tabascans to approach us. Or finally, we can move against them before they have the chance to strengthen their forces. Gentlemen, I will be guided by you."

He gave them a tight smile and sat back in his chair.

"We should leave here at once," León growled. "The actions we have taken are contrary to the governor's—my uncle's—orders."

"I agree," Ordaz said. "We do not have the men or supplies to conduct a full-scale land campaign against the Indians. We are heavily outnumbered. Look what happened to Grijalva last year."

"I say we attack these bastards now," Alvarado shouted. "We have given them enough time to find their manners! It does not matter how many of them there are: one Spaniard is worth a hundred Indians!"

"I agree with Alvarado," Jaramillo said.

"But we have no just cause to prosecute a war against these people," Benítez interrupted. "They believed they were defending their village against attack, no matter how misguided they might be. Let us move up the coast and look for a friendlier reception elsewhere."

"Where they will laugh at us for being women," Sandoval said.

Suddenly they were all speaking at once, and Cortés held up a hand to silence them. "So we are evenly divided," he said. He was disappointed with Benítez. After the fire he had shown in the river skirmish, he had expected more from him. In his mind he marked him as a potential troublemaker, like León and Ordaz. "I shall give the deciding vote to Alonso." He looked at Puertocarrero. "What say you?"

"I say we heed the advice of our commander," Puertocarrero said, softly.

Cortés smiled. As if the boy would say anything else. "Very well." He returned his attention to the map. "In my view we should proceed inland along this route until we make contact with the *naturales*. If they wish to trade and furnish us with provisions, we shall be pleased to greet them. If they wish for further punishment, we shall accommodate them in that also."

"I question who will take the greatest punishment," Ordaz growled.

"There is no need to fear the *naturales*," Cortés said. "We have learned important lessons from our recent encounter with them. We were outnumbered, perhaps as much as ten to one, and though many of us received wounds, our losses were slight. The *naturales* employ some manner of brittle glass for their swords and lances, and it breaks easily against a steel buckler or breastplate. Their shields are made of leather or wood, which is no hindrance to good Toledo steel. Furthermore, I have been questioning Brother Aguilar and the renegade, Norte, at length, about the Indian ways. It appears that their greatest honor in battle is not to kill but to capture, so the prisoner may be used in their infernal sacrifices." He glanced at Benítez. "Such a tactic works to our great benefit, does it not?"

Benítez had turned pale. He nodded. "Indeed, my lord."

"This appears to be the reason why so many of them were eager to throw themselves on the point of our swords." He looked around the table. "It seems to me that as long as we do not grow fatigued from killing them, our eventual victory is assured."

"Even so," Ordaz objected, "there must come a point when the odds are so great that we cannot kill them as quickly as need demands. The *naturales* must at this very moment be gathering a much greater army."

"Perhaps. But if two falconets fired into a swamp can make them scatter, imagine their reaction when we employ a full battery of cannons against their ranks. And," he paused and smiled, a gambler laying his final trump card, "they have yet to witness a warhorse in full charge."

✺ ✺

After his officers had left, Cortés leaned back in his chair and stared at his flagship, now framed by the temple entrance against the glittering waters of the bay. One day they will write ballads of me, he thought. I will be remembered in the same breath as Alexander or the Cid. In Cuba he was just another poor planter, a minion of Velázquez, the governor, but here he would become that other man, the man he dreamed himself to be.

Ceutla

Ordaz advanced the infantry through the fields of maize, his progress hampered by the network of irrigation channels and drainage ditches. On the other side of the valley were several thousand *naturales,* the plumes of their headdresses dancing in the wind like ears of corn. Benítez watched from their hiding place in the trees. The tumult of their whistles and drums carried to him on the wind.

Dear God, let me live to see the sunset.

Cortés turned in the saddle to address them. They were just sixteen, all the cavalry Cortés had. Yet he rode his horse, one hand on the reins, the other on his hip, like a duke at the head of thousands. *Does nothing terrify this man?*

"This day belongs to us, gentlemen," he shouted. "We shall wait for the moment before we charge." His chestnut mare tossed its plumed head, nostrils flared against the scents in the air, dust and fear. "Remember to aim your lances high, at their eyes, so they cannot easily pull you from your mount. And fear for nothing, for today we do God's work!"

On the plain the *naturales* had launched themselves at Ordaz's infantry. Benítez saw the sun flashing on steel armor, then a rolling cloud of flame and smoke as the culverins fired their first volley.

It was as if the Indians' front ranks had been swept away by an invisible scythe. The *naturales* hesitated only a moment, the survivors throwing great clouds of grass and red dust into the air in an attempt to cover their losses. A second squadron charged. Then a third. Still they came on. Some of them reached the Spanish lines, hundreds upon hundreds of brown bodies swarming forward over the piles of their dead.

Benítez fidgeted in the saddle, his nose wrinkled against the rank scent of the leather strappings, the grease from his armor, the sweat from his horse. His mouth was dry as bone. It was as he had always suspected: at heart he was a coward.

Cortés sat quite still in his wooden saddle, watching.

Ordaz and his men began to retreat, stumbling back through the ditches and bogs.

Cortés suddenly rose in the stirrups. *"¡Santiago y cierra España!* For Saint James and for Spain!"

They started to gallop forward.

✳   ✳

The *naturales* had not heard them over the din of cannon fire and their own drums and whistles. The main body of their army had their backs to them: they would be taken completely by surprise. But then Benítez realized with lurching horror that Cortés had not calculated well: their approach would take them directly toward the gridwork of irrigation ditches. His horse stumbled in one of the drains, and he saw other mounts around him rear up, their riders almost thrown from the saddle.

Benítez spurred on his own piebald mare. If their attack failed now, they would all die.

He remembered the bones in the temple at Potonchán . . .

Now he was on hard ground again, galloping fast. A cry went up, was taken up by other Indians until it echoed around the valley in one ululating shriek of terror. The *naturales* in front of him dropped their clubs and spears and ran. Benítez charged his horse among them.

At the finish of his charge, he turned, expecting to see the rest of the cavalry beside him. But there was no one. He was quite alone. The others were still mired in the mud.

Benítez shouted, this time in panic, but instinctively spurred his horse on to charge again. First a dozen, then a hundred, then thousands, they ran from him, like a ripple spreading from a stone dropped in the still surface of a lake. A cheer went up from Ordaz's beleaguered infantrymen.

He wheeled his horse around, charged again, his blood drumming in his ears. He pursued the great army of Indians like a dog after sheep.

Finally the rest of the *jinetas* arrived, and the retreat turned into
a rout. Benítez reined in, tasting the whirlwind of dust in his mouth.
He threw back his head to shout defiance at the blue sky, proclaim-
ing his victory, his joy, his relief, his disbelief, that he had dared so
much and survived.

✸ ✸

Norte wandered the battlefield, sickened to his soul. Such a wreckage of limbs, heaving and bloody mounds of meat still moaning with
pain, trying to crawl away. The Spaniards stood among them, still in
their armor, grinning and shouting and clapping one another on the
back. Thanks to Cortés they had achieved the impossible.

And yet Norte wished it had been otherwise. He had secretly
hoped the Indians would prevail, even though it would have meant
his own certain death. He was confident now that he could endure
his own end: it was the humiliation and despair of living that were
unendurable.

"Everything was lost," he heard one of the soldiers, Guzmán, saying. "Then I saw him. He came out of the dust on a white horse.
When the *naturales* saw him, they fled!"

"Who?" Flores asked him.

"*¡Santiago!* Saint James! I saw him there on the field for just a
moment, and then he vanished, into the dust. Disappeared!"

Stupid, Norte thought. The Spaniards were as stupid and as
superstitious as the *naturales*. "It was Benítez," he said.

Guzmán and Flores stared at him.

"What you saw was not Santiago. It was Benítez!"

"Do you smell something?" Guzmán said to Flores.

Flores turned his head to the wind. "Savages. I thought we killed
them all."

Guzmán leaned over one of the dead Indians and cut off an ear.
He tossed it at Norte's feet. "Breakfast," he said.

5

Potonchán

THERE WERE FOUR war canoes, garlanded with flowers and sitting low in the water. As they drew up to the bank, the Spaniards crowded around, laughing raucously, shouting and nudging one another with their elbows, behaving like schoolboys.

Cortés came down to the riverbank to greet the deputation, accompanied by Aguilar in his brown Franciscan habit. The *naturales* had sued for peace after the battle at Ceutla, and he had demanded a token of their goodwill. The spoils of his victory were in the canoes.

The *cacique* greeted Cortés in the traditional way, first dropping to his knees, then putting his fingers to the ground and touching them to his lips.

"He asks you to accept these small tokens of their friendship," Aguilar said, translating from the chief's Chontal Maya. "He also begs your indulgence for their foolishness in attacking you."

Cortés regally inclined his head. But his attention was not on the *cacique*. He was more concerned with what the delegation had brought with them in their canoes. In line with his demands, there was a certain amount of gold, some disappointingly small figurines worked in the shape of birds, lizards, and small animals. There were also some precious stones, earrings, and a pair of gold sandals, all of which the *cacique*'s slaves laid out on mats on the ground.

Cortés examined these objects. The pickings were not as rich as he had hoped, but he was surprised at the craftsmanship. From what he had seen so far, these people were not as primitive as Grijalva had believed.

He turned to Aguilar. "Ask him where the gold comes from."

Aguilar translated the query. "He says the mines are far inland. In a place called Mexico."

"Does this Mexico have much gold?"

"He says the king of the Mexica is the wealthiest sovereign in the whole world," Aguilar said.

Cortés took a moment to digest this piece of information, hoping not to betray his eagerness. "Does this king have a name?"

Aguilar asked the question several times, checking his pronunciation. "Motecuhzoma," he said finally. "His name is Motecuhzoma."

Their conversation was interrupted by a harsh bark of laughter from the river. He looked up angrily. The Indians had brought women in one of the canoes. They were being lifted ashore by the *cacique*'s slaves, and the Spaniards had moved in for a closer inspection. Jaramillo nudged Alvarado's ribs and made some ribald comment. More laughter.

Cortés's mouth twisted in contempt. Dogs! Even Alvarado with his fine manners and his coat of arms. At heart they were all dogs! None of them understood what it meant to be a knight in the service of a great king.

"The women are the most beautiful in all of Acalán," Aguilar translated for the *cacique*, who had noticed Cortés's interest. "He says he puts them at your service, to grind maize for you, mend your clothes, and..." Aguilar paused, and his cheeks flushed. "...and to perform any other services you desire."

There were twenty women in all. They were dressed in the Mayan custom: plain white tunics and cotton skirts, almost to their ankles, and held at the waist by an embroidered belt. Their ears, wrists, and ankles glittered with gold, their hair decorated with brilliant green quetzal feathers and pink flamingo plumes. But the gold trinkets and pretty plumes could not disguise the fact that most of them were squat and plain. Several were even cross-eyed—a mark of great beauty among the Mayan Indians, Aguilar whispered to him.

Really? Cortés thought. I see little there to get excited over.

And then he saw her.

She was no slave girl, that much showed in her bearing. Unlike the other girls, her tunic was richly embroidered at the neck and hem and was decorated with a design of reeds. She was unusually tall for a *natural*. The high cheekbones and aquiline nose lent her features an expression of arrogance that intrigued him. Instead of demurely studying the ground like the others, she stared straight back at him, her black eyes both a challenge and an invitation.

He felt the beast move in him. A delicious creature, his for the taking in other circumstances.

The *cacique* murmured something to Aguilar.

"He says her name is Ce Malinali Tenepal. Her first name is for the day of her birth. The first day of the twelfth month. It means One Grass of Penance. Tenepal is . . . well, it is a name you give to someone who likes to talk a lot."

Finally she lowered her eyes in submission. She had to be aware that he was still watching her. But she did not seem at all discomfited and did not giggle and chatter like the other women.

"The chief says she is very skilled with herbs and is a great healer," Aguilar said, but there was an edge to his voice that Cortés did not like. He looked around at the deacon, whose face was dark with silent accusation. These tiresome men of God.

"Thank him kindly for his gifts," Cortés murmured.

The *cacique*'s tone became more urgent. "He asks that you do not burn the town," Aguilar translated. "That is how the victors generally behave in this heathen country," he added.

"It is how victors behave almost everywhere. But you may assure the chief we do not intend any harm to him or his village. In return for our beneficence, he must renounce his false idols and the practice of human sacrifice. He will instead give obeisance to our Lord Jesus Christ."

There was a long and animated discussion. Finally Aguilar said, "I do not think he quite understands everything. I will instruct him further."

"Good. I leave the responsibility for their salvation to you and Father Olmedo."

Cortés returned his gaze to the women.

"My Lord."

"Yes, Aguilar?"

The deacon's face was still flushed. He stammered, unable to form the right words.

"What is it?" Cortés snapped.

"The women. The men must not . . . any form of . . . commerce . . . between a Christian gentleman and a . . . is forbidden by the Church . . ."

"I am aware of what the Church proscribes. You shall assist Father Olmedo in the morning. They will all be baptized into the true faith then."

Aguilar seemed appeased. "Thank you."

Cortés turned away and found the girl staring at him again. He saw something in her face, for just a moment. What was it? Curiosity? Fear? No, something else, impossible to define. She lowered her eyes again, but slowly. He felt a slow tingling, at the nape of his neck. Something had just happened. He was not sure what it was.

MALINALI

A GOD!

He has corn silk hair and blue eyes, and his skin is pale, almost pink. The *cacique* had ordered us to keep our eyes lowered, so as not to offend the Lords of Thunder, but I have to look, I cannot help myself.

As we women gather in the shade of a ceiba tree, the strange creatures cluster around us.

There, another god!

He is taller than the others, with a beard shaped like an arrowhead; but it is his hair that I find most startling. It is the color of fire, the color of the sun, which flashes on the gold medal at his neck and the gold rings on his fingers.

Everything here is dazzling, frightening, fascinating. Over there a dog, but unlike any dog I have ever known——a great, red-eyed, slavering creature with terrible teeth, a monster plucked from the realms of *Mictlantecuhtli,* a beast like that which guards the gates to the underworld. I try not to show it my fear, even as I hear the other girls shriek and draw away from it. The god with the fire-colored hair laughs raucously at their discomfort.

The ground thunders beneath my feet. I turn around, and

now I see for myself one of the great two-headed monsters that so unnerved and defeated our warriors. But I can see at once that the beast does not have two heads after all: the reality is far more astounding. For even as I watch, I see one of the gods dismount from the creature, which is as tall as a house and has feet of stone. It is breathing smoke. It seems the gods can sit astride these beasts and make them do their bidding. How is such a thing possible?

Out there on the river is the great canoe they speak of, flying a banner with the red cross of Feathered Serpent. There can be no doubt. The day has finally come.

"Look," I whisper to Rain Flower.

"I see it, Little Mother."

"I told you! It has happened!"

But still I cannot see *him*. I know he is not the god with the corn silk hair and turquoise eyes or the fire-haired one . . . not any of these other bearded, pink-faced creatures, many of them with faces pitted like lava stone, others with . . .

There!

For a moment it is hard to breathe. He is just as I have imagined him, as I saw him on the pyramid at Cholula, as he has been depicted a thousand times on statues and carvings and reliefs in temple walls: a dark beard, black hair falling to his shoulders, his face framed by his helmet, which is itself decorated with a quetzal-green plume. The gray eyes watch me intently, as if he, too, has experienced this same moment of recognition.

And now he approaches.

 6

THE GIRL FELL to her knees, touched the earth with her fingers, then brought them to her lips. Cortés returned the greeting, bowing and presenting her with the slightest smile.

"My lord *Quetzalcóatl,*" the girl said, in her own language. And then, in Chontal Maya, "Feathered Serpent."

Cortés turned to Aguilar. "What did she say?"

Aguilar stared at her. To Cortés's mind, he appeared suddenly flustered. "Just a traditional greeting," he said. But his eyes stayed on the girl long after Cortés had moved on to greet the others, and instinctively Malinali knew she had found an enemy.

MALINALI

THEY HAVE ERECTED a large wooden cross in the shade of two palm trees, and below it, hung from a nail on one of the trees, is a picture of a mother suckling a baby. It is clear to me what ceremony we are about to undertake. All Persons know that the cross is a symbol of fertility, and the painting on the tree makes it quite clear to us what they want.

The gods wish to mate with us.

I know I should be frightened. I heard the other girls whispering last night, wondering about our fate. Rain Flower said that the gods' penises had claws, which were as sharp as obsidian, and we would all die a terrible death, too horrible to contemplate. Another girl said that the gods' seed would not grow into a Person but into a jaguar, and when the time came for birthing, it would tear its way out of our womb with its teeth.

But they are just stupid Tabascan girls; even Rain Flower does not know what she is talking about. How could she?

The one called Brother Aguilar has tried to explain to us what is going to happen. But his words were difficult for me to follow. He talks in florid circles and intricate riddles.

Now, as we step out of the canoes, all these Lords of Thunder line the beach on either side of us. I feel the heat coming from them. Their eyes drink us in.

The pulse in my temple pounds with excitement, making me light-headed. I wish my father were here to witness this sublime moment.

Fray Olmedo and Brother Aguilar wait under the palms on either side of the cross. Feathered Serpent stands to one side. Behind him is the god with the astonishing turquoise eyes, Puertocarrero, and next to him the fire-god. It is silent save for the sound of the wind stirring the palm fronds and the whip of the banners flying from the pennons. The wind is from the east, as no doubt *he* has commanded.

Many of the Thunder Lords are wearing their armor. The sun reflects on the steel, hurting my eyes.

When I reach the cross, Aguilar orders me to kneel on the sand. Fray Olmedo stands over me, holding a small censer filled with water. He says something to me in a language I do not understand. I stare at him, mystified by these strange sounds.

"Say yes," Aguilar says to me, in Chontal Maya.

I do as he says.

Again Fray Olmedo makes these strange sounds, and again Brother Aguilar tells me how to respond. He then nods at Fray Olmedo, who sprinkles my hair with water and speaks quickly in this strange new language. Aguilar puts a hand on my shoulder. "You are saved, thanks be to God. Your new name is Doña Marina. Go in peace."

 7

TWENTY WOMEN: NOT enough for all the officers he had with him. The girls waited patiently under the ceiba tree, as they were baptized by Fray Olmedo and Brother Aguilar. Aguilar made each of them kneel in front of the cross, and Fray Olmedo asked them: "Do you renounce the Devil and all his works?"

Aguilar mumbled something to them in their devil's tongue and then nodded to Olmedo.

"Do you accept Jesus as your Savior and his Father, the Lord our God, as the one and only true God?"

Again, Aguilar whispered to them and gave his assent to the friar.

When the baptisms were completed, the men watched Cortés intently, wondering what he would do. He had proved to them his worth as a commander in battle; now he would have to demonstrate that he could be trusted with the spoils.

One by one he took the women by the hand and led them to one of his officers; he included potential troublemakers such as Ordaz and León in the division of the bounty yet did not forget staunch supporters such as Jaramillo and Sandoval. The less important officers such as Morla and Lugo and de Grado received the girls who were cross-eyed. There was much joking about this. Jaramillo advised them to put sugar bags over the girls' heads when they mounted them.

The resulting laughter offended Cortés, but he said nothing.

Next he wondered about Benítez. A good horseman, who had proved himself one of his most valiant at Ceutla. Yet in Cuba he had the reputation of a firebrand. A potential ally if handled properly, a thorn in the side otherwise.

There were three girls remaining, the three prettiest. Cortés chose for Benítez a tiny coffee-skinned girl with a hooked nose and bright, dark eyes, like a cat. She was pretty, but she had an arrogant tilt of her head that hinted at a fierce temper. There, that should keep him busy.

That left two, Malinali and one other, a young, heavy-breasted girl. Alvarado and Puertocarrero watched him, ready to be either pleased or affronted, depending on his choice. Would he exclude one of them for the benefit of himself?

He considered: Alvarado, reckless and loyal, and a good fighter; Puertocarrero, also loyal, but as he had shown in the river and at Ceutla, he had no taste for fighting. On the credit side of the ledger, he had excellent breeding and powerful friends at court.

He gave Alvarado the full-breasted girl and then returned his attention to Malinali. The bright black eyes looked up at him. Well, here was a thing: his ambition pitted against his desire. He felt a tide of anger at his predicament but promised himself that this would be a moment of deferment, not of loss.

He took her hand and led her across the sand to Puertocarrero. She seemed bewildered.

There, it was done. A murmur of approval among the men. Cortés had proved himself the perfect diplomat.

It was necessary, he told himself, turning quickly away so that the others could not see his bad grace. *There was nothing else I could do. But I will have her, finally, for there is something there that I must have.*

MALINALI

"HE SAYS HE will be gentle with you," Aguilar mumbles to me. He looks discomfited. I wonder if it is his intention to stay with me through the night to pass on my new husband's endearments as he penetrates me.

"Tell him I am a virgin," I say to Aguilar.

Aguilar seems both surprised and pleased with this news. "It is true? You still have your virtue?"

"No, but tell him anyway. He will appreciate it."

The candle gutters in the night breeze. These candles are a new wonder. The hot grease pools on the table, and shadows dance around the walls.

Aguilar clutches his Book of Hours to his chest. "He wants to know if there is anything you would like to ask him."

"I would like to know his name."

"His name is Alonso. Alonso Puertocarrero," Aguilar tells me. "He is a Spaniard and a Christian gentleman, of very good family."

I try this name on my tongue: *Alonso.* I repeat it several

times. The rest of Aguilar's gibberish, a stew of foreign and Mayan words, means nothing to me.

"Is there anything else you wish to know?" Aguilar repeats several times.

"Will you ask him for me if he's a god?"

Aguilar's cheeks flush to bronze. "There is only one God," he hisses at me. "We mortals are all born in sin. Alonso is a poor sinner like the rest of us."

Only one god. What nonsense. He must mean there is only one god among those here today, and by that he means, of course, Cortés.

Aguilar rises to leave. A strange man, a man of pale complexion and pungent sweats. "If he asks you to do any-thing ... unnatural ... you do not have to acquiesce."

This last utterance leaves me perplexed. Any matter con-cerning the cave of joy seems to unnerve this unlikely priest. "I shall gladly do whatever he asks me to do."

He hears this and flees from the hut.

8

AGUILAR STUMBLED AWAY through the darkness. These men— most men—were like beasts. Yet he needed these beasts if he was to do God's work in this dark and savage country.

He did not trust this Malinali. Some of the other Indian women—the fat ones, the homely round-faced ones, the ones with the unnaturally crossed eyes—well, if he tried, he could still imag-ine there was a soul in them needing salvation. But not this one; he saw the Devil behind those black and unfathomable eyes.

Nothing good would come of this. He was sure of it.

MALINALI

MY NEW AND violet-eyed husband sits down beside me on the sleeping mat of woven reeds. I study him more closely in the light of the candle. I reach out to touch the strange corn silk hair; his beard is wiry, but the hair on his head is surprisingly soft to the touch.

"*Cara*," he whispers. I wonder why Feathered Serpent did not take me for himself. Perhaps it is as Rain Flower said: no mortal woman can conjugate with gods and live. Despite what I know, I am still a little frightened.

Perhaps he senses my fear. He lays me gently on my back, strokes my hair, murmurs words to me in his own language. I do not understand him, but the soft timbre of his voice is soothing.

His body is terrifying and fascinating, at once. He fumbles with the strange fastenings of his clothes. His torso is not smooth, as a Person's: his chest and belly and thighs are covered in curly golden hairs, finer than his beard. I am relieved that Rain Flower's most macabre predictions are incorrect: his *maquauhuitl* does not have claws. But it is very large when it is swollen like this, perhaps because the Spaniards themselves are so big…

There is a smell about him I do not like, but then the gods and their consorts are not known for the beauty of their aromas. I try to ignore it, as I do when I am in the temple.

My violet-eyed god takes his time, something Tiger Lip Plug had never done. He couples with me face-to-face and not from behind, as I am accustomed to. After the first moments of stretching, there is no real physical sensation. I am too frightened and overwhelmed by his presence to feel anything.

Very soon I feel him shudder and spill his seed inside me. From this moment I know my existence on this earth has changed irrevocably: the river of my life has ceased its gentle meandering and is now crashing headlong over cliffs toward the ocean, the ocean that brought Feathered Serpent.

9

Tenochtitlán

THE THREE MEN crawled across the room on their hands and knees. They were barefoot and wore simple white loincloths.

"Lord, my lord, my great lord," one of them murmured in a shrill and broken voice.

Motecuhzoma received them in his full splendor. His carmine cloak was made of coyote fur and quetzal feathers and had been embroidered with a border pattern of geometric eyes. A gold lip ornament in the shape of an eagle glinted on his lower lip, and earrings of turquoise glittered in his ears.

He regarded the men in front of him with an expression of distaste. He turned and whispered something to his prime minister, Woman Snake.

"Revered Speaker wishes to know what it is you have seen that brings you here to his palace."

There was a brief silence as the three fishermen waited, each hoping that one of his comrades would be the first to speak. Finally the eldest of them said, "We come from the village of Coatzacoalcos in Tehuantepec. Just four days ago, gigantic canoes without paddles appeared in our bay. They carried the wind with them, wrapped in cloth bundles, and bore great banners emblazoned with crosses of scarlet! The next day we saw creatures with thick beards and helmets of gold that gleamed in the sun. They came ashore and asked for fresh water and food. We gave them all we had, some turkeys and some maize. They stayed for two sunsets, then sailed away again on their canoes toward the lands of the east."

Motecuhzoma's expression would doubtless have terrified the three fishermen if they had dared look up at his face, which they were forbidden under pain of death to do. And so they waited there on their knees unaware of the effect their words had had on their emperor.

Motecuhzoma composed himself and whispered another question to Woman Snake.

FEATHERED SERPENT ✳ 43

"Did they leave you anything in return?" Woman Snake asked the fishermen.

One of the men crawled forward clutching a piece of hardtack. He left it on the marble at the foot of Motecuhzoma's throne. "They told us it was their food," he said.

At a nod from Motecuhzoma, Woman Snake retrieved the piece of bread and handed it to him. Motecuhzoma weighed it in his palm. The food of the gods was the weight and consistency of a piece of volcanic rock. He tentatively bit at the edge with his teeth but could not break it.

He again turned and whispered to his prime minister.

"Revered Speaker wishes to know if these creatures said anything else to you."

"They told us that we must cease making human sacrifices to the gods," the man mumbled, "or else they would return and punish us."

Motecuhzoma gasped. In the great vault of the audience chamber, it sounded like the hissing of a snake. There could be no mistake. Feathered Serpent had returned, as prophesied.

His fist closed around the piece of hardtack. He murmured his instructions in Woman Snake's ear.

"You are to wait in the courtyard for Revered Speaker's pleasure. You are to speak to no one of this, under pain of death."

Relieved that the audience was over, the men shuffled backward toward the door, never once turning their backs on the throne.

After they were gone, Motecuhzoma again turned to Woman Snake. "Give them to the priests for sacrifice," he said. "Word of this must not spread."

"It will be done," Woman Snake said.

Motecuhzoma returned his attention to the divine sustenance now clutched in his fist. "What do you think of this story?"

"They are just fishermen. How can we believe the tales of such simple people? Perhaps these strangers are not gods at all. They may be ambassadors from some far-off place."

"How can that be? Tenochtitlán is the center of the one world. There is nothing beyond the sea except heaven." Motecuhzoma shook his head. "It is *Quetzalcóatl,* Feathered Serpent. These men spoke of a red-painted cross, his banner. He has come from the east, where he last fled into the dawn, and he carries the wind, his wind, tied to his canoe. And he spoke of human sacrifice! How can it be other than him?"

Woman Snake did not answer.

I have been doomed ever since I took the throne, Motecuhzoma thought. Strange, but now the moment had come, he felt a sense of relief. There would be no more living in dread of the future. The future was here.

He stared at the piece of hardtack in his fist, then handed it to his prime minister. "Have this placed in a golden gourd. We shall remove it to the temple of Feathered Serpent in Tollán. Should he return for it, he must see that we have treated his property with all reverence."

"Yes, great lord."

After Woman Snake had left, Motecuhzoma sat alone in the great audience chamber. The knife of fear twisted in his heart and he threw back his head and gave a small cry, like a captured and wounded animal.

Potonchán

She threw back her head and gave a small cry, like a captured and wounded animal.

By Satan's hairy ass, Benítez thought. A virgin.

The act of bedding a savage both appalled and aroused him. He had heard sailors speak of coupling with animals after long months at sea, and once this would have seemed just as appalling. Yet he had to admit she was clean, and the smell of her, though strange, was not unpleasant. She was young—he guessed no more than sixteen— and the days when he could entertain notions of bedding any sixteen-year-old virgin were long gone. It occurred to him that many men might indeed think him fortunate. But memories of what he had seen in that terrible shrine would not leave him.

Outside the hut the devilish shrieks of the howler monkeys rent the night, an unlovely chorus from hell.

Despite his misgivings he took her gently, trying not to hurt her more than was necessary for a woman's first time. In the dancing candlelight, he could see that she had a lovely body. At first he was startled by the fact that she had no hair between her legs, but even that did not displease him as much as he supposed it might.

The moment came quickly to him, and he gasped aloud with pleasure.

When he looked down into her face, he saw her cheeks were wet with tears. Because he did not have her language, he could not discover if she was crying from pain or some other reason beyond his fathoming. Perhaps she wept for a mother or sister or chaste love left behind forever at Tabasco, and he allowed, with some surprise, that this creature in his arms might not be as wild or barbarous as he had assumed. He stroked her hair, murmured words of consolation she could not understand, suddenly awkward in his act of violation; beast and savage lay entwined, but far apart.

Tollán

The omens had begun to appear soon after Motecuhzoma ascended the throne. In time they had become too numerous to deny: first a bloodstone appeared in the sky every night for a year, then vanished in the west, scattering sparks like a burning log, its long and fiery tail pointing to the east; lightning had struck the temple of the Hummingbird, setting it on fire; a phantom woman had been heard weeping in the streets at night; a few days ago a baby had been born with two heads.

Then Smoking Man erupted, belching smoke into the sky every day and at night burning in the mountains to the east like another sun.

It was time, it was time.

Why must it be me who bears this burden? Motecuhzoma asked himself in his misery. Of all the Great Speakers of the Mexica, why is it I who must face this moment?

✹   ✹

The priests had borne his litter on their shoulders all the way to Tollán. The ancient city had been Feathered Serpent's capital when he walked the earth many bundles of years before, but it was deserted now, abandoned on the sun-bright, wind-cold plain. The houses had long since crumbled away, and only the flat-topped pyramids of the temples remained, the truncated colonnades of the palace looking like the bleached rib bones of some long-dead giant. The streets were home to drifting tumbleweeds and rattlesnakes, mute testimony that even the greatest civilizations must one day fall.

Motecuhzoma stepped down from the litter and was borne up the pyramid steps by the priests. It was late afternoon, and the desert wind howled through the stones, throwing up clouds of grit and dust. Feathered Serpent, Lord of the Wind, was here; he was watching.

A phalanx of stone Toltec warriors, fifteen feet tall, guarded the temple roof. A crow, shivering in the desert wind, perched on one of the reclining *chacmooles*. It took to wing, screeching like a demon.

Another flurry of grit stung his face. To the east, behind the mountains, a lead-gray sky sparked and crackled with thunder.

The shrine itself, sanctuary of his god and ancient enemy, was in the heart of the pyramid, in a chamber below the summit. Motecuhzoma went down the steps alone, carrying the hardtack in a golden gourd, covered in rich cloth.

The wind moaned again.

✳ ✳

At the foot of the steps lay the Stone of the Sun, a round piece of gray-black basalt, intricately carved, as high as a man's waist and so broad two men could lie on it head to toe. On its wheel was a map of mankind's history . . . and future. Square panels showed the destruction of previous worlds. There had been four other suns before the present one: the first had been destroyed by tigers, the second by tempests, the third by fire, and the fourth by flood. And now, as every Mexican knew, they were living in the last days of the fifth sun, the final sun, the last spasm of this world before all ended.

At the center of the stone was the Sun God, *Tonatiuh,* a knife blade protruding from his mouth, for the last world would end by knives.

Feathered Serpent watched Motecuhzoma from the darkness behind the altar, a bearded snake devouring human skeletons, the living bodies of the Mexica.

Motecuhzoma felt his breathing quicken.

An owl blinked at him from the altar, fluttered blindly for a moment, trapped by the walls, then flapped away through the entrance into the gathering sky.

Another omen.

Motecuhzoma placed the gourd reverently on the altar, then stripped off his mantle and loincloth and knelt, naked, in front of the image of the Feathered Serpent. He picked up a small stone bowl, carved into the shape of a coiled snake, and the stingray spine that lay beside it. Holding his penis in his left hand, he carefully pierced it with the stingray spine, collecting the blood from the wound in the stone bowl. He repeated the process, piercing the flesh of his earlobes, his thighs, and his tongue, collecting as much of the blood as he could.

When he had finished, his body was bathed in sweat, and he was panting with pain. He stood, very slowly, and dashed the contents of the bowl in the face of the Feathered Serpent.

✺　✺

When Motecuhzoma left the temple, his rich golden mantle was stained with blood. He ordered Woman Snake to seal the shrine so that it might never be discovered, then allowed the priests to carry him down the steps and place him in his litter. He spoke not a word on the journey back to Tenochtitlán but stared morosely ahead, his eyes concentrated on some vision of future disaster. In truth he had already done all he could to propitiate the gods. If Feathered Serpent must return, he did not wish to forestall the inevitable. He might just as well have it done and finished.

 **10**

San Juan de Ulúa

THEY ARRIVED ON the morning of Easter Sunday, announced by the booming of snakeskin drums and the blast of shell horns.

There were fifty-two officials, one for each year in a sheaf of time. Sunlight flashed on golden pectorals and lip plugs; quetzal-green feathers danced in the morning breeze. They were shorter in stature than the Spaniards, but well muscled. They had broad, square faces and hooked noses, and their hair hung around their shoulders and low over their eyes in a fringe. The officials had their hair bunched on their heads in a topknot, held in place with a cotton headband. They were unarmed.

Cortés met them under the palm trees, a few yards from the camp. The leader of the delegation took a step forward. He was sporting a carved jade ornament worn through the pierced septum of his nose. Cortés fought to conceal his disgust at this barbarity.

The man put a finger to the ground then to his lips. Cortés bowed to him in turn and called for Aguilar to come forward and translate.

The *natural* finished his greeting, and Cortés waited for the translation. Aguilar seemed confused. He said something to their visitor in Chontal Maya. Now it was the Indian's turn to frown, bewildered.

"What is going on here?" Cortés demanded.

"I cannot understand this language," Aguilar said. "I have never heard it before."

"If you cannot speak for me, then what is the use of your being here?"

"I spent eight years among the Mayans," Aguilar protested. "What this man is speaking is not a dialect. It is a completely new language."

Cortés heard a voice behind him, a woman's voice. He turned around, saw the *camarada* with the black eyes whom he had given to Puertocarrero. There was a curious smile on her lips. "What did she say?" he asked Aguilar.

Aguilar scowled. "She says the language is called *Náhuatl.*"

"She understands what this Indian is saying, then?"

"It would appear so."

"Then bring her here!" Cortés waved the girl forward. "It may take an unconscionably long time for us even to say hello, but at least we may speak with one another. I shall speak with you, you shall speak with her, and she shall speak with our guest! Now, Aguilar, let us find out what these gentlemen want of us!"

MALINALI

THE STRANGER'S NAME is Teuhtitl—Aguilar pronounced it "Tendile"—and he is a Mexica, the governor of the province in which we now stand. He welcomes my lords in the name of the great Motecuhzoma, Revered First Speaker of the Triple Alliance, as he calls him. He himself, he says, is a vassal of Motecuhzoma, who is the greatest prince in the whole world and who lives across the mountains in a place called Tenochtitlán, as if Feathered Serpent did not already know this.

Tendile summons his slaves forward. They lay mats on the ground and present Feathered Serpent with the gifts they have brought for him: there is a handful of figurines, worked in gold, a few small jewels, and some cloaks decorated with green quetzal feathers, as well as ten bolts of fine white cloth. There is also food: turkeys, hog plums, and some corn cakes.

Aguilar tells me to thank Tendile for these gifts. Feathered Serpent says something to the lord Alvarado, who hurries back to the camp to do his bidding. I expect he wants to find something suitable to present in return.

Meanwhile Tendile addresses himself directly to me. "Who are your hairy companions? Are they human? What do they want with us here?"

I find his tone offensive, but I relay this question exactly to Aguilar, who confers with Feathered Serpent.

"Tell them we are sent by his most Catholic majesty Charles V, king of Spain, who has heard much of this great lord, Motecuhzoma. Tell him we have been sent here to offer him trade and friendship and show him the way to true religion."

What is he talking about? If only I could speak with Feathered Serpent directly! This Aguilar is a fool. He has twisted my lord's words to make them incomprehensible. I hesitate, give myself time to compose a more fitting reply.

Look at this Tendile, so full of his own importance, like all these Mexica. "The ancient prophecies are fulfilled!" I tell him. "Feathered Serpent has returned!"

There is a long silence. Tendile does not seem totally surprised by this proclamation. News of our progress up the coast must have preceded us. "Is he truly a god?" he asks.

"Look at his white face, his black beard. Do you not recognize him?"

Tendile returns his attention to Feathered Serpent, and the play of his emotions shows on his face. "Impossible."

"He has returned from the east on a great raft as he promised he would. Look at the way he is dressed, in Feathered Serpent's colors!"

Tendile seems bewildered. At that moment Alvarado returns, his curly red hair showing below his golden helmet. "Who is that man?"

What a fool! "That is not a man. His name is *Tonatiuh*. Sun God."

Aguilar interrupts me, betraying his impatience. "What are you saying to him?" he asks. "He looks excited. Does he wish me to tell him the mysteries of the Cross?"

The mysteries of the cross? The cross is a symbol of fertility. Does Tendile need to be enlightened on the making of babies? I think not. This Aguilar is obsessed with such matters. "He wishes to know more about where my lord is from and why he has returned."

"Returned? Ah, so they remember Grijalva's voyage of last

year!" He confers again with Feathered Serpent and then turns back to me. "Tell him my lord Cortés is the subject of a great king who lives over the sea from the direction of the dawn. My lord Cortés would like to know where and when he can meet Motecuhzoma in person and bring him the good news of the one true religion."

What *is* this nonsense? Aguilar speaks too quickly for me to understand everything he says, and his knowledge of our language leaves much to be desired. That Feathered Serpent should be served by such fools. I turn back to Tendile. "Feathered Serpent wishes to meet Motecuhzoma straight-away. As you can imagine, my lord, they have much to discuss. Principally, of course, matters concerning the gods."

Tendile blinks, battling to maintain the steely countenance of an ambassador now. "How can he ask to meet with the Revered Speaker?" he asks me. "He has only just arrived in our lands."

"They are his lands, so he may do as he wishes."

Aguilar interrupts us once more. "My lord Cortés wants to know what is going on."

I wonder how I may answer him without offending Feathered Serpent. These Mexica are such recalcitrant people. "He says he will pass on my lord's request to Motecuhzoma but does not know if he can arrange an audience straightaway. He says that my lord has only recently arrived on these shores and he will need to rest after his travels."

Another short conference.

"My lord Cortés says he is not easily fatigued and any errand he performs for his king cannot be delayed."

I have Aguilar repeat what he has just said, but it makes no sense to me. I wonder who this great god might be that Feathered Serpent serves in this way. He must surely be refer-ring to *Olintecle*, the Father of All Gods.

I turn back to Tendile. "Now you have made him angry," I tell him, and I am gratified to see him blanch. "He says he must meet Motecuhzoma and speak to him at once and with-out delay. He has been commanded this by *Olintecle* himself."

Alvarado brings up an assortment of gifts, carried for him by mole-slaves who are as shiny and black as obsidian: there is a casket of blue glass beads and a throne that has been attacked by sea worms.

Aguilar addresses me now: "Tell this Tendile that my lord Cortés hopes Motecuhzoma finds joy in these gifts. Perhaps he can use this throne as his seat when they meet with each other."

I pass on his words, and then both Tendile and I stare at the worm-eaten chair and the beads, and I believe we both have the same thought: Someone has just been deliberately insulted.

✻ ✻

I am asked to inform the lord Tendile that today is a very important and holy day to the Gods of Thunder and that he and his retinue are invited to witness the proceedings. They sit in the shade of the palm trees as Fray Olmedo and Brother Aguilar erect a large wooden cross in the sand. The friar then reads from his book while Aguilar rings a small silver bell he has brought from the ship.

"What are they doing?" Tendile asks me, as Aguilar and the priest raise a silver goblet to their lips. "What is that they are drinking? Is it blood?"

I do not know how to answer him. All I know of their customs is the gibberish spouted by Aguilar. "It is blood, but not human blood. The blood belongs to their god."

Tendile looks perplexed.

"Our gods demand blood from us," I go on, more confident now. "Feathered Serpent and his followers instead demand blood from their gods. The gods sacrifice themselves."

Tendile is silent. No doubt he wonders what Revered Speaker will say when he hears this.

11

CORTÉS STUDIED THESE Mexica. From the moment Tendile had arrived at the camp, two of his retinue had been at work, seating themselves on reed mats on the ground and drawing everything they saw. So, he thought, not only a delegation of welcome but a delegation of spies as well. Perhaps I can use this to my advantage.

After the holy Easter mass was completed, he turned to Alvarado. "Tell Benítez and the others to saddle their horses. And have Mesa prepare a charge for the artillery. We will give this pompous savage something to tell Motecuhzoma when he goes home."

Alvarado grinned and hurried away.

Cortés led Tendile and his entourage down to the beach. "Tell Malinali I have something to show my guests," he said to Aguilar.

Tendile followed Cortés, his face composed once more in the same stern visage he had assumed on his arrival at their camp. The other Mexica lords followed, too, their noses in the air.

Damn your arrogance, Cortés thought.

Suddenly, from a clear blue sky, a thunderclap shook the ground under their feet. All the Mexica fell to their knees, even Tendile. Another thunderclap, and another.

Cortés suppressed a smile. The little exhibition he had arranged had had precisely the effect he had wished. Tendile and his retinue cowered on the ground, the veneer of their arrogance destroyed.

Mesa fired another salvo from his culverins. On the other side of the bay, coconut fronds crashed onto the beach, palm trees snapped like twigs.

The guns fell silent. Tendile and his entourage got slowly back to their feet. Trembling like women, he was pleased to see. He nodded to Alvarado, who drew his sword and raised it into the air, a prearranged signal. From the other end of the beach came the *jinetas*, followed by the war dogs, galloping toward them in close formation, the horses' hooves thundering on the wet, hard sand.

The Mexica gasped in dismay. Tendile took a step back, his face a sickly gray. The others huddled around him. Thinking they would be ridden into the ground, the Indians screamed once more and threw themselves on the ground. Benítez and his cavalry spurred their horses so close to the Indians that the hooves churned up the sand mere inches from their heads.

Cortés looked back up the beach, saw Motecuhzoma's scribes frantically transcribing all they had just seen. Well, that should make a good impression.

MALINALI

I CANNOT TAKE my eyes from him. He is all that I have waited for. He fears nothing; even the Mexica tremble before him.

Feathered Serpent confers briefly with Aguilar, who then turns to me. "My lord Cortés wishes you to tell this Tendile that he hopes soon to have the great pleasure of looking on Motecuhzoma personally."

I pass this news on to my lord Tendile. See how the great Mexican lord sweats like a girl! At last I am no longer the struggling child tied with thongs in a storage hut, the helpless princess watching her father kick and tremble as Motecuhzoma's soldiers throttle the life from him. I am no longer dust on the ground. I am the obsidian wind, the breath of the gods. I am safe with Feathered Serpent, and together we shall crush these invaders with their savage, unnatural gods, these usurpers, these Mexica.

 12

THE LORD TENDILE took time to assume his composure and former dignity, regathering it around him like a cloak. He pointed to Alvarado.

"He asks *Tonatiuh* if he can have his helmet as a gift for my lord Motecuhzoma," Aguilar said to Cortés.

Alvarado laughed when he heard the request. He removed the cabasset and tossed it to Malinali. "He may borrow it for a while if he returns it filled with gold!"

Cortés thought to stop him, but Malinali had already translated what he had said. He wished sometimes he could control Alvarado's tongue. Such a request too baldly revealed their intentions.

Tendile frowned at Malinali, and there was an urgent discussion.

"What does he say?" Cortés asked.

"Evidently," Aguilar said, after conferring with Malinali, "he asked what is so very special about gold."

There was a tense silence. Several of the Spaniards exchanged glances.

Cortés considered a reply. "Tell him," he said, "that we Spaniards all suffer a terrible disease of the heart. Gold is the only cure. That is why it is so special to us; that is why we need it so badly."

"Amen to that," Jaramillo said, and grinned.

※　※

Tendile left, with a promise to return soon with word from Motecuhzoma. Cortés tried to suppress his excitement. This talk of gold had convinced him that he was close to the discovery he sought.

He looked at the Indian girl, Malinali. "Give her my thanks," he said to Aguilar. "In future she will stay by my side, to help me speak with the Mexica."

Aguilar started to protest. "But my lord . . ."

"Just do it, Aguilar," Cortés said, and walked away. More than a pretty face, he thought. He wondered what other secrets there were behind those black eyes.

MALINALI

FEATHERED SERPENT'S TENT has been pitched behind the dunes, in the shade of the palms. The royal-blue silk whips in the ocean breeze, the wind that he alone commands. He sits behind a wooden table, his valet and majordomo standing at his shoulder on either side.

I watch him, fascinated. He possesses magic; he has the eyes of an owl man, and when he holds you in his gaze, you cannot look away. For the first time, I notice the small scar on his chin and lower lip, which is partly concealed by his beard. Perhaps he was once attacked by the Earth Monster, as happened to another of the gods, *Tezcatlipoca*.

He says something to Aguilar, and Aguilar then turns to me. "He wants to know where you learned to speak the language of the Mexica."

"I am not a native of Tabasco," I answer. I wonder how much I should tell him. I am too ashamed to reveal all of it. "I come from a place called Painali. There we have the elegant speech—*Náhuatl*. When I was a child, I was...captured...and made a slave."

Feathered Serpent leans forward, his elbows resting on the table.

"He asks if you know of this Motecuhzoma," Aguilar asks me.

"I went to Tenochtitlán only once, when I was a small girl. He passed in the street, borne on a palanquin. I know only that he is the richest prince in the whole world. But he is also very cruel."

"This city, Tenochtitlán, what is it like?"

I direct my answers to Feathered Serpent, even though it is Aguilar who speaks. I want Feathered Serpent to see that I am a Person, and not afraid. "Tenochtitlán is built on a lake in the middle of a great valley surrounded by mountains. It is the most beautiful city in the world. Perhaps one hundred thousand people live there."

Aguilar smiles when he hears this. He thinks it is an empty boast; he thinks I see things with a peasant's eyes. I detest his smug smiles and cruel eyes.

"Are they a rich people?"

Now it is my turn to smile. "The Mexica own half the world, and half the world pays them tribute each year."

Feathered Serpent nods, satisfied. He is a god, and so he already knows the answers to these questions and is testing me.

"He says you will be well rewarded for your service," Aguilar tells me. Then he asks, apparently of his own volition, "When we were talking with the Mexica, with Tendile, . . . did you translate exactly what I said?"

I lower my eyes to the ground so they do not betray me. Does he suspect? I told the lord Tendile the truth, certainly, even though it was not exactly what this fool asked me to say.

"Yes, my lord."

"You are sure?"

I feel Feathered Serpent's eyes on me. I tell myself he does not understand what we are saying, yet I feel a thrill of fear. "I repeated everything as you said it to me."

"And they understood it?"

"They understood."

But what can he do? Aguilar is either a fool or a charlatan and for some reason wishes to subvert his lord Feathered Serpent's task. If only I could talk with him directly.

"Thank you, Doña Marina," Aguilar mutters, although he appears much less than satisfied with me. I am escorted out of the tent by one of the Spanish guards, but as I leave, I turn around and give Feathered Serpent one last glance, and I see that he is smiling at me.

I promise myself that I shall be his right hand, Brother Aguilar, I, not you!

Painali, 1507

I AM SEVEN years old, and my father is trying to explain to me why he had not changed my date of naming to a more propitious day.

"You will be Ce Malinali, One Grass of Penance," he whispers to me, "because you are fated to find your destiny in disorder and destruction. We have to destroy the Mexica so we can build a new nation."

At that age I am impressed more by the fact that he thinks I am important enough to speak to me alone and with such gravity than by the words themselves, which are incomprehensible to me. It is only when I am older that I remember them and realize that perhaps it is the reason my mother was glad to be rid of me: a daughter with such a name can only bring bad luck to those around her.

We are standing together on the summit of the Quetzalcóatl temple, staring at a blood-star falling down the night sky, its fiery tail pointing toward the Cloud Lands.

"That is your star," he whispers to me. "It comes to tell the world that the reign of the Mexica is over and the days of Hummingbird are numbered. It is a sign that Feathered Serpent is to come again."

I remember his voice, how soft and soothing it was, like a hand stroking my head.

"You are of the few," he says. "I knew this from the moment of your birth. You will be here when Feathered Serpent arrives, and you will help him rid us of the Mexica. I have seen it in the portents in the sky.

"You are both blessed and cursed with a destiny, my little one, my daughter, my One Grass of Penance."

 **13**

Tenochtitlán, 1519

IT WAS LATE, deep into the Sixth Watch of the Night, when Tendile and his fellow lords arrived at the royal palace. Motecuhzoma had given orders that he be woken immediately upon their arrival, and there was to be no waiting for audience. The delegation removed their sandals and stripped off their decorated mantles, replacing them with plain cloaks of maguey fiber. Then they were led up the great staircase to Motecuhzoma's apartments.

Revered Speaker awaited them in one of his private chambers. As they entered, they were assailed by the pungent musk of copal incense. Sandalwood glowed in a copper brazier, and *Tezcatlipoca*, Bringer of Darkness, watched them from the smoky gloom. Woman Snake lay prostrate in front of the altar. A young girl was spread-eagled, naked, over Motecuhzoma's own sacrificial stone, arms and legs hanging limp, her chest open, her heart cooking in the coals.

A skein of black smoke rose to the ceiling.

Tendile and his officers approached on their faces. Motecuhzoma stepped from behind the slab, his robes wet with blood from the sacrifice. He approached them with the basalt jaguar receptacle that held some of the dead girl's blood. He sprinkled it over his messengers, to purify them. After all, they had spoken with gods.

Motecuhzoma had hoped for good news but saw a terrible truth written on their stricken faces. "Speak," he said.

"The great rafts appeared off our coast five days ago," Tendile said. "We met with the strangers and have hurried day and night since to bring you news."

"Well?"

"They do not have the elegant speech; they speak some other language that sounds like the quacking of ducks. They have a woman who speaks for them: a Person, like ourselves. She calls herself Malinali."

"And what did this Malinali say to you?"

Tendile was trembling, and saliva leaked from his mouth onto the floor.

"What did she say?" Motecuhzoma shouted.

"She said that the ancient prophecies are to be fulfilled. She said . . . that Feathered Serpent has returned as promised."

Motecuhzoma pressed his knuckles to his forehead, as if trying to burrow his way inside his own skull. "Who was this woman?"

"I confess I do not know, my lord, except that she spoke most insolently to me."

"What did she say?"

"That Feathered Serpent wishes to speak with you in person, that he has been commanded to do this by *Olintecle* himself."

Tendile lay prostrate on the cold marble, waiting a hundred years for these few terrible moments to pass. *I will be sacrificed to Hummingbird for this,* he thought. *My skin will be flayed and thrown into the great pit at Yopico.*

Motecuhzoma took an agave thorn from the shrine and stabbed at his own flesh, repeatedly, until the blood ran down his arms. "Did you see this stranger who claimed to be *Quetzalcóatl*?"

"Yes, my lord. His skin was white, like chalk, and he had a dark beard and a straight nose. He was dressed in black and wore a green feather in his cap."

"A quetzal plume!" Motecuhzoma murmured. A god was known best by his headdress. A jade feather signified Feathered Serpent. And black was one of his colors. "What of the others who were with him?"

"Like him, they wore strange clothes that had a pestilential odor about them. Many of them had long beards and hair of strange and unnatural colors. Their swords and shields and bows are all made of some metal that shines like the sun. And yet, great lord, if they were indeed gods, their excrement was not of gold, as it should be, but like ours. For we waited after our meeting to observe them and—"

"What do you know of the ways of the gods!" Motecuhzoma shouted.

Tendile lay on his belly, silent. *Please do not kill me.*

"Did this woman tell you why this bearded lord wishes to speak with me?"

"She says it concerns matters of the gods."

"They spoke of religion?"

"No, but I saw them at their ritual, great Lord. They were drinking blood."

For the first time Motecuhzoma allowed himself to hope.

But then Tendile said, "Yet it was not the blood of a man they were drinking, or this is what she said, but the blood of a god."

"The blood of a god," Motecuhzoma repeated, his voice echoing around the marble walls.

"My artists drew pictures for you, great lord," Tendile mumbled.

One of Tendile's scribes crawled forward clutching several bark sheets, the paintings that he and his companion had made on the beach at San Juan de Ulúa. Motecuhzoma snatched them from him. He stared at the floating temples with their great banners of cloth, the logs spitting fire, the two-headed monsters, the angry beasts that followed them.

"What is this?"

"Great lord, the strangers possess stone serpents that shoot smoke and sparks from their mouths. If the serpent is pointed toward a tree, the tree falls. If it is pointed toward a mountain, the mountain cracks and crumbles away. The noise is like thunder, and the smoke has a vile smell that made us all sick. Some of them rode great stags, taller than two men standing on each other's shoulders, and these beasts carry them wherever they want to go. They breathe smoke from their mouths, and when they ran, it was as if the very ground trembled under our feet. They also possess dogs as no dogs we have ever seen, monsters straight from the land of the dead, with great jowls and yellow teeth."

What this woman called Malinali had told Tendile could not be denied. It was the Year One Reed, the day Feathered Serpent had been born and the day he had sailed away. The portents were there for even the most obtuse priest to read. The owl men had prophesied:

If he comes on one Crocodile, he strikes the old men, the old women,
If on one Jaguar, one Deer, one Flower, he strikes at children.
If on one Reed, he strikes at kings . . .

Motecuhzoma did not know how long he stood, staring at the shadows, lost in his own despair. Finally he remembered Tendile and the other lords, awaiting his answer.

"Is there anything else you have to tell me?" he said.

Another of Tendile's retinue crept forward. He was holding a metal helmet, made of some shining metal that resembled silver. *What is this?*

"One of the strangers gave us this headdress," Tendile said.

Motecuhzoma examined it. He understood why Tendile had been interested in such an object: it was similar to the helmet worn by Hummingbird on the Left, their own war-god.

"He gave you this as a gift?" Motecuhzoma asked.

"No, great lord. He demanded that we return it, filled with gold."

"Gold," Motecuhzoma said. "Why gold?"

"They said it was to heal a sickness peculiar to their kind. Indeed, they ignored all our other gifts, the finest cloth and feather work and some exquisite pieces of jade. Only the gold seemed to excite them."

Perhaps that is why they have come, Motecuhzoma thought. He started to giggle. Perhaps there was an answer to this after all ...

"You shall return to the coast tonight and give these strangers exactly what they ask. If it is gold they want, it is gold they shall have. We shall also discover if this Malinali's lord is truly Feathered Serpent or just a man, as you claim. There are ways we may divine the truth."

After they had gone, Motecuhzoma stared again at the pictures that had been painstakingly painted on the sheets of bark, and his fingers began to tremble uncontrollably.

One Reed. A bad year for kings.

San Juan de Ulúa

They had arrived off the coast on Good Friday, 1519. As the anchors rattled down, the Spaniards had gazed over a depressing horizon of sand dunes with sparse patches of straw-colored grass and a few groves of forlorn and wind-bowed palm trees. In the distance stood a range of blue mountains, dominated by a peak the local Indians called Orizaba, a volcanic caldera cloaked in great banks of cloud.

The Indian slaves whom Tendile had left behind helped them make shelters from green branches and palm fronds and thatch. The *naturales* made their own camp a little way off, a shantytown built overnight to service the needs of the Spaniards. They cooked fish and turkeys over open fires, and the women peeled fruit and prepared corn cakes under canopies of woven mats.

The Spaniards clustered around their own fires, shivering in the teeth of the northerly winds. Then one day the winds died and the weather turned unbearably hot. Now they were forced to huddle in the shade of the few gnarled trees, beating at the voracious clouds of tiny black insects that descended to feast on them and make their lives misery.

Only Cortés seemed immune to the discomforts. Day after day he patrolled the dunes, staring at the tangle of jungle beyond the plain to the forbidding range of mountains to the west, and waited and wondered and planned.

MALINALI

RAIN FLOWER PULLS off her *huipil*, the long tunic of sheer cotton she wears over her skirt. As she undresses, I see there are dark, plum-colored bruises on her arms and her breasts. She wades into the cold, black water of the pool, conscious of my stare. "My hairy lord is rough with me. I don't think he means to be. He is big and clumsy. When he is in the cave, he forgets how strong he is and how small I am."

She crouches down so that the water reaches her shoulders. I feel a sudden and powerful affection for her. In Potonchán

Rain Flower had been thought ugly. Her mother had neglected to hang a pearl from her cap when she was an infant, and so she had not grown up with the crossed eyes that the Tabascans found so becoming in a woman. Rain Flower's mother had in fact been Tiger Lip Plug's elder wife, and Rain Flower was only a few years younger than I. She was like a younger sister. Like me, she had a quick tongue and a quick temper that had been curbed only a little by the chili-smoke fires over which her father had upended her as punishment.

"I do not believe they are gods, Little Mother. Their bodies have a rank smell, and they spill their seed like any man."

"Your cave has opened for the first time, and now you know all there is to know of men. You are disappointed, then, that he does not have claws on his *maquauhuitl?*"

"I did not dare to look," she says, and dips her head below the water, stung by what I have said.

"Some men are not born gods," I tell her, more gently. "Sometimes the spirit of a god is born in them, or is given them, as it was with Motecuhzoma."

"And what of your god with the violet eyes?"

"He has three penises, and he keeps me awake all night! While the others are recovering their vigor, he always has one that urgently seeks the cave of joy. Then at dawn he turns into a cat and joins the other ocelots in greeting the dawn with their cries."

"You have a fancy tongue. I fear one day Motecuhzoma's priests may cut it out and roast it in their fires."

I have to smile at that. It is a warning I heard from Tiger Lip Plug many times. I think he considered many times offering me to the gods.

My Alonso is a better husband. He uses me gently and takes me in the way of the gods, with our faces and bodies pressed together. I see him only at night, for he does not try to speak to me through Aguilar, either because he does not wish to or perhaps because he finds Aguilar as tiresome as I.

And I know his only purpose is to teach me the way of the gods so that I can come to Feathered Serpent better prepared.

"Perhaps one day none of us will have to fear Motecuhzoma."

"Is that what you think?"

"Why else would our Thunder Gods have come here?"

Rain Flower ladles water from the palm of her hand over her shoulder, wincing at the small bruises on her flesh. "They are just men. They will take whatever they want and go back to the Cloud Lands."

"Perhaps they will take us with them. We will be better off than we were before. I do not wish to spend my whole life sewing cloaks and baking corn."

"What else should a woman do?"

How can I explain to her? I was not born to the ordinary woman's life of pounding tortillas and having babies. I knew in my heart that I was a warrior, a king, a statesman, a prince-maker, a poet. I am a woman with another destiny besides cook and concubine. I had always known it, and my father had known it, too.

"You hope for too much," Rain Flower said. "Life is just a dream. What happens here should not matter to a Person."

Lord Sun was sinking in the sky, to battle for another night against his sisters and brothers. Cicadas pounded a rhythm in the forest. A butterfly danced among the ferns, the spirit of a dead warrior playing forever among the flowers and reeds. "You may be right," I murmur, but I do not believe it. I do not believe it at all.

The water has grown black and very cold. We stand up and wade, shivering, toward the bank. I see a shadow running from a hiding place among the forest. It is one of the Thunder Gods: Jaramillo.

✳ ✳

My lord Tendile arrives with the usual fanfare: there are snakeskin drums, conches, clay flutes, and wooden clappers. But this time his heralds also bear green quetzal standards to show that the delegation carries royal approval.

"The lord Tendile, governor and voice of the Mexica,

appointed by the Revered Speaker himself, now comes! He brings greetings and friendship to *Malintzin,* newly arrived from the Cloud Lands of the east!"

Malintzin. In *Náhuatl* it means "Malinali's lord." So this is how they have decided to address him. So typical of Mexica ambiguity, skirting admission that he is either man or god.

Tendile is dressed magnificently in a mantle of sheer orange cotton, embroidered with geometric designs along its hem. His headdress is of flamingo plumes and is inlaid with gold. He is accompanied by a much larger retinue than before, both lords and slaves. Two young boys brush the insects aside from his face with feather fans while two priests walk ahead bearing braziers of copal incense. Behind him come the owl men, in their feathered cloaks and beaked helmets, skulls and human bones tagged to their cloaks. They scream like shrikes and blow clouds of colored smoke from clay censers.

"Who are they?" Aguilar whispers to me, clearly alarmed.

"Sorcerers. They are here to break the power of our great lord with their spells."

A sharp intake of breath, and Aguilar turns pale. "Witchcraft!" he mutters, and makes the sign of the cross.

Feathered Serpent receives them under the palms, seated on a heavy oak chair inlaid with turquoise. At my suggestion he again wears the black velvet suit and soft black cap with green plume he wore on the occasion of his last meeting with Tendile.

Tendile kisses the ground and puts a finger to his lips. Then his priests step forward and walk around Feathered Serpent and his retinue, fumigating them with incense. When it is done, Tendile announces to me, "I bring words of greeting and friendship to *Malintzin* from Revered Speaker."

I relay this greeting to Aguilar, who pronounces *Malintzin* as "Malinche."

"Revered Speaker has asked me to give *Malintzin* these gifts as a token of his friendship."

I realize what he is about to do. It is more, much more, than I had dared to hope. I turn to Aguilar. "Will you respectfully ask the great lord if he will stand? These men wish to dress him in ceremonial robes."

Aguilar can only frown. "To what purpose?"

"Will you do as I say! Let my lord ask to what purpose!"

Aguilar's eyes go wide. He would like to whip me for my insolence. But what can he do at such a moment? He must pass on what I have said. Feathered Serpent gets to his feet.

The Mexica lords step forward and knot a beautiful feathered cape at his shoulder, then place a collar of jade and gold in the shape of a serpent around his neck. Other lords bend down to put anklets of gold and silver on his legs. They give him a shield worked entirely from brilliant green quetzal feathers and place a miter of tiger skin on his head.

Finally Tendile himself produces a mask of turquoise mosaic, with gold fangs and a crossband of quetzal plumes, which he places on Feathered Serpent's head. It is the official regalia of a high priest of *Quetzalcóatl,* and so, by extension, the garb of the god himself. Motecuhzoma has just publicly recognized my lord as the incarnation of the god. *He believes also.*

The other Thunder Gods and their moles look on, bemused.

I had supposed that my lord would surely be moved at recognizing his very own emblems, but to my surprise and dismay, he immediately removes his garments and drops them at his feet, as if they are an impediment to him. He resumes his seat on his makeshift throne and barks a command at Aguilar.

"My lord Cortés wishes to know what else they have brought," Aguilar says to me.

I try to hide my confusion. Is it possible that Feathered Serpent is trying to hide his own identity? But to what purpose? This is not at all what I had expected.

I turn to Tendile, who seems similarly bemused. "Feathered Serpent wishes to see your other gifts."

"We have brought provisions for himself and his companions."

A line of slaves have been waiting his command. They

carry heavy baskets of food, which they lay on mats on the ground: baskets of guavas, avocados, and hog plums; panniers of eggs and roasted turkeys and toasted maize cakes.

All the food has been liberally sprinkled with a sauce made from human blood. I can smell it.

I hold my breath as one of the Thunder Gods, the one with the golden hair, steps forward and tears a joint from one of the turkeys. He holds it to his nose and sniffs, his face wrinkling in disgust. He throws the meat into the dirt.

There is a deathly silence, the Thunder Gods watching Feathered Serpent, waiting to see what he will do. I hold my breath. This is the moment when he will prove his identity to all, if he acts correctly.

He speaks softly to Aguilar, who then turns to me. "My lord asks you to thank Tendile for his gifts but says his religion forbids the eating of human flesh, as all men are born brothers. To break this commandment is considered one of the greatest sins in the sight of God."

I do not understand all of this long and confusing harangue, but I understand its meaning. I turn back to Tendile. "As you well know, Feathered Serpent has returned to abolish all human sacrifice. Do not be so transparent as to tempt his patience further."

Tendile seems disappointed, as well he might. I know what he is thinking: This *Malintzin* will not assume the trappings of Feathered Serpent yet has balked at drinking human blood, as would be expected.

He is as confused as I am. What will he tell Motecuhzoma?

The Thunder God with the golden hair says something to Aguilar.

"My lord Alvarado wishes to know if the Mexica have returned his helmet."

I pass on this request. Tendile raises a hand, and the rest of the porters—there must be more than a hundred—hurry forward. "My lord Motecuhzoma has done this, and more besides," Tendile says.

Straw mats are laid on the sand at Feathered Serpent's feet, and the helmet is produced, filled to the brim with gold dust. Then other objects are produced: gold figurines in the shapes of ducks, deer, jaguars, and monkeys; gold necklaces and bracelets; a gold wand studded with pearls; gold shields inlaid with precious stones; mosaics in turquoise and onyx; statues and masks carved in wood; jade pendants and brooches; fans of solid silver; a headdress of quetzal plumes studded with jade and pearls; capes of finest feather work; jewelry of shell, gold, turquoise, and jade; and five emeralds of enormous size.

The Thunder Gods and their moles are slack-jawed in astonishment. Then the final gifts are brought forward: two identical disks, each the size of a cartwheel and two inches thick, one of silver, the other of gold. The silver disk has the figure of a woman at its center, Sister Moon; the gold disk has the figure of Lord Sun on his throne.

The presents are arrayed there on the sand; the precious metals and jewels reflect the sunlight, hurting the eyes. There is complete silence save for the wind that murmurs across the sand, shifting grains across the mats and their treasures, as if my lord had commanded them to gently touch each piece in examination, without himself stooping or moving a muscle.

Finally he speaks, and Aguilar turns to me. "He wishes to know if that is all there is."

I do not know what to think now. I can scarce relay this sentiment to Tendile. Now it is my turn to wonder if Aguilar translates exactly everything Feathered Serpent says to me.

What can I say to the lord Tendile? "Feathered Serpent thanks you for your gifts," I manage, finally.

Tendile looks sour. "Perhaps now they will leave us alone."

Feathered Serpent speaks again, through Aguilar. This time I understand exactly what he requires of me. "My lord asks you to send his thanks to Revered Speaker for his generosity. It only remains now for my lord to thank Revered Speaker in person."

Tendile appears stricken when he hears this, as well he might. "That will not be possible. It is a long and dangerous journey to Tenochtitlán. Motecuhzoma asks that he take these few humble gifts as a token of his esteem and return to the Cloud Lands from whence he came."

I pass on these sentiments and wait for further direction. But I know what Feathered Serpent will say.

"My lord Cortés has traveled far for the great pleasure of gazing on Motecuhzoma's face," Aguilar says. "He has been ordered to pass on his greetings in person, and he cannot do otherwise without disobeying his king."

It is an effort to keep the smile of triumph from my face. With one hand Motecuhzoma dresses my lord as a god, with the other he tries to buy him off like a mortal man. How he must be trembling on his throne in the place of the Eagle and the Cactus!

"Feathered Serpent is a god and is not easily fatigued," I tell Tendile. "He must meet the Revered Speaker in person. He is guided in this by *Olintecle,* Father of All Gods and Mover of the Universe."

Tendile looks as if a great burden has descended on his shoulders. In a way, it has, for he must bear this news to Motecuhzoma personally, and at great risk to himself, if I am not mistaken. Perhaps in his failure here, he foresees his own death.

❈ ❈

After the Mexica had left, the Thunder Gods and their moles fall on the bounty. The beautiful and valuable quetzal feathers, intricately worked by master craftsmen; the prized shell jewelry; the sacred wooden masks; the fine embroidered cloths—all are trampled under the moles' boots as they fight one another to touch and admire the gold.

Feathered Serpent looks dismayed. I believe my god is ashamed of his cohorts. I recall what he had said about the heart sickness from which his followers suffer. It must indeed be terrible to be afflicted by such a disease, for it turns gods into monkeys.

14

ALREADY THEY CALLED this San Juan de Ulúa an infernal place, surely invented by the Devil, with all his talents for, and experience with, slow tortures. By day small groups of men gathered under the trees, grumbling to one another about the insects and the scorpions and the heat; when night came, they shivered in the sudden cold and scratched at their flea bites, tormented by the whine of the mosquitoes and the unearthly shrieks of the owl men in the nearby camp.

The morning after Tendile's departure, they gathered on the sand to watch Motecuhzoma's treasures being transferred to the fleet. Some dared to wonder aloud if they would ever see any of it again. As the great wheel of gold was lashed between two of the longboats, they whispered among themselves and threw suspicious glances at Cortés and his captains.

With the lord Tendile's departure, the attitude of the *naturales,* too, began to change. Each day there was less and less food.

Benítez heard some of the soldiers whispering among themselves: *What are we doing sitting here on this accursed beach? The governor's orders were to trade with the Indians and explore the coast. Here we do neither. The only gold we have seen so far Cortés has hidden away on his own ship. Any moment the* naturales *might swarm from the jungle and attack us . . .*

Since the battle on the Tabasco River, a dozen soldiers had died from wounds they received there. They had lost another two dozen to fever and the *vómito.*

There was talk about returning to Cuba. But if they went back now, would the governor, Velázquez, share the treasure with them, or would he keep it for himself?

Benítez suspected he knew the answer to that.

※　※

One morning they woke to find that the Indians had gone: their camp was deserted, fires still smoking, corn cakes burned to charcoal on the griddles. There had been two thousand of them, and they had all slipped away silently in the night, unseen, leaving them stranded there on the beach.

 **15**

THE TENSION WAS betrayed on sweating, bearded faces. Since the Indians had vanished, Cortés had warned them to expect attacks. Even at night they slept in full armor.

Now he called all his officers to an urgent meeting. Only Alvarado seemed unconcerned by their predicament, slouching at the entrance to the tent, a smirk on his handsome, golden face.

"I cannot understand what has happened," Sandoval was saying. "Why did the *naturales* run away? I thought we had made it clear we were their friends."

"They were happy to accept that friendship," León growled, "until Cortés insisted on a meeting with this Motecuhzoma."

Cortés accepted the rebuke in silence.

Ordaz was next to speak. "The men feel it is now time to go back to Cuba."

"But there is still so much more to be won," Cortés answered, his voice deceptively mild. "All of you saw the golden wheel Motecuhzoma presented to us. That is only the beginning of the great treasures I believe to be here."

León leaned both fists on the table. "The governor told us to explore the coastline and trade where we could. He expressly forbade us from sleeping on the shore. Yet we have been sitting on this accursed beach for weeks, leaving ourselves open to an attack from these treacherous Indians while our comrades die of the fever. We cannot stay here forever. We have already won far more gold and precious things than we could ever have hoped. We should return with it immediately to Cuba and present it to the governor."

A vein pulsed in Cortés's temple. Go back to Cuba? Going back to Cuba would ruin him. Velázquez would take the gold for himself, and he would not even be left with enough to cover his expenses. He had mortgaged all his possessions, exhausted all his lines of credit to finance this expedition. Moreover, the governor would probably arrest him and send him back to Spain in chains. Cortés could not countenance such a homecoming, disgraced and bankrupt after fifteen years of toil in the Indies.

An extravagant sigh. "I mean only the best for you and all of the men who have placed their trust in me. I am a Christian soldier and loyal subject of the king, and I shall do whatever you think is best. If you and your men wish to return to Cuba, then that is what we shall do."

"We did not agree to this!" Alvarado snarled, the golden smile falling away.

Cortés spread his hands, a helpless gesture. "It seems there is nothing more to be done. As these gentlemen have pointed out, the governor's orders were plain."

"You would listen to these two... ninnies?" Alvarado said, staring at León and Ordaz. The two men reached for their swords and had to be restrained by the others.

There was sudden, icy silence.

Finally Benítez said, "They are right about one thing. We cannot stay here and do nothing."

"If we go back to Cuba," Puertocarrero said, "we shall not see any of the gold."

Cortés held up a hand. "As I said, gentlemen, it appears we have no choice."

León and Ordaz exchanged glances. They had not expected to win so easily. Ordaz straightened. "I shall tell the men," he said.

With a glare in Alvarado's direction, León followed him out of the tent.

"You gave in too easily to those *Velazquistas*," Puertocarrero said.

"Am I to believe, then, that the rest of you do not wish to return to Cuba?"

Jaramillo looked sullen. "As you yourself said, what choice do we have?"

"Oh, we do have one choice," Cortés said. "Should you gentlemen wish to stay, there is another way we might play our hands."

✳ ✳

Without the lord Tendile's slaves on hand to bring them food, the Spaniards were faced with the possibility of starvation. After weeks in the holds of the ships, the cassava bread they had brought with them had turned to a foul and glutinous starch, crawling with maggots.

Now they had only what they could forage for themselves. The soldiers set out every morning to hunt birds and game with their crossbows while the Tabascan *camaradas* were sent off to scour the shore for crabs and wild fruits. Each day the hunt for food took them in broader sweeps, farther away from the camp.

Late one afternoon Rain Flower was alone collecting wild berries when she heard sounds from the rock pool where she and Malinali came each evening to bathe. Curious, she crept closer and peered through the ferns.

It was one of the Thunder Gods, the one they called Norte. He was naked, standing waist deep in the cool green water. She was astonished. She thought that the Spaniards never bathed. Malinali had said it was because they did not need to, but Rain Flower's own nose denied the veracity of that.

Norte, she had already noticed, was different from the others. They seemed to hold him apart; only the priest they called Aguilar ever spoke to him. It seemed curious to her that they called Aguilar their priest, because, of the two of them, it was Norte who possessed the tattoos and ragged earlobes of a holy man.

The water streamed off his skin as he rose from the water. He was hard and brown and smooth, not hairy like Benítez and Alvarado and the others. Her eyes lingered, and she felt an unnatural tingling in the base of her belly.

If any of these great lords were gods, then it was this one.

As he emerged from the water, he had his back to her. She supposed he could not possibly have seen her. But suddenly she heard him say, in her own language, "And how long do you intend to stand there staring at me?"

He knows I'm here!

She lowered her eyes and stepped from her hiding place, wondering what punishment she might receive for spying on him in such a manner.

"I am sorry, my lord. I humbly beg your forgiveness. You took me by surprise. I did not think a lord needed to bathe."

"Even gods sweat," he said. When he turned around, she saw that he was smiling.

"I did not think you had seen me."

He put on his breeches and a ragged linen shirt. "Obviously." His eyes were black and intense. He is beautiful, she thought, like one of those boys the Mexica sacrifice to Feathered Serpent on his feast day.

"What's your name?" he asked her.

"Rain Flower."

"Rain Flower," he repeated, slowly. "You were given to Benítez?" She nodded. He kept his eyes on her, his head cocked to one side, as if he were amused. "I interest you in some way?"

She looked at his ears.

He touched the ragged tatters of flesh, self-consciously. "Blood spilled for Feathered Serpent."

Rain Flower's eyes widened. "You are a priest?"

"Do I seem like a priest to you?" When she did not answer, he said, "I fear I am very much a Person, as you are. I had a wife with the same color skin as yours. She gave me two children."

"Why did you leave her?"

"I did not leave her; I was captured." He seemed to struggle with the words. "Even here you cannot escape your birthright, it seems. One day . . . they will always find you."

He was standing close to her, too close. Among her own people, the punishment for adultery was death. And she was married to one of the Thunder Gods. He reached out to stroke her hair, and she took a step back.

He lowered his hand. "I am sorry."

"You are not gods?" she whispered.

"No, we are Spaniards." He smiled again. "That's much worse." He gave her a curious smile and walked away, back toward the camp.

She felt suddenly short of breath. Now, there was a man she could have given herself to, willingly! Why couldn't the great lord have given her to Norte?

Life, as always, was too cruel.

☀ ☀

"Have you heard what the men are saying?" Aguilar asked Benítez. "Cortés wants to go back to Cuba and give Governor Velázquez all of the gold in return for clemency."

Benítez had heard this particular rumor. In fact, he had been there when Cortés told Alvarado to spread it. "Do you think it is true?"

"I cannot believe it of Cortés. He knows we have a mission here. We must bring these benighted souls to salvation. He is too much a good Christian to think only of himself at this moment."

"Yes, I am sure you are right," Benítez said.

☀ ☀

Cortés had the great oak table brought from his tent and placed in the shade of the palms. The entire expedition was gathered under the trees, eager to discover what had been decided for their future. They all fell to a sudden and deathly silence as Cortés appeared and climbed onto the table to address them.

"Gentlemen!" Cortés began, "I understand there are those of you who are growing frustrated at our delay here on the beach."

There were shouts of agreement.

Tread carefully, Benítez thought. The mood here is dangerous. This could turn into outright rebellion.

"I understand how you must all feel," Cortés went on. "I have suffered along with you these past weeks. However, before we make a decision, we should review all we have achieved. First of all, when we left Cuba, the governor directed us to secure the release of any Spaniards being held captive by the *naturales* of Yucatán." He allowed himself a small smile. "As Brother Aguilar and our comrade Norte will attest, this we have achieved.

"We were also charged to explore the coasts here, to observe the customs and religions of the natives, and to barter with them for gold. I believe that in all these things we have succeeded far beyond expectations.

"However, should we return to Cuba now, it may be that all your glory, and indeed the profits you have earned by your strength of arms at the Tabasco River and at Ceutla, will be taken from you. Do you trust Governor Velázquez to give you your fair share of the treasures? Many of you are here today because you were unhappy with your lives in Cuba and frustrated at the size of the *encomiendas* the governor awarded you. So why are you now so eager to hurry back to his tender mercies?"

"We are here under the governor's charter!" a man called Escudero shouted. "To go outside that charter is illegal!"

Cortés shrugged his shoulders, as if in agreement with the man. "You may well be right. But before we decide on this, let me tell you what else I have discovered."

A clever choice of words, Benítez thought. He is allowing the men to think that the final choice is theirs.

"These lands are ruled by a great prince who has wealth beyond your imaginings. Should we return to Cuba now, we turn our backs on more than just a few trinkets. I believe there are riches enough in this land that every man here might have his own wheel of gold!"

León could contain himself no longer. "We have no sanction here! Do we plan to march against an entire kingdom with five hundred men and a dozen cannons? I say we go back to Cuba!"

"We have to go back!" Ordaz shouted. "If we sit here, we will either starve to death or be wiped out by the Indians!"

Many of the men raised their fists in the air and shouted their agreement.

Cortés's shoulders slumped in defeat. He raised his hands for silence. "Very well. I want only to do what is best for all. We shall prepare for our return immediately."

There were ragged cheers. Cortés was about to descend his makeshift platform when Alvarado sprang onto the table beside him. "Wait! It is not yet decided! I say to return to Cuba now is no more than treason!"

Uproar. León and Ordaz tried to shout Alvarado down, but his voice was as loud as theirs.

Cortés finally restored order. When he could once more make himself heard, he said to Alvarado, "Will you explain what you mean, accusing us good men of treason?"

"If we leave, His Majesty King Charles may lose those possessions here that we have won for him. Can we be sure that next year the *naturales* will not have formed some great army ready to throw us back into the sea? If that is the case, our king will lose everything! No, we have a duty to build a fort here and consolidate the claims of the Crown!"

"I agree with Pedro," Puertocarrero shouted. "This land has proved it has many riches. Why should we not colonize?"

The word *colonize* galvanized the audience. León and Ordaz had to shout to make their own protests heard above the bedlam.

Even Cortés protested. "But we have no authority to do such a thing! I admire your arguments, gentlemen, but perhaps our comrades León and Ordaz are right. We have little food left, and we are facing a possible attack from the *naturales*. I must confess I am not in favor of our return. I will lose every *maravedí* I possess, since I have put everything I own into this voyage. But I must be guided in this by my officers and by the men with whose safety I am entrusted."

"You are not the only one who has invested in this expedition!" Puertocarrero shouted.

"But I have given my word to these men," Cortés said helplessly. "I have already told them they can go back, as they wish to do."

"Then let the ones who wish to go home do so!" Sandoval said, and others shouted their agreement.

"The rest of us will establish our own colony!" Jaramillo said.

"That's illegal!" Escudero bawled at him.

"I am afraid it is not," Cortés said, and there was silence. Everyone gaped at him. They knew that Cortés was trained in the law, that he had been a magistrate in the town of Santiago on Cuba. "Under law it is permissible for any group of Spaniards to found their own municipality if they seek and are granted royal sanction. They then become answerable directly to the Crown and to no one else. These men are within their rights."

"We do not have royal sanction!" Escudero protested.

"It could be quickly obtained," Cortés said.

León turned his appeal to the crowd. "We have our orders from Velázquez! We return to Cuba!"

"I am weary of this command!" Cortés shouted over him. "Whoever wants to return, I wish them Godspeed!"

"What about the gold?" someone shouted.

"The gold stays with those who won it, not with those who run away!" He jumped from the table and stalked off.

Uproar.

Benítez smiled. It was nicely done. None would have guessed that the idea to build a colony here on the sand dunes of San Juan de Ulúa had come from Cortés himself.

MALINALI

RAIN FLOWER'S HUSBAND, the one they call Benítez, is freezing to death in the stifling heat of the lean-to. The whites of his eyes are yellow, and his skin glistens in the lather of its own sweat. His body shakes and shudders in the grip of the fever, his teeth chattering violently in his head. Occasionally he cries out, raging at the phantoms that stalk the shadows.

Rain Flower kneels down beside him. "He has the marsh fever. One moment he boils, the next he freezes. The Thunder Gods' owl man came and took some of his blood for sacrifice to their god." She picks up his hand, strokes it as if it were a wounded bird. "He has been like this for two days."

I kneel beside her, surprised by this show of affection. "What do you want me to do, Little Sister?"

"You're a sorceress. You can help him."

"I am no sorceress. My father taught me about the medicine in herbs when I was small. There is no magic in it."

"But you can help him?"

"I thought you did not care for your hairy lord."

Rain Flower takes the cloth from his forehead, dips it in a bowl of water, and wipes the sweat from his face and chest as she struggles to answer. "So I should just watch him die?" she asks me, finally.

"If he dies, perhaps Feathered Serpent will give you to Norte."

She flinches. "You knew?"

"I have seen the way you look at him. You must be careful, Little Sister. To these lords, Benítez is your husband. If you share your cave with this Norte, who knows what they will do to you?"

Rain Flower bites her lip. Sweat beads at her temples.

"You still want me to help you?"

An almost imperceptible whisper: "Yes."

"All right, I will show you what to do. There is a plant that grows near the water hole where we bathe. You must crush its leaves, boil them in clean water, and make him drink the liquid. This is what I have done with all the lords who are sick with the marsh fever."

"It will cure him?"

"It has cured some of the others. If he does not pass through the Narrow Passage tonight, he may live."

I stand up to leave.

Rain Flower looks sad. "You see, Little Mother, he is no god."

"When Feathered Serpent left Tollán, he was helped across the mountains by an army of moles and dwarves. Gods seldom keep the company of other gods. These men are just his helpers."

"And are you one of his helpers now?"

A band of capuchin monkeys clamor in the palms overhead. A hot breath of wind whips the canvas of the lean-to. He is listening, so I do not answer.

"Your god would be mute without you," Rain Flower tells me. "Does that not seem strange to you?"

I think about what my father told me when I was a child, the promise and the prophecy he had made. "No, Little Sister. It does not seem strange. It seems like destiny."

 **16**

CORTÉS LOOKED TO the west. A droplet of sweat squeezed down his neck and worked its way along his spine. The weather was getting hotter, and great pillows of cloud swept in, obscuring the mountains and the great volcanic peak of Orizaba.

He fell on his knees before the wooden cross that Fray Olmedo had erected in the sands. A shrine had been constructed beneath it, a cairn of stones sheltering the image of the Virgin.

They were close, so very close. Yet many of his men had the marsh fever, and the *naturales*, who had at first seemed well disposed to them, had suddenly vanished. Although he had escaped, at least for the time being, from the shadow of Governor Velázquez, the morale of his men was low. Soon they would be clamoring once again to return home.

What could he do? He could not venture farther inland without food and water, not with just five hundred soldiers and a few horses. He had to find some excuse, some reason to remain.

He had to know what lay beyond those mountains.

Mother of God, help me . . .

A voice carried to him on the wind. He opened his eyes. One of the sentries was running toward him along the beach.

The *naturales* had returned.

MALINALI

THEY ARE NOT Mexica, not this time. There are just five of them, they have no escort, and their dress is plain. They wear white loincloths without decoration and white cotton capes, a vision altogether different from my lord Tendile's feather-work mantle and embroidered cloak. If their clothing is simple, their personal ornamentation is much more elaborate. Their leader has a polished jade turtle in his nose and gold rings in his earlobes; another piece of turquoise drags down his lower lip so that his teeth show in a permanent snarl. His companions also wear large and elaborate earrings and labrets.

They wait under the trees outside Feathered Serpent's tent. Alvarado reaches for one of them, grabbing at his lower lip. He seems excited by the man's labret, fashioned in the shape of a jaguar. My lord shouts at Alvarado, and he releases the man, albeit reluctantly. He steps back, glaring at the newcomer like a hungry dog eyeing a piece of raw meat.

Aguilar appears pained. "These people speak a language I have never heard," he hisses at me. "My lord Cortés sent for you."

He leads me over to these newcomers. One of them repeats the greeting he has made to Aguilar. I admit that I cannot understand him either, and Aguilar grins in triumph.

My lord's look of frustration and disappointment is like a knife in my heart. I cannot fail him now.

I turn back to the strangers. "Do you have the elegant speech?" I ask them.

After a moment's hesitation, one of them, the youngest, steps forward. "I speak *Náhuatl*," he admits.

I allow myself a shy smile in my lord's direction and a chill glance for Aguilar before returning my attention to the strangers. "We welcome you among us. Unfortunately I am the only one here with elegant speech. This dog behind me in the brown robes speaks only Chontal Maya, and the bearded god speaks Castilian, the language spoken in heaven. Can you tell us who you are and how we can be of service to you?"

The boy translates what I have said to his companions. They gape at one another in astonishment, then at Feathered Serpent. There appears to be some disagreement among them before the boy is directed on how to proceed. A lengthy and elaborate five-way conversation then takes place: I translate what they have to say into Chontal Maya for Aguilar; Aguilar, in turn, relays what is said to my lord in Castilian.

"We are Totonacs, from a place called Cempoala," the boy says. "The town is about a day's walk from here. We heard that *teules*"—he uses the *Náhuatl* word for "gods," I note with satisfaction—"had landed here on the coast. We have come to bid them welcome and invite them to visit our town, where they will be most joyfully received with feasting and presents."

Feathered Serpent smiles when he hears this. He says that he will be most happy to visit with them and asks if they are subjects of the great king, Motecuhzoma.

At the mention of Motecuhzoma's name, these Totonacs utter a string of curses in their own language. Finally the boy says, "We are most certainly his subjects, though we wish it otherwise. But is it true what we have heard, that Motecuhzoma sent tribute to your lord?"

"Indeed," I tell him, deciding I might better answer this question myself. True, it was more bribe than tribute, but it will not harm our cause for it to be seen this way. "He sent us a mountain of gifts, quetzal plumes, jade, and gold."

There is another excited exchange among the Totonacs. Then one of them, an old man, points to the feather-work pectoral that I have around my neck, something I salvaged from under the feet of my lord's moles the day Lord Tendile presented the golden wheel.

"My uncle wishes to know where you obtained this beautiful piece of feather work."

"It was part of their tribute."

The old man looks stricken.

"My cousin wore something like this when he was taken by Motecuhzoma's tax gatherers last year," the boy explains.

Aguilar shakes me roughly by the arm, and I jerk it free. I swear, if this brute ever touches me like this again, I will take a knife and cut out his heart myself.

"What's going on?" he demands of me.

"They are explaining to me how the Mexica steal their children for sacrifice."

Aguilar makes the sign of the cross and conveys this information to Feathered Serpent. He is customarily stern, but for a moment I see something else in his face, a flicker of excitement perhaps. Our eyes meet, and there is conspiracy between us; Aguilar does not exist for a moment, nor any of the others. His glance lingers on me, like a lover's.

Aguilar coughs, to remind us of his presence. My lord murmurs something.

"My lord Cortés wants to know," Aguilar says to me, "if the Mexica have many enemies inside their federation."

Why is he asking me this? Surely he already knows the answer to such a question. Why else would he be here? "The whole world hates the Mexica," I answer. "Everyone knows that."

Meanwhile the Totonacs are growing impatient with us. "Will these *teules* visit us at Cempoala?" the boy asks me. "It is only a day's journey to the north."

I relay the request to Aguilar, who in turn passes it on to Feathered Serpent. My lord seems not to be listening, his eyes fixed on some faraway time. He is seeing the future, I realize, and a chill passes through me.

Finally he speaks softly to Aguilar, who appears to hesitate, then gives me a look I cannot fathom. "He wants to know if you, too, hate the Mexica."

"He is my country now."

"That was not his question," Aguilar snaps.

"Just tell him what I said."

I receive a hateful look from him. Oh, he is so easy to read, this priest, this hater of women. But he does as I tell him, and I see Feathered Serpent smile, and I know he has translated my words precisely. Aguilar is too ingenuous to lie.

Feathered Serpent murmurs something else and gives me one last, appraising look before he turns and walks away.

"What did he say?"

"He praised you," Aguilar tells me.

"In what way?"

"Vanity is the enemy of the soul. You have been baptized into the faith, and you should practice modesty. Tell these Indians my lord Cortés will be delighted to visit them. We will leave tomorrow. That is all."

17

BENÍTEZ OPENED HIS eyes, slowly, painfully. He checked his senses, almost as if he were numbering them from an inventory. His mouth was dry and foul, his eyes sticky and swollen, and there was a dull pain behind his eyes. He stared up at the dark thatch of the roof, listened to the sonorous murmur of flies, recoiled at the rank smell of sweat and putrefaction and wood smoke.

How long had he been asleep? How long had he been lying here?

Rain Flower bent over him, dipped a piece of rag into a gourd of water, and wiped his forehead. She spoke some words he could not understand.

Norte's face thrust itself into his vision. "She asks if you are feeling better."

Benítez tried to sit up, but he was too weak. The room swam in and out of focus. He thought he was going to retch.

"Don't try to get up. You must rest."

Benítez wanted to speak, but his tongue would not obey him. It felt as if it were twice its size. Rain Flower held the wet cloth to his lips, and he sucked gratefully at the cool water, like a baby at a mother's breast. "Have I ... been ill?" he managed.

"You had the marsh fever," Norte said. "You came close to death. The whole world was about to grieve for one fewer Spaniard."

Benítez looked up at Rain Flower. He wondered how long she had been there with him. He could not understand for a moment why she might take it upon herself to nurse him. "Tell her ... thank you."

Norte shrugged. "She knows."

"Tell ... her."

A hurried exchange in a strange and exotic tongue. "She said it was Doña Marina's herbs that made you better," Norte said.

Benítez closed his eyes. A strange world. Sometimes it was impossible to decipher a person's motives. Why would these two Indian women help him? He was thirty-three years old, and he had seen little enough mercy in his life. As for the kindness of women, that had been rarer still. He did not delude himself: his features and his shy manners did not make him a ladies' man. This Rain Flower, given him as a *camarada,* a servant-concubine, had helped him not because he was rich or handsome but simply because she herself was kind.

How strange. How very strange.

MALINALI

WE SET OFF at dawn, the Thunder Gods at the fore, the moles stumbling behind, loaded down with armor and weapons. Our column snakes through the dunes, making hard work of it through the pebbled sand.

I follow on foot behind Puertocarrero astride his great beast of war. The sun and the muscle-breaking sand are not our only enemies: halfway through the morning, one of the men steps on a scorpion, and his screams carry to us, though he is so far distant, we cannot even see him.

Late in the afternoon, I stumble, my foot catching in a tree root hidden in the sand. I feel my ankle wrench and twist. I gasp in pain, but I do not cry out: after all, I have been taught from birth not to show pain. Puertocarrero rides on, ignorant of what has happened to me.

The moles tramp past; a few shoot curious glances in my direction, but they are too preoccupied with their own misery to worry about some lord's *camarada.* I rest my weight on my elbows and wait for the pain to subside. Finally I attempt to stand, but my leg will not support me, and I fall back on my haunches.

"Are you all right, my lady?"

A deep, rich voice. It is him. The sun is behind him, putting a golden aura around his head and glinting on his armor. I have to shield my eyes to look at him. He dismounts and leads his beast of war toward me.

"You are hurt?"

I do not understand the words, but I recognize the tone of gentle concern. I point to my left ankle. He bends down to examine it. His touch is soft; he has the hands not of a doctor but of a lover. He looks into my face. The gray eyes are penetrating.

I squeeze out a small tear for his benefit, although the pain by now is not so bad. I move my legs, allow my tunic to rise a little higher. But at that moment one of the other lords rides up on his horse and spoils the moment.

 **18**

ALVARADO REINED IN beside Cortés. "What's happening?"

"The lady Marina has injured her ankle."

"By the sacred balls of all the popes . . ."

"Order a stop. We will have the bearers make her a litter from tree saplings. They will have to carry her."

Alvarado shook his head in disbelief. "All this fuss for one *puta*? Leave her here. We can send the bearers back for her tomorrow."

"She is not a *puta;* she is a Christian gentlewoman. She is also our eyes and ears with the *naturales*. How will we communicate with the Totonacs or the Mexica without her? Would you rather have Brother Aguilar draw pictures for us in the sand? At this moment she is worth more to us than the cannons, even more than my second in command, perhaps. Should I leave you here and send her on ahead on your horse? I can have the bearers come back for you tomorrow."

Alvarado nodded, chastened and embarrassed by this harangue. "I will order a halt."

"I would be obliged."

Cortés turned back to the girl. She was smiling at him. *Bella*. An exquisite face framed by hair as black as a raven. And a delightful ankle, even when injured. Skin like velvet. Her tunic had ridden up, allowing him an uninterrupted view of the silky softness inside her thighs.

Well.

A native princess with a command for language and, I do believe, a flair for politics. Too much of a woman for the likes of Puertocarrero.

In time I must find a remedy for that.

✻ ✻

The next morning they forded a shallow river and turned inland; abruptly they left the barren sand behind and tracked through bright green fields of maize. They plunged into a forest, a riot of orchids and tangled, tendonlike vines. Huge *zapote* trees, their trunks sticky and shining with *chicle* gum, rose into a dense green canopy, alive with the brilliant flashes of tropical birds, scarlet-breasted macaws and blue-plumed tanagers. Occasionally there were ragged villages, aswarm with flies. The people, though, had fled before them.

And then, just after noon, they reached Cempoala.

✻ ✻

Cortés gazed at this new wonder before him.

He was not sure what he had expected; not this. A town rose from the heart of the jungle, thousands of thatched adobe houses clustered around a sprawl of palaces and temples that glistened with polished white limestone and stucco. A city, a wondrous city, not the run-down shamble of filthy huts he had feared.

God had rewarded his faith.

"By the sacred balls of all the popes," Alvarado shouted.

They were announced by a long blast on a conch shell from one of their guides, quickly answered by the beat of drums from inside the town.

The Cempoalans had prepared a welcome for them. As they rode through the streets, they were feted like returning heroes. The Totonacs crowded in, throwing garlands of flowers about their necks, tossing pineapples and plums to the foot soldiers, bouquets of roses to the *jinetas*.

Cortés worked his mount carefully through the press of brown bodies and white mantles. The Totonacs parted for him, wary of the horses. He found Malinali on her litter, Aguilar and Norte following behind her, as he had instructed.

"Ask her to what do we owe such a welcome," he shouted to Aguilar.

Malinali and Aguilar had to shout to make themselves heard over the noise of the crowd and the clamor of the drums and clay flutes.

"She says we are liberators, my lord!"

"Liberators?"

"I do not understand all of it. She says something about the return of a serpent god. Somehow these people know that we have come to save them from barbarity and lead them to salvation!"

A Totonac woman, braver than her fellows, ran toward Cortés and threw a garland of flowers at him, even had the temerity to touch his horse before she rushed away, giggling.

"Liberators," Cortés murmured. *Liberators!* Of course.

Yet in the triumph of the moment, he was distracted by something Aguilar had considered unimportant. *The return of a serpent god.* The words nagged at him and would not leave him.

There was more here than he supposed.

✳ ✳

His name was Chicomacatl, but Alvarado immediately nicknamed him *Gordo*—"Fatso." His standard-bearers came first, carrying long bamboo poles supporting fans of intricate feather work; then *Gordo* himself approached, leaning on stout canes, young boys supporting the great scallops of his flesh from behind. Other princes followed, their presence rendered insignificant by the great mountain of lard that preceded them.

"If they are all as fat as this," Alvarado said, "no wonder these people are cannibals."

Jaramillo grinned. "The whole of Salamanca could feed off his haunches for a month."

Cortés dismounted his horse and looked around. Like the great towns of Spain, Cempoala had its own plaza, surrounded on three sides by the courtyard walls of the temples, on the fourth by *Gordo*'s own palace. Smoke curled from the summit of one of the pyramids, doubtless to signify the completion of some barbaric ceremony. Cortés reminded himself that although the Totonacs had so far displayed friendship, at heart they were heathen.

May God protect them.

Malinali joined him, Aguilar beside her. The swelling on her ankle had diminished overnight, thanks to a herb poultice she herself had prepared. No bones were broken, and she was able to walk unaided, though with a pronounced limp. He smiled at her, glimpsed for a moment a look of fury on Aguilar's face. Envy, no doubt. Jealous of a woman, too. How unbecoming in a man of God.

Gordo waited while his surrogates fumigated Cortés and his officers with their copal censers, and then he stepped forward to embrace him. *Gordo*, like the town luminaries Cortés had met the previous day, wore gold ornaments through his ears and lower lips and had a turquoise stone through the pierced septum of his nose. Cortés did his best to hide his revulsion.

Gordo's slaves stepped forward and deposited at his feet a wicker basket containing bracelets, necklaces, and earrings, all worked in gold. *Gordo* then made a brief speech.

Aguilar listened to Malinali's translation and then said, "She says he apologizes for these few paltry gifts. It is all they have to demonstrate their friendship. He says the Mexica tax collectors have robbed them for years and left them with almost nothing."

Cortés considered. "Tell him we receive these gifts very gratefully."

It was now deathly quiet in the plaza, both the Cempoalans and the Spanish soldiers straining to hear every word that was spoken.

After the next exchange, Aguilar turned back to Cortés. "The woman..." Cortés noted the contempt in his voice; he could not bring himself to say Malinali's name. "... The woman says he makes great complaint against Motecuhzoma, that the Mexica have taken all their gold and feather work and jade in taxes, have stolen half their vanilla crop, and taken many of their young men and women to feed their priests' demand for sacrifice at their temples. He asks for your help."

Cortés solemnly regarded the fat simpleton standing across from him on the dusty plaza. *At last.* "Aguilar, please ask Malinali to inform Chicomacatl that we ourselves are subjects of a very powerful king, who has sent us here to free them from tyranny. If he agrees to become a vassal of King Charles V, he has paid the last of his taxes to the Mexica."

Gordo was sweating under the hot sun, despite the enthusiastic efforts of his slaves with their feather-work fans. There was another long harangue that passed through Malinali and Aguilar before it reached Cortés. "I think he wishes our help," Aguilar said, "but he is frightened because there is a garrison of Mexica not far from here. He says if he were to renounce his vassalship to Motecuhzoma, they would come here and burn the town and drag all the young men off to Tenochtitlán to be slaughtered in the temples."

"Tell him that if he obeys me, he need never fear Motecuhzoma again."

He heard the sharp intake of breath behind him. Puertocarrero began to protest, fidgeting on his horse, but Cortés silenced him with a glance.

He watched the fat Totonac lord. Was it possible for a man to look relieved, delighted, and consumed by abject terror at once? *Gordo* did a fair imitation of it.

Alvarado spurred his horse forward and leaned from the saddle. "Are you out of your mind?" he whispered.

"Have you ever known me to be reckless?"

"More times than I can count. That time in Salamanca you climbed the wall to that *doñita's* window, for instance."

"I still calculate the odds before I gamble. It will go well with us. You will see."

Alvarado sat back in the saddle, his lips a thin white line. "Whatever you say."

"Trust me. We have just been handed the key to Motecuhzoma's house."

MALINALI

A HUGE FEAST of turkey, fish, pineapples, plums, and corn cakes has been prepared for us. Afterward Feathered Serpent and the other lords are led to their quarters, a large palace belonging to a rich noblewoman.

The palace has a flat roof with a wide terrace that overlooks the plaza. The rooms are spacious, though there is little furniture, just some sleeping mats and a few low tables. Tapestries hang on the walls; others are strewn on the white stucco floors. Puertocarrero and I have a room to ourselves, as do the other Thunder Lords and their *camaradas;* the soldiers and moles are billeted together in the audience hall.

I cannot stop thinking about Feathered Serpent. During the meeting in the plaza, something angered him. Several times during that encounter, I saw his gaze return to the smoke rising from the pyramid, and I think I know what is troubling him.

I feel the stirring of a god.

✺   ✺

The next morning I am summoned to the patio, along with Aguilar and several of the Thunder Lords. Feathered Serpent's expression is stern. He is dressed in his suit of black velvet, he has his sword buckled to his hip, and he wears a silver medal around his neck bearing a picture of the goddess they call Virgin.

"Gentlemen, we are called to do God's work," he announces, and strides out of the gates and across the plaza, the rest hurrying after him, running to keep pace.

The temple here is very much like the one at Potonchán. There is a walled-off courtyard and a steep stone staircase that ascends a truncated pyramid to the ceremonial temple, a simple thatched hut of straw and bamboo. As we approach, the air becomes dense with the smell of charred meat.

The bodies lie at the foot of the steps, where they have come to rest after the priests have finished with them. The arms and legs are gone, and blood has congealed in a black jelly around the open cavity of their chests. Flies buzz in thick black swarms. Dead eyes gaze up, lifeless, at the blue sky.

"This one's just a child," Puertocarrero says to Feathered Serpent.

Fray Olmedo begins to mumble words from his book. Aguilar does the same.

The black-robed priests are watching from the shrine above us, clustered together like carrion crows. Feathered Serpent's face is terrible. I hear the rattle of steel as he draws his sword from its scabbard, but Puertocarrero puts a hand on his arm and whispers something to him, and he relents.

I watch, proud of his fury. Feathered Serpent had always promised he would abolish human sacrifice. Now I have witnessed his outrage and his despair, and I know I am in his presence. I wish Rain Flower were here, then she would believe also.

The Thunder Gods huddle behind him, their faces white as chalk, staring at the dismembered corpse.

Aguilar turns to me. "Is this how you care for your children in this land?"

How can I explain this to him? The child was probably malformed or taken from another village during war. "The sacrifice is for *Tlaloc*, the Rain Bringer. Unlike a man, a child weeps when faced with the sacrificial stone. The tears are like the falling rain. The more tears there are, the more rains there will be in the winter to feed the harvest."

Aguilar makes a sign in the air with his hand and mutters something in his own language. The others are looking at me as if this were my doing. I wish I understood what is going through their minds. But what mortal can truly fathom the ways of the gods?

 **19**

"SOMETHING MUST BE done here for the Lord," Cortés said.

Benítez stared into the face of the dead child. The others turned away, but Benítez remained behind. Cortés's words echoed inside his head. *Something must be done here for the Lord.*

He realized someone was standing behind him, watching.

It was Norte: Norte the renegade, Norte the traitor, Norte the savage, watching him with that unfathomable half smirk on his tattooed face.

"Another offering to your gods?"

"What is a god, Benítez? An invention of our own minds."

Heresy! They should hang this demon now before he infected them all with his devilish ideas. "What mind invented this?" Benítez said.

"A mind that has never been sure that its body will escape starvation."

Benítez shook his head. What kind of answer was that? "Did you witness rites such as these?"

Norte did not answer him directly. Instead, he said, "You have a fanciful morality, Benítez. You do not blanch when the Church's inquisitors break a man's arms and legs on a rack when he is still alive, but remove them when he is dead and you are suddenly offended. You will tear out a man's intestines with your pike on the field of battle, leave him there to die by inches, but to cut out his heart and kill him quickly appears to you a great barbarity. Your logic defeats me."

"This is just a child!"

"And women and children do not suffer and die in our wars?"

"Not in our churches. Our religion is not murder and cannibalism."

"No, our religion is gold."

Why do I justify what is holy to this savage? Benítez thought. No, he is worse than a savage, because he has known civilization and true faith and has knowingly turned his back on God to embrace this barbarity. "I have nothing but contempt for wretches such as you."

"You are supposed to have pity for me, Benítez. A lost lamb, a sinner who has strayed from the fold."

"Cortés should have hanged you."

"You see? You think human meat is so sacred, but you hold life so cheap. We have both seen men burned to death at the stake. Women, too. Why? In the name of God. Why is that so different from what has happened here?"

Benítez spun around. "You excuse this?"

"Are you asking me if I would rather expire screaming in my own funeral pyre or die quickly from one of these priest's knives? I think I know my answer."

"I pray that one day you will achieve your desire." He spat in the dirt and walked away. He had to be away from this infernal place, this unnatural man.

✳ ✳

They feasted in the square. The mats were heaped with the finest delicacies the Cempoalans could provide: venison with chilies, tomatoes, and squash seeds; roasted turkeys; locusts with sage; newts with yellow peppers. The Spaniards feasted riotously on the venison and turkey, but the other dishes were pushed abruptly aside. Dogs fought for the scraps of gristle and bone that the soldiers tossed over their shoulders while the Totonac girls serving the food flirted and giggled.

Cortés was seated beside *Gordo* on one of the feasting mats, Malinali and Aguilar behind them to translate. The Totonac chieftain was still enumerating his complaints against Motecuhzoma when his servants brought out a steaming tray of meats, which was placed reverently between him and Cortés. *Gordo* indicated that this dish was special and that Cortés should have the great honor of serving himself first.

Cortés's nostrils quivered, and he recognized the sulfurous smell of cooked human blood. There was a shocked silence, broken only by Fray Olmedo's murmured prayer for the dead.

"Tell him I cannot touch this," Cortés hissed at Aguilar. "Tell him that eating human flesh is an abomination before God."

Aguilar relayed Cortés's outrage to Malinali, who then leaned forward and whispered a few words in *Náhautl* to *Gordo*. The fat *cacique's* jaw fell open in astonishment.

"What has he to say for himself?" Cortés asked Aguilar.

"He asks what else might be done with prisoners captured in battle if one does not eat them. May God have mercy on his soul."

"Explain to him, if you will, Brother Aguilar, that these gods he serves are actually devils, and he will burn for all eternity in the fires of hell unless he desists from his heathen practices. Tell him we come here to bring him true religion, and that if he wishes to become a vassal of King Charles, he must learn to be a Christian gentleman."

Cortés watched Malinali as she spoke at some length with the Totonac chief. At first *Gordo* seemed confused. He whispered an answer to Malinali, who hesitated before relaying it to Aguilar.

"The woman says he will think about this," Aguilar said, "but he fears that if they do not give the gods due sacrifice, there will be droughts and floods, and locusts will come and devour all their harvests. But he is still happy to become your vassal."

Cortés felt himself losing his rein on his temper. This was not the answer he wanted to hear. "Tell him again—"

Fray Olmedo, who was seated next to Alvarado, leaned forward. "Perhaps, my lord, we need not suppress their barbaric rites immediately. We are in a tenuous position. We should speak gently to them over time, so that they—"

"We are here to do God's work!"

"Even God's work is not done in one day."

Now it was Aguilar's turn: "Fray Olmedo, with respect, I agree with our commander, the Lord cannot—"

The debate was interrupted by the blast of conch shells. The Totonacs leaped to their feet and began rushing from the square. A messenger hurried over to *Gordo* and whispered urgently in his ear.

Cortés looked at Malinali. The girl smiled and nodded, almost as if she had orchestrated this moment. What could have happened that pleased her and so greatly terrified the Totonacs? She whispered something to Aguilar.

"It seems," he said, "that the Totonacs are about to receive more visitors. The Mexica have arrived."

✺ ✺

From the panicked reaction they had evinced, Cortés had expected an army. Instead, there were just five officials with a handful of attendants. Their cloaks were knotted at their shoulders with the imperial seals of Motecuhzoma, and they each held the royal crook of office in their right hand; with the other they kept flowers pressed to their noses, presumably to ward off the stink of their hosts. Attendants kept the flies from their faces with broad feathered fans, while others held parasols to shade them from the sun.

They made their way across the plaza, *Gordo* and the Totonac nobility fawning in their wake. They completely ignored Cortés and the Spaniards, although a small army of bearded strangers encamped in the center of the town must surely have been the most remarkable thing they had ever witnessed in their lives.

It was a deliberate snub, Cortés decided. Well, there was an answer for that.

Cortés turned to Aguilar. "Ask the lady Marina to find out what she can for me."

"My lord, I—"

"Just do it, Brother Aguilar." The deacon was growing tiresome. Sometimes he wished he had left him on Cozumel with Norte.

Cortés looked at Alvarado. "May they repent their arrogance! They walk right past us as if we were peasants in a field."

"By Satan's hairy ass! I would like to teach them a lesson."

"And we shall. I promise you."

Perhaps the girl, Malinali, has reason to smile, he thought. The Mexica had arrived at a propitious moment. Even now a plan was taking shape in his mind. Very soon he would start picking at the corners of this great foundation that the Mexica had built, see if he could break off a small piece with his fingers. If it came easily away, then the rest would surely follow, a piece at a time.

✺ ✺

All the Spaniards heard the keening that came from the fat *cacique*'s palace. Malinali returned and reported that *Gordo* himself had spent much of the interview with the newcomers on his knees, crying like a baby. The five Mexica, she reported, were imperial tax collectors, and although she could not hear all of what was said, it appeared they were demanding a heavy tribute from the Totonacs because they had entertained the Spaniards so lavishly, against Motecuhzoma's express instructions.

Cortés watched from the roof terrace as the Mexica noblemen left *Gordo*'s palace, still sniffing the nosegays in their hands. The Totonacs had prepared quarters for them on the other side of the plaza. The rooms had been decked with hundreds of flowers, Malinali reported, food had been prepared, servants provided.

"Look at them," Alvarado snarled. "Like five bishops on their way to mass."

Aguilar and Fray Olmedo glanced around, thinking to rebuke him, but he ignored them.

Cortés looked around for Malinali. She was waiting, unobtrusively, at his right shoulder. Her dark eyes glittered, intelligent, watchful, and expectant. Ah, what an ally I have found here! he thought. And what a paradox. In this savage Indian, I have found more of a wife than I could ever have hoped for in a Spanish *doñita*, with her fluttering fan and precious manners. There is nothing at all behind the black mantillas but perfumes and a pretty face.

Aguilar noticed the look that passed between Cortés and Malinali and scowled.

What is it that troubles the young deacon? Cortés wondered. Does he fear her because she is a woman or because she is a *natural*? "Ask the lady Marina," he said to him, "why these people are so terrified of five unarmed men holding flowers."

Aguilar did as he was told.

"The woman says that it is not the five men they are frightened of, but the five thousand who will follow if they disobey them."

Cortés frowned. "So they are more frightened of the Mexica than they are of us."

"We should correct that impression," Alvarado said.

"Indeed." He turned back to Aguilar. "Ask my lady Marina to

go back to the palace and request my lord *Gordo's* presence here. Immediately."

What he planned was a gamble, but it was the best kind of wager to make: the stakes were high, and the coins were spilling off the table. Yet he himself had nothing to lose.

MALINALI

GORDO'S FACE GLISTENS like a piece of sweating dough, his jowls quiver below his chin, and he is wringing his hands like a woman. If it were not for the slave boys who hold him upright, his trembling knees would give way under him, and he would fall into a shapeless mass of fat on the floor.

I look at Feathered Serpent. His eyes are both beneficent and stern.

He speaks softly to Aguilar.

"My lord Cortés wants you to remind *Gordo* that he is a subject of King Charles of Spain, and he has nothing to fear from the Mexica. If he does as Cortés commands, he will be safe."

I turn to *Gordo* and tell him in *Náhuatl,* "Feathered Serpent says he will protect you. But you must do everything he says."

"The Mexica have demanded twenty of our youths and girls for sacrifice because we have disobeyed Motecuhzoma! They insist that three of my own children be among those surrendered to them!"

"Feathered Serpent says you are under his protection now," I repeat, trying to be as patient with him as my lord.

Gordo stares at me in panic. "Tell me what we must do."

My lord whispers to Aguilar, who appears to question his instructions, as if he cannot quite believe what he has heard. My lord's tone becomes impatient.

"My lord Cortés wants you to tell him..." Aguilar hesitated. "... Tell him his men must seize the Mexica immediately, bind them, and put them under guard."

At last, the struggle is to commence.

This time I convey my lord's words precisely, and when *Gordo* hears them, I fear that he is about to faint away. His legs collapse beneath him, and his page boys grunt and struggle to keep him from sinking completely to the floor. His face has the look of a cornered animal. "I cannot!" he shouts at me, his voice shrill.

"You must do as Feathered Serpent commands."

"If we lay a hand on them, Motecuhzoma will slaughter us all!"

What a spineless coward. Does he not realize he has the power of a god to help him? "He refuses," I tell Aguilar.

Feathered Serpent leaps to his feet, and his anger is terrible to witness. "My lord Cortés says that if he does not do as he commands, he will leave immediately and never return," Aguilar says, almost shouting in his agitation. "It is his choice. But if he wants to save the lives of his children and free himself from the Mexica, then he must do as he says!"

It is the moment I have been waiting for. I round on *Gordo*, and now I am shouting, too. "See! You have angered Feathered Serpent! Unless you do as he asks, he will return to the Cloud Lands, and your sons and daughters will have their hearts ripped out on Motecuhzoma's altars!"

Gordo makes gasping noises as if he were choking. He really has no choice. Why is it men find it so hard to make a leap of faith, even when there is no other way? If he cannot surrender to a god, then all his religion is just stupid superstition.

"Well? Any moment Feathered Serpent will leave here and sail back to the east. What is your decision?"

 **20**

THE MEXICA WERE bound to long poles, hand and foot, like the carcasses of wild deer. But these trophies were very much alive, their eyes wide, grunting protests of outrage through the rags in their mouths. Totonacs rushed from all over the plaza for a glimpse of this terrifying and extraordinary spectacle.

Cortés himself watched from the parapet of their quarters with Alvarado, Puertocarrero, and the rest of his officers. *Gordo* stood beside him, his jaw slack with terror. He said something to Malinali, who relayed it to Aguilar.

"He wants to sacrifice them immediately," Aguilar said. "He believes that once they are dead, there is less chance that Motecuhzoma will discover what has happened."

Cortés shook his head. "They are to be kept alive. I may wish to question them later. Tell him to separate them and put them under close arrest. I will send men to help guard them." Cortés felt a fire of excitement in his belly. At last he was in control. "Also, tell him that he is now free. No more of his sons and daughters will die on Motecuhzoma's altars, and there will be no more tax collectors to steal his possessions. From now on I regard him as my own brother, and he should put his trust only in me!"

MALINALI

THERE IS A feeling of exhilaration and pride as I have never experienced before. Finally it has happened, and in his fury he is as magnificent as I had imagined. The Feathered Serpent has returned to break the hold of the Mexica, and I shall be a part of it, as I was promised.

"Enjoy this moment, Little Mother," a voice whispers in my ear. "Before Sister Moon rises a second time, we will all be on our way to the temple stone in Tenochtitlán!"

I turn around. It is Rain Flower. What will it take to convince her?

"He is a god."

"He is not a god; he is a madman." Her hand reaches for mine. She is frightened. I press her hand tightly, try to pass on some of my own strength, my own confidence in him. I know this in my heart: we are witnessing not only the end of the Fifth Sun but the dawn of a new and blood-red day.

As my father prophesied.

✳   ✳

Puertocarrero shakes me roughly awake. His corn-colored hair shimmers in the light of the candle. It is deep into the Fifth Watch of the Night, but he is fully dressed. He indicates to me that I am to follow him. I rise from the sleeping mat, put on a skirt and tunic, and follow him down the cloister. Shadows dance in the flickering torches of pitch pine on the walls.

We stop outside my lord's private chamber. Puertocarrero pulls me inside.

I look around, still only half awake, at the bearded faces of the Thunder Gods, dressed in their golden armor, torchlight glinting dully on their steel pikes and swords. My lord sits behind a heavy wooden table in the middle of the room, several of these other lords around him, Aguilar, too.

He looks up and gives me a gentle smile of encouragement. Three of the Mexica tax gatherers stand in front of the table with heavy wooden collars around their necks. Not so haughty now. Their hands are roped behind their backs, their eyes lowered to the floor in shame for their condition.

But what are they doing here? What is happening?

Aguilar, looking pale and pious, is first to speak. "My lord Cortés wants you to ask these men who they are, where they are from, and why they were seized by the Totonacs."

"But he knows the answer to all those questions."

"Just do as he says!"

I hate it when he speaks to me this way. But I obey. I address myself to the one by whose cloak and adornments I judge to be the highest ranking of the three here. "Feathered Serpent wishes to know who you are and why you are here. He also asks why the Totonacs have taken you as their prisoner."

The man raises his head and regards me down the length of his parrot's-beak nose. Still too proud for his own good. He also resents being addressed by a woman. "We are *calpisqui*—tribute gatherers—of the great Motecuhzoma. As to why we were taken prisoner—and you will all suffer tenfold for our humiliations—it was done at the behest of your great lord!"

What is the point of this charade? I wonder. My lord knows all this. But I dutifully translate the *calpisqui*'s reply for Aguilar.

He confers with Cortés, then says to me, "My lord Cortés answers that he certainly did not know what the Totonacs were planning. But when he learned that they were preparing to sacrifice their Mexica prisoners to their gods, he decided to intervene. Tell him this is because Cortés considers Motecuhzoma a friend, for he knows he is a great lord like himself and has sent him many gifts."

Well. What am I to make of this? But it is not for me to comprehend the mind of a god. I instead take great pleasure in seeing the Mexicans blanch when I mention the Totonacs' planned "sacrifice." How fitting it would be to see you three stretched across a slab!

"The Totonacs told us that our capture was executed on the orders of your lord," the *calpisqui* answers, though he seems less sure of himself now.

When Aguilar repeats this to Feathered Serpent, he contrives to look mystified.

Aguilar turns back to me. "My lord Cortés says the Totonacs must be a perfidious and devious people, for he certainly knew nothing about it."

I stare at Feathered Serpent. His face is blank, and when I look for some secret communication in his eyes, as we have shared before, he will not meet my gaze. Why should he lie about this? But again, I convey his words exactly as Aguilar has spoken them.

The Mexica seem as mystified as myself. One of them says to his fellows, "Perhaps he is telling the truth. Why else would he have gained our freedom for us?"

While they are debating among themselves, I turn back to Aguilar. "What is happening here?"

"You do not have to know that. You are only here to translate."

Oh, may you be buggered by a leprous porcupine! Do not deign to speak to me this way! I am more, much more, than translator for Feathered Serpent—as we both know!

Feathered Serpent whispers something to Aguilar, who turns back to me with a silken smile. *I know what you have been trying to do,* the smile says, *but I am still his confidant. You are just an Indian and an outsider.* "Tell them my lord Cortés is pained to see their austere selves brought to such straits. As they are servants of the great Motecuhzoma and have been arrested with no just cause, they are to be released immediately. Furthermore, he places himself completely at their disposal."

As I tell them this, the Thunder Gods step forward and release the thongs at their wrists and remove the heavy wooden collars around their necks. For the second time this day, the Mexica are taken quite by surprise.

The *calpisqui* turns to me. "Thank your lord for his service," he says, as unsure of what is happening as I am. "But tell him that although he has freed us, we cannot leave. The Totonacs will snatch us again as soon as we walk from your protection through the doors of this palace."

It seems my lord is prepared for their answer, and Aguilar already has instructions on how to respond to it. "Tell them they should not fear. Our soldiers will remove them to the coast, disguised in Spanish capes, and they will be escorted out of Totonac territory aboard one of our ships. They can then go about their business in peace. All my lord Cortés asks is that when they stand once again in the pleasing presence of the lord Motecuhzoma, they shall remind him that Cortés is his friend."

I convey this to them, but I stumble over this last sentiment. How to tell the emperor of the Mexica that Feathered Serpent, the traditional enemy of Motecuhzoma's own gods, is actually an ally? I am sure Aguilar must be mistaken. But I convey his words as best as I am able and leave the *calpisqui* to make of it what he can.

The three Mexica tax gatherers are ushered from the chamber. Suddenly all the Thunder Gods are grinning at one another. I stare at them, confused. Why should my lord release these monsters and so betray *Gordo*, who placed himself in his trust? Why are they so pleased with what has been done?

Feathered Serpent turns to me, and I detect another curious smile, allowing further conspiracy between us, but then Puertocarrero has hold of my arm and is ushering me out of the chamber.

I cannot help but wonder what *Gordo* will say when he discovers that three of his Mexica prisoners are gone. I wish, again, that I could speak the language of the gods and know what he plans to do. He is surely as unpredictable as a god.

The one thing I am sure of: he is no friend to Motecuhzoma.

✳ ✳

The next day *Gordo* does indeed appear the shell of the man who met us in the plaza just a few days before. He stands quivering before Cortés like a fresh heart in a bowl.

I pass his first utterances to Aguilar, who then whispers to Feathered Serpent. On hearing what *Gordo* has to say, my lord rises from his chair in a rage, his hands bunched into fists at his sides. "What! You let them *escape*? Were all your guards *asleep*?"

The *cacique* is trying to explain to me that he does not understand how it has happened and that those responsible have already suffered the consequences, that their hearts are roasting in a brazier at this very moment. But my lord does not wait for my translation. After all, he knows far better than *Gordo* how the escape was managed. During the First Watch of the Night, Guzmán and Flores approached the Totonac guards with a jar of Cuban wine, which *Gordo's* men had found very pleasant. When the Spaniards returned two hours later, they were snoring like pigs. The three Mexica had then been led away, still bound.

But now my lord paces the room like a caged animal, beating his fist into the palm of his hand. I know his rage is feigned, and I wonder at the reason for his perfidy.

"My lord Cortés says this is an unmitigated disaster," Aguilar is saying to me. "Tell this dog he must hand over the other prisoners to us immediately, for he obviously cannot be trusted. We will put them in chains and have them transferred to one of our ships."

Gordo agrees. Of course. Anything the great lord desires.

"My lord Cortés also insists," Aguilar adds, while my lord raves on the other side of the room, "that *Gordo* must this day swear allegiance to himself and the king of Spain, his most catholic majesty, Charles V, in the presence of the royal notary. He must also agree to join forces with us against the Mexica, placing all his warriors at his disposal. Should he fail to do either of these things, my lord Cortés shall abandon him to his fate."

Suddenly I understand what has been done. I stare in admiration at my lord. He portrays rage so well. He is indeed a god, for he can wear so many disguises so well. He has played this *Gordo* like a flute.

I convey my lord's terms to the Totonac chieftain: he is to place himself utterly at Feathered Serpent's command. There is a long and deathly silence as the *cacique* imagines the consequences if he should now be left to face the wrath of Motecuhzoma alone. He nods his acquiescence so vigorously, his jowls shake.

"Well?" Aguilar asks.

"He agrees," I say. "You have given him no choice."

21

Tenochtitlán

ON OCCASIONS OF national importance, the Supreme Council of the Mexica gathered in the House of the Eagle Knights, inside the Great Temple complex. The room was furnished with low stone benches, decorated with carved reliefs of serpents and warriors. A clay brazier fashioned into the likeness of the god *Tlaloc,* Rain Maker, warmed the room. *Mictlantecuhtli,* the God of the Dead, his bones protruding through his clay flesh, watched over the deliberations of these emperors and kings, reminding them of the ephemeral nature of life and of their power.

Motecuhzoma presided over the gathering, as always. Beside him was Snake Woman, his prime minister. Also in attendance was his nephew; Lord Maize Cobs; the king of Texcoco; and Motecuhzoma's brother and heir, Cuitláhuac, the lord of Iztapalapa. The chief priests of the temple and the most senior Jaguar and Eagle Knights had also been ordered to this council. All of these great nobles and priests wore only robes of plain maguey fiber in the presence of their emperor, who was himself resplendent in a turquoise cloak of the finest cotton, decorated with a pattern of writhing serpents.

Pine torches crackled on the walls.

"My army is ready to march, as you ordered," Lord Maize Cobs said. "You have only to give the command."

"That unfortunate remedy may not be necessary," Motecuhzoma answered. "There has been a new development. Three of the *calpisqui* have been released. They were escorted through Totonac lands by *Malintzin's* own soldiers."

The gathered Mexica nobles shook their heads in bewilderment.

"They brought a personal message from this *Malintzin.* He has conveyed his feelings of friendship to me and has promised to punish the Totonacs personally for the offenses they have committed against our tribute gatherers."

There was a long silence. What to make of such a thing? Incomprehensible.

"Then, just a few hours ago, their two companions also returned to Tenochtitlán. They, too, have been saved from the Totonac sacrificial stones by this *Malintzin,* who conveyed them to safety on his own war canoes. They said these lords treated them most gently."

"What does it mean?" one of the old warriors said aloud.

"This woman he has with him," Woman Snake began, "this... Malinali. She says *Malintzin* is a god. She says he is Feathered Serpent returned."

A deathly hush.

"We cannot be sure that what this woman says is true," Cuitláhuac murmured. "*Malintzin* does not have the elegant speech. They are not his words, they are hers."

Lord Maize Cobs nodded. "He may only be an ambassador from some far-off place. If that is the case, then we must welcome him with good hospitality and hear what he has to say."

Falling Eagle, Motecuhzoma's nephew, shifted irritably on his bench. "You should not let into your house someone who will try to throw you out of it."

"If this *Malintzin* is indeed an ambassador of another country," a general of the Jaguar Knights said, "then we should give him the hospitality he is due, as Lord Maize Cobs has said. If he comes dishonestly, we have brave warriors who can defend us. What do we have to fear, we millions against a few hundred?"

"And yet Lord Teuhtitl does not believe them to be ambassadors. He thinks they are invaders, come in the guise of gods."

"Invaders?" one of the chief priests interrupted. "How can so few men invade all Mexico?"

Motecuhzoma, who had sat in sullen silence during this debate, now raised his hand for silence. "The *calpisqui* overheard the Totonacs also calling them gods."

"The Totonacs were fathered by monkeys," Falling Eagle said.

Motecuhzoma silenced him with a stare. "This *Malintzin* and his followers behave as incomprehensibly as gods. He has come in the year that was prophesied, One Reed, and he landed on our beaches on the day of his name, Nine-Wind."

"What should we do, then? If we send our armies against him and they are victorious, what should happen to us?" He looked around the room, seeing other worried faces. "If we destroy Feathered Serpent, we destroy the wind, and without the wind there will be no clouds, no rain, and no crops in the fields. To vanquish him would be to vanquish ourselves."

For a long time the only sound was the hissing of burning green logs in the brazier.

"Now he has proclaimed himself my friend and given proof of it. To take up our arms against him would be a needless folly."

"What if he is not Feathered Serpent?" Lord Maize Cobs asked.

"What if he is?" Motecuhzoma countered. "No, for now we will do nothing. We will wait."

He rose to his feet to indicate that the council was closed. The gathered nobles fell to their knees as he left the chamber, each of them more frightened now than when he entered the room. Their emperor seemed paralyzed by indecision while somewhere on their borders a mischievous hand was manipulating events. Either as a god or as a man, this *Malintzin* was manifestly dangerous. Only the priests seemed satisfied with the interpretation Motecuhzoma had placed on events; the rest of them, the soldiers and the statesmen, by instinct did not trust what they did not understand.

But they must be guided by Revered Speaker; they must believe, as he did, that they might yet be spared the doom that had been foretold.

MALINALI

OUR ALLIANCE WITH *Gordo* and the Totonacs is done with great public ceremony in the plaza. One of my lord's moles writes everything down in his book, as Feathered Serpent wishes. *Gordo* then announces that the Cempoalans will cement this alliance in the normal way.

"The Totonacs and your Thunder Gods will now make a bond that will last forever. We now present our finest daughters as their wives!"

I turn to Aguilar. "There is to be more mounting of women," I tell him with a slow smile.

"What do you mean?"

"He is offering my lord more women for his pleasure. Perhaps this time you should ask for one for yourself."

Aguilar now uses a word in Chontal Maya that he thinks means "whore," but it does not carry the same power or stigma in our language. Then he turns away from me and gives the news to Feathered Serpent.

"My lord Cortés wants you to thank *Gordo* for his generosity," he says to me after consultation, "but you must remind him that the young women must first be baptized in the Holy Spirit before they can . . . accompany a Christian gentleman."

"They are to be sprinkled outside and in, yes, Aguilar?"

His face turns the color of a ripe chili.

I know it is not politic to goad him, but I cannot help myself. Besides, I am growing anxious now, and Aguilar is an easy target for my frustrations. What if my lord Feathered Serpent should choose one of the women for himself, over me?

✳   ✳

Eight young women are led into the plaza, dressed in sheer cotton mantles and wearing several golden collars and earrings. So much for the destitution to which the Mexica had apparently condemned the Totonac nation. But never mind. I am sure my lord is aware of their perfidy; as long as they are unaware of his.

Seven of the women are presented to my lord's captains; my violet-eyed Puertocarrero and *Tonatiuh* are rewarded with a second wife. My husband's is especially beautiful, the daughter of *Gordo*'s own prime minister, Lord Cuesco. She is immediately sprinkled with water by Fray Olmedo and is now to be called Doña Francisca.

Then *Gordo* proudly presents my lord with his own niece.

There are stifled guffaws among the moles. I feel a surge of relief. The princess is not as fat as *Gordo*. Not quite. Give her a few months. She approaches in a wobbling gait like an overfed turkey and looks utterly ridiculous in her bridal finery, covered from head to foot in flowers, a garden on the move.

I dare a glance at my lord. He silences the titters of his captains with a hard stare and then steps forward and kisses his bride gallantly on the hand. I wonder at his manners and his kindness. My heart goes out to him, beating wildly.

Then he looks at me, and I see laughter in his eyes but not on his lips. He whispers something to Aguilar.

"My lord Cortés wishes you to tell this girl's uncle that his generosity is huge." I smile at this, but it is evident Aguilar cannot see the joke. In my translation I change *huge* to something approximating *boundless,* as I am sure my lord would have wished me to do.

Gordo's niece is the last to submit to the sprinkling of the water.

Aguilar seems pleased. "Tell *Gordo* that now he has sworn fealty to his most Catholic majesty the king of Spain, he must abandon these damnable blood sacrifices and tear down his devilish idols."

I turn to *Gordo*. "Feathered Serpent says that you must now abandon human sacrifice, as he preached when he was last here many sheaves of years ago."

Gordo gapes at me, astonished. "But surely a few slaves, some prisoners taken in battle, this is not unreasonable to ensure a good harvest or when the rains are late..."

"Feathered Serpent says it is a crime and must be stopped immediately. You must also tear down your images of his great enemy, *Tezcatlipoca,* Bringer of Darkness."

"But if we destroy our gods, there will be no more rains, no more crops in the fields..."

An angry murmur passes through the crowd. Like a ripple on a pond, the whispers pass from mouth to mouth.

"What is *Gordo* saying?" Aguilar wants to know.

"He argues like a woman at the market. Let me have one

more moment with him." I return my attention to the *cacique*. "All these years you and your ancestors have waited for Feathered Serpent's return, and now you reject his teaching! First you welcome him back with a great procession, and then you betray him! What if he decides not to bother with you any further? What do you think Motecuhzoma will do when my lord is no longer here to protect you, when he has gone back to the Cloud Lands in disgust?"

Gordo hesitates.

I turn to my lord Feathered Serpent in frustration. He gives a signal to the Thunder Lords waiting on the other side of the plaza.

A clap of thunder. The crowd gasps, some fall to the ground in terror, others start to run. I see *Tonatiuh* and some of his fellow captains sprint up the temple steps, holding swords and heavy iron bars. When they reach the top, they knock aside the priests, and then a dozen of them lever one of the stone idols toward the edge. It is Serpent Skirt herself.

Even as I silently will them on, I concede it is a terrible sight to witness. The goddess falls, lurching sideways onto the topmost steps, and then comes crashing down toward us. Serpent Skirt is broken in three pieces by the time she reaches the plaza, stone splinters landing a hundred paces from where she finally comes to rest, bloodying some of the crowd.

Already the Thunder Gods are attacking Rain Bringer and Maize Mother. The crowd spills back into the plaza, moaning like a giant wounded beast. They want to rush the temple to protect their gods, and they spill forward in an onrushing tide, only to retreat again in fear as Bringer of Darkness rumbles down the steps, gathering speed before shattering into pieces at the bottom.

It is a moment I had thought never to see in my lifetime, a sacrilege that leaves me breathless, exhilarated, and terrified. I smell smoke. They have overturned Lord of Fire, and the sparks from his crown have ignited the thatched roof.

A black pall of smoke hangs over the temple. The wails of

the Totonacs echo from the adobe wall, deafening. They will turn on us at any moment, are only waiting for a signal from *Gordo.*

The Thunder Lords have already formed a defensive perimeter around Feathered Serpent and the fat *cacique,* their swords and pikes and thunder sticks trained on the crowd. It seems impossible that a few moments before, they were giving us their women and their devotion. *Gordo*'s fat niece is running comically in circles, wailing at the top of her lungs. Fray Olmedo is on his knees, hands clenched and thrust up at the sky.

I must admire Aguilar, though I detest him. In the face of this wild crowd, he clutches his precious book to his chest and regards the Totonacs who wish to kill him with the benign forbearance of a schoolteacher.

For myself I do not fear anything. My father had told me never to fear chaos. *In destruction you will find your destiny.*

22

CORTÉS DREW HIS sword. "How many innocent women and children have been butchered by these heathens?" he shouted over the baying of the Indians around him. "How can we count ourselves as Christians and honorable Spaniards if we let this continue? Let us count our lives as nothing if we fail God in this venture!"

The soldiers kept their order as the crowd surged forward. Benítez shouted a warning and pointed to the royal palace. Totonac archers were assembling on the roof.

Cortés grabbed *Gordo* by the arm and held his sword to his throat.

"Lady Marina!" Aguilar shouted over the din. "Cortés says you must inform their *cacique* that he is about to die unless he restores order!"

Cortés forced *Gordo* to his knees. The sharpened edge of his sword had already drawn a trickle of blood from his doughy flesh. Malinali put her face in front of his and whispered to him in *Náhuatl*. He nodded his acquiescence, babbling.

It took four of his own slaves to get him back to his feet. He addressed the mob, his voice a wavering tremolo, and gradually a silence fell over the plaza.

MALINALI

THE NEXT DAY the Totonacs drag their shattered gods from the plaza with ropes. Rain Bringer and Maize Mother and the rest disappear into the forest. They will not be smashed and buried as my lord has ordered, of course. The Totonacs will steal away, from time to time, to the secret hiding places. But it is enough for now that their power has been challenged, their hold on the people broken.

On the summit of the pyramid, another thatch is already under way over the ashes of the old, and the bloodstained temple walls have been whitewashed. A new shrine is to be established, this one brightened with fresh flowers and illuminated by the candles that the Thunder Gods make from beeswax. The priests have been made to exchange their blood-encrusted black garments for new white vestments. Their hair, which they have allowed to grow long and is caked stiff with dried blood, has been sawed off with the sharp blades of the captains' swords.

In the place of the old stone gods, a cross and a picture of the goddess Aguilar calls Virgin have been placed in the temple. Feathered Serpent himself carried the picture up the steps.

I must confess, this new shrine disturbs me. My lord is truly like no other god I have ever imagined. He is divine, and yet he bends his knee each day before the gentle image of a mother and child; he rages against human sacrifice but instead drinks the blood of his own god, *Olintecle*.

He is Feathered Serpent as I always imagined him to be—and yet in some ways he is not.

He is not faultless, but then no god is without fault. Sometimes a god will find his way inside a man, as with Motecuhzoma. And if a god may find his way inside a man, could the divine not also find a warm place inside the heart of a living woman?

 **23**

Cortés made the decision to abandon San Juan de Ulúa and build his new colony on the plain seven miles to the north of Cempoala. Alvarado took possession in the name of King Charles V of Spain. He named it the Rich Town of the True Cross, *Villa Rica de la Vera Cruz*.

The men cheered him, even those who had formerly wished to go back to Cuba. After all, as Cortés had said, the gold wheel must be only the beginning, and if they continued to create new colonies, soon every last one of them imagined that one day he would be an *alcalde* himself.

After the ceremony the position of chief justice and captain-general of the new colony was declared vacant. The post was unanimously offered to Hernán Cortés, who humbly accepted.

The next day they set to work on the building: there were to be a church, a marketplace, warehouses, a stockade, a hospital, a town hall, and an arsenal, all protected by a high stone wall with watchtowers, parapets, and barbicans. They would also construct kilns to make clay bricks, and smithies from the ships were put to work forging wrought iron. As part of the treaty Cortés had made with *Gordo*, thousands of Cempoalans were recruited as native labor. But all the

Spaniards helped with the work, digging foundations or carrying earth to the kilns; Cortés himself put his back into the hewing of logs for the new buildings.

Malinali and Rain Flower were put to work in the hospital, assisting the Spaniards' only doctor, Mendez. Now that they were away from the marshes, there were fewer cases of fever and *vómito*, but Malinali proved her worth, preparing herbal remedies for a variety of ailments.

As the months passed, the new colony took shape. The Mexica waited and watched.

MALINALI

CORTÉS KNEELS BEFORE the wooden trestle that serves as an altar in the half-finished church. A wooden cross has been fixed high on the wall above a picture of Aguilar's goddess and her baby. Cortés fingers the beads he holds in his right hand, his face serene, oblivious to the banging of nails and the shouts of the moles around him.

I watch him at his devotions. It moves me to my core that such a great lord will fall to his knees before the image of a woman with an infant. It is testament to both his gentleness and his strength. The picture seems to serve as inspiration to him, for in his last incarnation, Feathered Serpent had been a priest, serving the gods. Now he has returned to destroy those gods and bring us a new divinity, a gentle god, not a bringer of war and destruction and deception.

Seeing him like this renews and restrengthens my faith in him. How can a goddess with a suckling baby be the harbinger of anything but good? Would such a goddess demand blood and burning?

As I leave the church, I see Norte, bare-chested, heading

across the plaza, carrying some rough-hewn timber over his shoulder.

I call out to him in Chontal Maya. "Norte! Will you help me?"

He lays down his burden and looks up, surprised. "If I can, Doña Marina."

"Come here, please."

He approaches, cautiously. "How can I help you?"

"I want you to talk to your lord for me."

"Why me? What about Aguilar?"

"Because I want *you* to speak for me, not Aguilar."

Norte seems unsure, but he reluctantly agrees. He follows me back inside the half-built church, and we wait for my lord to finish his devotions.

He stands up, appears both surprised and gratified to see me, but frowns when he sees Norte.

"Please beg his forgiveness," I say to Norte, "and tell him I did not mean to disturb him while he was with the gods. But there is something I must ask him."

There is a swift exchange between the two men. "He says that there is nothing to forgive. He is very happy to see you."

I smile at this gallantry. But I hesitate. How can I tell him what I wish to say? "Tell him...tell him that I know...that I know he is Feathered Serpent."

Norte stares at me. "What?"

"Have you not guessed?"

"This man is no god, believe me."

"Just tell him what I say."

Feathered Serpent watches this exchange and appears puzzled. Norte turns back to him, finishes the translation as I have asked him to. When it is done, my lord stares at me for a long time without speaking. Finally he murmurs something to Norte.

"There, I told you."

"What does he say?"

"He says he does not know what you are talking about. He asks me who Feathered Serpent is."

"I don't believe you."

"He's just another Spaniard, as I am. Except a little more greedy and ruthless than most."

My lord speaks again.

"He wants you to leave him in peace," Norte says to me. "You're to leave, and I have to remain here. He'll probably have me flogged for this."

I do not understand. Is it possible that a man might become a god and not know of it? Or is he trying, for some reason, to conceal his true identity? From whom?

"Go!" Norte urges me. "Don't anger him further. You don't know this man as I do."

I look at Feathered Serpent, but there is no secret smile of conspiracy, no glint of amusement, as I have been offered in these past weeks when I have helped him in some way. I have offended him.

I hurry away.

24

CORTÉS STUDIED THE unappetizing creature in front of him, his ragged ears and tattooed face. Like a demon from hell rather than a good Spaniard. A traitor, to his mind, and more than likely a heretic. But for the time being, he was useful. "Do you understand what that conversation was about?"

"She thinks you are *Quetzalcóatl*—the Feathered Serpent. He is one of our ... one of *their* gods."

Cortés noted this slip of the tongue for future reference. "And why does she think that?"

"Your appearance, perhaps. Feathered Serpent is tall, as you are, with a fair complexion and a beard. But mainly it was the manner of your arrival. The people here ... they believe that one day Feathered Serpent will return on a raft from the east and save them from the tyranny of the Mexica. Among the people of the coast, it is almost an article of faith. A cult, if you like."

"So that is why they received me in Cempoala as a liberator."

Norte lowered his eyes.

"You knew this?" Cortés asked him.

"It is just Indian superstition."

"Still, I would have regarded it an act of loyalty if you had reported it to me before now."

"I thought it meant nothing."

A thin smile appeared on Cortés's face. Norte must think me very dull. Or perhaps that is the best excuse he can think of. "And you, Norte, do you think I am this Feathered Serpent?"

"I am a Spaniard, my lord."

"You were once. Who knows, perhaps one day you will be again. But you have not answered my question."

"I think you are a Spaniard like me, my lord."

"A Spaniard, yes, but not a Spaniard like you. May God strike me dead if I ever become like you. Thank you for your service. Now you may return to your work."

MALINALI

SUNLIGHT DAPPLES THE surface of the water, I can hear the howl of the spider monkeys as they bounce and glide through the canopy of trees. I am bathing alone in the stream when Aguilar appears on the bank, his face flushed from running, his robes stained with sweat. He is looking for me. I see him steal a guilty glance at my body before he turns away.

"I need to talk to you!"

"I am listening."

"You must dress."

How delicious. This man worships icons of fertility yet is

reduced to a child by the sight of a woman without clothes. "I can listen to everything you say as easily when I am wet as when I am dry."

I can imagine why he wishes to speak with me so urgently. Norte has told him of my conversation with my lord in the church. Well, if I must listen to his rant, then I can at least keep him at a disadvantage. Let him try and intimidate me with his back turned.

"Who is this Feathered Serpent?" he demands.

I cup some water in my palm, leisurely anoint my shoulders and breast. "Feathered Serpent was once a man, the priest-king of the city of Tollán, before the time of the Mexica. He was a just and kind leader who abolished all human sacrifice and made Tollán the most wonderful city in the world. But his great enemy, *Tezcatlipoca*, Bringer of Darkness, was jealous of his power and tricked him into drinking too much *pulque*. He made him so drunk, he seduced his own sister. The next day Feathered Serpent was filled with remorse and sailed away on a raft of serpents into the east. He always vowed he would one day return and reclaim his throne, in the Year One Reed. This is the Year One Reed."

"This is witchcraft! Witchcraft and heresy! There is only one god!"

I dip my head in the water, wring out the long tresses of my hair. Aguilar is such a fool. How can there be only one god? I wonder why my lord keeps company with him. If not for his ability with tongues, which is only a limited talent, it seems to me he serves no useful purpose at all.

"Is this what you have been telling the Mexica about Cortés?" he shouts at me. A man ranting at the trees. If only he knew how ridiculous he looks.

"I only ever repeat what you yourself say to me."

"And the Totonacs?"

"I do not tell the Totonacs what to believe."

"Then they do believe he is a god? Do you realize you will destroy him? A man—no man—may lay claim to divinity!"

"If the people think he is Feathered Serpent, it is no fault of mine."

Aguilar is so agitated, he spins around to face me just as I am rising from the water. He groans when he sees I am naked and turns away again. "You . . . you . . . you don't understand! If these pe . . . pe . . . people believe Cortés is a god, then they do not believe in Christ. It means they are not true Christians and they will roast forever in eternal torment! That is what you have done! That is the sin on your head!"

I dry myself at my leisure on a cotton cloth. I am in no hurry to dress. Let Aguilar continue to address the ferns and *zapote* trees. "You accuse me wrongly. I have only relayed your words, Aguilar."

"I pray that you are right!"

"You must know that I would never do anything that would harm my lord." I take a step closer to him, put my hand on his shoulder. I feel him stiffen. He is frightened now, more frightened of one naked woman than he was of the whole mob that wanted his blood in Cempoala. "Do you understand about things between men and women?"

"I know you are given to Alonso Puertocarrero."

"We are given to some, we belong to others. It was not for me to choose."

"What are you saying?"

"If you really understand about these things, you will know it is not just that a woman's body is different from a man's. It is much more than that. It is like the sun and the moon, the land and the ocean, laughter and tears. One exists to counterweight the other. In this way I cannot exist without my lord. That is why I would never do anything to hurt him."

When Aguilar speaks again, his voice is hoarse with great emotion. "I will pray for you," he says, and walks quickly away without a further backward glance.

A strange man. Why is it so terrible for a man to be a god? I do not comprehend the reasons for Aguilar's anguish, but I do understand the warning I have been given. From now on I must be very careful.

It is clear that these Thunder Gods and their moles and dwarves do not know that my lord is Feathered Serpent. He himself wants to hide his identity from them; that would explain his reticence in the church. It is not for me to understand his reasons for doing this, so I must tread carefully until I do.

 **25**

His new quarters were not the palace he had imagined for himself: the floor was beaten earth, the walls clay brick, the roof constructed of thatch. But it placed him firmly in this new land. There could be no going back now.

Cortés put the quill and parchment aside, interrupting the letter he was presently writing to the king of Spain, and regarded his two visitors.

His prize, his treasure, Malinali, kept her gaze demurely to the floor. How he would like to warm himself by that particular fire. Those black eyes and proud nose were sufficient challenge to any man. How he would like to know what she was thinking.

And then there was Aguilar, awkward and thin, sweat like dewdrops in his thinning hair, his hatchet mouth a study in piety. Cortés slapped at an insect on his neck. How he hated churchmen!

"I want you to ask Doña Marina," he said, addressing himself to Aguilar, "to tell me more about the capital of the Mexica, this place they call Tenochtitlán. She has told me that she went there once, as a child."

Malinali replied softly to the question.

"The woman asks what it is you wish to know," Aguilar said. "She will do her best to search her memory."

Cortés smiled and nodded. "She has told me the city is built on a great lake. Can the city then only be reached by boat?"

"She says Tenochtitlán is connected to the mainland by three causeways," Aguilar answered. "There are bridges on the causeways, made of wood, which can be removed quickly in the event of an attack, making the city impregnable."

Impregnable, Cortés thought with a smile. How often had he heard men say that about a woman or a city? "And what is the city like? Is it like Cempoala?"

Malinali became animated. Cortés thought she would never stop talking, words spilling from her in a rush. Aguilar spoke quickly also, to try and keep up with the translation. "She says it is much bigger and incomparably more beautiful than Cempoala. She says on the outskirts of the city are what the Mexica call *chinampas,* islands of mud that have been built in the water and that are used to grow crops. The suburbs are adobe and thatch houses, similar to the ones in which the Cempoalans live, but at the center of the city, there are many large temples and palaces, too many to count. She says that the population is numbered not in thousands but in hundreds of thousands."

Cortés was disappointed. All Indians were prone to exaggeration, and it seemed even this Malinali was guilty of it. If she was to be believed, such a city would be the largest in the known world, and it was quite obviously impossible for savages to construct anything on the same scale as, say, Venice or Rome or Sevilla. He decided to confine his questions to military matters: "I wish to know more about these bridges. Ask her, if a force of men were able to get over one of the bridges, could the city then be easily invested?"

Malinali understood intuitively what he was asking.

"She says it is impossible to take Tenochtitlán by frontal assault. The houses all have flat roofs and parapets, like *Gordo*'s. The warriors could use them as forts."

So, they would have to find some other way inside.

"Thank her for her wisdom," he said to Aguilar. "Even as a child, she was obviously a very bright and observant little girl." He saw her smile with pleasure at this flattery.

Aguilar leaned forward. "Should we pay so much attention to the word of an Indian girl?"

Cortés smiled thinly to disguise his anger. This deacon had to learn his place. "I shall be the judge of that."

"But my Lord—"

"Be silent or you will regret it!"

Aguilar obeyed. Cortés drummed his fingers on the table.

"I have one more question to ask of her," he said. "I need to know more about the relationship the Mexica enjoy with their neighbors. Are the Totonacs the only peoples who struggle under their yoke?"

Malinali had much to say on this subject.

"She says the Mexica have many enemies inside the federation," Aguilar translated. "I think what she is saying . . . I do not quite understand everything, but it would seem that the Mexica are regarded as upstarts in the valley of Mexico, that they have attained their dominance through brutality. She says they demand heavy tribute from all the tribes under their dominion, and there is great resentment against them. There is even one republic permanently at war with them."

"Indeed?"

"She says it is called Tlaxcala, the Land of the Eagle Crags. It is situated in the mountains between here and Tenochtitlán."

"I see." *A kingdom divided against itself cannot stand.* "Well. Thank Doña Marina kindly for me, Brother Aguilar. She has been most helpful. Tell her I may wish to speak with her again later, but that is all for now."

As Malinali rose, their eyes met. There was no mistaking that look from a woman, even a *natural*. I am her chosen, whenever I decide to take what is offered. But I must tread carefully. He looked back at Aguilar, who had not missed this moment of commerce. He was waiting, apparently thinking that he would now be consulted privately.

"You may go also," Cortés said to him, and took satisfaction from the look of wounded pride on the deacon's face. Churchmen. All the same.

He considered his position. The idea that had insinuated itself in his mind was not so much a plan as yet another gamble, perhaps the biggest wager of his life. But why not take it? He was thirty-three years old. What else was there for a man of his years but to die or claim his fame and fortune? So many men worried over danger, as if they would live forever, and left their destinies unclaimed. Of one thing he was sure: if a man did not choose his moment of risk by the time of his middle years, the rest of his life would pass by in a moment and be done. He had promised himself, when he left Extremadura, that he would either dine with trumpets or die on the gallows.

Though it might be a gamble, in this particular game he was in possession of the only ace in the pack. And her name was Malinali.

※   ※

They crowded into Cortés's headquarters, stained with sweat from laboring at the construction work, exhaustion etched into their faces. They waited for Cortés to address them, all of them wary, excited, and a little afraid.

Cortés has hatched some new plan, Benítez thought. I can see it in his eyes.

"The construction of the new colony has gone well," Cortés began. "In a few more days, the most important work will be done." He paused to look around the room. They were all there, his most senior captains, as well as Fray Olmedo and Brother Aguilar. His war council. "Yet while we remain here, we earn ourselves no merit in the eyes of the Lord or the king of Spain. The glory and the riches we seek remain in the capital of the Mexica, this Tenochtitlán."

"Then we must lay siege immediately," León said, his voice thick with irony.

Cortés smiled thinly, as if amused by León's humor. "There are many ways to catch a hen," he said. "Sometimes by giving chase, sometimes just by holding a few grains in the palm of the hand and having the hen come to you. Either way, we will not get our dinner by sitting here. As soon as construction of the fort is completed, I suggest we remove ourselves to Tenochtitlán."

Benítez wondered if he had heard correctly. What Cortés proposed was breathtaking. Breathtaking and suicidal.

"We are five hundred against millions," Ordaz reminded him.

"We are five hundred generals," Cortés said. "For every Spaniard here, I believe we can raise an army from those *naturales* in the countryside whom Motecuhzoma has oppressed. From what I have learned from the Lady Marina, the emperor of the Mexica has more enemies than a dog has fleas."

"To a dog, fleas are only an irritation," León said.

Cortés's face underwent a sudden change. "You call yourselves gallant gentlemen, but you are all of you consumed by your own fears."

"Better than being consumed by Indians," Ordaz said.

"We have already demonstrated, at Ceutla, that we can defeat any number of *naturales* in battle. I am not proposing a war; we do not have to fight this Motecuhzoma. If we can win our way inside his city, we may be able to do our good works by other means." He waited for the others to support him, but even Alvarado and Puertocarrero were strangely silent.

Cortés slammed his fist on the desk. "Have you forgotten the gold wheel that lies in the hold of the *Santa María*? There will be one there for each of you if you support me in this!"

Puertocarrero began, "If there were more of us—"

"There are more of us! There are our Totonac allies. And as we walk the road to Tenochtitlán, there will be many more along the way! Do you not see? We come here as saviors! These people look to us to save them from the Mexica! They will support us, in their thousands, in their tens of thousands." He paused again, to look around the table. "Not only shall we do God's work, gentlemen, but there shall be fame and fortune here for every man, enough to last him his whole life through!"

"I say we go with Cortés," a voice said. They all looked around. It was Aguilar, of all people.

Alvarado grinned, suddenly. "I agree. I shall not let you carry back all that gold on your own."

"Alonso?" Cortés said.

Puertocarrero nodded, ashen-faced.

"I will go," Sandoval said.

"I will go also," Jaramillo said.

Cortés looked around at Benítez.

Madness, Benítez thought. But what choice was there? He could not go back to Cuba empty-handed. What would be the point of that? Nor would he stay here in the fort and catch jungle rot and die of the *vómito*.

"Yes, all right. Why not?" he heard himself say.

We're all infected by this madness. We caught the fever the day the Mexica brought that great golden wheel to us on the beach. It is going to kill us all . . .

26

THE RUSH OF water drowned out all sound. Butterflies danced in the shadows of the silver-barked cotton trees; dragonflies hovered in the green gloom of the waterfall. A blue hummingbird hovered around the flowers of a *zapote* tree.

Norte stripped off his shirt and breeches and jumped into the pool. Rain Flower watched him, crouched among the ferns. She had been more careful this time, and she was sure he had not seen her. Why did I follow him here? What do I hope to find? Hadn't Little Mother Malinali warned her of the dangers?

But she could not help herself. She was obsessed with him, this beautiful Spaniard with the ways of a Person and the saddest eyes she had ever seen.

She watched him bathe. Afterward he rose from the water and picked up his clothes. But instead of dressing, he walked naked to the mouth of a cave partially concealed by the waterfall at the far end of the pool. He disappeared inside.

Rain Flower suspected what might be in there, and her heart quickened in anticipation.

She crept from her hiding place and picked her way carefully over the rocks, stopping in the shadows at the lip of the cave. She crouched down and peered inside.

A niche had been cut into the rock on the far wall as a shrine for a small clay figure of Feathered Serpent. Norte knelt before it. He took out a small gourd and a stingray spine that he had concealed in his clothes. He plunged the spine without warning into the fleshy part of his penis. He held the gourd below his groin to collect the blood that dripped from his thighs. The sweat that glistened on his skin was the only sign of his pain.

When the bleeding had finished, he stood and dashed the contents of the gourd into the face of Feathered Serpent, and the offering was complete.

Rain Flower turned to go; as she did so, a rock slipped from under her feet, and she almost fell. Norte spun around.

There was no point in trying to hide from him now. She stood up so that he could see her clearly, outlined against the sun-dappled pool.

He said nothing, waited to see what she would do.

He is beautiful, she thought. The sweat-sheen on his bronzed skin outlined every muscle on his chest, his shoulders, his legs. His face was gaunt and hungry, and she knew what he wanted. She wanted it, too. Wasn't that the reason she came here?

She reached down, pulled the *huipil* over her head, removed her skirt and undergarment, and stepped into the cave.

"You put yourself in danger," he said to her.

She knelt down in front of him, licked the blood from his *maquauhuitl*, gently sucking on the wound. She heard him groan. Mali had whispered to her of this: *caressing a man with flowers*. She had never done this before, tasting that which had been intended for the gods. The organ grew huge in her hands, richly engorged with the blood he had held back from Feathered Serpent.

Now he dropped to his knees also. There was blood on her lips, and he licked it away with his tongue. She turned away from him, placed her hands on the cool, slippery rock of the shrine. He held her by the hips, penetrating her slowly, moment by golden moment, like a hummingbird dipping its tongue into a flower, quick, tiny, darting movements. His final possession of her evinced a gasp of pain and pleasure. My death will be this way, she thought. When she opened her eyes again, she saw *Quetzalcóatl* watching her, his beaked face and scaled body mute in the shadows, as their bodies coiled and intertwined like serpents above the dusty floor.

⁂ ⁂

A chill and violet sunset. They sat at the mouth of the cave, watching the jungle turn dark, listening to the symphony of the night, the rhythm of insects, the snarl of a jaguar somewhere in the mountains.

Rain Flower shivered, and he drew her closer. From the cave they could make out the glow of the campfires at Vera Cruz.

"We must go back," he whispered.

She kissed him once more, then dressed quickly and ran ahead alone. A dangerous flirtation. She must keep this secret even from Little Mother.

✳ ✳

Flickering shadows, the smell of wood smoke. Cortés toured the guard posts, sharing a jest with those gambling with dice around the fires, reprimanding any sentry found dozing at his post. He came upon Puertocarrero standing alone on the parapet. He was watching the moon rise over the jungle and the black slopes of Orizaba.

"Dreaming of Cuba?" Cortés said.

"Of Spain."

Spain. For him Spain was the flat horizons of Extremadura, sparse groves of cork oaks and olives, the baking heat of summer with its intense light that hurt the eyes, the terrible cold of winter and the biting winds that hissed across the plains and almost froze you to the saddle of your horse. Spain was the genteel poverty of his father's *hacienda*, great oak doors with bolts of iron, cavernous halls without furniture, a vast kitchen with few servants and no food.

"You have been talking with the men?" Puertocarrero said.

"I played the hale and hearty commander. I was hoping to gauge their mood."

"Some of them are frightened."

It is you who are frightened, Cortés thought, but he let it pass. He saw a familiar silhouette hurry across the courtyard below. Her face was illuminated for a moment by a pine torch. *Doña Marina.* And then she was gone.

"You are happy with the services of the Lady Marina?"

"Of course, *caudillo*."

"What is she like?"

Puertocarrero seemed embarrassed by the indelicacy of the question. "She is very beautiful to look at. But she has no passion."

No passion? Cortés thought. That has not been my impression. Perhaps she simply has no passion for you, my friend.

"I admit she has been very useful to us as an interpreter."

"Yes," Cortés agreed, "very useful." More than useful. Without her we would not have come this far. I could not have secured so much gold from Motecuhzoma's lords or manipulated the Totonacs. She is the key in the lock.

He thought again about the lacustrine city she had spoken of and wondered.

"Do you think the men will follow us willingly to Tenochtitlán?" he said.

Puertocarrero shrugged his shoulders. "No, but I think you will find a way to persuade them."

 27

AGUILAR WOULD HAVE liked to conduct his lessons in the church, but the noise of the hammers as the roofing neared completion was deafening. Instead, he took his charges a little way off and sat them down in the shade of a jacaranda tree. Rain Flower watched him, sweating in the heavy brown robe, his sacred book still clutched to his breast. His audience, the cross-eyed beauties from Potonchán, sat on the ground at his feet staring at him in stunned bewilderment. The Totonac women had been excluded from his Bible classes, as he called them, as none of them could speak Chontal Maya.

Occasionally he would look up and glance at Rain Flower, and once he invited her to sit and join the others, but she shook her head, preferring her own company.

Today's teaching was a confusing harangue, and she could not follow it all. It appeared that the Spaniards had just one god, but there were three gods in this one god. These three gods who made up one god had a son who was also a god. There was also another man called a pope who was also a god but wasn't. But it appeared to her, from what Aguilar said, that none of these gods were as powerful as the Spaniards' own king.

Aguilar finished his lesson by making the women recite a prayer praising their own fathers.

When they had all drifted away, he turned around and seemed surprised to find Rain Flower still there, watching.

"Doña Isabel," he said, calling her by the name he had given her on her baptismal day, "I am pleased to see you have discovered a thirst for God."

"I listened to your speech. When you spoke of your gods, you did not mention my lord Cortés."

"Cortés?"

"Is he not one of your gods?"

By the look on his face, she might have struck him from behind with a war club. He even swayed a little on his feet. "Of course not."

"Then I was right. He is just a man, like the rest of you."

"I do not know where you come by such blasphemies. Cortés is our leader, and his mission is blessed by Pope and by almighty God. But he himself is just a man."

"You are not from the Cloud Lands?"

"We were born in a great and powerful country called Spain. But we came here from Cuba, an island across the ocean."

Well, Rain Flower thought, that makes as much sense as anything else you have to say. "Why did you come here?"

Aguilar bestowed a smile that Rain Flower did not much care for. "We came here to teach you about God. We want you to be saved."

"From what?"

"From the Devil."

The Devil. Perhaps he meant the Mexica's god, Hummingbird on the Left.

Poor Malinali. She was wrong, then. But what was the point of trying to convince her? She must have asked these same questions of Brother Aguilar. She did not want to believe that Cortés was just a man like all the rest. She clung tenaciously to her fancy and would not give it up.

But did it matter? Let her dream. They had been given to these Spaniards, and their future was out of their hands anyway. Unlike the Totonac women, they were far from home and could not slip away in the night.

And did it matter if Motecuhzoma's altars were waiting for them at the end of this journey? Life was just a dream itself, a short post-ponement of death.

She stood up and started to walk away.

"Wait," Aguilar called breathlessly after her. "I can read to you from my holy book!"

But Rain Flower was not listening. She was planning when she might next steal away to the pool with Gonzalo Norte.

✳ ✳

"We must send a deputation back to Spain to petition the king for the right to establish our own colony here. Alonso, as my most trusted friend and ally, I want you to return to Spain to plead the case on our behalf."

Puertocarrero looked neither surprised nor unhappy with this news. He does not have the stomach for soldiering, Cortés thought, or the temperament to survive long in these fevered lands. His breeding and manners were more suited to the royal court, which was why Cortés had chosen him for this errand.

Well, perhaps not the only reason.

But his officers would find his logic irrefutable. To obtain official recognition from the king, they would need to send someone who knew the ways of the court. Puertocarrero was by far the best candidate, the nephew of a prominent justice of Sevilla and related to the count of Medellín, one of Charles's most powerful and influential grandees.

Cortés passed across the table his *carta de relación,* sealed with wax. "In my letter I have described to the king all that has happened here since our arrival three months ago. I have informed His Majesty how we have been forced into our recent drastic actions because of the arrogance and greed of Governor Velázquez in Cuba. It also relates the enthusiasm of all members of our new colony to serve the king."

"I will return as soon as I can, with the king's endorsement."

Cortés smiled. He would miss Puertocarrero: he was a loyal and trustworthy comrade. But he would still rather have Alvarado with him if it came to a fight. "To help the king arrive at his decision, I am sending with you all the treasure we have won so far." Well almost, Cortés thought. Not the gold that *Gordo*'s niece was wearing the day he gave her to me, nor certain items of dress that Tendile's lords hung on me. They are rightfully mine. "The value of the gold and jewels alone I place at two thousand *castellanos*."

"I am sure His Majesty cannot fail to be impressed."

"We will leave in the morning for the coast. You will take my flagship from San Juan de Ulúa. Alaminos will be your pilot."

Puertocarrero rose to leave, hesitated. "About the girl," he said.

Cortés strived to appear puzzled.

"Doña Marina," Puertocarrero said.

"What about her?"

He smiled. "Treat her kindly."

MALINALI

THE GREAT WAR canoes of the Thunder Gods roll on a gentle tide, the sun just risen on the water. A smaller canoe waits at the beach, to take my husband away.

A few of my lord's soldiers stand around, watching me. I hear them mutter and spit in the sand.

My husband strides down to the strand in high leather boots. The morning sun brings out the gold in his hair and his beard. He says something to Aguilar, who then turns to me.

"He says he does not know when he will be back."

"Tell my lord I wish him well and thank him for his kindness." I am almost too excited to play my role this morning. I know that Feathered Serpent has arranged this. It is not unknown for a person to have his own brother instruct his bride in the ways of the cave before he takes her to his own bed, and I am sure this is what my lord intended. Now his task is completed, my violet-eyed husband is returning to the Cloud Lands.

Still, he seems sad to be leaving.

"He wishes you well." Aguilar yawns.

"I wish him well also. Tell him my cave of joy will be a place of great emptiness without him."

Aguilar takes a deep breath. "I cannot tell him that."

"You cannot tell him that I wish him well?"

"I cannot . . . the rest of it."

I try not to grin. This man is so discomfited by natural things. Such a fool. "Then tell him may the God of Wind hurry onward the great canoe bearing him to heaven."

"Castile is not heaven," Aguilar mutters. He speaks a few curt sentences to my husband, who smiles and answers in his own language.

"You did not tell him what I said," I say to Aguilar.

"How can you know what I said? I said that you would miss him and that you wished him well."

"And he wished me well also."

"That much you may have guessed."

"And the rest?"

"That was all."

"There was more."

Aguilar is about to debate further with me, but then he shrugs his shoulders and admits, "He also asked that you do the best you can for his friend Cortés."

"I would do anything for my lord."

Aguilar snorts with derision and walks back up the beach, leaving us to finish our farewells alone.

My husband kisses my hand and walks down the sand to the canoe. Some moles push the boat through the shallows. He waves to me once, then takes his position at the stern. I know I shall never see him again.

✳   ✳

The Feathered Serpent comes to me in the night, slipping and hissing through the darkness like the wind. As I knew he would, as he knows he must.

He whispers to me: my sacred one, my sweet one, the one desire of my heart.

The desire is urgent, and the heat of our bodies fills the little room where I sleep. He ignites me. I am like cold water thrown against a hot wall.

I whisper to him also in the elegant tongue: my lover, my lord, my destiny here on this earth.

What our bodies do is a mirror of our minds. I wish desperately to be a part of him, need him to fill me up. He takes possession of me quickly, striking like a serpent, in a rush. I am left breathless, woken from sleep, and he is lying between my legs, his breath hot and labored on my cheek, my body tender and bruised from his onslaught.

"I have wanted this from the moment I saw you," he murmurs.

He thinks I do not understand him. He does not know that from that very first day, I have been learning the language of the gods. I wonder when I will tell him how much I hear, how much I know.

Not yet. It suits my purpose, for the moment, to be a shadow on the wall.

There is a candle burning in the corner of the room, and I can make out the chiseled lines of his face, even the flecks of gray in his beard.

"I wish I knew what you were thinking. Such liquid eyes I have never seen on a woman." He laughs. "Alonso said you were cold."

The candle dances in the draft.

"You don't understand a word I'm saying, do you?" he says, and looks disappointed. His hand cups my breast. "I wonder if we are all the same to you."

He is gone before dawn, and the sunrise is still, without a murmur of breeze. I lie awake; I have not slept. I am planning to capture the wind. I am laying schemes, weaving dreams; my life is pregnant with possibilities now, a squealing litter of hopes, blind and thrusting.

28

GUZMÁN WAS STANDING in the doorway. Cortés looked up from the dice. One by one the officers gathered around the table grew silent.

"What is it?"

"The woman, Doña Marina. She is outside, *caudillo*."

Alvarado grinned. "Perhaps without Puertocarrero she has an itch to scratch," he said, and the others laughed.

Cortés silenced them with a glance. "Bring her in," he said.

Guzmán went back outside and moments later reappeared with Malinali.

"Get Aguilar," Cortés said to Guzmán.

"No," Malinali said, in Castilian. "No Aguilar."

The Spaniards stared at her in astonishment.

"Leave us," Cortés said to Guzmán. He returned his attention to the girl. *Well.* "You can speak Castilian?"

"Speak slowly ... for me ... please. Then ... I understand."

Cortés laughed. What a wonder. But of course, she had been with them for nearly three months now, living with Alonso as well as nursing their sick and wounded. A bright girl like this, she would not have spent the time idly. He wondered how long she had been able to understand what was being said around her and why she had only now decided to reveal her secret.

"You are to be commended," he said.

She ignored his praise. "They will steal ... your canoe. Tomorrow."

Cortés stopped laughing. "Steal?" He suddenly realized that by *canoe* she meant one of the *naos,* or brigantines, in the anchorage. "Who plans to steal from me?"

"León . . . Ordaz . . . Díaz . . . Escudero . . . Umbral."

They all stared as she recited the names of the conspirators. Alvarado cursed under his breath.

"How do you know this?" Cortés said.

"They talk . . . they do not take care . . . what they say. They think . . . I do not understand."

"Traitors!" Sandoval hissed.

Cortés smiled. "Indeed. Fortunately God has sent an angel to watch over us."

"What are we to do?" Alvarado asked him.

"We have been patient long enough. It is time we removed our velvet gloves and showed them the iron beneath." He turned to Jaramillo. "Get Escalante and a dozen men. Arrest all of the conspirators now. No, wait. Leave Father Díaz. Just the other four. Bring them to Alvarado in the stockade. We shall learn the truth of this matter."

Alvarado nodded eagerly. "It will be my pleasure, *caudillo.*"

His captains rushed from the room, eager for the chance to finally revenge themselves on the *Velazquistas.* Cortés was left alone with Malinali. Once again you have saved me! he thought. And once again I have underestimated you.

"Thank you," he said.

This time she did not lower her eyes. Instead, she spoke some words in *Náhuatl* that he did not understand: "You are Feathered Serpent. My destiny is with you."

29

ALVARADO'S SHIRT WAS stained with perspiration, and there was blood on the cuffs. He looked fatigued from his night's work. Cortés had not slept either. He sat behind the great table, his face dark with anger, his decisions already made.

Outside the first gray light of dawn crept up the horizon.

"What did you discover?" Cortés said.

"Escudero proved to be stubborn."

"How stubborn?"

"Oh, he talked," Alvarado said. "Finally." There was a jar of Cuban wine on the table. He poured some into a pewter mug and slaked his thirst. The red wine stained the corners of his mouth and soaked into his beard. "They all talk eventually. A piece of sail canvas and a few buckets of water and they all talk."

"Who was with him in the conspiracy?"

Alvarado appeared reluctant. The news cannot be good, Cortés thought. Alvarado pushed a list of names across the table. Cortés scanned them quickly and sucked in his breath. He was shocked. He had not realized the *Velazquistas* had so many in sympathy with them. He must keep this knowledge private or risk the loyalty of the rest. Besides, if his future plans were to come to anything, he would need every man he had.

Well, almost every man. One or two would need to be sacrificed in the name of discipline. "So many?"

Alvarado picked at the dried candle grease on the table. "They planned to seize one of the brigantines and make their way back to Cuba under full sail. They hoped to warn Velázquez of Puertocarrero's mission and have him intercepted."

A vein swelled at Cortés's temple. "Who was to be their pilot?"

"Juan Cermeño."

"Cermeño," he muttered. Pilots, at least, were expendable, for he had no plans to sail anywhere. He looked up at Alvarado. "We must not allow the other men to know the extent of the mutiny. We will make an example of the ringleaders and pretend Escudero kept silent for the rest. Those who are not punished will give thanks to God for their good fortune and be especially diligent with their loyalties in the future." He considered a moment, his eyes on the list. "Hang the pilot, Cermeño. I can spare a few sailors on a land campaign. And of course this dog, Escudero."

"What of the others?"

"Any mariners on this list, give them two hundred lashes. The sailors are less use to us than the soldiers."

"What about Fray Díaz? And then there's Ordaz and that goatfucker León."

"We cannot touch a churchman. Let Díaz think we do not know of his involvement. As for the other two . . . León is a good fighter, and Ordaz is a veteran of many Italian campaigns. We need them. It behooves me to show clemency. They can sweat in the stockade until they agree to a formal oath of loyalty, duly notarized."

"So just Cermeño and Escudero, then?"

Cortés consulted the list again. "There are many good men here."

Alvarado frowned. "Still, it would be better if we had one or two more swinging from the tree to remind the others of what their fate might have been. What about Norte?"

"I do not see his name on the list."

"Does it matter? He's a troublemaker, and he's dispensable."

Cortés nodded. "All right. Let Norte join the others on the scaffold. None here will weep for him. Do what you have to do."

✳ ✳

The two men waited on the scaffold, the heavy manila rope looped around their necks. The pilot, Cermeño, was crying and had to be held upright by the soldiers. Escudero remained defiant, staring over the heads of his comrades who had gathered to watch his execution. There was blood on his shirt, and he looked ill.

A court-martial had been hastily convened an hour before. The chief magistrates of the town council, Grado and Ávila, had pronounced sentence.

There was a table in front of the gallows, and the official warrant of execution lay on it, as yet unsigned. Cortés finally appeared, accompanied by Alvarado and Diego Godoy. He wore the suit of black velvet he had worn to welcome the Mexica. He walked slowly across the plaza, his head down. He stopped in front of the table, looked up at the men on the gallows, and appeared to hesitate.

The sun had just risen over the ocean, throwing long shadows over the fort.

"You must sign these warrants of execution," Alvarado said.

"This is indeed a heavy duty," Cortés whispered.

Alvarado appeared both desperate and angry. "*Caudillo*, these men committed rebellion against you. They have betrayed every one of us here. There is only one course of action open to you."

Cortés leaned over the table and picked up the quill. "Better that I had not learned to write than to use my signature for the death sentences of men." He signed his name to the warrants and walked away.

The drums rolled.

Three men stood behind each of the victims. At a signal from Alvarado, they hauled on the free ends of the ropes, and Cermeño and Escudero rose into the air, legs kicking at the air.

Rain Flower watched, her eyes locked on the death throes of the two Spaniards. There was a look of naked pain in her eyes. Norte was to be next.

⬟ ⬟

It took some moments for his eyes to adjust to the darkness inside the stockade after the harsh light of the plaza. Norte was huddled in a corner of his cell, his head between his knees, his shirt bathed in sweat. It was already breathless hot inside the jail, one small window high in the wall the only ventilation.

His wrists and ankles were in fetters.

"Did they hang Cermeño and Escudero?" Norte whispered.

Benítez nodded. "Two hours ago."

"Fray Olmedo has already come. He wanted my confession. When I would not give it to him, he seemed concerned that I might not find my proper place in heaven among the saints. He even sent Aguilar to plead his case for him."

"That is not why I am here. Your confession is a matter between you and God."

Norte looked up. "Is it time? They have kept me waiting long enough. Do they know how frightened I am? Is someone enjoying this?"

"There has been a stay of execution."

Norte made a sound that could have been laughter or tears. "Why?"

"I pleaded your case. I said you had language skills that might yet prove valuable to us. I made the point that although your time with the *naturales* had left you soft in the head, you were not dangerous. I struck a bargain on your behalf."

"Why?"

"I am not a complete barbarian."

"But you despise me."

Yes I do, Benítez thought. Why could he not keep his mouth shut and let this dog hang? But every man has his own honor, and he could not let this stand.

He had been present at the court-martial that morning; there was nothing to be done for Cermeño or Escudero. If Escudero had had a brain in his head, he would never have joined the expedition. Years ago, when he was a constable in Santiago, he had arrested Cortés, at Velázquez's request, on a contrived charge of sedition. Putting himself in reach of the *caudillo*'s claws on such a journey was the hallmark of an arrogant fool.

Norte was another matter. Jaramillo had been present at Escudero's interrogation, and he had told Benítez that Norte's name was not on the list of plotters. Norte was innocent, and for Benítez that was the heart of the matter.

No matter what else I think of him, justice should be inviolable. A man should not hang for a crime he did not commit.

"I am helping you because what they wish to do to you is not just. That is all."

Norte thought about this a moment. "You said something about a bargain."

"You are to swear an oath of loyalty to Cortés, and you will then be placed in my charge. You must also agree to take up arms and fight under our banner. Do you accept the terms?"

"You are a strange man, Benítez."

"Because I believe in justice?"

"Because you don't use justice for your own ends."

"I am still waiting for your answer. I shall not wait too much longer."

Norte rested his head against the wall. "Among the *naturales* I was merely an amusement for the first years, a novelty, a foreigner, an outcast. I wished myself dead many times. But the body is tenacious with life." He sighed. "I agree to whatever you say, Benítez. If you think I am worth saving, save me. I don't know why it should be, but it is too hard to die."

30

"SHE WANTS YOU to go with her to the river," Norte whispered.

Benítez frowned at him, then looked at Rain Flower. "Why?"

"To bathe."

"It is unhealthy to bathe. It is how one catches the fever."

"The *naturales* bathe all the time, and they don't get sick."

The roofing on the church had been completed. Benítez was in his shirtsleeves, watching Fray Olmedo perform the dedication ceremony. Priests and their nonsense. Hundreds of Totonac laborers had been herded inside and were staring in dumb bemusement as Fray Díaz and Brother Aguilar moved along the aisles with copal censers. Their incantations in Latin were incomprehensible even to most of the Spaniards.

Benítez took Norte's arm and moved toward the doorway. "But why does she wish me to bathe?"

"You don't know your own stench. Even a vulture would be offended."

He grabbed Norte by the throat. "I piss on your mother's grave!"

"I mean no offense," Norte gasped. "These people bathe every day to wash the sweat off their bodies. Rain Flower only desires that you do the same."

Benítez wondered if they were making fun of him. Or was it some sort of trick?

He released his hold, and Norte massaged his neck. "It is no business of mine if you go with her," he said. "It is what she wants."

Rain Flower stood fearfully to one side, awaiting the outcome. Benítez looked at her, and she gave him an encouraging smile. *By Satan's ass, this is ridiculous!* Still, it was that or stay here and listen to Fray Olmedo droning on all afternoon. He nodded his assent and followed her across the deserted and timber-strewn plaza, and out of Vera Cruz.

✳ ✳

She took off her clothes and waded into the pool. The water glistened like dew on her hard, brown body. It was cool in the green shadows, and her nipples were hard and erect.

Benítez felt suddenly unsure of himself.

She shouted something in her own language and waited. He just stood there. Impatient now, she got back out of the pool, water streaming from her limbs, and started to peel off his clothes. He pushed her away and finished the job himself. He felt a little ashamed to be standing naked with a woman in the daylight. He imagined his comrades watching from the bushes and laughing at him. Or sneering. Was this the first step in his degeneration to a savage, like Norte?

He followed her into the water. Rain Flower was holding a piece of soap-tree root. She rubbed it between her hands and smeared the grease from it over his body. She cupped the water in her hands, poured it over his chest and shoulders, then pulled him to a deeper part of the pool to wash off the residue.

After she had finished bathing him, she turned and swam away from him, to a wide, flat rock. The shade had moved from that part of the glade, and the stone had been warmed by the sun. She lay on her back and beckoned him to join her.

✳ ✳

"You are big and ugly," she said in Chontal Maya, knowing he could not understand, "but you are also kind and just. What you did for Norte was a good thing."

He pulled himself up onto the rock beside her. The water streamed off his chest and belly. She noticed that when it was wet, the hair on his body looked like the pelt of an animal. He shivered in the dappled sunlight. His skin was cool to the touch.

"What am I to do?" she said to him. "My lover is beautiful and a Person, and he understands the ways of the gods. You are clumsy, but you are kind. The Spaniards have made you my husband. What am I to do?"

She kissed him, felt his thick arms wrap around her. They lay back on the sun-warmed stone. She stretched herself on it, imagining it was Motecuhzoma's altar stone and she was a sacrifice. Is this how it will feel? she wondered, gazing up at the washed blue sky.

She pulled his mouth to her breast. His beard was wiry and rough against her skin. "Look at you," she whispered, "you are so hairy. Your *maquauhuitl* is like a purple fist punching its way through a forest."

She wrapped her arms and thighs around him, entangled her fingers in his hair. "But at least now you do not smell like a corpse. Now you can enter the cave redolent of water and the forest, and I will enjoy the closeness of you also."

"*Cara,*" he whispered. "*Cara mía.*"

She wondered what the words meant. She would ask Little Mother.

With Norte words were no barrier. But she had not been given to Norte.

So she would make the best of things, show her lord and husband what she liked, help him to be gentle, make him smell sweet, even teach him some words of her own language. And perhaps, in time, she might even grow a little fond of him.

31

EVERY MAN NAMED on Escudero's list had been sent north to Cempoala. Cortés had told them it was a routine patrol. Alvarado was placed in charge.

When they returned some weeks later, they were shocked and dismayed to find the bay empty. They were informed by their comrades that the entire fleet had been hauled up onto the beach and scuttled.

There was no way back to Cuba now.

※ ※

Cortés stood on the sand, the sea at his back. Father Olmedo stood beside him, holding a large wooden cross. A nice touch, Benítez thought, the empty sea and the cross. The *caudillo* had a flair for such theatrics. He knew how to make his point without a word being spoken; he was telling them to have faith, for there was no way back.

The mood was volatile and hard to gauge. Looking around at the men, Benítez saw fear, resignation, anger, resentment. The expedition had already taken much longer and traveled much farther than any had anticipated when they left Cuba.

"Gentlemen," Cortés began, "I know you are distressed at hearing what has happened to our ships. But here is the report from the master mariners in charge of our fleet, which I received while some of you were away in Cempoala. It states that this accursed climate had rotted out the timbers of every ship and that the predations of water worms and rats had made the hulls unsound. Our pilots therefore told me that the boats were no longer safe for ocean voyage and that my only recourse was to have them beached so that we might salvage what we could."

Benítez had seen this document. The pilots had indeed reported the condition of the boats just as Cortés had described it. They had done this because he had paid them well to do it. The subterfuge was a matter of small significance to Benítez personally: he had already made the decision to stay. By the time the boats were scuttled, he no longer had any interest in them.

"While some of you were absent, I made the decision to ferry sails, ironwork, and cordage here to the shore," Cortés was saying. "What could not be salvaged was scuttled there in the bay. It was a heavy decision to make, but it was forced on me by my advisers. There was simply no other choice."

He weighed the silence, the breeze rustling the papers he held in his right hand.

"In the sober light of reflection, you will all realize that this unfortunate incident should not distress us unduly. With misfortune also come many benefits. The loss of the ships means that we have gained a hundred good men for our expedition, as our mariners will no longer be required to man the fleet. They have this day pledged their allegiance to us and will assist us, by the grace of God, in our enterprise.

"And let no one doubt that glory is still ours for the taking. The *naturales* of this land esteem us to be a superior race of beings, and I see no reason to discourage them in their prejudice."

Benítez spared a glance at Aguilar. The deacon gave Doña Marina a look of pure venom.

"I swear this day to make each of you rich beyond your wildest dreams," Cortés went on. "All we need is courage—and faith. For remember, although we go to seek our fortunes, there is another mandate we carry, that of our Lord Jesus Christ. We have all seen how these heathens engage in the most unnatural practices. We shall tear down their infernal temples wherever we find them and bring salvation and true Christianity to these savage lands. So, you see, in our adventure we are in the happy position of serving not only our own interests but those of God Almighty.

"So let us go on, knowing that while we do God's will, we cannot fail! With the loss of our ships, the die is cast. We go on—to Tenochtitlán!"

There was a moment's hesitation. A critical pause when all might have been lost, Benítez thought. But it was then that León unsheathed his sword and held it high in the air. The shadow of the noose and Cortés's gesture of mercy had brought about a radical change in his character.

"On to Tenochtitlán!" he shouted.

The rest of the men, without a leader to champion their fears and complaints, let themselves be carried with the tide. From hundreds of throats came the cry: "On to Tenochtitlán!"

Yes, on to Tenochtitlán, Benítez thought.

And may God have mercy on us all.

 **32**

August, the Month of the Falling of Ripe Fruit.

Cortés left one of his junior captains, Juan Escalante, in charge of the fort at Vera Cruz, his garrison those soldiers too sick or too old to endure the rigors of the journey. The rest left with Cortés.

Cristoval, the standard-bearer, rode at the head of the column on a dappled gray, followed by the *caudillo,* his crest and breastplate shimmering in the sun. Malinali followed on foot, alongside Father Olmedo, who held aloft a great cross studded with turquoise stones extracted from the ears and noses of his Totonac converts. Behind them came the main body of the infantry, six companies of fifty men each.

Totonac and Cuban bearers hefted the Spaniards' heavy steel armor or hauled the wheeled carts that carried the artillery. Behind the artillery came the pikemen, harquebusiers, and crossbowmen. An army of five thousand Totonac warriors, resplendent in their feathered regalia, took up the rear. A hot sun bounced off steel helmets, the muskets of the harquebusiers, and the brass-studded trappings of horses.

Madness, Benítez thought. An army of five hundred and a few thousand natives with tasseled clubs and shields made from turtle shells setting off to conquer an entire nation.

Utter madness!

✳   ✳

The road from Cempoala led them first through ripening fields of maize, then up damp and winding jungle trails strewn with wild passion-fruit vines. The soldiers panted and cursed in their heavy armor. Those Tabascan women who had not been left behind in Cempoala fled into the jungle at their first opportunity. Only Malinali and Rain Flower remained.

They camped in a broad and fertile valley planted with vanilla and cochineal, and the next day they made the steep climb to Jalapa, the Town of the Sand River. They left behind the steaming jungles and distant fever coast; in front of them now, the land rose in surging crags and snowy passes.

Jalapa was no more than a cluster of stucco buildings that clung to the walls of a verdant, thickly forested valley. The inhabitants had been warned in advance of their arrival, and the stone gods had been hastily removed from the temple to a hiding place in the jungle in anticipation of Feathered Serpent's wishes. The priests had cut off their blood-matted hair and were dressed in new cotton robes. The nobles threw open their fine houses to the Spaniards as barracks. A feast was prepared.

So far it had been a triumph, a procession. But tomorrow they would leave the lands of the Totonacs and take their first steps in the lands of the Mexica.

MALINALI

THERE IS MIST in the valley; the dark forest is thick with tree ferns and orchids. Steam rises from the flanks of a chestnut horse. An owl blinks from its hiding place in the shadows, its head cocked to the small cries of humans.

I slip off my tunic and skirt, lie down on the hard floor of the cave, raise my arms above my head in sacrifice to a god. My lord kneels between my legs. There is sweat on his face, and his eyes glitter in the darkness. There is a third figure watching us unseen, in the darkest corner of the cave: Feathered Serpent with his bared fangs and snarling tongue, fired clay given life with polychrome paint.

My lord hovers like an eagle above its prey. His hair is dark and matted like a priest's. In the gloom of the cave, his medallion gleams with gold; it hovers above me, the image of a mother with child, potent and rich with meaning at this moment of conquest, this instant of possession, this hour of conception. I embrace my invader, welcome him in.

Feathered Serpent slides into the cave. I entwine with my god, my destiny won.

 **33**

FROM JALAPA THE road snaked upward. The jungle was left behind, and they climbed through cool forests of cedar, oak, and pine, traversed by rushing streams. They passed under the shadow of a great volcano. Forbidding and snow-swept mountain fastnesses reared up ahead of them. The scantily dressed bearers began to shiver with cold.

They reached the Totonac frontier town of Xicotlán. The chieftain's name was Olintetl, and he seemed unimpressed by their horses and their dogs of war and instead told them of the army of one hundred thousand men that Motecuhzoma had waiting for them in the valley of Mexico.

The thunderheads were growling over the Cofre de Perote. The Totonacs, their eyes turned to the horizon in dread, bought or stole every blanket in the town.

They marched on under a leaden sky. The pennons of the cavalry and the banners of San Diego whipped in the wind, and the beat of their drums echoed around lonely passes.

✺   ✺

Rain fell every afternoon; cannons became bogged in the mud, and the horses fought for their footing in the defiles. Their army disappeared into the clouds at a high col they named the Nombre de Dios. The rain turned to sleet and hail. Several of their Cuban porters froze to death.

They came upon an occasional miserable pueblo. The villagers would flee on hearing them approach, leaving just a few scrawny Xolo dogs to yowl at their heels before they were silenced by the soldiers' swords and butchered for the evening meal. In the deserted temples, they found the remains of human bones.

At each shrine Diego Godoy dutifully read the *Requerimiento*. Fray Olmedo and Brother Aguilar erected wooden crosses on each summit. Buzzards screeched overhead.

The tree line was far below them now. The path flattened, and they reached a barren plateau, a vista of salt lakes broken only by the spiny claws of huge maguey cacti and a few gnarled trees. There was no food to be scavenged, no fresh water to drink. More of the bearers died, from pneumonia, from starvation, or from thirst.

Cortés urged them on. "We are nearly there!" he shouted to them. "The end of the journey is just over the next rise!"

✳ ✳

There was no earth in which to plant the tent pegs. They threw their sleeping blankets down on basalt rock, huddled next to one another for warmth, tried to sleep as best they could. The wind shrieked over their heads, and icy needles of rain slanted down from a black sky.

Benítez drew Rain Flower closer. He had thrown his cloak around her slender shoulders, wrapped his body around her to give her some of his warmth.

We're going to die here, he thought. We're going to freeze to death in this wilderness, and the buzzards will pick over our bones until there is nothing left. What a fool I have been. Why did I ever leave Cuba? Why did I follow Cortés here? León and Ordaz were right about him all along.

He heard the rumble of a landslide somewhere in the mountains.

Rain Flower clung to him, moaning something in her own pretty speech over the rushing of the wind and rain.

Norte lay close by. Benítez could hear his teeth chattering in his head.

"What did she say?" Benítez asked him.

"She wonders," Norte said, his voice barely discernible over the howling of the gale, "since we are so intent on throwing ourselves on Motecuhzoma's altars, why we wish to suffer so much first."

PART II

HUMMINGBIRD ON THE LEFT

Every Spaniard should have in his pocket a charter

of rights consisting of a single item framed in these

brief, clear and striking terms. "This Spaniard is

authorised to conduct himself as he chooses."

—CANIVET

 **34**

BELOW THEM LAY a broad valley, green with maize, patchworked with fields of pale lavender flowers. The wind had shifted to the west, clearing the sky and warming the shivering men as they made their way down from the mountains. Cortés went down the line barking orders, tightening formations. They marched into the town of Zautla in close order as a victorious army, not one that had nearly frozen to death on the high passes.

Cortés was given the best house in the town for his living quarters. A great oak table and his favorite carved wooden chair, which was inlaid with brass and turquoise stones, had been carried all the way from Vera Cruz; these were set down in the middle of the beaten earth floor.

That morning's council was the usual gathering of captains, Benítez noted, but with one exception: Malinali was there, and without Aguilar to translate for her.

The mood in the room was optimistic. They had feasted well on roasted turkeys and maize cakes, and that night they had slept warm and dry with roofs over their heads. Already the horrors of their journey were receding into memory.

Cortés looked around the room. "Gentlemen, we have a decision to make. There appears to be some dispute on how we should proceed."

"What are our choices?" Alvarado asked.

"There are two routes we may take. Last night I spoke with the *cacique* of this town, and he pressed me strongly to go by way of a place they call Cholula. He said that we may be certain of an enthusiastic welcome. However, the Totonacs advise me that the route is longer and more difficult, and they suggest we instead pass through the land of Tlaxcala."

"By the Virgin's ass," a voice said. "You cannot take the word of a Mexica over a Totonac."

They all looked around. It was Malinali.

Benítez grinned. Her education in Castilian was progressing well, though perhaps she had been spending too long in the company of men like Jaramillo and Sandoval and Alvarado.

Cortés himself looked stricken by her outburst. "We will have to replace your tutors," he said, by way of rebuke.

"What do you know of these Tlaxcalans, Doña Marina?" Alvarado asked her.

"They have been at war with the Mexica for as long as anyone can remember. Most of the hearts that are torn out each year on Motecuhzoma's altars belong to Tlaxcalan captives. They are his mortal enemies."

There was a silence when she finished speaking. Cortés looked around the room. "Is it Tlaxcala, then?"

Every man nodded his assent.

"Then I shall send four Totonac envoys to Tlaxcala to explain our mission and offer them alliance against the Mexica. How can they refuse? When they join us, we will have two great nations with us. I predict that by the time we enter Tenochtitlán, Motecuhzoma will already be isolated and besieged, without one of us drawing his sword from its sheath."

They nodded and grinned at one another, mesmerized by Cortés's words. He made it seem so easy. Even Benítez imagined himself returning to Extremadura clothed in velvet with gold on his fingers and jewels in his pouch. What had seemed impossible on the coast was suddenly attainable here in the mountains. It might really be as simple as Cortés told them. Like picking a ripe plum from a tree.

✳ ✳

The four Totonacs set out the next day, wearing the official regalia of their rank: double-knotted cloaks, special cotton wraps, and a buckler. They also had with them a letter of greeting, signed by Cortés and sealed with red wax, as well as some special gifts: a Toledo sword, a crossbow, and a red taffeta hat fashionable in gen-teel Cuban society.

The leader of the delegation took with him a further, and vital, accoutrement: a tiny piece of jade, carved in the shape of a heart. He concealed it by sewing it into his hair. It would pay his passage to the Yellow Beast of the Underworld should the Tlaxcalans prove less accommodating than the Spaniards believed.

After all, everyone knew the favorite food in Tlaxcala was ambassador stew.

 **35**

THE ENVOYS WERE conveyed to the Council of Four in Tlaxcala with all courtesy. They proffered their gifts and letter of greeting and explained how Feathered Serpent had returned to assist the Tlaxcalans in their struggle against the Mexica. They were thanked for the troubles they had taken and escorted to the quarters that had been prepared for them.

But during the night they were seized and thrown in wooden cages to await sacrifice to Smoking Mirror the next day. Two of them managed to escape and arrived back in the Spanish camp, filthy and exhausted, two days later.

Cortés had his answer. There would be no alliance. The Tlaxcalans would not be intimidated as easily as the fat *caciques* of the Totonacs.

✻ ✻

Norte lay on his back, staring at the sky, thousands of stars tossed across the firmament like chips of diamond on velvet. His mind broke free of Zautla, found itself in a small village in Yucatán, watching two little boys without a father. Remembering them now, he had to admit they were not like the sons he had once imagined for himself: their hooked noses and the dark copper color of their skin were uncompromisingly Indian. But they were his blood, and he had loved them.

The cold pain in his chest returned.

He did not remember when the Old World had slipped away from him and the New World had insinuated itself into his soul; there was no absolute moment when the yellow sands of Cozumel Island had become more important to him than the marketplace of Sevilla. The Christian gentleman who had sailed from Palos eight years ago was a stranger to him now. Like an actor on a stage, he fumbled for his lines as he tried to remember how to play that man.

This feeling was not new to him, this black crow of dislocation and loneliness. What an irony it now seemed, how he had once wandered the beach, looking to the sea and praying earnestly for a sign of his countrymen from Castile and Extremadura. He had thought himself a Christian gentleman, abandoned among heathens. Now he saw himself as he truly was eight years before: a pirate and a thief and a hypocrite, rank with the insufferable smell of his own sweat.

As he tossed sleeplessly on his sparse straw bed, he imagined two tobacco-colored children standing on the beach at Yucatán. He had loved them as much as he had ever loved anything. He wondered what they were doing now, if they had wept for him, whether they had already keened the funeral rites for him . . .

In his memory their mother was scolding them for some infraction and threatening them with chili smoke. She was a squat woman with a plain, square face, a shy smile, and little conversation. A flower her father could afford to toss aside. But he had made children with her, thankful that he had not finished his life, like his comrades, on the sacrificial stone.

It was the birth of his sons that had bonded him to the Mayans; it was his own flesh, still there in Yucatán, that tore at him now.

He closed his eyes but could not rest. Around him his comrades were snoring and farting in their sleep. Like sleeping in a sty, he thought. How he hated them.

He thought about escape, as he had done every night since they had taken him from the beach. But if he ran away, Cortés would send men after him, would not hesitate to hunt him down again. The pride of these Spaniards would not allow that one of their own would prefer the company of the *naturales* to that of Christian gentlemen. But it was impossible. He could find his way back to Yucatán as easily as he might find his way to the moon.

The only one of this band worth his spit was Benítez. And right now he would have liked to slit his throat over another woman.

✳ ✳

They left Zautla, made their way through the thick forests to the west. Everywhere they found figurines in wood or clay, smaller versions of the devils they had found in the temples, left by the side of the road, placed in niches cut into the trunks of large trees, inside hilltop shrines. The soldiers also wondered over the brightly colored threads they found strung between the pine trees, and they stopped to examine them, frankly curious. The Totonacs stared, wide-eyed with trepidation.

"Bad-luck charms," they said. "Motecuhzoma's owl men have been this way, making their sorcery."

The Spaniards laughed at them and marched on.

✳ ✳

They followed a fast-running river toward the neck of the valley, gray ramparts closing in on either side. A wall loomed in front of them, an impossible sight in the middle of this raw plain.

Cortés reined in his horse and gazed at this new wonder in awe. It had been built of the same granite as the cliffs on either side and stretched from one side of the valley to the other.

"By Satan's ass, it must be three leagues wide," Benítez murmured.

Cristoval was sent ahead as scout. The wall looked to be more than nine feet high, Benítez decided; even seated on his horse, Cristoval could not see over the parapet.

Cristoval wheeled his horse and rode back. "It is not defended, my lord. There is only one entrance, but it is like no gateway I have ever seen. It is curved and so narrow that only one rider may enter at a time, and no faster than walking pace."

"It's a trap," Sandoval muttered. "By the pope's holy balls, it has to be a trap."

Norte ran forward, whispered something to Benítez as he sat astride his horse.

"What does he say?" Cortés asked him.

"He advises caution, my lord."

Cortés stared at Norte. "Well?"

"*Caudillo*, the first aim of all warfare in this country is to entice your enemy into a place where he cannot escape. That way, when you are victorious, you have more prisoners to sacrifice to the gods."

Cortés stared at the wall and did not respond.

Alvarado walked his horse forward a few steps. "Did the Totonacs not tell you of this wall?" he whispered.

"I thought they exaggerated the extent of it. Who would have thought these *naturales* capable of such a thing?"

The horses tossed their heads and stamped their hooves. The brass on their strappings jangled.

Benítez joined them. "We defeated the Tabascans only with difficulty. Are we then to face a much more powerful enemy with a wall at our backs?"

"We do not want to fight them. We want them as our allies against the Mexica."

"Even so, we should perhaps take the other road, to Cholula."

"Are you afraid, Benítez?"

"I am not afraid to die. But I did not come here to throw my life away to no good purpose. I came here for the gold."

"And there is gold! If we show no fear, there will be more gold than any of you ever dreamed of!"

"I agree with Benítez," Jaramillo said. "We should go back."

"If we go back, what do we go back to? I tell you, if we ride up to the Devil and spit in his face, he will run." He pointed to the feathered ranks of the Totonacs at their rear. "But by my conscience, if we show one scrap of fear, these dogs, too, will be at our throats."

Benítez thought, He is right. We are even outnumbered ten to one by our allies.

Cortés twisted in the saddle. "Remember the Cid, gentlemen, in his battles against the Moors? Would he have turned back, faced with his first wall?" Cortés snatched the banner from Cristoval and held it aloft, then wheeled his chestnut mare around so that he faced his army. "Gentlemen! Let us follow the banner, the sign of the Holy Cross, and by this we shall conquer!"

He galloped toward the wall and disappeared from view through the entrance. Benítez looked at Alvarado and Sandoval. Alvarado shrugged and spurred his horse after Cortés. None of them knew what was on the other side.

But they had no choice except to follow him.

MALINALI

A VAST AND empty plain. An eagle circles above our heads, black and solitary against an overcast sky.

Cortés points at a score of Indians wearing cloaks of red and white. When they see us, they run toward the defile at the far end of the valley.

"We will cut them off," Cortés says. He turns to Benítez. "Take Martin Lares and four other horsemen and block their retreat. We will parley with them. Malinali, follow me. We will need you to help us talk with them."

I think not. I try and shout a warning to him, but my lord has already spurred his horse forward. What difference will it make now? Our armies are engaged, but my lord does not know it.

Benítez and his fellow *jinetas,* as the Thunder Gods call them, flank the Tlaxcalans easily, round them up like turkeys in a pen. But they do not cower at the sight of the horses, as the Tabascans had done; instead, one runs screaming toward Benítez, swinging a great war club studded with volcanic glass. He is taken by surprise, and the club swings into his mount's shoulder. The beast screams and rears back.

Lares rides forward, driving his lance into the Tlaxcalan's chest.

Now two more come on, their spears raised. Benítez tries to regain control of his horse, but this huge animal, which I once thought invincible, is bucking with the agony of the wound. It is impossible for Benítez to maneuver his lance and defend himself, so he lets it slide from his grasp and draws his sword. He hacks at the first of his attackers, and the second is deterred by the horse's flailing hooves.

Just then one of the *jinetas* wheels his horse around and gallops away.

Jaramillo.

The rest join Benítez and Lares in the melee, but the Tlaxcalans stand their ground. One of the great warhorses crashes to its knees, defeated, after a blow from one of the war clubs. Its rider crawls away, clutching at his leg. I hear a gasp from the Tabascans behind us. This is something none of us thought to see.

Cortés has galloped ahead, and I run after him. I hear Lares shout a warning. The horizon is moving toward us, transformed now to a solid line of red and white, stark against the pine trees. There are thousands of them, streaming from the defile, their war whoops faint but growing stronger on the wind.

36

THEIR FACES WERE painted as death's heads, their bodies striped in red-and-white grease. The sound of their ululating war cries was unnerving. Benítez tightened his grip on his sword. *Stay calm.*

His mare was lame. A flap of flesh hung loose from her shoulder, and blood had sprayed along her right foreleg. He could not ride her with such a wound. He looked to his left. The cannons had been unloaded from the carts and primed. Mesa stood by one of the culverins, waiting for Cortés to give the order. Ordaz and his infantry were drawn up behind, ready to protect the guns if the Indians broke through.

"Look at them," Ordaz shouted, making a gesture toward the advancing Indians. "It is always the ruffians and cannon fodder who make the most noise. Real soldiers go about their business quietly."

FEATHERED SERPENT ✳ 163

Ruffians? Benítez thought. They do not fight like ruffians. Not many men would stand and face a charging horse as these *naturales* had done.

Cortés gave the order to fire.

The cannons roared, and the front rank of the Tlaxcalan charge disappeared. When the powder smoke cleared, they saw a few survivors milling around in dazed confusion. But instead of retreating, they tried to drag away their dead and wounded.

Cortés gave another signal, and the remaining *jinetas* spurred their horses among them, cutting them down with their lances and swords, wheeling clear of the carnage before they could be engaged, then charging in again at full gallop.

But the Tlaxcalans still would not leave their dead.

"Why don't they just run?" Benítez murmured, sickened.

The cannons had been reloaded. As he charged back to the lines, Cortés gave the order to fire again.

✳ ✳

Acrid smoke on an empty plain.

The Tlaxcalans had finally retreated into the valley reaches. Ordaz hawked deep in his throat. "I told you, Benítez. Cannon fodder."

Cortés walked his horse back through the cannons, a bloodied sword hanging limp in his right hand. "Perhaps now they will parley," he said.

I hope so, Benítez thought. If they do not, we are all dead. A horse is supposed to be worth three hundred men. If that is true, then this small engagement has cost us six hundred dead and nine hundred wounded.

Jaramillo waited until Cortés had moved out of earshot, then leaned down from the saddle. "What kind of Indian is not afraid of a horse?" he whispered.

Benítez did not respond. He did not have the answer.

MALINALI

WE HAVE FOUND another broad plain and a green panorama of maize plantations. The villagers have abandoned their farms before us, taking everything with them but a few small and hairless dogs, which were immediately slaughtered for the pot.

We have set up camp near a small stream. Night is falling quickly, black and cold. It starts to rain.

Four of the *jinetas* were wounded in the clash with the Tlaxcalan scouts, and the Thunder Gods have their owl man, who is called Mendez, cauterize the wounds with hot steel. The men's screams make the hair rise at the back of my neck. Rain Flower and I offer our services to Mendez and show him how to dress the men's wounds with the fat from a dead Tlaxcalan warrior.

Sentries are placed around the camp and the Thunder Gods try to sleep, but I watch them start at the screech of every night owl and wildcat that prowls these dismal mountains. Their moles roll their eyes and shiver under their blankets. Even their beasts whimper and fret at the night.

✳   ✳

A candle burns in Feathered Serpent's tent. Here he holds his war council. I smell fear on them all.

"We should go back," León is saying.

"We cannot go back, even if we desire it," my lord rebukes him. "Put your noses to the wind, gentlemen. Do you not smell it? That is the sweet aroma of boiling pine sap, coming from the east. The gate through which we entered is no longer deserted. The Tlaxcalans await us there, and if we try to retreat, we shall receive a bath of scalding pitch as we pass under the walls. How often must I remind you? Our Indian allies support us because they think us invincible. Should we prove otherwise, we will no doubt find ourselves adding a few pounds to *Gordo's* girth even if we escape this particular trap."

There is a profound and somber silence.

"I have discussed today's events with Doña Marina, and there seems to me no cause for gloom."

"Well, there is no need for her to be gloomy," Alvarado mutters. "She does not have to fight these devils."

I cannot believe my ears. How dare he talk to me this way? "Give me your sword and I will dispatch these whoresons as well as you," I tell him. "In return *you* can cook my lord's dog for dinner." And then I add, for good measure, a new word I have just learned: "Goatfucker!"

Alvarado's eyes flash in anger, but the other Thunder Lords grin and turn their heads to hide their laughter.

"Before you give yourself over to your temper," Cortés says, trying to mollify him, "hear what she has to say."

The Thunder Lords all turn toward me. At least my lord shows me proper respect, as it should be. I serve Feathered Serpent, but that does not make me vassal to any of these others.

I gather my thoughts in the strange tongue they call Castilian. "Some of you are wondering why the Tlaxcalans returned today for their dead and wounded. This is because a warrior believes that if he leaves the corpse of his comrade on the place of flowers, the Lord of Darkness will curse him until the day he dies. He also believes the enemy will eat these dead bodies and absorb their valor and strength so tomorrow he will be twice as fierce."

"Their belief in this witchery cost them twice as many dead today," Benítez says.

"It is true," I tell him. "But whether he is Mexica or Tlaxcalan or Totonac, a warrior has a strict code that must be obeyed on the place of flowers. To kill, as you do, with your great iron serpents at a great distance,...to a Person, this is unnatural...and dishonorable. A coward's way."

Alvarado looks perplexed. "Is she insulting us?" he asks my lord.

"What she is saying is that if he has the stamina, there is no reason why one man should not kill scores of *naturales*, perhaps hundreds. If they were a conventional army, their numbers would be enough to crush us—and swiftly—but these Indians have no military discipline, and their glass spears shatter on our steel armor." He slams both palms on the table. "Let them come on tomorrow. We shall show them what Spanish arms can do, as we did the Tabascans. After that they will come to us, begging for an alliance."

I watch their faces, and I do not understand why they are so afraid. They are just dust, after all, borne on the wind of the gods, the east wind of *Quetzalcóatl,* Feathered Serpent. They are privileged to rise above the ordinary lives of men, of planting and tilling, birth and death. If they cannot sacrifice their bodies in the service of a god, what other end is there to life?

 **37**

THE WIND HOWLED over the black plain. As he left the *caudillo's* tent, Benítez saw a dozen soldiers huddled around a meager fire. He stumbled over a body in the darkness.

"I piss in your mother's grave," a voice hissed at him.

"Norte?"

"Ah, my apologies, my lord," Norte grunted. "If I had known it was a captain who stepped on my head, I would have kept silent."

Benítez could not see the other man's face clearly, but he could imagine his mocking smile. Norte was shivering, just a thin blanket wrapped around his shoulders. "Why aren't you with the others?"

"Why do you think?"

Benítez found a cob of maize he had saved from Cortés's table and pushed it into his hands. "Here. Take it. Go on, it's not poisoned."

Norte snatched it, mumbled his thanks. Benítez blew into his hands. He wondered how much suffering lay ahead of them. Perhaps not so much if they all died tomorrow.

"How is your horse?" Norte asked, his mouth full of corn.

"Lame."

"You're lucky you're still alive. These Tlaxcalans have a reputation for fighting. Cortés must try and talk his way out of this. He won't defeat them in battle."

"He thinks we can."

"Once they get used to the noise of the cannons, we won't beat them back as easily as we did today."

The wind moaned across the plain, a dirge for the dead. "They could have killed me easily today," Benítez said. He was awed by how the Tlaxcalans had fought. They might be savages, but they lacked nothing in courage.

"They did not wish to kill you. A true warrior is only interested in capture, the glory of having a sacrifice to offer to the gods. What is the point of wars otherwise?"

"To win."

Norte laughed, a hollow sound like the bark of a frightened dog. "That is the Spanish way of thinking. For these people a battle is a gathering of . . . of duels. You understand? One man against one, a thousand times."

"Is that why they do not help one another? They could have overcome me easily if they had attacked together."

"The battlefield is the only way a young man can raise himself above his station in life. If he wins enough captives, he will wear rich cloaks and have his own harem and live in a beautiful house. *That* is why they do not help one another. You do not rob a comrade of his one chance of a better life."

Benítez listened, fascinated and repelled by these ideas. "Is that how you fought for the Maya?"

"I had other uses. I gave them another bloodline."

"And will our great lover fight for us tomorrow?"

"I must. Or the Tlaxcalans will kill me, won't they?"

"Even though they are your people?"

"The Maya were my people. These are Tlaxcalans."

"They're *naturales*."

"Must you continually bait me, Benítez? Do you want me to say the words? All right, it's true, I despise you, all of you. I even despise myself, for I am a Spaniard. If I could, I would go back to live with the Maya. But I can't. Is that what you wanted to hear? Will you hang me now?"

The wind died for a moment, and Benítez heard a wild dog's mournful howl somewhere on the plain. Why will Norte not understand that for a civilized man to live with heathens is an abomination before God? How can a Spaniard say that he prefers to live like a savage? How can a man find happiness among the reek of their temples, prostrating himself before clay idols?

Without another word he stood up and walked away. He had no time for priests, but before this expedition was through, he was determined to make his own conversion here. Norte would see that he was right.

Then he would let them hang him.

MALINALI

I watch Cortés kneel before the goddess Virgin, his lips moving in silent prayer, tiny beads clicking softly between his fingers. He is totally absorbed by his devotion and does not notice that I am awake. He finishes the prayer and makes the sign of the cross in the air.

He reaches for his gauntlets and sword. Last night he undressed to explore the pleasures of the cave, but when we were done, he had replaced all but his steel armor. I swore to him that the Tlaxcalans never fought at night, but he said that a good commander never assumed anything. He ordered patrols for the perimeter and told all the men to sleep ready in their armor, as he did.

"Is it morning so soon?" I whisper.

His eyes shine in the gray light, luminous as a cat's. "I did not mean to wake you."

"It was not you who woke me." I sit up, pull the rough

woolen blanket about my shoulders. "I heard the ocelots call-ing to one another in the valley."

He buckles his sword, takes the helmet he calls a burgonet, with its long green plume, from the table. The morning wind whips at the silk of the tent. He hesitates before going outside. "Will the Tlaxcalans yield, Marina? If we vanquish them today, will they sue for peace?"

"I cannot say, my lord. All I know is that they have never yielded to the Mexica."

He looks suddenly sad. "I do not wish to fight them. They have forced me to this. What am I to do?"

What kind of god is this, I ask myself, who fights his ene-mies only when they bring him to it? Who weeps over every drop of blood spilled? Why can the Tlaxcalans not see that he is their salvation and not their enemy?

I hear the murmur of soldiers' voices outside: they kneel before Fray Olmedo and Fray Díaz by turns, whispering strange and strangled prayers, as they have been doing through the night. The Tlaxcalan drums start to beat some-where in the early dark.

I catch his wrist. "My lord, when you plan the battle, remember that they do not fight as you do. If they lose their commanders, they lose heart. Remember this."

"I will remember it." He kisses me gently and leaves the tent.

I watch the shadows fade to gray, hear the mountain cats howling to welcome Feathered Serpent as he strides to his horse. The ocelots are sacred to my dawn lord, and they have awaited him especially on this day of all days to acclaim his coming.

But for the first time, I feel a little afraid. If he should be defeated today, he will return to the Cloud Lands to await a more propitious time. But for me there will be no other days, nor would I wish there to be. Why survive to spend the rest of my life at the loom until I am old and withered? Rather a glo-rious death with *Quetzalcóatl* than a wearisome life without him.

❊   ❊

And this is what happened.

The entire plain is covered with the *naturales,* their plumes waving in the breeze like ears of maize in a cornfield. There are the Otomí in their war paint of red and white, the Tlaxcalans striped with the yellow and white of the Rock Heron clan, the generals sporting the great battle standards of their lord, Ring of the Wasp. The sun flashes on thousands of obsidian blades. I hear the blast of whistles and conch shells, the ululations of their war cries, the beat of the snakeskin *teponaztli* drums: *ta-tam, ta-tam, ta-tam . . .*

My lord forms his tiny army into a square, the artillery at the wings and his *jinetas* at point. He rides his warhorse ten paces to the front and himself reads out the strange god-language that the Thunder Gods call the *Requerimiento.* His voice is all but drowned by the battle cries of the Tlaxcalans as they move toward us across the plain.

My lord spurs his warhorse around so that he is facing his soldiers. "Gentlemen. The cavalry will make their charge by three. Keep your lances high . . ."

The Tlaxcalans come on, the hammering of drums and the blast of whistles deafening now. My lord must raise his voice to make himself heard.

". . . Remember, they wish for captives, not for kills, and their glass lances will shatter on your armor. Do not concern yourselves with being overwhelmed, for only the front rank of the Indians will fight, and no more than one Indian will confront you at any one time. Your only enemy today is fatigue . . ."

The Tlaxcalans are almost within bow range.

"The harquebusiers and the crossbowmen will stagger their fire so that they are not overrun." He turns his horse to face the enemy and draws his sword. *"¡Santiago y cierra España!"*

I realize our Totonac allies have not understood a single word of my lord's speech. So I clamber on one of the thunder serpents and raise my voice in the elegant speech: "People of the Totonac! Feathered Serpent promises us victory today! You cannot die! He has promised to make you invincible!"

They raise their war clubs and cheer wildly when they hear this.

Aguilar grabs me by the arm and shakes me. "What are you telling them?"

I tear myself free of his impudent grip and ignore him.

"What did you tell them?" he screams at me, but his words are lost in the bedlam. A shower of arrows, darts, and stones rains down on us.

✻ ✻

The Indians come on one squadron at a time, perfect fodder for the thunder serpents. Their bodies are shredded in smoke and flame. As they try to drag themselves and their comrades from the field, the *jinetas* gallop among them and scythe them down.

But still they come, rank after rank. Death on the field of flowers is glorious, and they know they will be transported to the paradise of butterflies and waterfalls.

As my lord had warned, fatigue is our greatest enemy, and as the day wears on, the weight of numbers wears us down. A squadron of Tlaxcalan warriors, their bodies and faces streaked with the yellow-and-white paint of the Rock Heron clan, break through our lines. I see Guzmán fall, an arrow in his thigh. He lies there helpless as a Tlaxcalan warrior stands over him, a broad two-handed club raised above his head.

"No!" Guzmán screams, as shrill as a girl.

The *natural* brings his war club down on the mouth of the iron serpent, hoping to kill it. Guzman crawls away, clutching at his bleeding leg. I snatch his pike from the ground and run toward the warrior, the weapon aimed at his chest.

It is like driving into wood. The point of the blade sticks fast, and I cannot remove it. I look into the warrior's face, and I realize he is younger than I. He still wears a *piochtli*, a lock of hair at the nape of his neck to show he has not yet taken his first captive. He falls back against the iron serpent, gasping like a beached fish.

Flores helps me wrench the spike from the warrior's chest, then pushes me out of the way. Other soldiers rush past me to protect the precious serpents.

I see Aguilar staring at me. Why does he look so horrified? All these men here are fighting for their lives and their histories; why can I not fight for mine?

 **38**

THE NATURALES RETREATED toward the gorge.

"¡Santiago y cierra España!" Cortés shouted, and ordered the cavalry in pursuit of the stragglers. Benítez's horse was still lame from her wound and could not keep pace with the rest. He fell farther and farther behind, and from his position at the rear, he saw what was about to happen but was powerless to stop it.

The Tlaxcalans had drawn them into a trap. Thousands of Otomí had been kept in reserve, hidden on either side of the ravine. As the cavalry entered the defile after the retreating Tlaxcalans, they swept down in an avalanche of red and white. Cortés shouted to retreat, but his voice was lost in the bedlam of drums and whistles and screams.

Everything happened very quickly after that.

Benítez found himself surrounded. Hands clawed at his legs, as the naturales tried to drag him from his horse. He slashed wildly with his sword, trying to force the Indians back, but then one of them leaped into the air swinging a great club tipped with razor-sharp obsidian, a two-handed blow aimed not at him but at his horse. It almost severed the mare's head, and she dropped to the ground, instantly dead.

Let me die now, Benítez thought as he hit the ground. Let them kill me, but do not let them take me captive!

His sword was jarred from his hand as he fell, and the breath

went out of him. They were on him straightaway. They grabbed
him, started dragging him away. He kicked out, biting like a wild
animal. His own screams echoed in his ears.

Suddenly he heard shouts and the sound of steel crunching
through a flimsy wooden shield. A Spanish pikeman had driven into
his attackers, forcing them back. The soldier used the butt end of
his weapon to knock one of them to the ground, then turned and
slashed again at the encircling Indians.

Norte.

Clumsy and inexpert with his weapon, he had used his agility
and the ferocity of his charge to unsettle the Indians. It won Benítez
a moment's grace, time enough to struggle back to his feet and find
his sword. But now they were surrounded once again by a sea of red
and white. Benítez retreated until he was back-to-back with Norte.

Two of the Otomí stepped forward.

✳ ✳

And so it went. The Indians came at them two at a time, one to
Norte and one to Benítez, until ten of them lay at their feet, either
dead or wounded so badly they could not continue. Benítez wondered how much longer he and Norte could survive this. He could
not see any of his comrades. Perhaps the rest of the cavalry had
already been slaughtered or taken captive. If Cortés was dead, they
were lost anyway.

Then he heard Norte scream, felt him fall.

Benítez finished his own opponent and swung around. An Otomí
was dragging Norte away by the hair. He was unprepared for
another attack, thought his part of the battle done. Benítez drove his
sword deep into his chest and stepped back, his feet planted on
either side of Norte's body to defend him.

The Otomís snarled and screamed, and another left the group to
face him.

✳ ✳

It was Sandoval who reached him first, driving his mare among the
Indians, a running wedge of pikemen following him in. He reached
from the saddle and held out his hand.

Benítez pushed the hand away, stood his ground over Norte's body. This renegade had saved his life, and honor demanded he must die rather than leave the field without him, alive or dead.

As any good Indian would do, he found himself thinking, and the thought made him laugh aloud.

MALINALI

AS THE SUN sinks, the valley is filtered in shades of gray. My lord's soldiers limp from the field of flowers, supported on the shoulders of their comrades; others sit on the ground, their heads on their knees, spent. Bodies, two or three deep, litter the ground in front of Mesa's artillery, a twitching, moaning mass. The reek of the iron serpents' breath hangs heavy in the air, acrid and foul.

The man I speared lies on his back beside one of these iron monsters, still living. I can hear the noise of his breathing. I wish one of these moles would finish him, but they are concerned with their own wounds and with those of their comrades and do not worry about the suffering of a single Indian.

"You must confess." I turn around. It is Aguilar, clutching his tattered book to his chest, his greasy hair plastered to his skull with sweat. "You have committed the mortal sin of murder."

This madness echoes in my head. How can it be bad to kill your enemy on the battlefield?

"We must pray for your soul. It is a sin to kill."

"Look around you, Aguilar. All that has been done this day is killing."

"Cortés's soldiers have purchased a special dispensation from the pope. What they do is in Christ's name."

I turn away. This Aguilar is a madman and talks in riddles.

"You must ask forgiveness from God!" he shouts at me.

Flores, tiring of the noises coming from the dying Indian, slashes quickly with his sword, and there is silence. Brother Aguilar makes the sign of the cross and moves on.

39

THE ROOM STANK of blood. Men lay on the floor in their own ordure crying for their mothers. Fray Olmedo and Fray Díaz could be heard murmuring in the candlelight, taking confessions, administering the rites of extreme unction. Mendez and Malinali were busy with more practical needs, binding the soldiers' wounds as best they could.

Norte was sobbing with pain. His face was gaunt, the stubble on his cheek stark against the pallor of his skin. Rain Flower knelt beside him, holding his hand. She had bound a poultice of vinegar-soaked herbs to the wound in his side. She was weeping.

Benítez had come as a brother comrade, to whisper words of thanks and say a prayer for his recovery. But when he saw Rain Flower, he felt as if he had walked into a wooden post. He stood at the foot of the litter, stunned.

What a fool I am, he thought. This Norte has been my intermediary with this girl. Stupid of me not to realize that it allowed him the opportunity to be so much more. He could now imagine what they had done and how they must have laughed at him behind his back.

His shadow fell across Norte's face, and Rain Flower looked up, startled. She wiped away the wetness on her cheeks with her sleeve. Too late.

Benítez knelt down beside the wounded man's pallet. "Norte," he whispered.

The wounded man's eyes flickered open. He blinked, trying to focus.

Benítez leaned closer. "There is something I must tell you. First, I have to thank you for saving my life."

Norte tried to speak, but no words came.

"The second thing I want to tell you—I hope you die. I hope you die in the Devil's own searing agony."

He walked out.

The rain beat a steady rhythm on the woven roof; rivulets of water ran down the ridgepole into the churned and bloodstained mud at the entrance. He took a lungful of air, glad to be away from the sweat and the stink and the crying in there. All right, Norte had saved his life, but he had owed him that much. Benítez had saved *him* from the noose at Vera Cruz. But the girl was a different matter. That was betrayal of the most desperate kind.

Forget about it, he told himself. She is just a *natural* and a *puta*. What does it matter? Still, he was glad that Norte was suffering. Damn him.

And damn her, too.

MALINALI

WE ARE CAMPED at a place called the Hill of the Tower. The moles have found some supplies of maize and spiced our meal with meat from the village dogs. My lord suspects that the Totonacs are supplementing their own diet with Tlaxcalan prisoners, but Fray Olmedo has dissuaded him from confronting them on this vexing question. He rightly pointed out that we cannot afford to antagonize our only ally in our present dire straits.

We have fought two pitched battles with the Tlaxcalans in the last three days. My lord's soldiers are exhausted, their fragile morale shattered. He has withdrawn his forces from the plain and decided to wait.

The finer dwellings in this abandoned village have been requisitioned by the Thunder Lords for their personal use.

Feathered Serpent himself has laid claim to one of the few houses built from adobe. His oaken table and favorite studded chair are set up in a corner of the room, and he sits there now, writing on a piece of parchment with quill and ink.

His face looks haggard in the light of the candle.

We have lost forty-five soldiers from a force of four hundred. Another dozen are ill with disease, and of the rest almost all have at least two wounds. Another battle like the last will probably finish us.

There is sweat soaking his linen shirt despite the bitter wind that moans through the cracks in the walls. His hand trembles violently with fever. It is as much as he can do to hold the quill to the paper, but he is determined to finish the missive before he surrenders to the black exhaustion that envelops him. He wishes to demand of his *Olintecle* the right to be king of the Mexica when he captures Tenochtitlán. I do not see how the gods can do otherwise. These lands, after all, have always been his.

The funeral chant of the drums from the Tlaxcalan camp are carried to us on the night wind. They are sacrificing the Totonacs they captured today.

The letter is done, my lord seals it carefully with blood-red wax, and then his shoulders seem to collapse under the weight of a great burden. "What am I to do?" he whispers.

I place my hands on his shoulders, willing strength back into his tired muscles. It is obvious to me what he must do, but he is too tired to see it. "Free the prisoners your soldiers took today," I tell him. "Send them back to Lord Ring of the Wasp. Tell him you will pardon everything if he will embrace you and join you in your fight against Motecuhzoma."

He stares at the candle flame for a long time, not speaking. He appears not to have heard me. But then he calls for his majordomo, Cáceres, and tells him to send in two of the Tlaxcalans his men have captured today.

Sandoval leads them in. They are hog-tied: their wrists are bound behind their backs, and the rope is looped and knotted around their necks. They have been stripped of everything except loincloths. They spare a glance around the room from under black fringes of hair, eyes hooded, expecting death.

My lord waits, composing his thoughts.

"Tell them," he says to me, "tell them I do not wish to make war on them."

"May your wives all grow fangs in their caves of joy," I begin, using the elegant speech. "You have made my lord very angry. He came here in peace, and instead you have attacked him and vexed his patience."

The Tlaxcalans do not raise their eyes from the ground.

"They must tell their chief," my lord continues, "that I am on my way to Tenochtitlán for my reckoning with Motecuhzoma. If the Tlaxcalans continue to make war on me, I will come and burn all their houses and kill all the people."

His audacity takes my breath away. Our soldiers are barely able to stand, they are so exhausted. Yet what else shall a god say to his enemies when he is vexed? "Tell the blind white bird who sees wisdom in the darkness that Feathered Serpent is returned to claim the Lands of Bread. Let him pass quickly on his way to hasten Motecuhzoma's destiny, or the Mexica's fate may be your own."

These warriors' eyes go wide. Finally they raise their heads to stare at the shivering, bearded figure at the table, and I see them wonder if this might indeed be *Quetzalcóatl.*

My lord nods to Sandoval, who steps forward and cuts their bonds with a knife. He hands each of them a string of glass beads that the Thunder Gods have brought with them from the paradise world of water and boats they call Venice. My lord's prisoners stare at this treasure in bewilderment.

"This is a gift from Feathered Serpent himself," I tell them. "In the Cloud Lands they are more valuable than the most precious jade. Now go and tell your chief what Feathered Serpent has said."

Sandoval bundles the Tlaxcalans from the room. My lord dismisses Cáceres also, with a nod.

When we are alone once more, he allows his head to drop

to the table. His hands ball into fists. The fever has all but broken him.

I help him undress and put him to bed. His body shakes with chills; his eyes are shining, unfocused. I take off my clothes and warm his body with my own, cradle his head against the softness of my breast. His limbs curl around me, and he sucks at my nipple like a baby.

I continue to hold him through the night, and now I see not the god but the man who clothes the god's essence, with all his imperfections. It confuses me, for I am no longer sure whom I love more: the god or the man in whose skin he shelters.

 **40**

THE CANDLE FLICKERED in the draft, threw deep shadows on the cracked adobe plaster. The room was bare except for a table and a few threadbare tapestries.

It was an impromptu council, each of the participants spurred to meet with his fellows from alarm at their precarious situation. Alvarado and León both sported wounds from the day's battle: León's beard was matted with blood from a slash on his cheek; Alvarado had a blood-soaked rag wrapped tightly around his lower arm. Benítez, too, had a deep wound in the muscle of his shoulder.

"Where is Doña Isabel?" Alvarado asked Benítez as he entered.

Benítez hesitated. Was he worried about spies, or did he know about Norte and his treacherous Mayan bride? "She is helping Mendez in the hospital."

"The hospital," León repeated. "Where Cortés should be."

Sandoval nodded. "He has the fever."

"What he has is love fever," Alvarado snapped. "He spends too much time alone with Doña Marina. She exerts too much control over him."

"They say she has been his mistress since Jalapa," Sandoval said.

"He covered her the moment Alonso got on the boat back to Spain," León said. "By Satan's great spotted ass, he treats her as if she were a Spanish *doñita*! He has assigned her her own page and even a litter for when we travel on hard terrain."

"Aguilar says that she has told the Indians he is a god," Alvarado said.

There was an embarrassed silence. "We cannot know the truth of that," Benítez said. "But I have never heard those words pass his own lips. Never."

"What are we to do?" Sandoval asked.

"What can we do?" Benítez said. "As Cortés says, there is no way back. We must be victorious here or die."

"It is the girl's fault," Alvarado said. "She led us to this. She has bewitched him."

"Bewitched or no, let us pray he is better tomorrow," León said. "Without Cortés we are lost."

"I can lead you in battle as well as Cortés," Alvarado said.

Another silence. The men stared at the table.

"You will see," he hissed. He turned on his heel and went out.

"As you say," Sandoval murmured, "without Cortés we are lost."

✷   ✷

She watched Cortés from a corner of the room. She was bathed in watery light, and her face was exactly as he had imagined it, serene and very pale. She wore long purple robes and held an infant in her arms. This chimeric vision reached out a hand toward him, and Cortés tried to grasp it, his fingers outstretched. He murmured the words of a prayer he had learned in boyhood from his grandmother as they knelt before the image of the *Señora de los Remedios* in the cathedral in Sevilla.

"You have been blessed by God," the vision said. "You will have me beside you, wherever you go and whatever you do."

"They will not relent," he murmured.

"They will all break before you. You must fear nothing, for this kingdom is already yours. You will win it for me. This is your destiny."

"My destiny," Cortés repeated.

"You are not like other men. That is why I chose you. You will be my champion. You will bring these people to me, and I will reward you a thousand times."

He would have touched her robe, but a hand pulled him back onto the bed. "You're hot," Malinali whispered. "Your skin is burning."

"María," Cortés murmured.

"Who are you talking to?"

Cortés looked again for the woman in the purple robes, but she was gone. There was only the darkness and the numbing cold of the room. The sweat on his skin felt suddenly chill, and he started to shiver again. Malinali lay on top of him to warm him while he shuddered and cursed.

Finally he slept.

When morning came, he had forgotten the lady in the purple robes. The memory of her remained buried, something glimpsed and quickly forgotten, a match struck in a darkened room in a dream.

MALINALI

I RISE NAKED from the bed. The blanket is dank with cold sweat. I throw it aside.

The plain is still in darkness. The morning star, emblem of Feathered Serpent, is risen in the east, and the ocelots are calling welcome. My lord breathes in deep and peaceful rhythm. The fever is passed.

I put a hand to my belly and wonder if Feathered Serpent's seed already grows inside me. Tonight I thought I felt it move, though it is too soon; it is just my desire, my imagination. What a wonder it would be, to be mother of a god, the womb of a new dynasty for the Toltec kings.

Already my lord's soldiers are moving about the camp,

wraiths dressed in rags, hunched for warmth over the smoldering embers of their fires. A mist of rain seeps down from the mountains.

I feel someone's eyes on me, a man with a jar of wine cradled on his lap. I cannot see his features clearly in this gray dawn light, but I guess that it must be Jaramillo.

My skin feels hot, as if it were crawling with fire ants. I hurry back inside.

 41

MEN LAY ON mats on the bare earth floor, their wounds covered in blood-soaked bandages, shivering under thin blankets. Some stared hollow-eyed at the rafters; others moaned and tossed and called for their mothers. Benítez moved slowly through the slaughterhouse stink, looking for Norte.

Rain Flower was still with him, crouched beside him on the straw mat where he had lain for almost a week. His face was hollow, covered with a pelt of beard. Before he had been wounded, it had been his habit to shave his face every day with a piece of obsidian, Benítez remembered, a practice he had apparently taken up while living with the beardless Mayans. At last he looked like a real Spaniard.

Rain Flower saw him and quickly averted her eyes.

Benítez knelt down. The stench of old blood and waste was overpowering. *Our renegade no longer smells so sweet.*

"Norte," he whispered.

His eyes flickered open. He tried to speak, but no sound came. Rain Flower raised his head and held a small gourd of water to his lips.

"Well. You have a beard now," Benítez said. "You are one of us."

Norte managed a strained smile. "You . . . come here . . . to insult me?"

"If possible." *He is better since yesterday,* Benítez thought. *The* yellow has gone from his cheeks, and his breathing is better. "I hope you are suffering."

"Thank you, yes. The wound is...not deep, but I have broken...ribs. It is difficult to breathe, and the pain...is very bad."

"I find that most satisfactory."

Benítez looked up at Rain Flower. She would not meet his eyes. The little Tabascan girl looks thin and ill, he thought. Like the rest of us.

Somewhere in the darkness, a soldier was babbling at the phantoms that had come to haunt him.

Norte's eyes went to the girl. "...You know?"

Benítez nodded.

"What are you going to do?"

"I have not decided. The way things are, perhaps I will not have to do anything."

Norte reached for Rain Flower. "Be kind...to the girl. She...does not deserve...to suffer."

"No?"

"Had you plans for her?...You would never...be able...to take her back with you...to Castile. Except as...a novelty."

"That was not my thought."

A ghost of a smile on Norte's face, and then it was gone. He might have imagined it. What was my thought? Benítez wondered. Have I really grown fond of an Indian?

Mendez had begun an operation on a wooden table in the corner of the hut. Four soldiers had been recruited to hold down the patient, who had been liberally soused with Cuban wine.

"Why did you save my life?" Benítez asked him.

"You saved mine."

The man on the table let out a piercing scream. Benítez tried to shut his ears to it.

"Was that reason enough to kill your fellow Indians?"

"I told you,...they are not...my fellow Indians. I cannot...escape my skin. I am a Spaniard...like you. I have a beard and...blue eyes. Why deny it?"

Rain Flower whispered something to Norte. He turned to Benítez.

"She wants to see...your arm."

"It is nothing."

Another whispered exchange. "She says wounds get infected . . . easily here. She would like to . . . take care of it for . . . you."

"What is the point? As you say, we are all going to die here."

Norte's breathing was becoming labored. The effort of talking had exhausted him. "You should try . . . and learn a little . . . of her language. If you are kind to her, she . . . will be kind to you."

"Why would I need her kindness?"

The man on the table had finished screaming, had thankfully passed into unconsciousness.

"I discovered," Norte said, ". . . among the Maya . . . that every man . . . is two men: what he is born to and . . . what he can become. Most follow the road . . . they were born to."

"What are you saying?" Benítez said.

"Perhaps you are not . . . at heart . . . a Spaniard."

He wasn't going to listen to this anymore. He stood up and hurried outside.

Damn him. Damn him.

Damn him because it was all an act, this hate. Norte was right: he did not hate the renegade as a true Spaniard should hate him. It was his right to have them both punished for their crimes against him, and yet he did nothing. His slowness to vengeance had unmanned him. *They* had unmanned him.

Clouds raced across the moon, the smell of camp smoke and rain on the air. Feelings of confusion, exhausted yet unable to sleep.

 42

RAIN FLOWER EXAMINED the wound in the light of the candle. As she removed the filthy bandage, her nose wrinkled at the taint of infection. A Tlaxcalan lance had sliced cleanly through the skin and deep into the muscle, and the lips of the wound were swollen and inflamed. A watery discharge wept from the flesh.

Benítez gave a small grunt of pain.

Rain Flower had brought with her a foul-smelling poultice of herbs. She placed it on the wound and bound it tightly with cloth strips. When she had finished, she looked up at him and did something he had not expected her to do.

She smiled.

Despite himself, he found himself reaching out a hand to stroke her hair.

So beautiful, he thought, once you became accustomed to this coppery skin. More beautiful than any Castilian women he had ever courted. But then, he was not as experienced as others in such matters. He was not what most women thought of as an attractive man: he was clumsy, his nose was too large, and his features were too coarse. He was not like Alvarado or even Cortés, who had a reputation for chasing every *doñita* on Cuba. No, he had never been a ladies' man, had never possessed the wealth or the power or the personality that could have outweighed the shortcomings in his appearance.

He was suddenly overwhelmed by the force of his own loneliness. Here he was, alone with a beautiful woman, yet he could not even talk to her in the simplest terms. He wondered what she was thinking. About Norte no doubt, he thought with a stab of anger: Norte with his torn ears and tattooed face, Norte who could speak her language and could remind her of her own ways and her own gods.

But it was no good. He could not sustain the same force of rage he had felt when he first discovered her betrayal. Now there was just the pain of his own clumsiness. He had never been able to keep beautiful things; it was his fault, not hers. And Norte? Hard to hate a man when you have stood back-to-back with him in a fight.

Her fingers touched his cheek.

"*Cara,*" he whispered. But of course, she could not understand.

She kissed him. Gently. Not a kiss of obligation or even of reward. Indeed, no woman had ever kissed him quite that way. Be careful, a voice said to him. Do not pretend to yourself that you can fall in love with a *natural*. You simply take what is offered, when you can. That is the nature of soldiering.

He pulled her gently down beside him on the mat.

MALINALI

THE MAN IS dressed only in a loincloth. I can see each muscle and sinew of his body rippling beneath the skin. He is on his knees, his feet roped together, and one of the Thunder Gods, Jaramillo, has a foot on the rope; his right hand holds the bonds that are looped around the man's neck and wrists. He keeps it taut, forcing his prisoner's arms up between his shoulders while simultaneously choking him.

Alvarado has another rope around the man's upper arm, an iron spike knotted in the cord as a lever. He twists it tight so that it bites deep into his prisoner's arm, cutting off the supply of blood. The limb is swollen and purple.

The young man gasps and writhes but does not shame himself by crying out. Not yet.

He had been captured during the night attack. The moonlight had betrayed the Tlaxcalan's movements; a sentry had seen them and given the alarm. This warrior was not to be as fortunate as their other prisoners. Instead of gifts and offers of peace, Feathered Serpent has decided on quite a different tactic.

I look up at him. Can he not stop this? I fear the bout of fever has changed him somehow. He no longer behaves as a god but as a man.

"Ask him if he knows who I am," he says to me. He has a look on his face I have not seen before.

"Feathered Serpent asks if you recognize him," I say to the young warrior. "You must tell him and stop your suffering. He is very angry."

Jaramillo takes the tension from the rope to allow him to reply. Our warrior gags and coughs, fighting to catch his breath, froth spilling down his chin. He rakes air into his lungs. After a few moments Jaramillo jerks on the rope to remind him of the question.

The Tlaxcalan looks up at me, his eyes silently pleading with me to make them stop the torture. Death in battle or on the sacrificial stone holds no fears for any warrior. But this... "Some say... he is indeed... a god,... others that... he is a man. Lord Ring of the Wasp... is unsure."

I turn back to my lord. "He knows who you are."

"Ask him, then, why his people are fighting us."

When our young warrior hears this question, he shouts, "Because you are on our land! You are thieves and... murderers! Soon we will... roast all your hearts and feed them to the gods!"

Jaramillo does not understand what is said but hears the defiance in his prisoner's voice and jerks hard on the rope, forcing his head back, silencing him. I look up at my lord. Why does he allow this? To kill in battle is glorious, but to inflict such torment deliberately is shameful.

"What did he say?" he asks me. There is a sheen of perspiration on his forehead, even though it is deathly cold in the room.

"He says... he thinks we are invaders."

My lord sinks into his chair; the small effort of standing even for so short a time leaves him exhausted. After a few moments he looks up at Jaramillo. "Cut off his nose and hands, tie them around his neck, and send him back to his village."

No! I cannot believe what he has just ordered. I cannot speak against him in front of the other Thunder Gods, so I silently implore him with my eyes to revoke the order. He looks straight through me, dead to all kindness. Could this be my Feathered Serpent, the god who weeps for suffering, the commander who looked so forlorn when he signed the death warrant for the traitors at Vera Cruz, who prays every night on his knees in front of a painting of a mother and child?

"Mali, before we send our prisoners back, you must give them a message for Lord Ring of the Wasp. They are to tell him that I have lost all patience with them. I will give them two days to come here in peace, or I will march to their capital and burn it to the ground."

Outside Jaramillo is setting about the task Cortés has assigned him. He holds the man's hands on a chopping block, grinning into his face as Guzmán wields the pike. As the blade crunches into the wood, our unfortunate young warrior screams, blood spurting rhythmically from his wrists. Jaramillo plunges the stumps of his arms into a bucket of hot pitch to cauterize the wounds.

He is still screaming when Jaramillo cuts off his nose with his knife.

It is worse, much worse, than anything I have witnessed in the temples. Our prisoners are not even allowed a warrior's death and the certainty of afterlife. They will go to the underworld as old men and cripples.

Why, why has my Lord of Gentle Wisdom allowed this?

"My lord—"

He dismisses me with a wave of his hand. "I am tired. I have to rest. Just do as I say." And he signals to his majordomo to send me out of the room.

43

YOUNG RING OF the Wasp shook his head. "I still do not believe they are gods."

The Council of Four no longer shared his conviction. "Then how do you explain our defeat?" Laughs at Women said. "Even if they are men, as you say, then they must surely have a god leading them. These *teules* can see at night as well as read our minds."

"We can defeat them," Young Ring of the Wasp insisted.

"No," his father said. The old *cacique* was tired of this, tired of these endless debates, tired of hearing the funeral drums for his young warriors. "You are wrong. We cannot vanquish them. We have fought them through the whole Month of Sweeping, and still they will not retreat. First they send us words of peace, claiming they wish only to fight the Mexica; now they send back our young warriors without hands and faces." He sighed. "He is unpredictable like a god, and if he is Feathered Serpent, then we have tried his patience too far. These *teules* offer us an alliance against the Mexica. What if this is true? For fifty years Motecuhzoma and his ancestors have drained the blood of our youth on their altars. At last we will have the opportunity to free ourselves from their arrogance and cruelty. When these *teules* return to the Cloud Lands, we will be the masters of the valley."

Young Ring of the Wasp began to protest, but the old *cacique* put up a hand to silence him. "You have had your chance, my son. We have made war, without effect. Now we must sue for peace."

MALINALI

THEY ARE SHABBY, compared to the Mexica. Indeed, some of their robes must have been stolen from enemies: you can see the bloodstains. The rest of them wear poor mantles of maguey fiber.

I stand behind Cortés's chair as he receives them, ready to offer my translations from the elegant speech. There are perhaps as many as fifty in the delegation, and judging by their feathers and jewels, they are all senators of the Tlaxcala republic. Their leader is as tall as a Spaniard, his skin spotted by disease. He identifies himself as Ring of the Wasp the Younger, son of the Tlaxcala chieftain.

"We have come to ask your lord Malinche for forgiveness," the young chief begins, his face a sullen mask. "At first we thought he had been sent to invade us by our great enemy Motecuhzoma. We thought this because you were accompanied by their vassals, the Totonacs. Now we see that we were...wrong." He seemed to choke on the last word.

I relay his sentiments to my lord. If he is relieved to hear these soothing words, he does not show it. "Tell them they have only themselves to blame for this war," he answers. "I came here in friendship, and they attacked me and caused much disruption. Now my officers want to burn their town, and I do not know if I can keep them from it."

A churlish and astonishing reply. Burn their town? Our soldiers can barely light a cooking fire at night.

But his reply seems to cause Young Ring of the Wasp great consternation. "Please remind your lord Malinche that he entered Tlaxcala without our consent. We would be less than men if we had not fought to defend ourselves. However, we regret this misunderstanding, and our Council of Four offer him their friendship if he will make an alliance with us."

But my lord is sulky when I tell him this, couching Young Ring of the Wasp's words in more pleasantries than I heard from his lips.

"I see no reason to forget past injuries," my lord says, and his fingers drum impatiently on the arm of his chair.

"So what should I tell him, my lord?"

"Tell him that my terms for peace are these: that he must submit to me immediately and offer his allegiance to His Majesty King Charles of Spain. If he refuses, I shall come to Tlaxcala, burn it to the ground, and make all the people there my slaves."

I take a moment to compose my thoughts. "Feathered Serpent says that you must agree to obey him, in everything he says, or he will come to Tlaxcala and punish you all."

Young Ring of the Wasp stares at Feathered Serpent, then at me. "Are they really gods?"

"What does he say?" my lord wants to know.

I lean toward him so that no one else can hear, though I see Aguilar crane his neck trying to eavesdrop. "He asks if you are a god, my lord," I whisper.

"Tell him I am a man, as he is, but I serve the one and only true God."

What can I say? If I tell the Tlaxcalans he is not a god, they will want to fight us again, and this time they will surely win. I look into Feathered Serpent's wild gray eyes and wonder why he tries to conceal the truth about himself this way.

I turn to Young Ring of the Wasp and give him the only answer that makes sense to me. "He is just a man, but he has a god inside him. That is why he cannot be defeated in battle."

And now I see my lord's wisdom, for it is the only answer that this young warrior will accept. Yes, that is possible, I can see him thinking. *Sometimes gods return as men. Feathered Serpent had been a man when he ruled the Toltecs.*

It is an answer for the Tlaxcalans, but is it answer enough for me? Can a man really be a god and not know of it? Or is there some mystery here greater than I have so far divined?

Painali, 1508

The Yucatán is a place of scrub and thorn, a low plateau of lime-stone nestled against a coast of salt pans and lagoons. In places the rain percolating through the stone has caused underground caverns to collapse and form deep wells we call cenotes, *where the rain gods live.*

One day my father takes me by the hand and leads me to the litter that waits for him outside our house. My mother watches us leave, and I see the poison in her eyes. She wishes Motecuhzoma had chosen me for his altars instead of my brothers, and I know also that she is jealous of the time my father spends with me.

You should understand that my father was a man of some importance and renown in our district and had a litter to carry him everywhere. He was of striking appearance. His head had been bound with boards as an infant so that his skull had the elon-gated shape of a nobleman. He was a man of distinction among us. His hair was bound in four plaits, and there were expensive jade ornaments in his ears, nose, and lips. His body was painted in the blue of a priest, and his front teeth had been sharpened to points and capped with expensive topaz.

I adored him.

When we reach the water hole, we climb from the litter, and he leads me by the hand down a steep and crumbling path. The shadows close around us, and the water is black and very cold. Butterflies dance in the emerald twilight; a hummingbird dances from flower to flower.

But this is no paradise garden. We step over a skeleton moldering at the base of a cliff, and the air is sickly and tainted with rotting flesh. A column of ants is busy at work, harvesting the latest prize.

When the rains do not come, the priests bring a sacrifice here, and they are thrown from the top of the cliff as offering. Our gods are not greedy. One or two slaves and they are mollified.

"You are wondering why I brought you here," my father whispers.

He points to a ledge above us, halfway up the cliff.

"When I was as old as you are now, the rains did not come. The maize crops shriveled in the field. Clouds gathered on the horizon, but they shunned us and would not venture in from the sea, frightened away by Tlaloc, *Rain Bringer, who was angry with us. Scores of slaves were sacrificed here, but still* Tlaloc *did not relent.*

"So it was decided to offer a true sacrifice, the son of a freeman. The one they chose was me."

He was silent, the past relived behind his black eyes. When he spoke again, his voice was hoarse.

"I did not understand what was happening, of course. I was too young to understand death. I remember only a feeling of importance, briefly enjoyed, and then the terrible fear as the priests led me toward the edge of that cliff.

"I remember the priest told me that when I met the gods, I was to ask humbly for rains and knowledge of the future. That when this was done, I could return to Painali. And then I remember falling.

"That ledge saved my life, of course. I do not remember much of what happened. When I woke up, it was night, and I was in terrible pain; something was broken in my leg. In the morning I managed to crawl out, and the villagers found me. And that day it rained.

"The rain was my destiny. I was immediately raised to the

priesthood. From that day on, I also enjoyed the gift of prophecy, and it elevated me above other men.

"Mali, my gift has shown me that one day soon Feathered Serpent will return from the Cloud Lands to break the hold of the Mexica and bring peace and golden times, as he did before. I know why I was saved from death on the ledge, because one day I would have a daughter and you would one day grow up to be guide and consort of Feathered Serpent when he returned from the Cloud Lands."

I cannot tell you how I felt. I should have been shocked by what he told me, but I must confess I had been born with this same sense of destiny. It was as if I had always known that I would not spend the days of my life pounding tortillas with an infant strapped to my back.

"Do not fear the end of things, Mali. From death and drought, I emerged reborn and bowed down with gifts from the gods. Look for destruction. When it comes, welcome it. It is your destiny."

The litter carried us back to Painali, and we rode in silence. A golden future spread before me, rippling in the wind, like a field of ripening maize.

Tlaxcala, 1519

A silver river snakes across the valley below us. White stone buildings cling to the hillsides as if balanced there by weather and time, well-tended gardens clustered about the high walls. To the surprise of my Thunder Lords, Tlaxcala is even more beautiful than Cempoala.

The entire population comes out to welcome us. The day before, these people were our bitter enemies; now they crowd the streets and roofs, throwing flowers, and they are beating drums and blowing their conch horns in welcome instead of war.

We enter Tlaxcala on the first day of the month known as Return of the Gods.

Ring of the Wasp the Elder waits in the plaza to greet us, seated on a palanquin, a great train of lords and servants behind him. He is very old, his face so nut-brown and wrinkled that he looks like a small monkey. Gold ornaments and bolts of cloth are spread on mats in front of his litter. Not a great treasure, but an offering, of sorts.

My lord dismounts his horse, and Old Ring of the Wasp is helped to his feet by his attendants. He makes a short speech. My lord turns to me for translation.

"He welcomes you to Tlaxcala and offers you these poor gifts in tribute," I say, indicating the gold and the cloth. "He says he would like to offer you much more, but Motecuhzoma keeps him besieged here in the mountains, and so his people are very poor."

Today Feathered Serpent, smiling and radiant, has returned. Perhaps it was just the fever that stole him away from me for those few hours. "Tell Ring of the Wasp that I value his friendship more than I value all the gold in the whole world. Tell him also that he shall suffer under the yoke of the Mexica no longer, for I have been sent by a great Lord to free men from the tyrannies of kings."

I relay his words in the elegant tongue, and Old Ring of the Wasp answers: "He thanks you for your kind words. He wishes very soon to confirm this alliance by offering you and your officers some of their women in marriage. But for now he wishes to touch your face."

"My face?"

"He is blind, my lord. He wishes to see you."

My lord shrugs aside a certain repugnance at having the old man's fingers on him. He gives his assent, standing rigid while the old chief runs his gnarled fingers across his lips and eyes and beard. The *cacique*'s face splits into a beatific smile.

"*Quetzalcóatl,*" he says.

"What was that?" Cortés asks me.

"He spoke the name of one of our gods, my lord."

"Which one?"

"Feathered Serpent."

I see a flicker of fear on his face and wonder what has been the cause of it. "Well, my lord?"

"Yes, Doña Marina?"

"What shall I tell him?"

"Tell him nothing. He knows enough for now."

※ ※

That night Aguilar waits for me in the darkness.

"I need to talk with you," he says, falling into step beside me. I can smell him, fervent and rank. A priest is like any other, whether he is a god or a person.

I walk faster, trying to outpace him.

"Cortés does not make me privy to his deliberations any longer," he says.

"That is not my concern."

"I fear for him. He is a good man, but there are some things he does not understand."

"What things?"

"He trusts too much. For instance, he trusts that you translate exactly what he says to these lords and chieftains."

"What is it you think I do? Recite poems about butterflies?"

"You must take care, Doña Marina. You are playing a dangerous game."

I wheel around. Look at him! That tattered book he clutches to his chest, the ridiculous fertility symbol he wears at his neck. How much can he possibly understand about the Mexica, and about my lord? "I will do nothing to harm him. Ever."

"Then be careful what you say. You will destroy him."

"He cannot be destroyed. Not by me, and certainly not by you."

"You are wrong. He is just a man, and any man may be destroyed. Especially by a woman."

44

Tenochtitlán

MOTECUHZOMA WAS HUDDLED on the *ypcalli*, a fur cloak wrapped around his shoulders. He stared into the distance, his eyes unfocused.

Woman Snake lay prostrate on the floor in front of him.

The emperor struggled with the latest news: the Spaniards had defeated the Tlaxcalans on the fields of flowers and had forced them to surrender, something their own armies had failed to do in a bundle of years. How could a few hundred men defeat an army of tens of thousands? How was such a thing possible?

It was not possible, of course. Unless these Castilians were led by a god. Unless this *Malintzin* was *Quetzalcóatl*, the Feathered Serpent.

A god had to be propitiated. But Feathered Serpent was not one of their own gods, was not the source of the Mexica's power, and therein lay the problem. When Motecuhzoma's ancestors had reached this valley many bundles of years before, they had come under the protection of *Huitzilopochtli*, Hummingbird on the Left, the God of War; and *Tezcatlipoca*, Smoking Mirror, Bringer of Darkness. Both were bitter enemies of Feathered Serpent. It was Smoking Mirror himself who had plotted Feathered Serpent's expulsion from his ancient city of Tollán.

Unlike Feathered Serpent, they both demanded human blood as sacrifice.

Motecuhzoma considered the terrible implications of these recent events. What if his people were caught in a direct confrontation between the gods? A clash of these titans would either destroy the sun or bring an end to the wind and rain. Whoever won, it would mean the utter destruction of the Mexica, and he, Motecuhzoma, was solely responsible for preventing this cataclysm.

He had always known it would come to this. When he had taken the throne, he had commissioned the building of a shrine to Feathered Serpent in the court of the Great Temple in the hope of allaying this moment. But even as it was being built, he had known, deep in his soul, that disaster was inevitable.

The weight of his responsibilities overwhelmed him, and he started to giggle with fear.

 **45**

Tlaxcala

A PRINCE'S RANSOM in gold and silver and precious stones lay on the floor at his feet. Cortés tried not to look impressed.

"They wish to congratulate you on your victory over the Tlaxcalans," Malinali said.

"Thank them for their kind words. But tell them it was all a misunderstanding. Insist that I have not come to make war on anyone, that I have come here in peace."

She relayed this sentiment to the leader of the Mexica, an Indian with more pride than was good for him. He regarded Cortés down his great parrot's beak of a nose. He had thick jades and opals on his fingers, even more jade through his ears and lower lip. On his head was a great fan of quetzal feathers, which gave him the look of a strutting peacock.

I should like to teach you some humility! Cortés thought.

"He says you should not trust the Tlaxcalans," Malinali was saying, "for they are a perfidious and unworthy people, and he is greatly concerned that we may all be murdered in our beds."

Cortés smiled. How sweetly we talk to one another! "Thank him again for his concern on my behalf. But tell him that if the Tlaxcalans should think of dealing treacherously with me in any way, I would know of it in advance, because I can read men's minds."

Another rapid exchange. Malinali seemed surprised at what the Mexica had to say and appeared to verify it.

"What is it?" Cortés asked her.

"He says that the Revered Speaker of the Mexica, the great Motecuhzoma, would like to offer you annual tribute to demonstrate his friendship. You yourself may set the amount in gold, silver, jade, and cloth, payable each year. But Motecuhzoma insists that it is too dangerous for you to travel farther toward his capital, since there are many treacherous republics like Tlaxcala between here and Tenochtitlán. He therefore asks that once you collect your tribute, you return to the Cloud Lands in the east."

He is afraid of me! Cortés thought. He is afraid of me, and it must be because he, too, thinks I am this mysterious Feathered Serpent! First he sends his ambassadors to plead with me; now he offers me rich bribes to leave his lands as if I were the commander of great armies and he the captain of a few hundred men! Above the Totonacs and the Tlaxcalans, there is one ally here that I have so far overlooked, an ally far stronger than any of them.

Motecuhzoma's own mind.

These *naturales* really believe that men can become gods! A blasphemous notion. But divinity is a role that will serve me well for the present, as long as I tread carefully.

"Mali, ask him to convey to his great lord my most devout friendship. Tell him I would dearly wish to accede to his lord's wishes, but I must convey my words to Motecuhzoma in person. I cannot turn back without disobeying my own king."

The Mexican ambassador seemed dismayed at this reply. There was another long exchange. What is she saying to him? Cortés wondered. How much does she embellish this myth that I am not mortal? A dangerous game. No matter what these Mexica believe, not a word of heresy or sedition must be seen to emanate from my own lips. I must remain blameless.

"What is his reply?" he asked Malinali.

"He says that if you must approach, then he asks that you travel by way of Cholula, for there you can be certain of a welcome befitting a great lord. He is even willing to act as your guide."

"Thank him most kindly for me. Tell him I will think on this, and he will have his reply in due course."

The Mexican ambassador and his retinue bowed and left. Cortés stared after them, lost in his own thoughts.

MALINALI

Painali, 1510

THE MEXICA ARE to dedicate a new temple in their capital, Tenochtitlán, and there is to be a day of celebration demanding many sacrifices to their insatiable gods. Below us, in the market square, are gathered together those whom they have chosen as suitable gifts for Huitzilopochtli, *the best of our young men and women.*

Hate, real hate like this, is a new experience for me. My legs are trembling with the force of it so that I have to lock my knees and clench my fists. It is only when you feel such powerlessness that you lust for power, real power, ache for it, pine for it. I think this is what happened to me at that moment; I think that was the beginning. I want to watch their beating hearts blacken and burn and see their faces suffer in agony and death.

I am ten years old.

Down there among the milling prisoners are two of my brothers and a sister; down there five friends I have played with since I walked my first steps; down there one hundred boys and girls little older than myself. I hear their mothers shriek in grief, see the blank faces of fathers powerless to protect them.

I understand, of course, that if rain is to fall and maize is to grow, the gods must have their due. Here in our own temples, our priests offer up a slave from time to time. But this wanton slaughter of Persons is savagery beyond comprehension.

My father stands beside me. His face betrays no emotion.

"Quetzalcóatl, Feathered Serpent, will return in the Year One Reed," he whispers to me. "He will return on a raft from the east, as he has done before, and he will put these vermin, this plague on our people, to the torch. The hours of our suffering are almost past."

Later this became my creed; but then I barely heard him. I watched my brothers and sisters file from the plaza, roped together, a hundred hearts for Huitzilopochtli, *the warm blood humming through their veins soon to be dashed in the face of Hummingbird on the Left.*

I rushed away to vomit. Pure bile. May Feathered Serpent hasten his return. Bring them down in pain and suffering and terrible, shrieking death.

I am ten years old.

 **46**

Tlaxcala, 1519

THE BEAT OF drums, the whistle of flutes, the tantalizing odors of warm food and spice. Heaped dishes of maize cakes, roasted rabbit, and beans with chili had been placed on the mats in front of them. Acrobats cartwheeled across the floor of the great hall, and dwarves tumbled and danced.

Ring of the Wasp the Elder whispered something to Malinali.

Cortés had eaten very little, his eyes darting everywhere. He saw this exchange and wanted to know what the old chief had said.

"He says you should not go to Cholula," Malinali told him.

"The Mexica have assured us of a hospitable welcome."

She conferred briefly with the Tlaxcalan chief in *Náhuatl*, then turned back to Cortés. "He says he would trust a rattlesnake not to bite him before he trusted a Mexican's hospitality. If you go to Tenochtitlán, you must go by way of Huexotzinco."

Suddenly everyone is concerned for our welfare, Cortés thought. How things have changed in the past few days. "I will have to think about this."

"Of course you will think about it," Malinali said, "but then you must go to Cholula."

Alvarado and Benítez overheard the conversation, and they both stared at her in stunned silence. "Damn your eyes," Alvarado muttered, "you cannot speak to the *caudillo* in such a manner."

Cortés smiled. "But she is right," he said. "I have to go to Cholula."

"But why, *caudillo?*" Benítez asked him.

Cortés did not answer him.

"Ring of the Wasp wants to cement the alliance we have made with him," Malinali was saying to Cortés. "He is offering women for all your captains." She hesitated. "He would like you to have his daughter."

Ring of the Wasp indicated the five women sitting demurely on the other side of the hall. They wore beautifully decorated *huipiles,* and fine pieces of jade had been worked into their hair.

"They are all from families of important Tlaxcala lords. The one Ring of the Wasp claims as his own daughter is the one on the right. Actually she is his grandchild. He is being vain."

Cortés studied the women critically. "What do you think, Mali?"

"My lord?"

"Should I accept his kind offer? Should I bed his granddaughter?"

He saw a flicker of uncertainty, of pain, on that inscrutable face. His little Indian princess was jealous and possessive after all. Like all women. Suddenly she seemed to have lost her tongue.

"Tell him it is a most gracious offer and I thank him for it. But I cannot accept his daughter, although she is indeed quite lovely, because I am already married, and my religion permits me just one wife."

He returned to his food, but he felt her stillness, her silence. Several moments went by before he heard her relay his words to Old Ring of the Wasp, and when she did, her voice was not the same.

"Please inform him, however, that my other captains would be greatly honored to accept these beautiful ladies into their households after they have been baptized into the Christian faith. Remind him also that he is an old man and must soon think about death. And because he is my friend, I would like him and his fellow chiefs to also take the sacrament and renounce their old gods, so their souls might find peace in heaven."

Malinali seemed shaken by this outburst. Cortés listened to her stammer through her translation, with many pauses. When she had finished, Old Ring of the Wasp's toothless grin was gone.

"He answers you this way," Malinali said. "He is very happy for his daughter to be sprinkled with water if that will make you content. But for himself, he could not renounce his gods even at the forfeit of his own life. Should he do so, there would be an insurrection among the people."

Why were these people so stubborn? Cortés wondered. He thought Fray Olmedo and Fray Díaz had explained this matter thoroughly to the *naturales,* had made them see their errors. "If he becomes a Christian, he will find eternal happiness in heaven. But if he dies without the sacrament, he will be thrown into the infernal pit and roast forever in agony. He must renounce these blood sacrifices—"

Fray Olmedo leaned forward and put a hand on Cortés's shoulder. "My lord, perhaps now is not the time. We should be more gentle in our approach."

Cortés stared at his friar. "Am I to be prevented from spreading the word of Christ by a priest? Which of us is the man of God?"

"I only wish that you moderate your remarks."

"You always seek to hold me back!"

"I believe it is better we bring God to these people slowly than rush at this and, by doing so, lose all the ground we have gained."

Alvarado leaned forward. "He is right, *caudillo.* To force our hand when we have only just found peace with these people would be suicide."

Men were such cowards. On a subject as important as salvation, what did it matter if men came to the truth willingly or at the point of a sword? But if his churchmen would not stand with him on this, there was nothing he could do. He turned back to Malinali. "Tell Ring of the Wasp we shall be happy to take his brides. We will talk more on matters of religion at some future time."

❉   ❉

Benítez, seated just a few feet from Cortés, had been holding his breath, sensing a disastrous confrontation. He let it out now in a long sigh. Even Fray Olmedo was trembling. They had won so much; he thought Cortés had been about to throw it all away.

Perhaps he still might.

✼ ✼

As a concession to his new friends, Old Ring of the Wasp allowed Cortés to convert one of the city's temples into a Christian shrine, and it was here that the five young Tlaxcalan princesses were baptized in a special ceremony before being given to Cortés's captains as *camaradas*.

Ring of the Wasp's granddaughter was christened Doña Luisa and given to Alvarado; Cortés had softened his rejection of her by telling the old *cacique* that the red-haired giant was his brother. Cortés chose Sandoval, Cristobal Olid, and Alonso de Ávila to receive the other women; the most beautiful of them all, another granddaughter of Ring of the Wasp, was given to León and rechristened Doña Elvira.

A good tactical choice, Benítez thought, giving her to León—a way to reward a onetime enemy and make him a firm ally. Cortés never stopped thinking politics, even in bed.

MALINALI

I LIE BESIDE him on the sleeping mat, his honey still sticky in the cave. Through the window I see Sister Moon, beheaded by her brother *Huitzilopochtli*, slipping defeated down the night sky. Cortés is silent, staring at his brother stars, lost to me for now.

"You have never spoken of a wife."

He stirs but does not answer.

"Is she very beautiful?"

"She is not like you. I do not love her."

"But she is your wife. Why is she not here with you?"

"Come here? She would not get out of bed in the night unless she had a maid to hold her hand."

I wrap my thigh over his, put my cheek against the strange, coarse curls of his chest. "What is her name?"

"I do not want to talk about her."

"Do you have children with her?"

"No. There are no children."

No sons yet for Mexico, then. "Will she come here and join you when we reach Tenochtitlán?"

"Why all these questions? I told you, I do not love her."

"But it would have been better if you had told me."

"Why? Perhaps one day I will have a better wife."

"Me?"

"Who else?"

I know there can be no one else, but I want him to say the words—that the new Tollán will come through me, his spirit, my bone. I wait for one glimpse of his heart, I hold my breath, I can hear his heartbeat and mine. But he is silent, and after a while I realize he has fallen asleep.

I lie awake long into the night, thinking. My lord may be divine, yet gods are unpredictable by their nature. Even my gentle Feathered Serpent may demand sacrifice of me, and I must decide if I am willing to offer up my heart for him.

47

SOME GASPED ALOUD when they saw the city of Cholula spread before them in the Anáhuac Valley: hundreds of white towers, pyramids of the gods, soaring above a sprawl of flat-roofed stone houses that seemed to go on forever. If this is a town only for pilgrims, Benítez thought, what must the capital, Tenochtitlán, be like? Just when he had seen something he thought could not be surpassed, a new wonder proved him wrong.

They camped that night in the dry bed of the Atoyac River in the dark shadow of Sleeping Woman. A dusting of snow glittered in the moonlight below the peak, like a necklace of pure white on the throat of a princess.

MALINALI

THE CHOLULANS COME out to meet us, their senators and priests dressed after local custom in fringed and sleeveless cotton cassocks. Their arrival is announced with the blowing of conches and flutes, and slaves run before them with fans and censers of copal incense.

Feathered Serpent waits for them, the morning sun bright on his golden armor. I stand at his right shoulder, his Thunder Lords behind me.

The leader of the Cholulans steps forward, touches the ground and his lips in formal salutation, and makes his greeting.

"He says his name is Angry Coyote," I tell my lord in a loud voice.

I hear Alvarado whisper to Jaramillo and Sandoval, "He looks more like a slightly aggrieved duck," and there is laughter.

My lord silences them with a stare. "Thank him for his greeting," he says to me. "Tell him we have come in the name of his most catholic majesty Charles V to bring news of the true religion and put an end to the Devil's works in this country."

I turn to Angry Coyote and tell him, in words he will understand: "Feathered Serpent has returned to rest in his city. He has been sent by *Olintecle*, Father of All the Gods, to reclaim his throne and bring an end to human sacrifice."

Angry Coyote's face betrays nothing. His reply, which appears to me to be carefully rehearsed, is just as I expected. These people are such hypocrites! They feign devotion to their god, and yet, when he finally returns to them, as he promised, they do not even recognize him! What kind of religion is that?

"What does he say?" Cortés asks me.

"He says you are most welcome in their city. They are happy to receive you. Quarters have been prepared, and food will be provided." I hesitate, wondering how to tell him the rest of it. "He says they will be most interested to hear all you have to say. But he also insists that they must not upset their other gods, who already provide them with everything they need."

Laughs at Women, in his rough maguey cloak, approaches one of the Cholulan senators and is fingering his mantle acquisitively. It is made of a beautiful dyed cotton of a quality his own people cannot obtain because of Tenochtitlán's embargo. The nobleman who is the object of his attentions looks uncomfortable and tries to shuffle away. Laughs at Women holds on, leering at him.

Angry Coyote turns back to me. "If this Lord Malinche has come in friendship, why has he brought such a large army of our enemies with him?"

"Angry Coyote is frightened of the Tlaxcalans," I tell my lord. "They and the Cholulans are traditional enemies."

"Tell him they are accompanying me on my journey to Tenochtitlán. They intend no harm to him or his people."

I pass this on, but Angry Coyote is not mollified. He demands that when the Spaniards enter Cholula, they leave the Tlaxcalans outside the city.

"Never," Alvarado says when he hears this.

"It's a trick," Sandoval says.

I wait, wondering what my lord will decide.

Cortés shrugs. "If I were Angry Coyote and strangers appeared with my sworn enemies—the French, for example—I should also ask that they remain outside my city."

"*Caudillo,*" Alvarado hisses, "we cannot agree to this!"

"I am aware of the risk." He looks at me. "Tell him we accede to his request."

Suicide, I think. Once again, he behaves exactly like a god, with complete arrogance.

"Feathered Serpent agrees to your request," I tell Angry Coyote, "but he warns you not to test his patience. He is able to read men's minds and will know everything you plan."

Angry Coyote gives me a look of sweet contempt. "I do not see Feathered Serpent here."

"Revered Speaker has seen him," I answer. "He has sent him a mountain of gold and jewels in tribute."

My lord interrupts our exchange and demands to know what is being said.

"It is nothing. He was just being insolent."

I see Alvarado and Sandoval exchange a glance. It is clear they do not like my conducting private conversations with the *naturales*. But my lord does not seem concerned. "Tell him we shall look forward to being received in his city," he says.

After Angry Coyote and his retinue have left, my lord takes me aside. "Should I trust them?" he whispers.

"Only if you wish your army to be destroyed, my lord."

"As I thought."

He walks away, joins the other Thunder Gods. Later I see a wild rabbit dash across the path from the bushes. It is an omen. Something bad is about to happen.

48

HUGE CROWDS GREETED the Spaniards as they marched into the city. Young women threw bouquets of flowers; acrobats ran in front of their column turning somersaults; priests ran alongside blowing conches and flutes and beating drums. But there was a sense of unease among Cortés's men.

The major part of their army, their fierce Tlaxcalan allies, was still outside the city, camped at the riverbed.

Benítez saw Norte struggling to keep pace on foot, his arm still in the sling. Rain Flower hurried along beside him. She looked up and shouted something at Benítez.

"What did she say?" he called to Norte.

"She said enjoy your fame while it lasts," Norte answered. "They are going to kill us all tomorrow!"

✳ ✳

An eerie silence as they crossed the temple court, the echo of their boots on the stones and the metallic chink of their steel swords the only sounds to be heard. The crowd parted for them.

Cortés led the way up the stepped walls of the pyramid. It was a long climb and a steep one, and they were all wearing heavy armor. When they reached the summit, they were all panting for breath, and their faces were streaked with sweat. The priests, dressed in cloaks of white and red, huddled together, watching them.

Cortés marched past them into the shrine. Benítez followed.

It took some moments for his eyes to grow accustomed to the light. Benítez realized he was staring at a giant coiled serpent carved from stone. It was dressed in a mantle of white, emblazoned with red crosses, similar to the garb they had seen on the priests outside. The snake's body was studded with jade stones, but its head was not that of a snake: it was instead that of a man with long hair and a beard.

"So this is Feathered Serpent," Cortés said.

Benítez felt his flesh crawl. He could make out the visceral gleam of fresh, dark blood on the sacrificial stone. The smell of death was everywhere.

The *caudillo*'s eyes shone strangely in the gloom. He looked as if he had drunk too much wine. He turned to Alvarado. "Some of these people think I am Feathered Serpent." He vaulted onto the shrine beside the bearded idol so they could make a comparison. "Do you think he looks like me?"

Alvarado spared a glance at Fray Olmedo. This might be construed by some as blasphemous. "You should not talk this way, *caudillo*," he said.

"It is the Devil," Fray Olmedo said.

"The Devil? Oh, I rather think it looks like Aguilar," Sandoval said, and laughed. "Or maybe Pedro," he added, looking at Alvarado.

"You should not say such things," Alvarado muttered.

Benítez put a hand to his sword. He did not like the way the priests had crowded around the entrance, blocking their retreat. "Let us leave now," he said. He wanted to be away from there before

Cortés incited them further. He had become dangerous and unpredictable of late, certainly not the same man who had left Santiago de Cuba seven months before.

Cortés turned to Fray Olmedo. "Father, you shall be my witness. Today I vow to throw down every idol in this kingdom and scrape every drop of blood from these walls! For there is no god but God, and I am his servant. Amen."

"Amen," Fray Olmedo echoed.

Cortés leaped down from the statue and strode toward the entrance. The priests backed away. Benítez and the others hurried after him, eager to be away from that accursed place.

MALINALI

I WANDER THE marketplace, Flores and a handful of my lord's soldiers following behind, as escort. I am dazzled by this place; everything is for sale here: stone and lime and wooden beams for building, cooking pots, obsidian mirrors, kohl for darkening the eyes, herbs for curing sick children, feathers, salt, rubber, bitumen. Merchants haggle over cacao and maize; porters with tumplines across their foreheads carry wicker panniers of mantles or embroidered skirts or fiber sandals; a prostitute raises her skirts to prospective customers, displaying her tattooed legs. Old women squat on the ground beside the corncobs and strings of peppers laid out for sale on reed mats. I can smell the savory aroma of *tamales* and gourd seeds toasting over braziers.

The crowd ahead of us parts for a woman in a beautifully embroidered cloak, her wrists and throat and fingers adorned with onyx jewelry. She is surrounded by a coterie of slaves. I recognize her at once from the arrival celebrations: it is Bird in the Reeds, the mother of Angry Coyote.

Bird in the Reeds waits while one of her slave girls barters for a hundred sheets of bark paper. The price is finally set at 120 cacao beans.

I tell my escort to wait and approach her courteously, lowering my eyes, showing her proper respect. She glares back at me imperiously.

"I need to speak with you, Mother."

"What would we have to discuss?"

"I need your help."

This declaration brings a change to the woman's demeanor. Her expression softens. She spares a glance over my shoulder in the direction of my lord's soldiers.

"It is quite safe, Mother. None of those dogs has the elegant speech. They cannot understand a single word we say."

"What is the matter, child?"

"I have to get away from these devils."

Bird in the Reeds seems alarmed but not surprised, as if she had anticipated this predicament. "You are a slave?"

"I have royal Mexican blood in my veins, and I was the daughter of a great and noble lord until some specks of dirt kidnapped me from my home in Painali. Now I am enslaved to these bearded monsters. Will you help me?"

Another furtive glance at the soldiers. "Not here. Tonight. At my house." She walks on, her entourage trailing behind her.

 **49**

"For the second day running, there has been no food brought to us," Alvarado said. "The men are hungry. What are they to eat? The promises of the Cholulans?"

Benítez leaned both hands on the table. "Norte has spoken with the Totonacs. They say they have found pitfalls in the roads leading out of the city. They are lined with sharpened stakes, which will impale any who fall in them. They also say there are stones stockpiled on the flat roofs of the houses, ready to be hurled down on any trying to escape through the streets below. We have been lured into a trap."

Just three days after their carnival entrance into Cholula, and the feasting on turkeys and maize was already a distant memory. Now, instead of bouquets of welcome, they received only sneers and murderous looks.

Their discussion was interrupted by the blast from a conch shell, from the temple close to the palace where they were quartered. Another sacrifice, another heart offered up to *Huitzilopochtli*.

The sound of it sent a chill through the room. None of them spoke for a few moments.

"They have evacuated all the women and children," Jaramillo said. "I saw hundreds of them leaving this afternoon, heading toward the foothills."

"We should go back to Vera Cruz," de Grado said.

Ordaz folded his arms and grunted to show his contempt for this remark.

"You were one of those who called loudest for our return a few months ago," de Grado reminded him.

"Since then I have seen the gold piling up in the wagons, and our *caudillo* has brought us victories and fame I did not believe possible. Besides, we have been through this many times before. We cannot go back."

"Then we should have brought the Tlaxcalans into the city with us," Alvarado said.

Cortés had been oddly silent through this debate. Now he stirred. "They may not love us, as the Tlaxcalans do, but I am yet to be convinced that they intend to betray us." He turned to Malinali. "Well, Doña Marina, what do you think?"

✳   ✳

The moon fell below the hills. A shadow down in the street, hurrying inside a darkened doorway. A servant answered the timid knock and escorted the visitor across a wide patio and into a torch-lit audience chamber.

The house was silent; the city slept.

"Did the Spanish devils follow you here?" Bird in the Reeds whispered.

"I was very careful, Mother. I waited until the guards were asleep."

Bird in the Reeds made space for her visitor beside her on the reed mat. Another servant brought foaming cups of *chocolatl*. Malinali's hands shook as she took the hot spiced drink in its earthenware cup.

The girl is terrified, Bird in the Reeds decided. Those barbarians! They dare to come here with those murderous Tlaxcalans, their leader masquerading as Feathered Serpent. Death is too good for them.

She studied her visitor closely. She was thin, but that was not unexpected after her tribulations. Her features were not displeasing to the eye. There was the danger that she might carry these barbarians' seed in her. That might be a problem.

"Tell me about yourself," Bird in the Reeds said.

Malinali kept her eyes respectfully on the floor. "I was born in Painali, a day's march from Coatzacoalcos. My mother was Mexica, the daughter of a great nobleman, a descendant of Lord Face in the Water, Motecuhzoma's grandfather. My father was a *chilan*, a priest and a soothsayer of much reputation."

Bird in the Reeds felt her heart leap. She had been right to trust her instincts. If this Malinali had royal blood in her veins—and that could be verified—she would be a great asset as a wife. The only hope for advancement in the royal court these days was to be a proven blood relative, however distant, of the current emperor.

"I was kidnapped from my village and forced to live with the Maya at Potonchán. I was sold to these Spaniards, as they call themselves, and they forced me to stay with them against my will. When they discovered I had the elegant speech and knew also the animal grunts of the Mayans, they kept me as their interpreter. They forced me to learn their barbarian language also, so I could communicate with them directly."

"What of this *Malintzin*, who professes to be Feathered Serpent?"

"I confess I believed the legend was true when I first saw him. He has some physical resemblance, and his men have magical powers, like their firesticks and the iron serpents that breathe fire and smoke. But I have since learned that they are mortal, as we are. They want only to steal our gold and chocolate and jade."

"I knew it!" the old woman said. "I knew he was not a god!" She took Malinali's hand. "You must have suffered greatly."

She nodded. "If I try and run away, I am afraid they will kill me. I don't know what to do."

"Perhaps I can help you. You are a pleasing-looking girl, and you have been well educated. With your Mexican blood, you could attract a good husband. You deserve a kinder fate."

"First I have to escape these Spaniards."

"I could hide you here."

"They would not rest until I was found. It will only make trouble for you."

Bird in the Reeds wondered if now was the right time to speak. But she could not contain herself. "They will not be able to make trouble for me, little Malinali, because they will all be dead."

"Dead?"

"I should not be telling you—"

"What can you not tell me? What is going to happen?"

Bird in the Reeds hesitated. She had been sworn to secrecy, but what could she do? Why should a fine daughter of the Mexica die with the rest of these devils? It was her duty to save her. And if they could verify her bloodline, one of her sons might soon find himself among the elite of Tenochtitlán.

She lowered her voice, as if there were eavesdroppers in every corner of the empty room. "My husband and other senators have been communicating secretly with Motecuhzoma. Our Revered Speaker wants the strangers killed. They are to be starved out of their quarters and slaughtered as they try and leave the city."

Malinali gaped at her.

"Why should you die with them? I have a son, and he is of an age to marry now. Provided you do not have a monster in your belly from these Spaniards, you can knot your cloak to his and learn to live like a Person again."

"I wish that I could, but it is hopeless. You cannot beat them. They defeated the Tlaxcalans even though they were greatly outnumbered. They are devils."

"They may be devils on the field of flowers, but when they are marching in single file through our city streets and are trapped there, they will not be such formidable enemies."

Malinali leaned forward eagerly, and her hands clutched at the old woman's. "I shall dream of that moment, Mother. But how can I get away? What should I do?"

"For now you must do nothing. We shall wait until the last moment, for we do not wish to raise their suspicions. As soon as they make preparations to leave, you must hurry to me here, and I will hide you until it is all over."

Bird in the Reeds laid a hand on her arm.

"Did they hurt you? Did they make you do many terrible things?"

"I really thought they were gods," she said. "I have been such a fool." She began to weep.

Bird in the Reeds held the girl in her arms. Poor, dear child.

✻   ✻

The next day Cortés sent a message to the two *caciques* of Cholula, the Lord of the Here and Now and the Lord of Below the Earth, to advise them that he was leaving the city the next morning. He asked for food for the journey as well as porters to carry these provisions and one thousand warriors as protection. He also requested that they and all the chief lords of the city attend him in the court of the temple of Feathered Serpent for a ceremonial farewell.

MALINALI

ALMOST TWO THOUSAND Cholulan warriors and porters shuffle into the broad court, led by their most senior chiefs and senators. When they are all inside, the Spanish soldiers close and bar the gates behind them.

These Cholulans look around at the black maws of the iron serpents, at the Thunder Gods with their firesticks on the steps of the pyramid and the ramparts of the walls. The silence is terrible.

My lord rides out on his great warhorse, and I follow behind him on foot. He stops a few paces from the Lord of the Here and Now and the Lord of Below the Earth, and they wilt in his presence. He addresses himself first to me.

"Greet these gracious lords of Cholula," he says, and I can hear the anger in his voice. "Tell them they are most kind to bid me farewell on this fine morning. It is one of the few kindnesses I have received from them. I came here as their friend, and I did not expect to receive such scant hospitality."

I pass these sentiments to the Lord of the Here and Now, who is openly dismayed to hear them. "The Lord Malinche is not happy with the lodgings we provided for him and his men?" he asks me.

I repeat what he has said to my lord, and our eyes meet. It is as if he is looking to me for further verification. But what more can I tell him? Everything I know I whispered to him last night in our bed.

"Ask him why he has tried to starve us out of his city."

When he hears this question, the Lord of the Here and Now looks panicked. "The orders came from Motecuhzoma himself. What were we to do?"

Oh, he is an extraordinarily good liar, but I do not think it will do him any good now. "He says the orders came from the emperor."

The great beast my lord sits astride snorts and stamps its foot, as if it understands what is said and is angered by it. The brass trappings jangle in the silence. My lord stares down from the saddle, his face a stony mask. "Tell him you know all about his lies."

I face the assembly of Cholulan lords, see Angry Coyote watching from behind the Lord of Below the Earth. "I warned you before we arrived at this city that my lord could read your minds as well as he can hear your words. That is how he knows that you have taken Motecuhzoma's gold in return for setting a trap for us as we leave this city. He knows about the stones piled on the rooftops and the pitfalls in the streets—"

Angry Coyote steps forward. "My mother's idle gossip!" he shouts. "She heard it in the marketplace! There is no truth to it!"

The Lord of the Here and Now and the Lord of Below the Earth look around, startled, then turn back to me, their faces betraying shock and bewilderment. "We were afraid," the Lord of Below the Earth shouts. "Our lifelong enemies were camped outside our gates, and you have Totonacs with you right inside our city. Could you blame us for making preparations to defend ourselves?"

I wonder if that is the real reason so many of their women and children had been sent out of the city. It might be fear, not treachery, after all.

What if am I wrong about this? What if all the Cholulans' plans were just the mutterings of an old woman?

"Motecuhzoma asked us to attack you," the Lord of Below the Earth is saying, "but we refused. How could we harm Feathered Serpent in his own city?"

"What are they saying?" Cortés asks me. I hear the tension and uncertainty in his voice.

"They deny everything."

My lord is breathing fast, struggling with the decision.

"It is Motecuhzoma who is at fault!" the Lord of the Here and Now shrieks at me. "Not us!"

If he had only stayed still.

But he sees the look on my lord's face, understands how close he is to death, and loses faith in the truth, if that was what it is. He turns and makes to run.

Immediately Feathered Serpent draws his sword and brings it down in a sweeping arc, the prearranged signal for what follows now.

❈ ❈

Some of the Cholulans escape the bloody slaughter of the iron serpents and firesticks and arrows and flee into the plaza, where they find the lancers waiting for them on their warhorses. They set about dying while the rest of the city is waking from sleep. When it is done, the soldiers make their bloody sweep through the town. They find no army waiting for them on the rooftops, no ambush lying in wait.

The people of Cholula flee the city gates, onto the waiting obsidian spears of the Tlaxcalans, who are eager to settle old scores.

Meanwhile, in the court of the temple of *Quetzalcóatl,* I watch the Thunder Lords complete the work they have begun. My lord's soldiers seek out those still moaning and twitching and fillet them with the dexterity of a temple priest.

I look around for Feathered Serpent, but he is gone.

 # 50

SMOKE ROSE FROM the blistered beams of a roof; a swarm of flies buzzed around the blackened leg of a corpse. A coyote looked up at Benítez's approach, then returned to its feast. A bloody handprint smudged an adobe wall.

He saw Norte staggering toward him. There were clots of blood on his sword, and he was grinning.

"For the glory of God, Benítez!"

Benítez said nothing. He had been a soldier for just a few months, and he had thought the worst he would ever see was the carnage on the plains of Tlaxcala. He had never imagined anything like this. His heel skidded in a pool of gore, and he almost fell.

What if we imagined it all? he wondered. All we had as evidence was the sum of our own fears, enhanced by the words of an old woman and the slander of the Totonacs. We bowed to the urgings of the Tlaxcalans, who only wanted an excuse to grab the women and the plunder and take their revenge on the hated Cholulans.

"Nothing like the slaughter of innocent women and children for the glory of God, Benítez?"

Benítez grabbed Norte's tunic and forced him against a wall. "They planned this same slaughter for us!"

"I beg your leave. I quite forgot the reasons for our killing here. I have lived with barbarians for eight years and forgot that it is the sacred duty of a Christian gentleman to butcher the ignorant and the unprepared."

"There is blood on your sword also."

"It belongs to one of our allies. A Tlaxcalan. He was trying to rape a child. You always said I could not be trusted. Would you have me hanged for it?"

Benítez released him.

"The Cholulans were right, weren't they?" Norte hissed at him. "They said they were afraid of the Tlaxcalans. They had reason to be. Our new friends are like wild beasts."

Benítez pushed him away, stumbled on through the rank and loathsome streets. Coyotes screamed and vultures circled in the sky.

"It was Malinali!" Norte screamed after him. "Malinali persuaded him to do it!"

MALINALI

IT IS LATE in the Fifth Watch of the Night, and the glow of the burial fires can be seen against the black sky. My lord is on his knees before a portrait of the Mother and Babe. He hears me enter and opens his eyes, carefully unfolding his hands from prayer as if he were putting aside a pair of delicate silk gloves. "Gods are sometimes beneficent," he murmurs, "but there are other times when they have no choice but to punish. Is that not the way?"

"They are even killing the children," I tell him. It is impossible to describe to him the turmoil I feel inside. It is as if I have woken from a vivid dream to find myself in a world inhabited by shadows: everything is gray, nothing has shape, and nothing is what it once seemed.

My lord gets to his feet. There is a strange light in his eyes. He grabs me by the arm, hurting me. "I did not want this. They brought this on themselves."

"I don't know what to think."

"But it was you who told me of this plot! I trusted you! You said you were sure!"

"I thought I was sure." I try to pull free, but he is too strong. "It had to be done! Now there will be no further rebellions against us. Already other *caciques* have sent us messages asking for peace."

"But so much death."

"It had to be done," he says, as if hoping to persuade himself. He strokes my hair, and suddenly his arms are around me. I do not resist him. He lifts me easily and lays me on the scrap of bed. "It had to be done," he says, a third time.

He is not gentle. He mounts me, and I cling tightly to him, hoping that the act of loving him will heal the pain, that his kisses and embraces and the murmur of his endearments will heal me.

Afterward, as I lie on my back, his body sprawled across me, I strain my ears to the silence. It is no good. I can still hear the screams.

I thought only to expose the Cholulans and their complicity, not to turn their city into a vast butcher's yard. My lord rolls away from me, but still I feel the crushing weight on my chest. Perhaps it is the burden of the dead.

51

Tenochtitlán

FLAMINGOS PICKED THEIR way fussily through the shallows, rose-pink colors reflected in the still ponds; parrots of carmine and royal blue flashed through the greenery to hang squabbling in the vines. A tiny blue hummingbird hovered at the mouth of a trumpet flower; an eagle picked over a raw carcass brought fresh from the temple earlier that day.

Woman Snake hurried through the royal aviary and up the steps to a gallery that commanded a panoramic view over the entire zoo. He was surprised to find Motecuhzoma in a light mood. After the news from Cholula, he anticipated another of his tearful rages. Instead, he seemed relaxed, even confident.

"Lord, my lord, my great lord," he murmured, approaching on hands and knees. "You required my presence."

"I want you to send a message for me to Cholula."

"As you command."

"Send our envoys with presents for Lord Malinche, and tell them to congratulate him on punishing these Cholulans. He is to be assured that I had no part in any plot made against him. Ask him also to convey himself with all speed to Tenochtitlán, for I long to meet with him."

Woman Snake wondered at this change of heart. "But, great lord, until now we have done our utmost to discourage him."

"We have nothing more to fear from this Malinche. Any anger he may have harbored against us has been spent on Cholula. Let him hasten here if that is what he wishes."

"As you command."

Woman Snake departed on hands and knees.

Motecuhzoma smiled. News of the massacre had allayed his fears. Although Feathered Serpent was the Lord of Enlightenment, like any beneficent god he also had a dark side. This slaughter at Cholula was retribution for all the human sacrifices that had been made there in his name. It was proof of his divinity.

Now Motecuhzoma was certain he was dealing with a god and not a man, he felt strangely calm. He spent the rest of the day alone, listening to the birds, and did not return to the palace until long after nightfall.

MALINALI

I LIE AWAKE for a long time, my lord's warm breath on my breast. I feel bruised in all my secret places. But why should I expect him to be gentle? Men are rarely gentle. Besides, I am sucking the honey not from a man but from a god.

He is awake but lies quietly. Soon he will rise to put on his armor and go out to patrol the sentry posts, as he has done every night since the massacre. Since Cholula he has become quarrelsome, anxious. I wonder if he is afflicted by the same terrible dreams as I.

I cannot forget my betrayal of Bird in the Reeds. Was it as Angry Coyote had said, just the rambling and gossip of an old woman? Was it mindless prattle that had consigned all those thousands to their deaths?

And what of my lord? He claims he is not a god, and yet he surely behaves like one, bewildering and unpredictable by turns. One moment he is gentle, kneeling before his Mother and Babe picture, taking terrible risks to throw down the sacrificial stones in Cempoala; yet he will, at a whim, sentence men to have their faces and limbs destroyed, order a whole town slaughtered and burned.

So where shall I now seek out my Lord of Gentle Wisdom? For the first time I realize that though he must surely be divine, the god in him may not be Feathered Serpent.

But what can I do? There is no turning back, for I have come too far. Without his protection, I am a heart roasting in a brazier; without the means to realize my father's promise, I have nothing to live for.

I feel as if I have woken in the forest at night: I cannot trust the darkness, and I do not know which way to run. I can only wait, and wonder from which direction the monsters will come.

 ## 52

CORTÉS STARED AT the new bounty Motecuhzoma had seen fit to send him: the gold and jewelery at his feet must be worth two thousand crowns, and that did not include the pile of richly embroidered cloaks beside it, tall as a man.

It seems the more Indians I slaughter, the more generous my lord Motecuhzoma becomes.

He caught Malinali's eye and wondered what she was thinking. Hard to read her these last few weeks. Since Cholula she had become withdrawn and sullen. And yet it was her word that had led him to give the order for the town's destruction. What was he to make of her? Motecuhzoma's latest envoys watched in silence as he considered.

"Give them my usual greetings," he said to her, "and ask them what message they have from their king."

She conferred with them and then turned back to Cortés. "Their lord Motecuhzoma sends you his greetings and regrets that the Cholulans have annoyed you. The Revered Speaker has always found them a tiresome people and thinks you have probably been too gentle in dealing with them. He now wonders why you still endure the miserable company of the Tlaxcalans and asks instead that you make haste to his capital, where he will do his best to entertain you. These men offer their services as guides and will ensure that provisions for the journey are provided along the way."

"Well, this is a different song."

"It may be a trick."

"I do not doubt it. Everything in this land appears to be no more than an illusion."

He massaged his temples with his fingers. There was a nagging pain behind his eyes. He had not slept well since the slaughter. Fray Olmedo had assured him he had acted in the only manner open to him, in the best interests of the Church and the State, and that much good had come of his actions, for those Cholulans who had survived had immediately converted to Christianity. Cortés had made his confession and been granted absolution.

Yet sleep had been difficult these past weeks.

"Thank them for their presents and tell them I look forward to the great pleasure of gazing on their emperor's visage soon," he said.

After the envoys had gone, he was left alone with Malinali. Her black eyes were liquid, impenetrable.

She had become much more than his mistress. Without her he could not have won over the Totonacs or the Tlaxcalans; without her he would have fallen victim to the perfidy of the Cholulans. He needed her now as he had needed no woman in his life. If she should fail him, he would be abandoned to the darkness of this Motecuhzoma, and no power on earth could save him.

At this moment she held sway over his life's destiny, and it terrified him.

He ran his fingers through her hair. "Well, *cara,* on to Tenochtitlán."

"Yes, my lord," she answered, "Tenochtitlán." She returned his embrace, but it seemed to him that lately there was neither warmth nor affection in it.

✳ ✳

The wax candles burned in ruby cups, were reflected in the breast-plate of Benítez's armor hanging on the wall. Rain Flower sat on a reed mat, Benítez beside her, picking from a platter of roasted rabbit and maize cakes. Norte, his arm still strapped, sat apart from them by the curtained door, his expression sullen.

Rain beat on the roof, and the storm wind brought with it the moldering breath of the jungle, of things dead and rotting.

Rain Flower had painted flowers on her feet, and there was cinnabar on her lips and eyelids. Her eyes flashed in the candlelight, predatory, primitive. Norte wondered if this display was for the benefit of Benítez or for him, her true lover.

"I want to make love with you," Norte said to her, in Chontal Maya.

She did not answer.

Benítez looked up sharply. "You have something to say?"

"I merely asked her what she was thinking, my lord."

Benítez's inaction had made Norte reckless. It would have been easier if he hated him; but it was impossible to properly hate a man who has saved you from the gallows and faced death with you on the battlefield.

Norte looked up at the ceiling, where men were being devoured by a great snake, their endless torment forever etched into the dark volcanic stone. Something strangely beautiful in it. The other Castilians had expressed their revulsion at this savage art. Norte himself wondered how a Mexica gentleman would react if he walked into a Christian home, where the centerpiece of every wall was a naked man being tortured with wood and nails.

"Will you ask my lord when we are to leave this place?" Rain Flower said.

Norte turned to Benítez. "She wants to know when we are leaving Cholula."

Benítez finished eating, licking the juice from his fingers. "When Cortés is ready. I don't know when that will be."

"Tell him I hate this place," Rain Flower said. "It has the stink of death."

Benítez nodded when he heard this. "I feel the same way. But it is not my decision."

What is he really thinking? Norte wondered. It is a subtle game he is playing here. Too easy to simply have me put to death; better to torment me this way, have me watch him with her every day. Or perhaps I do him a disservice; it may not be in his nature to condemn me to death out of spite. It would offend this damnable man's sense of justice.

"My body aches to hide in your cave," Norte whispered to Rain Flower.

She pretended not to hear him. Instead, she asked him if they would one day go back to the coast.

"She asks where we go from here," he said to Benítez.

"I believe my lord Cortés intends us to march on Motecuhzoma's capital."

Norte shook his head. "Then he is a madman. Can none of you captains convince him to turn back?"

"One does not tell the wind which way to blow."

"Do you know anything at all about the Mexica, Benítez?"

"Do you?"

"Only what I have learned from Rain Flower."

"Then tell me. I would like to hear it."

"A century past these people were living in the desert eating vermin. By nature they are savages. Everyone knows it, even the Mexica themselves."

"How did they come to be so powerful so quickly?"

"Because they have always been great warriors. It is the one thing they have to recommend them, apparently. They now have a formidable army."

"Of how many men? Twenty thousand? Fifty thousand?"

Norte consulted with Rain Flower. Even he seemed surprised at her answer. "She believes a hundred thousand, at least. So . . . do you still want to follow Cortés to Tenochtitlán?"

Benítez looked shaken. He can already imagine his insides roasting on a brazier before Hummingbird's altar, Norte thought.

"She obviously has no understanding of numbers," Benítez said.

"On the contrary, she says she counts only the Mexica. She does not count the other armies of the Triple Alliance, the Texcocans and the Tacubans."

Norte doubted very much if this summation of their enemy would deter Cortés. He supposed he had already learned this much from Malinali himself and was keeping it from the rest of his officers.

He turned his attention to the sleeping mat, where tonight Benítez would lie with Rain Flower. If only it were me, he thought. Sometimes he imagined himself back on Cozumel Island, but instead of the squat and homely girl they had given him, his wife was Rain Flower...

Since Tlaxcala there had been few opportunities to be with her. But now he had found a place just outside the city where they could slip away, unseen, with a little complicity on her part. But lately she would not catch his eye, and whenever he tried to speak with her, she moved away.

She was afraid of what Benítez would do if he discovered them, he supposed.

"I am tired," he said. "May I have leave to go bed?"

Benítez nodded, and Norte got to his feet.

"There is one more service you can perform for me," Benítez said, almost as an afterthought. "I want you to tell Rain Flower here... tell her that if we survive this expedition, and we are able to return to Cuba... tell her I would like her to come with me. I will make her my wife in a Catholic church and be proud to do it."

Norte stared at him. By the Devil's spotted and hairy great ass! You would be proud, would you? How generous of you! And what of Rain Flower? How might she find such an arrangement? What do you understand of these *naturales*, as you call them? You just want to make them more like you.

Rain Flower waited for him to speak.

"He says that he likes you very much and he is happy to have you in his bed. But you must understand he already has a wife in Cuba. After Tenochtitlán he wishes you well and hopes you will go back to your people and not bother him anymore."

He pushed the curtain aside and went out, into the night.

❋   ❋

"I have just received ambassadors from Motecuhzoma," Cortés announced. "They have invited us to visit him at Tenochtitlán."

There was a sullen and shuffling silence. Cortés looked at his second in command. "Alvarado?"

His captain thrust out his jaw. "We have been talking among

ourselves," he said, and looked at Benítez for support. "It seems these Mexica are far stronger even than we anticipated. It is said they can raise an army of one hundred thousand men—"

"We are not going to Tenochtitlán to fight a war."

"After the slaughter here, surely they will not open their arms to us?"

"That is exactly what they will do. Because they are afraid of us."

"Even the Tlaxcalans advise against it," Benítez said.

"The Tlaxcalans are not our war council."

"We think we should go back to Vera Cruz," de Grado said.

Cortés could not believe his ears. If he could teach a parrot to talk and put a helmet on its head, it would be as much use as de Grado. "Oh, very well, then," he said, and he sat down.

"Caudillo?" Sandoval said.

"I said, very well. Go back to Vera Cruz. Sit there in the swamp and breathe in the bad airs of the coast and catch fevers and die, if that is what you want. And then, no doubt, some of you will harp again about going back to Cuba—where, no doubt, you will be forced to heap all the treasures we have so sorely won into the hands of the governor."

Silence. No one could look Cortés in the face.

"We have come so far, and at every turn you want to go back. Have you forgotten we have God's work to do?"

"Cortés is right," Sandoval said. "It is too late to turn back."

"What of our allies?" Alvarado asked.

"The Totonacs have expressed a wish to return to Cempoala. They lost many of their men in the war against the Tlaxcalans, and now they are weighed down with the booty they have taken in Cholula. As I cannot persuade them to stay, I have given them leave to do as they wish."

"What about the Tlaxcalans?" Sandoval said. "Will they desert us also?"

"On the contrary. Laughs at Women has received word from Ring of the Wasp the Elder that we may have ten thousand of his finest warriors to accompany us when we visit Motecuhzoma."

Alvarado smiled. "Well, that is a little better."

"I have refused his offer," Cortés said.

Alvarado gaped at him. "Are you mad?"

"*Caudillo!*" Jaramillo gasped.

"Ten thousand men is not enough to wage a war against a whole nation, but it is enough to enrage their emperor. He cannot allow so many of his enemies to march across his territory unchallenged. When we enter the valley of the Mexica, we must be seen as friends and not enemies."

"So we are to go alone?" Sandoval asked.

"I have agreed to two thousand Tlaxcalans, on condition they keep their weapons hidden and pretend to be our porters."

De Grado started to protest.

Cortés jumped to his feet. "May you repent your intransigence! What do you all wish from me? You wanted me to found a colony, and I did as you asked. You asked me to find gold; I have won for you all a fortune from Motecuhzoma himself. You prayed for deliverance from the Tlaxcalan armies. Did I not obtain for you their surrender?"

Benítez bit his tongue. It seemed no one but Cortés was to get credit for anything. But he despised de Grado and so kept his silence.

He turned and looked at Malinali. He saw in her face the same uncertainty that he felt himself. *Without Cortés we have no hope. With him we face certain death.*

What sort of choice was that?

Cortés looked around the room. "I shall be guided by you, gentlemen. You are, after all, wise and Christian captains. If you wish to return to Cuba as paupers—that is, if the Totonacs and Tlaxcalans do not slaughter you all—then I shall lead you back. If you wish to do God's work and find your life's fortunes in Tenochtitlán, we shall follow Christ's banner to that city. Let me know your decision."

And he walked out.

✳ ✳

They left Cholula on the first day of the Month of the Flamingo. Their Mexica guides led the way into the high passes between Smoking Man and Sleeping Woman, the volcanoes that guarded the gate to the valley of the Mexica.

Pennons snapped in the wind. There was a breath of ice in the air.

They were all afraid.

Even, perhaps, Cortés.

 **53**

THE MIST EMBRACED them long before they reached the col, a gray shroud that hid them from one another and transformed their march into a series of lonely struggles. They entered a world of lizards, of trees gnarled and twisted into bitter fingers by the winter winds.

The column halted at a high and rocky stream. Rain Flower bent to drink, grateful for the rest. She splashed water on her face, cupped the icy water in her palm to slake her thirst. Another woman bent down to drink beside her.

"Little Mother," Rain Flower whispered.

Malinali squeezed her hand. "Little Sister."

"I had hoped that you might persuade the great lord from this."

"It would be like chaining an eagle to the earth. If he was not on the road to Tenochtitlán, I think he would disappear."

"You still think he is Feathered Serpent, then?"

"Not the Feathered Serpent we dreamed of as children, perhaps."

"I can still hear the women screaming in Cholula."

Rain Flower saw one of the Tlaxcalans, Laughs at Women, watching them from the baggage train. His face was streaked with the yellow-and-white paint of his clan. She wondered what he was thinking. He would not talk to her, out of contempt or out of awe, she did not know.

"It was not our Thunder Lords who slaughtered the women and children in Cholula," Malinali said.

"Your lord allowed it to happen. I do not love the Cholulans, but

I wonder if these Thunder Gods of yours are any better. Their swords are just as sharp as the knives of Motecuhzoma's priests."

Malinali did not answer. As she stood up, Rain Flower clutched at her wrist. "You can break this spell! It is in your power. He cannot speak to Motecuhzoma without you!"

"You think we are better served by the Mexica?"

"I think you are wrong about these Thunder Lords. They are not kind."

"You expect kindness from the gods? Look around you. If gods were kind, would little children die of disease, would we all starve when the crops fail?" She ran her fingers through Rain Flower's thick black hair, tender as a mother. "You once told me, life is just a dream, it lasts only a moment, that all our fears are shadows on a wall from a child's hand. So we must follow our hearts. In the end nothing matters anyway."

The column had resumed its march. Malinali ran to catch up with Cortés at the van. Rain Flower stared after her until she was swallowed by the mists.

MALINALI

MY LORD SITS astride his great warhorse at the crest of a hill. He takes a magical charm from the pocket of his long-sleeved doublet. Our Mexica guides murmur among themselves, pointing.

I clutch at the stirrups of the beast, no longer afraid of its size, its smell. "Our guides would like to know what is in the box you are looking at."

"It is a compass," he says, and shows it to me. "The needle always points to the north. This way I can judge in which direction we are headed."

It is a ridiculous answer and one I cannot repeat to men of

position and intelligence. I turn back to our Mexica guides. "It is a mirror for looking into the future," I tell them. "It can also read men's minds."

The Mexica stare at Cortés, and their eyes go wide.

 54

THEY STOPPED THAT evening at a village hunched in the shadow of the great volcanoes. Billowing clouds of ash rose vertically into the sky despite the howling winds. Another omen.

His men were crowded together into the few poor houses while the Tlaxcalans crouched around campfires in the open, shivering in their cloaks.

When night fell, Cortés called his captains to a conference in the adobe house he had requisitioned for his own use. Malinali was nowhere to be found, and when the parley ended, she still had not returned. Cortés was about to order a search of the camp when she appeared in the doorway, flushed and anxious.

"Where have you been?" he demanded.

"The *cacique* sent word that he wished to speak with me privately."

Cortés frowned. "Oh? What did he want?"

"He says that Motecuhzoma's soldiers have laid an ambush for us on the road to Chalco."

"I see. And is this road the only way to the capital?"

"There is another passage through the mountains, but the Mexica have blocked it."

What sort of treacherous dog am I dealing with here? Cortés thought. By my conscience, I shall make this Motecuhzoma repent the trouble he has given me! "Why does the *cacique* tell us this?"

"My lord, like everyone, he hates the Mexica. They have seized much of his good land, taken the most handsome women for concubines and the strongest men as slaves. And once a year, at the feast of the Rain Giver, he takes their sons and daughters for sacrifice on his altars. Naturally the *cacique* does not want our guides to know of his enmity, but he hopes that if he helps us, we will give him redress."

"This Motecuhzoma is certainly a popular fellow."

"There are very few in this empire who do not have cause to hate him."

Cortés considered for a moment. "Go back to the *cacique*. Thank him for the good service he has done us and tell him the time will soon come when his people will not have to fear the butchers of Tenochtitlán. Then return here to me. I would like to talk to you."

MALINALI

WE LIE HUDDLED under the blankets, listening to the icy wind moan through the alleys of the village. I rest my head on his chest. I can hear the beat of his mortal heart, the pulsing of quick blood.

"What is it you haven't told me, Mali?"

"I don't know what you mean, my lord."

"You can speak freely. Your secrets are safe with me."

"My lord?"

"You are Maya. How did you learn the language of these Mexica?"

I am reluctant to speak of this, even now. "From my mother, lord."

"How?"

I think he knows, or suspects. Impossible to hide such things from a god. I take a deep breath. "Because she herself was a Mexica, my lord, and highborn."

He takes my hand, holds it to his lips, and kisses my fingers. "Tell me all of it."

"After my father was murdered, my mother married again, bore a son by her new husband. It was soon clear to me that this man did not want me to inherit any of his lands or to interfere with my new half brother's claims even to my own father's estates. My mother felt she must decide between her new husband and me." I feel my throat tighten. "One day there was a sickness in the village. I became very ill, as did one of our slave girls. One night, as I lay in a fever, I heard my mother kneel down beside my bed and pray to Smoking Mirror to let me die. It would have solved all her problems, of course. But I did not die. Our slave girl succumbed, but I survived.

"My mother had a devious mind—she was raised, after all, as a Mexica—and she was yet able to find an ingenious solution to her problems." It is as if I have swallowed a stone. He pulls me closer, and I continue, as best I can. "She must have told everyone I had died . . . so they placed a piece of jade between my lips and wrapped my body in a cloak, head to toe, in the traditional manner . . . and they threw Ce Malinali Tenepal on a funeral pyre. Only the body in the burial cloak was not mine. It was our slave girl."

"How could they succeed with such a deception?"

"Slave traders came to our town the night of the funeral. I am sure now that it had been prearranged. They trussed me with wet rawhide and carried me away. I was sold to a wealthy Tabascan lord at Potonchán. I have no idea how much profit my mother made on this arrangement. I fetched a good price, I believe. I hope the traders did not try and cheat her."

"*Cara . . . ,*" he murmurs. He holds me tightly to his chest.

"My Tabascan master got a handsome bargain. I had already received rigorous training in song and dance, and I had royal Mexica blood in my veins. If my feelings on this commerce were discounted, everyone involved was greatly pleased."

"Royal blood, Mali?"

"My mother was a descendant of Motecuhzoma's grandfather."

"And your father? He was a lord also?"

"My father was from the royal house of Culhuacan, long

ago conquered by the Mexica. They pay Motecuhzoma rich tribute every year. But my father was a priest, much revered and very wealthy. He owned much land and many houses."

My lord falls silent. He strokes my back with his hand. His skin feels hot against mine, as if anger has ignited a fire inside him. "How did your father die, Mali?"

It takes me a long time to answer. "My father was a follower of the cult of Feathered Serpent. . . . He also understood the passage of the stars and could foretell the future by the portents in the heavens. He publicly prophesied the end of the Mexica."

"Motecuhzoma punished him for that?"

"Some soldiers came. They murdered him, in the square, in front of everyone."

I think he understands me better now. He holds me more tightly. "So you would number yourself among Motecuhzoma's enemies?"

"My lord, I am the greatest enemy he has. And he does not know it."

 **55**

THEY REACHED A fork in the road: one way led down to the valley, to a place called Chalco; the other, toward Amacameca and the high saddle between the volcanoes. Pine trees had been felled across the Amacameca road, blocking the way.

Cortés halted the column, walked his horse up to the van, where Malinali waited with their Mexica guides. "The old chief was right," he said.

Malinali nodded but said nothing.

"Ask our guides why the road is blocked."

She did as he asked. "They say you should not concern yourself over it," she answered. "The road to Chalco is easier, and you can be assured of a warm welcome there."

"Very warm, if the *cacique* is to be believed." The Mexica watched him, their cloaks pulled tight around them in the gray, cold mist. "Tell them we will take the Amacameca road."

Their guides received this news with consternation.

"What are they saying now?"

"They cannot understand why you wish to take the more difficult route. I told them you had consulted your magic mirror and this is what it had told you to do. They say Motecuhzoma will be displeased with them for putting you through such hardship."

"I shall take full responsibility for my actions when I meet their lord." He turned around in the saddle. "Bring up some men with axes," he shouted to Alvarado. "We should not be delayed here more than an hour or two. We will soon see this Tenochtitlán."

✳ ✳

As they climbed above the timberline, the driving rain turned to hail. The wind whipped ice and tiny pieces of volcanic rock, as sharp as glass, into their faces.

Then the hailstones turned to snow.

The Castilians stumbled snow-blind through the high passes, leaving scores of their Cuban porters behind them in the defiles, frozen and dying. Even two of their own soldiers, hampered from their wounds in the Tlaxcalan battles, succumbed to the cold. More would have given up, but always there was Cortés, spurring his horse up and down the column, driving them on.

Finally they were over the high sierra, and the road led down again, through forests of mulberry and cedar. Below them they saw cultivated fields of maguey and maize and, in the distance, a great lake, shining like burnished steel, before the clouds drew a veil across the vista.

They camped at Merchants' Meeting, a cluster of simple shelters built for the use of the caravans of the *pochteta,* Tenochtitlán's wealthy merchants. They built fires of green pinewood inside the open thatched huts. Cortés barely had time to post sentries and organize his patrols when Alvarado galloped up with startling news.

Motecuhzoma was on his way.

MALINALI

BEHOLD: A PALANQUIN richly decorated with shimmering green quetzal feathers and burnished gold, borne on the backs of eight Mexica lords, a great column of attendants following. But the wail of flutes and drums and conch shells is all but lost to the rush of wind.

My lord has had no time to prepare himself. He is still buttoning his black velvet doublet as he stumbles outside. Alvarado and Sandoval and Benítez are at his shoulder. We were not expecting this. Would the Revered Speaker of the Mexica really travel so far from his own capital to meet us this way?

"Is it him?" my lord whispers. It is the first time I have seen him truly anxious. "I have to know. Is it him, or is it another of their tricks? Give me the truth! Our lives depend on it."

How can I know the answer to this? I visited the center of the world just once, when I was a child. Motecuhzoma passed on his way to the Great Temple that day. But my father told me to keep my eyes lowered to the ground. He whispered to me later that the sentence for gazing on the emperor's face was death.

"Is it him?" Cortés says again, his voice uncharacteristically shrill.

I dare a glance at the emperor's face as he descends from his litter. Even though I am under my lord's protection now, it requires an effort of will, for the memory of my childhood experience is still so vivid.

Well.

He is younger than I expected, but magnificent to look at, and he carries himself with almost breathtaking arrogance. He has no beard and a nose like a parrot's beak to complement his haughty bearing. And his clothes! He is wearing a headdress of quetzal plumes, the like of which I have never seen, and a huge golden lip ornament in the shape of a serpent, no doubt in homage to my lord. His cloak is a rich carmine with gold thread that shimmers as he moves. As he comes toward us, his attendants sweep the ground in front of him with feathered whisks.

"Is it him?"

I look into my lord's face. I see panic. I have only these few moments to decide.

I turn my attention to Motecuhzoma's courtiers and attendants. Some are staring transfixed at the Thunder Lords, but others—even the attendants with the rolled mats and fly whisks—are watching the emperor. There is my answer. It is as if my heart has started to beat again.

I turn to my lord and give the slightest shake of the head.

"Thank you," he murmurs. His body sags with relief. "Tell them to go home."

I turn to the parade of frauds and clowns before us. "Who are you, and what are you doing here?" My voice seems to echo all the way down the high valley. Such power. I am no longer a woman: I am the voice and ears of a god.

"Do you not know us?" one of these Mexica shouts up at me. "This is Revered Speaker, divine lord of the Mexica. He comes here to greet the Lord Malinche and bid him welcome to the center of the world."

"This is not Revered Speaker," I answer. "This is some monkey you have dressed in gold sandals. Do you think my lord is a fool?"

Silence. The howling wind whips at the plumes and cloaks of the delegation. For a moment I wonder if I am mistaken. But it is not a mistake; I can see it on their faces.

Only a god would have known, they must be thinking.

"Tell them I look forward to the great pleasure of gazing

on the true Motecuhzoma very soon," my lord says, once
again assured of himself, and of me. "Until then, I bid them
farewell." He deliberately turns his back on them and walks
back inside the merchant hut.

I tell the Mexica what my lord has said, smiling at their
confusion. When this finds its way to Motecuhzoma's ears, I
can believe it will ruin his appetite, his sleep, and with luck,
his potency.

 **56**

Hall of the Jaguar Knights, Tenochtitlán

THE HEAD OF Juan de Argüello gaped at them from the low table in
the center of the hall. It was a large head, with a black, curly beard,
encrusted with dried blood, which glistened in the torchlight like ruby
stones. It was already starting to rot, and a foul odor permeated the air.

"Now we are doomed," Motecuhzoma murmured.

Woman Snake felt the cold claws of panic tearing at his insides.
During his time as prime minister, Motecuhzoma had been by turns
rigid, cruel, even monstrous. But he had been a strong prince, and
that was what the gods and the empire required. It was most certainly what was needed now.

But with the appearance of these strangers on the eastern shores,
the emperor's character had changed. One day he was the confident,
decisive leader he had always been; the next he was as he was today,
vacillating between depression and tears. He rarely slept and had
lost all appetite. Neither his wives nor his acrobats and musicians
could distract him.

Motecuhzoma pointed to the head of Juan de Argüello. "Get it
out of my sight!" His voice was a shrill scream.

"Shall we convey it to Tollán, to the shrine where we placed the
god's food?" Woman Snake asked him.

"I don't care what happens to it! Just remove it!"

Attendants were called, and it was hastily carried off. There was a long silence as the gathered lords and priests waited for Motecuhzoma to compose himself.

"My lord," the chief high priest of the temple finally ventured, "Feathered Serpent has appeared many times before. He first came with the secret of fire, then returned to demonstrate the making of paper and teach the writing of poems. If he has indeed decided to visit us once more, it may only be to bring us some other great gift. Let us take what he has to offer, find out what he wishes for himself in return, and send him back to the Cloud Lands. The important thing is that we do not offend Hummingbird or Smoking Mirror, for they are stronger lords, and if he challenges them, they will out-wit him, as they did at Tollán."

"On the other hand," Woman Snake said, "they may not be gods at all. It is possible they are merely ambassadors from some land we know nothing of, and this girl they have with them ascribes him powers he does not possess. If *Malintzin* and his followers are indeed envoys, we should receive them with all due hospitality. But we have no reason to be so afraid of their approach."

Neither of these arguments seemed to stir Motecuhzoma from his gloom. "If he is just an ambassador," he said, "how is it that he knew of the ambush your generals had prepared for him on the road to Chalco? How is it also that when we sent my lord Tziuacpopocatzin, disguised as myself, he knew immediately that he was an impostor?" He looked around at his council. None of them had an answer for him. "Our spies who guide him say he has a mirror with him that looks into men's souls. Is this like any ambassador you have ever known?"

"These things are indeed mysterious, but I still think this Lord Malinche is neither god nor ambassador," Cuitláhuac protested. "I believe they are invaders and we should attack them now, while they are in the open."

"I agree," Lord Maize Cobs said.

"Invade us?" one of the generals jeered. "With a few hundred men?"

A terrifying and high-pitched sound filled the chamber, breaking off the argument. All eyes turned to Motecuhzoma. He was giggling, his face contorted into a grimace, fat tears rolling down his cheeks.

"It is Feathered Serpent," he said, "come as prophesied. If we destroy him, we destroy one of the gods. If we let him come on, who knows what mischief he will bring? There is nothing we can do. It is the Year One Reed." He made a gasping sound, deep in his chest, as he fought to catch his breath. "The prophecies foretell that we shall all die at his hands and those who survive shall be his slaves. I shall be the last of the Mexica to rule this land."

He got to his feet and staggered from the chamber.

Snake Woman hung his head. Unless they could convince Motecuhzoma to act, they were all helpless. How had it come to this? A nation of warriors and now they were rendered impotent by, of all things, a priest.

 **57**

ANOTHER PALANQUIN STUDDED with jade and gold and silver; another richly cloaked prince in a great headdress of emerald quetzal plumes. Servants again swept the dirt from his path with plumed whisks. As the Mexica made his greeting, Cortés kept his eye on Malinali's face, wondering if this was another trick.

But on this occasion, she seemed impressed. "My lord, this is Motecuhzoma's own nephew, Lord Maize Cobs. Revered Speaker has sent him here in person to greet you."

Cortés bowed. At last! "That is most gracious of him."

There followed a long exchange between Lord Maize Cobs and Malinali. Cortés grew impatient at the delay. "What does he say?"

"My lord, he says that Revered Speaker is angry that you have approached so near to his capital and now asks that you return at once to the east."

What game are they playing with me now? Cortés wondered. "Remind him that I am here at his emperor's own invitation."

"I did this, my lord. But he insists there is not enough food in Tenochtitlán to feed us all, so he says that we must go back to the coast at once."

"By my conscience! What is going on, Mali?"

"I do not know, my lord."

Cortés looked at Alvarado, who was standing at his shoulder, listening to this exchange. "Let's run him through with a pike," Alvarado said, grinning.

Cortés turned back to Malinali. "Tell this Lord Maize Cobs that he should not upset himself on the subject of provisions, as my men can survive on very little. But repeat that I must meet his king in person and I shall not be swayed."

Another, more heated, exchange. Even Malinali appeared exasperated by it.

"What is he saying now?"

"He says that Motecuhzoma has a large private zoo and some of the lions and alligators have recently escaped. He is afraid that if you approach too close to the city, these animals may attack you and tear you to pieces." She took a deep breath. "This goatfucker lies like a Muslim."

Alvarado and Jaramillo grinned at this obscenity. Cortés felt a stab of irritation. "My men have been giving you more Spanish lessons, I see."

"My lord?"

"I will have to instruct you further in the ways of a Christian gentlewoman. For now you will again repeat to Lord Maize Cobs that I must meet with his lord Motecuhzoma personally. Remind him I have already taken very many risks, and the threat of alligators or lions does not deter me."

When he heard this, Lord Maize Cobs sighed and gave a signal to his attendants: the retinue of slaves that had accompanied him came forward, one by one, and laid their burdens on the ground in front of Cortés. He heard Alvarado and Sandoval gasp when they saw what they carried.

"By the sacred balls of Saint Peter," Alvarado murmured.

"Gold," Sandoval hissed.

Gold, indeed: pannier after pannier of gold objects—necklaces, bracelets, and exquisitely carved statues—perhaps as much as two or three hundred pounds in weight.

With this cornucopia spread before him, Lord Maize Cobs spoke again.

"He says this gold is for you alone," Malinali said. "There is a separate hoard for each of your captains if you will but turn around and return to the coast."

Cortés stared at the treasure. With each step I take toward Tenochtitlán, the bribes increase. Nothing could persuade me to turn back now. "This Motecuhzoma is indeed a fickle ruler. In Cholula I was told to make all haste to the capital. Now he offers me a king's ransom to retreat."

"What will you do, *caudillo*?" Alvarado asked him.

"Malinali, thank my lord Maize Cobs for these fine gifts and the trouble he has taken to bring them to me. But I cannot neglect my duty. My king has commanded me to convey his messages to Motecuhzoma in person. Assure him that we come as friends and he has nothing to fear."

There was one final, long exchange.

Malinali turned to Cortés. "He says that in that case, he will guide you the rest of the way to Tenochtitlán. He also asked me . . . he wanted to know if you were the god, Feathered Serpent."

Cortés heard Aguilar intone the words of a prayer somewhere behind him. There, it was said now, loud enough for them all to hear, and his response must be as plain, for one day it would find its way to the king of Spain and the Holy Inquisition. "What did you tell him, Mali?"

"I said you were a Spaniard, my lord, and that put you one rank above the gods."

Even Alvarado laughed at that.

 **58**

THE GREEN SLOPES were veiled in mist, creating a world at once mysterious and magical. As the shrouds parted, they saw a great lake, houses built on stilts over the steely water, and lush gardens that floated on its surface, anchored by lines of weeping cypress.

Their march had taken on the appearance of a pilgrimage. Crowds flocked to greet them. Men and women and children lined the road, some cheering their approach, others staring in sullen silence or slack-jawed wonder. A number even joined their procession, thinking they were witnessing the return of the gods. Their column swelled to twenty, thirty thousand.

The road down the mountain led to a causeway that took them across the lake. They found themselves on a peninsula at a town called the Place of the Precious Black Stones. Motecuhzoma's lacustrine city, of which they had heard so much, remained invisible, hidden in the mists; but they could now see, in the distance, trailing wisps of smoke from the altars of the Great Temple.

Motecuhzoma was just a few hours' ride away.

※　※

Benítez stood on the roof terrace looking around in awe. He had never imagined any place as beautiful as this. In every direction there were forests of oak and sycamore and cedar, fields of maize and maguey cactus. The town itself was a marvel, white adobe houses with thatched roofs, some perched on stilts over the mirrored waters of the lake. Sculptured terraces of lily ponds, arbors, and fruit trees led down to the water. The warm scents of frangipani and hibiscus were carried to him on the evening breeze.

Not even Salamanca or Toledo—considered the most beautiful towns in all Spain—could compare to this place.

He was astonished at the architecture. The palace they had been given as quarters was built of cedar and an ocher-colored volcanic stone and was as solid as any grandee's palace in Castile or Andalusia. The sandalwood beams used to reinforce the ceilings also gave off a fragrance that sweetened the rooms. Colorful tapestries and brightly painted frescoes enlivened the walls, and there were spacious patios where vivid-colored macaws and parrots chattered in hanging bamboo cages.

A paradise.

He prayed that there would be no fighting to endanger this fragile beauty. He consoled himself instead with what Cortés had told him many times on the journey: they had not come here to make war but to bring peace, salvation, and true religion.

✳ ✳

Norte joined Benítez on the terrace, and for a while they shared an uneasy silence.

"Where are you from, Norte?" Benítez said, suddenly.

Norte seemed surprised at the question. "It was a village called Barajas in Castile."

"When you were there, did you ever imagine a place like this?"

"No, my lord. The slum I lived in bore no relation to this. Even the poor people here live better than I did. Yet the Mexica appear to have done all this without initiation into the secrets of Christ or the Virgin."

Benítez felt a prickle of irritation. Why had he ever ventured to ask Norte's opinion? "Every time you open your mouth, it is to utter a blasphemy," he said.

"Is it blasphemy? It strikes me as the truth. Eight years away from Christian society gives a man a different perspective."

"I agree with you that these people may not be as backward as we at first supposed. But we come here armed with the true faith and trusted with a sacred mission."

"Because we are victorious does not make us saviors. Barbarians have conquered Rome before now."

Benítez was about to argue with him further, thought better of it. The panorama before him did not incline him to be disagreeable. So they returned to their silence until at last the sun fell behind the distant mountains and it grew too dark to see.

MALINALI

Painali, 1511

I AM ELEVEN years old, and my life is abruptly separated, as you would chop a maize cob in two with a machete, neatly parting the two halves.

In one hand the gods held my childhood; in the other my destiny.

It happens with the arrival of the Mexica *calpisqui,* the tribute gatherers, and a squadron of Mexica warriors. There is no warning of their arrival, and they are not expected.

They know where my father will be. They drag him from our house, throw him in the dirt at their feet to humiliate him while the whole town watches. They slash at him with their obsidian knives to hear him scream.

Then one of the warriors, their lieutenant, drops a great rock on his head, crushing his skull. As if he were a thief, an adulterer.

There they leave him, in the plaza, the flies crawling over the bloody mess that had once been the man I loved and adored and revered most in the world.

His crime was to prophesy against Motecuhzoma and to foresee his end. My father's gifts are well respected, and his murmurings have reached even to Tenochtitlán.

You might ask me how I feel at that moment. I feel only numb. I try to summon the rage and grief that consumed me the day my two brothers and sister were led away for sacrifice. I want desperately to feel something, but grief does not exact its bitter due until much later.

Instead, I stare at my father's body, and something dies in me; something else is born to take its place.

I carry it with me, even today. It is black and secret and lives in my heart. Its taste is foul and its course implacable.

59

Place of the Precious Black Stones, 1519

THE FIRE HAD been lit in the stone hearth outside, and now the wall glowed with heat. Rain Flower led him into the bathhouse, took off her clothes, and indicated that he should do the same. Then she sat him down on a stone bench.

There was a trough in the corner of the room. A drain had been cut in the wall to allow water to flow into the trough from a well outside. She took a clay dipper, dashed some water onto the shimmering wall. Immediately the room filled with steam.

She sat down on the bench next to him and examined his naked body. The wound on his arm had healed well, she noted with satisfaction. The heat in the room was opening the pores on his skin, and she took a handful of grass and began to wipe the sweat from his back and chest.

Her naked body had aroused him, and his hands were everywhere on her. But so gently. She liked his kisses on her face now, even though his beard tickled her, and she liked the way his hands stroked her. She had shown him what she enjoyed, and he had been an adept pupil. But after a while she wriggled away, dashed more water against the wall. The steam filled the tiny room in a hissing roar.

Suddenly he was behind her. Their skins were slick with perspiration, and she felt his *maquauhuitl* slide sweetly between the clefts of her body. She heard him groan. She threw back her head for his kisses. He lifted her under her arms, and she parted her thighs for him, was surprised to find that her cave was ready. For the first time she found herself enjoying him as she imagined a wife would enjoy her husband. She reached behind her and clung to him, and he joined with her easily.

As he reached his moment, she wondered if her baby would look like Norte or like this hairy Castilian. But she would not have to worry about such a predicament: long before that day came, Benítez would have returned to his wife in the Cloud Lands, or they would all be dead on Motecuhzoma's altars.

✳ ✳

Motecuhzoma stared at the dishes that had been laid before him, each prepared in the finest red-and-black Cholulan earthenware and warmed over tiny clay braziers filled with burning charcoal: fried fish that had been swimming in the eastern ocean just the morning before, brought to him across the plains and the sierra by a relay of specially trained messengers; crow, quail, venison, and grasshoppers, each one a delicacy; rattlesnake and agave worms from the desert; larvae nests and salamanders from the lakes; armadillos from the forests. There was a foaming cup of *chocolatl*, cacao beans mashed and boiled with cornmeal and seasoned with honey.

None of it tempted him.

The plates were returned to the kitchens untouched, and the gilded screens that guarded his privacy while he ate were removed. His private theater of freaks and monstrosities performed for him: dancing hunchbacks, juggling dwarves, a one-legged man who lay on his back to spin balls into the air. His musicians played flutes and snakeskin drums.

They scarcely warranted attention.

A servant lit his tobacco pipe, and he puffed on the smoke, lost to the byzantine wanderings of his own thoughts...

...As much as he had always feared the coming of Feathered Serpent, another darker interpretation of recent events had occurred to him. It had been suggested by a chance remark of one of his spies, who had reported that *Malintzin* had with him a small mirror in which he could look into the souls of men. As a former priest, he knew that Feathered Serpent did not own such a mirror; but his rival, Smoking Mirror, certainly did.

Tezcatlipoca, Smoking Mirror: the god of affliction and anguish and disease, whose particular pleasure it was to disguise himself in many forms in order to bring misery and suffering to human beings on earth. Like Lord Malinche, he was greatly interested in personal riches, and whenever he appeared on earth, he caused confusion and anguish—exactly as Lord Malinche had done.

A confrontation with Feathered Serpent was terrible enough, but at least he had known the parameters of his dilemma; but what if this was instead a test of his steadfastness? What if Smoking Mirror had for some reason grown dissatisfied with his people, the Mexica, and had come to punish them? What should he do to save himself and his people? How should he act?

He could find no answer to this riddle. All he knew was that tomorrow he must go out and face this terrible and bewildering divinity and nothing in his training, either as a priest or as a prince, had prepared him for such an encounter.

 **60**

DAWN. MIST DRIFTED across the steely surface of the lake, keeping Tenochtitlán yet hidden from view, but the Spaniards could hear the cry of the city's boatmen and the echo of their wooden clappers as they steered their canoes along the algae-green canals between the *chinampas*. The stench from these floating gardens belied their ethereal beauty: the crops were fertilized with frequent applications of human manure.

They were on a broad causeway, made of earth and stone flags. Their guides led the way, followed by the cavalry, in full armor, pennons hanging limp from iron lances. Cristóbal del Corral, the standard-bearer, rode behind, tossing his banner from side to side so that it fluttered and whipped in the still morning air. Then came the infantry, led by Ordaz, swords drawn, shields over their shoulders. Cortés was in the rear, Malinali on foot on the left of his great chestnut mare; Brother Aguilar and Father Olmedo followed on his right, bearing aloft great wooden crosses. Finally came the great wicker standard of the White Heron, the emblem of Tlaxcala. Some of the

Tlaxcalan warriors dragged the wooden carts that held the lombard guns; the rest marched in their traditional cloaks of red and white, jubilant at the prospect of entering the capital of their ancient tormentors.

The sun rose over the dark blue ridge of Mount Tlaloc. As the mist burned away, they saw Indians darting across the lake in their canoes to witness this remarkable sight. Soon the lake was filled with boats, some with just a single fisher, others huge, holding two or three score people, all paddling as close to the causeway as they dared for a better view, faces silent and awed. Some ventured too close, and one of the war dogs ran barking to the edge of the causeway with foam dripping from its jaws, and they shouted in alarm and paddled frantically away to a safer distance.

Sunlight glinted on newly polished armor and brass trappings and steel lances; the pipers began to play, were answered by the whistles and shouts of the Tlaxcalans.

Then the mists burned away, and they were afforded their first view of the towers of Tenochtitlán.

✳ ✳

At first Benítez thought it must be an illusion, a trick of the light and water. Scores of stone pyramids floated on the haze created by the early morning cooking fires. Skeins of smoke drifted skyward from the temple shrines, to signal more dawn sacrifices to the Mexican idols.

The sun rose up the sky, and it was as if a veil had been lifted away. He twisted in the saddle and realized that there were towns and villages all around them, linked by the causeways and *chinampas*, a vast and vibrant economy supported entirely by the great lake.

Suddenly he wanted to turn back. None of them, perhaps not even Cortés, had imagined they were going to find a civilization as large and as complex as this.

Cortés says we have come as saviors. Why, then, do I feel like a sheep being herded to the slaughterhouse?

✳ ✳

They reached the Fortress of Chaloc, a twin-towered castle guarding a fork in the causeway. The iron shoes of the horses clattered on the wooden bridge.

Snake Woman came out to meet them, wearing a cape of elaborately worked flamingo feathers. He had with him perhaps a thousand of the city's most prominent noblemen, a shuffling sea of copper skins, feathered capes, elaborately worked cloaks, and waving plumed headdresses.

Do not look in the least impressed, he told himself. They must not suspect that you find anything in the least wonderful here.

It took almost an hour for this first ceremony of welcome to be completed. Finally they passed through the gates of the fort and headed north toward the capital.

※   ※

An hour later they halted in front of the Gate of the Eagle, at a spot known as *Malcuitlapilco,* the Tail End of the File of Prisoners. Cortés knew of this gate; Malinali had told him of it the night before. At the inauguration of the Great Temple, so many prisoners had been offered up as sacrifice to the gods that the line of prisoners had finished here, with the main gate of the capital still half a league distant. Malinali said that twenty thousand men, women, and children had had their hearts torn out on the altars during that festival week.

The shriek of conch shells and the thunder of *teponaztli* drums echoed across the lake. A great procession appeared from the gates, another carnival of plumes, jaguar skins, the feathered beaks of eagles. Dwarves hurried ahead, spreading cacao blossoms on the ground.

And Cortés had his first glimpse of Motecuhzoma.

His litter was carried by four of the most senior princes of his empire, including Cuitláhuac and Lord Maize Cobs. A further four nobles supported an elaborate canopy of shimmering quetzal plumes, bossed with gold and silver, with pearls and green chalcolite stones suspended from the fringe. Other *caciques* walked ahead of the procession, sweeping the ground and unfolding golden carpets.

The procession halted, and Motecuhzoma stepped down.

The *Tlatoani*—Revered Speaker—of the Mexica was younger than Cortés had expected. He was between forty and fifty years old, Cortés guessed, tall for an Indian, and slim. His skin was the color of cinnamon, and his black hair was cut to the nape of his neck. He did not have a beard, but a few long hairs on his chin had been allowed to grow in imitation of one.

He wore a blue-and-white mantle, richly adorned with pearls, turquoise, and opals, the ends of his cloak gathered in a knot at his right shoulder. On his lower lip was a turquoise labret in the likeness of a hummingbird; his ears and nose were also studded with precious stones. Most stunning of all was his headdress: feathers of green quetzal and blue cotinga, perhaps four feet high, a breathtaking sight.

He was ceremonially supported by his brother and his nephew, and all eyes except those of the most senior princes were turned to the ground.

✳ ✳

A gentle breeze stirred the pennons on the lances and the plumes in the helms of the Spanish captains. Save for the jangling of brass trappings on the Spanish horses, there was utter silence as the two men regarded each other.

Cortés dismounted and approached, Malinali at his right shoulder. He thought to embrace the emperor, but the two princes who accompanied him stepped forward to block him, alarmed. Cortés took a step back.

Instead, he offered Motecuhzoma a collar of cheap glass *margajitas*, strung on gold filament and scented with musk. Lord Maize Cobs accepted it on Motecuhzoma's behalf. In return he placed over Cortés's head a necklace of sea snails, carved from pure gold.

"My lord," Malinali whispered at his shoulder, "these are the emblems of Feathered Serpent."

He noticed that the emperor's hands were trembling. Here he stands at the gates of his capital city, surrounded by tens of thousands of his own vassals and warriors, and he quakes! At this moment I hold him and his entire nation in my thrall. The Virgin is with me. God has made me invincible.

Motecuhzoma spoke his greeting. "He says he kisses your feet, my lord," Malinali said.

"What?"

"It is a traditional greeting of the Mexica, my lord. It means nothing."

Motecuhzoma spoke again, a longer soliloquy this time. Cortés waited impatiently. When he had finished, he looked at Malinali. "Well?"

"It is difficult, my lord."

"Difficult?"

"I do not know whether his meaning is literal . . . or poetic."

"Just tell me what he says."

"He says you have suffered great fatigue on your journey, and he calls on you to rest here awhile. That part is a formal greeting—protocol, if you like. But then he says . . . he says he has been troubled for a long time and that whenever he gazed into the east, he knew one day you would come to instruct your servants further. Now the prophecy has been fulfilled, and he is glad. He says he has guarded your noble seat for you and now offers you the throne."

Cortés heard Alvarado swear under his breath. "By Satan's black and spotted arse, is he offering to make you *king*, my lord?"

"Mind what Mali says," Cortés reminded him. "He may only be gracious." But his own mind raced ahead, calculating.

He considered before he spoke again. "Tell him that I, too, have long wished to gaze on him in person. Tell him to fear nothing from us, for we love him greatly and think on him as a friend."

Malinali relayed his message. Motecuhzoma's face underwent a dramatic change. The transformation was unmistakable. What Cortés saw on the king's face was relief.

❊   ❊

They entered the capital down a broad avenue lined with white adobe houses. The city was eerily quiet. Cortés felt eyes watching them from behind the windows and from the roofs, but apart from the official welcoming delegation, the streets were empty.

It seemed to him that they were being received as conquerors and not as guests. He knew he was tantalizingly close to doing as he had promised his officers, which was to win this great city without firing one shot from the cannons or having one man draw his sword. Here was the kingdom he had always dreamed that one day he would possess, and it was within his grasp. All he had to do now was close his fist around his prize.

 **61**

THEY ENTERED THE great plaza of Tenochtitlán. On one side stood the rose-colored walls of Motecuhzoma's own palace, on the other the Great Temple itself. Directly ahead of them, beyond Motecuhzoma's private zoo, was the palace of Face of the Water Lord, Motecuhzoma's father. This was to be their new quarters.

Cuitláhuac himself escorted them there.

It was a paradise: a great court, heavy with the scent of flowers, surrounded a man-made pool seeded with large fish and adorned with painted statues. The palace itself was vast and brilliant with light, the stone walls dressed with lime and polished till they glittered like silver. They looked upward: the ceilings were buttressed with cedar. They looked down at their feet: the walls and floors were covered with huge tapestries of feather work and cotton.

Fragrant sandalwood burned in the braziers; pallets of woven straw had been laid out for sleeping. The room set aside for Cortés himself contained a throne of beaten gold, inlaid with precious stones.

Cortés was stunned. The palace was so vast, a man might easily get lost in its corridors; private rooms opened onto vast audience halls, which in turn opened onto patios with steam baths and fountains and gardens. It was beyond imagining. Even the palaces of Toledo and Santiago paled by comparison.

But he must not allow the splendor of these surroundings to

blind him to the reality. Despite Motecuhzoma's fine words, nothing had yet been decided.

As soon as they were settled in their new quarters, he followed his soldier's instincts and posted sentries around the walls, ordering everyone to remain inside the palace. For good measure he had the falconets carried to the roof, where his gunners fired a salvo of blank rounds, which thundered over the city, acclamation of their arrival and warning to their hosts.

✹ ✹

Cortés was barely settled in his room when Cáceres announced that Fray Olmedo and Brother Aguilar were outside, wishing to speak urgently with him.

Cortés rubbed a weary hand across his face. "Very well. Bring them in."

Olmedo looked abashed, as he often did when coming to Cortés with petitions, while Aguilar wore his usual expression of painful forbearance. Cortés felt a stab of irritation. No doubt they were here to remind him of his religious duty. How he hated churchmen!

"Well?" Cortés said.

The two men looked at each other. It was Fray Olmedo who spoke first. "Brother Aguilar has raised a matter of great concern," he said.

Cortés kept his silence and glared at them.

Olmedo was intimidated by this tactic; not Aguilar. "I fear that Doña Marina has led the natives of this land to believe that you are a god," Aguilar said.

Cortés felt a vein pulse at his temple. *You and your hair-shirt morality! I should have left you on the beach in Yucatán! You have been more trouble to me than that renegade Norte.* "You both hear for yourselves what I command her to say. What proof do you have that she has falsified my position?"

"From where else could the belief that you are a god have sprung, my lord?"

"I do not know, Brother Aguilar. We are dealing with a people of many superstitions. That is why we are here: to rid them of their devils and bring them the good news of the one true faith."

"And she confounds our good works at every turn! She has told the people you are this Feathered Serpent!"

"You have no evidence of that."

Aguilar clutched his Book of Hours to his breast. "You must let me act as your interpreter once more," he said. "It is the only way you can be sure that your message is not corrupted."

"You do not speak their language."

"But some of the Mexica speak Chontal Maya. We can——"

"We can what? Spend all day listening to you chattering away like a bird? It takes long enough to communicate with these people as it is! You fear that our message becomes corrupted? How much worse will it be when it is conveyed through the minds and tongues of four different people!"

"We only fear that you put yourself in jeopardy, my lord," Fray Olmedo said, trying to pacify him.

Cortés slammed his fist on the table. "By my conscience! How do I place myself in jeopardy? What would you accuse me of? Treason? Heresy? Or is it blasphemy?"

Father Olmedo withered in the face of his anger. "It is only that mischievous minds could perhaps say of you——"

"Say what of me? Well? What more would a reasonable man have me do? Wherever I could in this land, I have destroyed their diabolical idols and impressed their shrines as houses of God. And I would have done more, much more, and yet it was you——you!—— who stayed my hand. And now you accuse me of blasphemy——"

"That was not my thought, my lord——"

Cortés rounded on Aguilar. "And you! You try my patience too far, Brother Jerónimo."

Aguilar blanched. "My lord, I do not fear what is, only how it may seem to be."

"How it seems to be is how it is! I have brought God to this land under the banner of Christ and furthered the interests of my king to the very throne of a great empire! I may soon be in a position to give this great kingdom intact, not only to the king of Spain but to God himself! When others wished to turn back, I alone furthered the cause of our crusade. Do you dispute that?"

"No, my lord," Fray Olmedo said, quickly.

"You have no cause to distrust me or Doña Marina! What must I do to prove to you that I am committed to our cause?"

Fray Olmedo did not speak. It was Aguilar who, with typical bullishness, tried to have the last word. "You must convince them that you are not a god," he said.

"I will mind my duty, Brother Jerónimo. Be sure to mind yours. And do not fear on my account. I shall prove to both of you that I am Christ's champion. I shall prove it to you in such a way that you need never doubt it again."

 **62**

WHEN BENÍTEZ ROSE the next day, it was still dark. He dressed quickly and went up to the terraced roof. Dawn was yet a violet stain on the eastern horizon behind the mountains. Light seeped slowly into a world of alien terror and breathtaking beauty.

Canoes drifted unseen through the mist; the *tap-tap-tap* of the steersmen's wooden clappers echoed on the still water. In the street below, shadows were moving silently toward the temple, carrying burning coals for the temple braziers, cakes of corn for the priests' breakfasts.

The first blinding shot of gold appeared dramatically behind the sierra, was greeted by the boom of snakeskin drums on the *Templo Mayor*. Moments later the blast of conch shells reverberated over the rooftops as the first sacrifices were made.

He gaped like a country boy in the city. This was like no town or city he had ever been in: there was no creaking of cart wheels on cobbled streets, no snorting or stamping of horses—all the goods these people needed were carried on foot or by canoe; no cussing of traders in the market or crying of beggars—the streets were completely ordered and silent.

As it grew lighter, he could see that the roads were laid out in a grid pattern, some of them broad enough for a dozen horses to ride abreast. Others had canals running down their center. Ordaz, who had fought many campaigns in Italy, had compared the city to Venice, which, he said, also had canals instead of streets. "But," he added, "this place does not stink like Venice." Indeed. Instead of the smells of ordure and rotting garbage, common to any large town in Spain or Italy, there were instead the sweet aromas of pimentos and herbs, flowers and lilies, the pungent drift of incense from the temples.

Street cleaners were at work damping down the beaten earth with water. A Mexica in a broad cloak walked slowly past, chatting with a neighbor who kept pace with him in a canoe.

Heathens, he had called them when he had first stepped on this soil at the Grijalva River. Savages. This was delicate savagery indeed.

A terrible growl interrupted his reverie. Motecuhzoma's private zoo was close by, and the sounds of the early morning feeding shattered the quiet as jaguars and ocelots and coyotes fought over raw carcasses. Rain Flower said that the animals were fed on the remains of human sacrifices from the temples.

Here was the first taint on this earthly paradise: the sharp sulfur smell of blood from the *Templo Mayor*. The sluices carved into the steps of the pyramid were already flowing.

He had almost been seduced by the Devil's sweet ways; here was the real heart of darkness.

MALINALI

MY LORD WEARS a suit of black velvet. On his head is a cloth cap with a medal, engraved with a depiction of a Thunder

Lord slaying a terrible beast. Around his neck is a chain of gold with another medallion bearing an image of the goddess Virgin. There is a large diamond on his finger.

Satisfied with his reflection in the mirror his chamberlain holds for him, he turns his attention to me. "This morning I have an audience with the emperor," he says. "I command you to be diligent in your duties."

"As I am always, my lord."

"Mali...," he begins. His voice trails away. For once, I see him at a loss for the right words.

"My lord?"

"This morning you must translate my words exactly as I say them. Exactly."

Now I understand what is wrong. That fool Aguilar has been whispering in my lord's ear!

"I think that in the past you have claimed more for me than I have for myself."

"I have only put your words into language my brothers and sisters can understand."

"You have told them I am a god."

I lower my eyes and contrive to appear contrite, but I do this to disguise my anger. You are a god. You have let your moles persuade you otherwise, but you are.

"Do you know what would happen to me if my king should discover that I claimed to be a wizard of some sort?"

"The blame is mine, not yours, my lord."

"If it is a lie and I allow you to tell it, then the calumny might as well have come from my own lips." He continues, his voice softer. "I know you mean well, but this must stop. Today you must add no embellishments of your own." He crosses the room, gently strokes my hair. "You must promise to do as I say."

Such a promise will destroy us all. I understand what has happened, for Smoking Mirror has taken on many disguises in the past in order to destroy Feathered Serpent. This time I fear he has returned as Brother Aguilar.

"I will do as you command," I promise.

He smiles, thinking he has tamed me. "Good. Then let us be on our way. We must not keep the emperor waiting."

✳   ✳

The royal house shimmers in the morning sun, more dream than real, a chimera in rose-colored stone. Over the main door a painted rabbit symbolizes the day—One Rabbit—that the palace was completed. Polychrome stone serpents stand sentinel on each side of the entrance. Gods and eagles and Jaguar Knights watch us from the frescoes. We have stepped into the maw of the Mexica.

I hear one of the Thunder Gods mutter in awe.

We step into a huge hall, fully two hundred paces long, the walls faced with marble and a porphyry the color of jade; I look up, there is a paradise world in wood: friezes of flowers, birds, and fish carved into the broad cedar beams.

My lord is oblivious, but then he is a god and not easily impressed. He strides ahead, and I hurry after him. I am frankly worried. He has brought just four of his Thunder Lords with him on this morning's adventure and only five of his soldiers as escort. At the moment he holds Motecuhzoma in his mesmeric gaze; should it fail, we are utterly at the mercy of the Mexica.

The building we are in is the heart of Motecuhzoma's empire; around us are his law courts, tribute storehouses, arsenals, reception rooms, and kitchens, as well as quarters for the thousands of servants and retainers he employs. I feel as if I have shrunk to the size of an insect and now find myself in the middle of a nest of ants; we pass through a crawling mass of Motecuhzoma's drones, his fetchers and carriers, scribes and worriers. Around us I hear murmurs of astonishment; for a moment we have brought the business of the Mexica to a halt. Everyone stops their frantic activity to stare.

There is no time to stare back; my lord hurries ahead, into a court of luxuriant gardens and bubbling fountains. But he has no time for the flowers and is bounding, two steps at a time, up a broad stone staircase that leads to the second floor of the palace and the emperor's private apartments.

※ ※

Into the presence of Motecuhzoma himself.

Revered Speaker, resplendent in a turquoise cloak lined with coyote fur, reclines on a throne sculpted from a single block of stone. Beside him is another throne, woven from reeds. He indicates that my lord should take his ease in this. Other low wooden *ypcalli* have been arranged for the other Thunder Lords.

Dwarves and musicians go tumbling from the room, summarily dismissed. Of Motecuhzoma's court, just four remain in attendance: Woman Snake, his prime minister; Motecuhzoma's brother, Ciutláhuac; and his nephews Lord Maize Cobs and Falling Eagle.

Motecuhzoma claps his hands, and Falling Eagle steps forward with the gifts the emperor has chosen for his guests: my lord receives a casket of golden jewels, while his captains each receive two golden collars and two cotton cloaks.

At my lord's behest, I thank Motecuhzoma for his gifts and for his hospitality. Motecuhzoma responds by asking how he might please my lord further.

"Mali," my lord says to me, "you must tell him that I am not a god but a man like himself. Tell him that I have been sent here by a great king who rules many lands. He wants Motecuhzoma to abandon his false gods, who are only demons, and become his vassal so that he may enjoy his friendship and embrace the true faith." He pauses in this pretty little speech to stare at Fray Olmedo and Brother Aguilar, ensuring his point is well made. "Please relay my words exactly as I have said them."

"I shall, my lord." But I will certainly do no such thing. Brother Aguilar will get us all killed.

I turn to Revered Speaker, who has watched this exchange intently and no doubt wonders what to make of it. "My lord wishes you to know that he has come from the Cloud Lands at the behest of *Olintecle,* Lord of All Lords. He is here to reclaim the throne, as is his right. He wishes you to obey him in all things."

Motecuhzoma does not seem at all surprised to hear this request; if anything, he appears resigned to it. "As you know, your lord's coming has been prophesied for many generations. I have kept his seat for him. But I hope he will allow me to continue to lead my people. In all other things, I put myself entirely at his service."

For a moment I cannot breathe. It appears with these few words that we have won. My heart is thumping painfully against my ribs, and I want to dance and scream. I turn to my lord: "He says that he hopes you will allow him to continue his rule, if only as your instrument."

There is a moment of awed silence. The Thunder Lords look at one another, their thoughts and feelings transparent to everyone. Only my lord remains inscrutable. "Those were his words?"

"I translate his words exactly," I say, remembering our earlier conversation. "No embellishments."

"Does he mean what he says?"

"I don't know," I answer, keeping my eyes lowered. "All I can do is translate exactly what he says. No embellishments."

"Mali!"

"My lord, I do not know the mind of the emperor!"

He concedes the point. "All right, tell him, then, that I will be happy to accept his vassalage, on the king's behalf. But if he accepts Charles as his political sovereign, he must also accept him as his spiritual guide. In that case he must abandon this abhorrent practice of human sacrifice and be baptized into the holy faith. He must also tell his people to abandon their false gods and learn of the one and true religion."

I do as he asks. Motecuhzoma's demeanor immediately undergoes a dramatic change. He seems both afraid and angry at once. "Tell the lord Malinche that I have received many reports of his new religion and of the crosses he has erected in our temples. I am sure his gods are very good to him. But my gods are good also, and I cannot risk offending them even for him. I hope that we can be friends and that we do not have to talk about this delicate subject any further."

Ask a god not to talk about religion? How can that happen? I do not want Motecuhzoma and my lord to be friends. My destiny is chaos.

"He says that he cannot risk offending his gods further. He recognizes that you are a great lord, but he hopes you will not mention this subject again."

My lord's captains look at one another, confused.

"First he surrenders you the throne," Alvarado growls, "then he deigns to threaten us. What game do we play here?"

My lord looks to me for guidance now. How can I explain it to him, in front of everyone here? Motecuhzoma still suspects that you are Feathered Serpent, so he offers you the throne. But he wishes only to placate you with baubles and fine words. His loyalties both from need and from conviction lie with Smoking Mirror and Hummingbird.

"He means that you may be king of this place, as long as you do as he commands."

My lord's eyes blaze with anger, as I hoped and as I anticipated. "Tell him that he lives his life in error, that there is only one God, and that these idols that he worships are in fact only devils! All men are descended from Adam and Eve, which means we are all brothers, and so this practice of sacrifice and cannibalism is an offense against man and against God! Tell him that we have come here to save him and his people. Unless he accepts Christ as his savior and turns his back on his idols, he will burn in the fires of hell for eternity."

I have heard this speech before, from Fray Olmedo and Brother Aguilar, but I had never expected I might have to repeat it to the emperor of the Mexica. If it is incomprehensible to me, what will Motecuhzoma make of it? "You wish me to say that to him exactly?"

"They are my words."

And so I do as he asks. Motecuhzoma receives my speech with a mixture of confusion, terror, and outrage. My lord had told him that he came as a friend, in peace; now he is harangued and threatened in his own palace. By a god, yes; but by a lesser god. And worse, all this comes through and from the lips of a woman, who looks directly at him, like an equal. Such humiliation must be hard to bear.

"Tell Lord Malinche that my own gods have served me very well. I will obey him in all other things. But what he asks is impossible."

I pass on Motecuhzoma's words. Alvarado and the rest of the Thunder Lords appear terrified; the monkeys who love only gold are trapped now by religion. I watch as my lord struggles with the moment. He knows the dangers, but he cannot draw back.

Fray Olmedo steps forward. "My lord," he whispers, "I fear we should not press him. Enough that we have broached this subject, for now. Let us progress by stages, consolidating as we go."

"It was you who urged me to show more piety, Father," my lord says to him, his voice strained now.

"We do not doubt your piety, my lord. But I think in this case we should not be too rash in our fervor."

"Just yesterday you dared lecture me that I am not fervent enough!"

"I think Fray Olmedo is right, *caudillo*," Alvarado says. "Let us leave off for now."

My lord sighs. "Very well," he murmurs, with bad grace. He returns his attention to me. "Thank Motecuhzoma once again for his gifts and his hospitality. Tell him we shall take our leave of him now."

I feel a rush of disappointment. I have for a long time prepared myself for the great collision between god and prince. I cannot believe that my lord has been persuaded from it by his own priests. They force him to deny his own divinity every day.

Motecuhzoma smiles thinly as we take our leave of him. It is all I can do to hide my contempt for him. There will be another day; my lord will not delay forever. I will be at his side when he finally confronts you with your cruelty and lays claim to your throne, his throne, which you and your kind have usurped.

 **63**

FALLING EAGLE WATCHED the Spaniards take their leave. He had noted that during the exchanges with his uncle, the girl had been careful never to call this stranger Feathered Serpent by name, as she had done on the coast and at Cholula. Instead, she used the honorific *lord*, which could be applied to either a prince or a god. So it was still not clear whom they were dealing with.

For himself, he was now convinced that this Lord Malinche was mortal, a man like himself; even so, a man with more cunning than any god.

Hall of the Jaguar Knights

"He has asked to see the temple," Woman Snake said.

High above them the priests sounded the conches from the shrine of the Great Temple. It was the last watch of the night, and before the dawn could come, it was the priests' duty to tear the heads from hundreds of quail and use their blood to salute the rising sun. The quail were chosen for this ceremony because of their markings: speckled white on black like the stars in the sky, the same stars that Hummingbird, the Sun God, must defeat before he could rise in the east.

"What does he wish to find in the temple?" Cuitláhuac asked.

The question remained unanswered.

Falling Eagle felt helpless with rage. So far these intruders had shown scant regard for their gods. What could be their purpose in seeing the temple but to offend them further?

Like Motecuhzoma, he, too, was worried about the portents. These strangers had chosen to enter their city on the Day One Wind, the sign of Feathered Serpent in his guise as the whirlwind. One Wind was also the sign of sorcerers and thieves who chose this particular day to hypnotize their victims before taking over their houses, eating all their provisions, raping their women, and stealing all their treasure.

Ever since their arrival, an oppressive silence had hung over the city, everyone waiting for a cataclysm to erupt. Meanwhile, here they sat, the cream of the nation's princes and warriors, helpless to intervene.

"I do not believe this Lord Malinche is really Feathered Serpent," Falling Eagle said.

"Revered Speaker believes it," Lord Maize Cobs answered.

Falling Eagle turned to the prime minister. "What do you think, Woman Snake? Is he perhaps just an ambassador from some land we know nothing of?"

The prime minister shook his head. "If he were an ambassador, he would have presented us with his credentials. He has not done this. Instead, he intimates that he is rightful king of Tenochtitlán. If Motecuhzoma accepts his word, as he seems disposed to do, what is to become of us?"

There was silence in the audience chamber. Despite their frustration they all balked at the next step, that of disobedience and rebellion. Motecuhzoma was their *Tlatoani*, Revered Speaker, chosen ruler for life. His right to govern them was as indisputable as the hierarchy of their gods, and to defy it was unthinkable. Slowly, one by one, the great lords stood up and left the chamber until Falling Eagle was left there, alone.

Our empire was founded upon the sun, he thought. But now the sun grows weak. I fear for Mexico.

Templo Mayor

At the foot of the temple steps, the mutilated body of a naked woman was strewn in a circle some four paces wide. This was Moon Goddess, Malinali explained, daughter of Serpent Skirt, mother of the Moon and Stars. When Serpent Skirt was pregnant with the Sun God, Hummingbird, the Moon Goddess had tried to kill her. Instead, Hummingbird had leaped, armed and fully formed, from his mother's womb to save her. He had cut the Moon Goddess down with his sword, as he now had to do each night in order to be born again. Here she lay, at the foot of his shrine, her gory fresco placed precisely so that she could accept the bodies as they rolled down from the sacrificial stone at the top of the steps.

Benítez tore his eyes from this blood-caked and evil stone and gazed in awe at the towering stone pyramids that soared around him. Less than fifty paces from where they now stood was the church of Feathered Serpent, his temple quite different from the others that surrounded it; instead of a pyramid like the others, it was rounded, Malinali explained, so that it provided no impediment to the Lord of the Wind, allowing his breath to flow where it would.

Its appearance was similar enough to a proper church to appear beautiful, if it had stood alone. But close by it were the skull racks—the *tzompantli,* as the Indians called them—thousands of heads, some still oozing blood and flesh, others bleached by the sun, testament to the voracious appetite of the Mexica's gods.

Feathered Serpent's church was not their goal this morning. Cortés had announced they were to climb the Great Temple itself. Benítez shielded his eyes to gaze up at its peak, which was by his estimation taller than the spire of the cathedral at Sevilla. The steps that led to its summit were so steep that they seemed to ascend almost vertically to the clouds. Two painted stone serpents stood sentinel on either side.

The Mexica who accompanied them indicated to Malinali that they would carry Cortés up the steep incline, but he waved them away and strode up the steps toward the summit unaided. Benítez followed him, his breath burning in his chest as he tried to keep pace with him.

Dear God in heaven, Benítez thought.

✳   ✳

Motecuhzoma was waiting for them at the summit, comfortable, rested, gloriously attired, at his advantage. Cortés was breathing hard from the exertion of the climb, and sweat shone on his forehead. One by one the rest of his officers appeared, gasping in the thin air.

"Revered Speaker asks if you are tired from your climb," Malinali said to Cortés.

"Tell him . . . we never tire," Cortés snapped.

Perhaps you do not tire, Benítez thought, but my own lungs are on fire, and I believe they can hear my heartbeat in Cuba. But he attempted to look unconcerned, as Cortés did, tried to slow the heaving of his chest.

The panorama of the city was laid out in front of them, a grid work of streets and canals and white thatched-roof houses stretching beyond the rose-colored palaces. Other pyramid temples soared above the plaza, the ocher and blue of their decoration vivid against the snowcapped volcanoes of Sleeping Woman and Smoking Man. The lake was crowded with canoes, beetling their way between the city and the distant shore. The day was clear and bright, and in the far distance Benítez could even make out the pine forests and high col through which they had marched just a week before into this great valley of wonders.

"Have you ever seen anything like this?" Ordaz breathed at his shoulder.

"Not even in my dreams," Benítez answered.

"I have fought all over the known world, I have seen the great cities of Europe—Rome and Venice and Naples, even Constantinople—but I have never seen anything to compare."

Benítez was reminded for a moment of what Norte had said: *barbarians at the gates of Rome.* He had a troubling thought: If God has indeed chosen us as the blessed, how is it that we have never created an earthly paradise like this one? Perhaps he intends for us to bring our cathedrals and our religion and make this paradise a better one. That is the reason he has led us here.

Motecuhzoma was pointing to a nearby island, another temple city with great arcades and markets, which Malinali told them was called Tlatelolco. He showed them an aqueduct that carried fresh water from a place called the Hill of the Grasshopper all the way down to the city.

This is like a dream, Benítez thought, one wonder after another.

He forced himself to look away, his gaze drawn reluctantly to the sacrificial stone before Hummingbird's shrine. The stone itself and the steps in front of it were black with dried blood. Beyond it he saw a gathering of crows in human form, the priests of the temple. Their black robes were embroidered with human skulls, their waist-length hair clotted with human blood, their ears ragged from repeated self-mutilations. They stank of sulfur and rotting flesh; even from a distance their odor made him want to retch.

He looked up: Hummingbird's aerie was painted ocher, and a frieze of white stone skulls was carved at the peak. There was another shrine on the summit: it belonged to *Tlaloc*, the Rain Bringer, Malinali told them. It was painted blue and white and was guarded by stone frogs and the reclining polychrome figure of a *chacmool*, messenger to their devilish gods. Malinali took pains to point out the bowl carved into the *chacmool*'s back where roasted human hearts were placed as sacrifice.

The emperor said something in his own monkey tongue, and Malinali translated: "Motecuhzoma asks if you would like to step inside the shrine of their great god, Hummingbird on the Left."

Cortés gave a slight nod of his head, and they followed the emperor into the temple. Nothing had prepared them for what was to follow.

64

THE HOUSE OF the Beast.

Stepping out of the bright sun, he was blind for a moment; as his eyes grew accustomed to the gloom, Benítez was aware only of the stench, the dreadful, choking taint of a slaughterhouse.

He was aware of a pair of luminous eyes watching him. He took a step back, against his will, then realized the eyes were two huge glasslike stones set in a gold mask. Below the mask was the statue of a warrior holding a golden bow and arrows, his body encrusted with jade and opals and pearls.

"This is *Huitzilopochtli*, Hummingbird on the Left, God of the Sun, Decider of Wars," Malinali translated for Motecuhzoma. "He says that the Culhua-Mexica are his chosen people and that he protects them and brings them great victories. The collar he wears contains the skulls and hearts of kings they have defeated in battle, wrought in silver by their finest craftsmen."

Benítez fought back the bile in his throat. There was blood everywhere, clotted in thick black layers on the walls and the floors. The smell, the terrible smell . . .

Motecuhzoma led them through a pair of curtains—made from human leather, Malinali announced—and hung with tiny copper and silver bells. The tinkling sound they made was eerily reminiscent of the Eucharist.

Benítez was breathing shallowly and fast, trying to keep the stench out of his nose. He came upon three fresh human hearts quivering and blackening in a brazier of copal incense. Another beast lurked in the gloom: it had the face of a bear, its eyes glittered with obsidian mirrors, and its body was ringed with devils with long tails. Malinali introduced them: *Tezcatlipoca,* Smoking Mirror, Lord of Hell, Lord of Darkness, prince of wizards and sorcerers, and ruler of eagles.

Benítez needed no further acquaintance: this was Satan.

"I think I am going to vomit," Alvarado said.

Cortés, his face black with rage and disgust, turned on his heel. They hurried after him, out of that infernal nest and into the fresh air, the leering faces of these stone devils imprinted forever on their memories and their dreams.

MALINALI

MOTECUHZOMA HAS TURNED pale with the force of his outrage and humiliation. Yet there is pleading in his eyes. He wishes to avoid this confrontation, though he must know it is impossible.

My lord, too, is consumed with rage. I see the god in his eyes now; there is no mistaking his presence.

"Tell this creature that I cannot credit how he can debase himself before such idols, which are only manifestations of the Devil himself. With his permission I shall remove the demons that live here and replace them with the sign of the true cross and a picture of our Savior in the arms of the Virgin."

I turn to Motecuhzoma, eager now to have done this final confrontation, which is his destiny and my own. "My lord is very angry. He is astonished that a great prince such as yourself persists with these evil human sacrifices. Surely you realize these idols you serve are monsters. He wishes to consecrate this temple to his own religion immediately."

As I make my speech, I am gratified to see our Revered Speaker tremble. "If I had known Malinche would use this occasion to insult our gods, I should not have invited him here."

My lord has his hand on his sword. I feel a shiver of excitement. Yes, let us do it now. Hack off his head right here, throw down the idols, murder the priests, sack the temple. *Do it now!*

But one of the Thunder Lords puts a hand on his arm. "Not here, *caudillo*," Benítez whispers. "This is not the time."

"This is not religion," my lord shouts, pointing at the black-robed priests. "Look at them! It is a gathering of vultures!"

"I agree with what you say, my lord, yet I fear the good captain is right." It is Fray Olmedo speaking now, his normally ruddy features pale with fright. "Let us not precipitate a fight when it is not to our advantage. We have only just arrived in this city. The Lord does not expect us to overthrow the Devil and all his works in just one day."

My lord removes his hand from his sword. He turns to his captains. "What do you think, gentlemen? The beauty of our surroundings is there to deceive us. Here is the capital where the Devil has his main seat. Once this place is mastered, the rest is ours to conquer."

He turns and walks off the summit. I hurry after him. Whatever ailment had afflicted him in Cholula is gone. The god has returned, magnificent in his anger.

Yet I had thought the moment had come. Motecuhzoma was at our mercy, and my lord's hand had been stayed. As I follow him down the temple steps, I cannot but feel angry with him and the rest of these Thunder Lords, impatient to have it done.

 **65**

Motecuhzoma watched them go. He felt the eyes of his priests on him, felt their condemnation, for instead of assuaging the gods, he had only angered them further. He went back inside Hummingbird's shrine to make a blood offering as penance.

He pricked his tongue and ears with maguey spines and placed the bloodied thorns into a ball of plaited grass.

What was he to do?

The lord Malinche's initial show of friendship had not been sincere. Soon the news would be all around the city how the strangers had defiled the temple. Who were these Thunder Lords? This Malinche seemed concerned only with religion and the abolition of human sacrifice, and in that he certainly behaved like a god, like Feathered Serpent. And yet the servants Motecuhzoma had sent to the palace of the Face of the Water Lord to cook and care for the strangers claimed that they did not behave like gods at all, that their excrement was not of gold, as it should have been, and that they smelled like dogs.

What was he to believe? The burden of the Culhua-Mexica lay on his shoulders like a yoke. The future of the men of Aztlan depended on his interpretation of these omens and signs. Why must so much depend on him alone?

He went beyond the curtain and threw himself on his face before the image of Smoking Mirror, and prayed for an answer to his dilemma:

"O master, O our Lord, Lord of the Nigh, Lord of the Near, open my eyes, open my heart, advise me, set me on the road to wisdom, inspire me, animate me, incline thy heart, guide me, show me what I must do . . ."

66

PULSING HEARTS ROASTING *on the coals. The terrible eyes of the Beast, the fetid stink of his breath. Benítez fled down the labyrinth corridors of the palace. His handprint left a bloodied smudge on the wall. Headless corpses pursued him, screaming his name, blaming him. His legs were trapped in the mud of the lake. He couldn't move.*

He sat up, eyes wide, staring into the darkness.

The priests were sounding the conches from the summit of the *Templo Mayor*, bleeding themselves to ensure that in the morning the sun would rise again for another day.

He took a deep breath. Just a dream. "Just a dream," he said aloud, to reassure himself. His shirt was soaked in sweat.

He lay down again, and Rain Flower wrapped herself around him, whispered words in *Náhuatl* he did not understand, trying to comfort him. When had she become so precious? This woman made him wish to live a little longer yet. Yet he doubted there would be time for them. They were lost to the world he knew and trusted, and the hours and days that lay before them were steeped in blood.

✳ ✳

It was one of the carpenters, Alonso Yañez, who found it. He had been directed by Cortés to build a chapel inside the palace, and while selecting a suitable site, he found a patch of wall that had been very recently covered over with lime plaster. He decided to open it and see what lay beyond.

✳ ✳

Cortés held the lamp above his head, the beam illuminating, piece by piece, cameos of the fabulous treasure: tumbling hills of jade, opals, and pearls; cascades of necklaces worked in gold and studded with precious stones; fallen regiments of statues, worked from pure silver; a pile of great golden platters very like the one he had been given at San Juan de Ulúa. He gazed at the cornucopia before him, scarcely crediting the evidence of his own eyes.

The Mexica had tried to hide their wealth under their very noses. All of the gifts they had received to this point paled by comparison. Here was the treasure he had promised himself, what he had promised them all. Possession of it would eclipse even the wealth of certain crowned kings of Europe.

An awed silence, each alone with his dark and private rumination.

"By Satan's black and hairy ass," Alvarado murmured.

"How will we keep this secret from the men?" Jaramillo said.

"We will not," Cortés answered. "I want everyone to see this. Every last soldier."

"But *caudillo*," Alvarado protested, "this will only sharpen their greed. There will be dissension—"

"Why do you think these men are here? Because of greed. When they know what we now possess, they will fight like demons to protect it. Do as I say. Bring them here, three at a time. Let everyone see what this Motecuhzoma has tried to conceal from us, that which is rightfully ours by his own words. When it is done, have this chamber resealed immediately. We must think further on this. It is one thing to find a treasure; it is another to keep it."

✳   ✳

Once again men huddled in small groups, whispering among themselves. The disease that had afflicted them all at San Juan de Ulúa was rampant again; this time the cause was not the mosquitoes from the swamp or the bad water but sickness of the heart brought on by the sight of gold.

Cortés paced his quarters, took his meals alone in his rooms, planned, fretted, prayed to God for guidance, and looked into the darker places of his own soul for his ambition.

 **67**

A CHARCOAL BRAZIER burned in the corner of the room, for the nights were cool. The sounds of flutes and drums drifted on the cold November air; the *naturales* were dancing and singing in the streets, an ominous sign. The fear that had gripped the city on their arrival had dissipated. Once again there were rumors among the Tlaxcalans of a planned attack by the Mexica. It was Cholula all over again.

Cortés stood to address his council.

"Gentlemen, we are presented with an exquisite dilemma. At this moment we are all of us rich beyond our wildest dreams, and yet we might as well be as poor as heathens, for we are trapped here in this city with our fabulous treasure. If we are not free to leave and take our gold with us, we might as well be back in Cuba with just our dreams.

"When we first arrived here, the emperor agreed to vassalage under our majesty the king of Spain and relinquished his throne to us, in accordance with the *Requerimiento*. Yet I believe he played us false, for we have been in Tenochtitlán these five days and he still clings to his old powers while we are treated as no more than honored guests. Have any of you gentlemen suggestions on how we should proceed?"

"Should we not wait further and see what transpires?" Jaramillo asked.

"If we play such a game, we are likely to fall victim of it. Although these Indians love us now, their hearts are fickle. Already it seems they find their initial hospitality too lavish. All of you here have seen how our provisions decrease day by day. Should they wish, they may at any time remove the bridges from the causeways, and instantly we become not their guests but their prisoners. They do not even need to attack us; they might as easily starve us out and then offer our hearts to their devilish idols. Motecuhzoma could, if he chooses, poison the food he gives us. At this moment we are at their mercy."

To have the situation so baldly stated sent a shiver through everyone in the room.

"Let us steal the gold and leave by night for Vera Cruz, then," Ordaz said.

Cortés gave his infantry commander a chill smile. "You forget that between here and the coast is a place called Tlaxcala. Should Ring of the Wasp the Elder discover that we have abandoned his warriors to their fate inside Tenochtitlán, he may decide we are not the allies he had wished for. Is there any here who ardently desires further battles with the Tlaxcalans?"

Cortés seemed to be taking a sadistic delight in defining their dilemma.

"We do not have to return by way of Tlaxcala," Sandoval murmured.

"No, we can flee through territory belonging to the Mexica," Cortés said. "Is it your opinion that they will let us leave here peaceably, our pockets weighed down with their treasure? In the unlikely event that we outrun and outmaneuver Motecuhzoma's armies, it will take us months to build boats to return us to Cuba. And when we arrive there, my lord the governor will take all our riches from us anyway."

Depression settled over them like a fog.

"There is a further complication," Cortés went on, relentlessly. "Before we left Cholula, I received a message in secret from the coast, from Juan Escalante, who commands our fortress at Vera Cruz."

This is not going to be good news, Benítez thought.

"The local Mexica governor attacked a force of our comrades in arms who had entered his territory. They were routed on the battle-field, together with our Totonac allies. Nine of your fellow Spaniards died from their wounds. Many more were wounded but were able to flee to Vera Cruz, by the grace of God."

There was an appalled silence. Until now the one thing that had stood between them and the Indians was the myth of their invinci-bility on the battlefield. Now the Mexica had put the lie to that. If Motecuhzoma's armies had attacked them on the coast, what was to stop their routing them in their own capital?

"Why did you not tell us this news before?" Benítez said.

"To what end? If you had known in Cholula, you would have wanted to turn back, and the Tlaxcalans would have slaughtered us. There never has been any other choice but to come here."

They all looked at one another. This appalling man, Benítez thought. What has he done?

"Then there is only one course of action open to us," Alvarado said.

Benítez looked up, suspicious. This sounded too easy, too rehearsed. Perhaps Cortés had tutored him in this, as he had seen him do before.

"We must do as we did at Cempoala," Alvarado continued. "We must hold a knife to their chief's throat."

"You mean Motecuhzoma?" León said, appalled.

"We must take him hostage. With the emperor in our power, we will be masters of our own fate once more—and of Tenochtitlán."

"This is a dangerous adventure," Cortés said, as if such a suggestion had never occurred to him. "We should think carefully before we act."

Benítez could not believe his ears. *Utter madness.* "We are just three hundred Castilians and a few thousand unpredictable Indians. You think that by holding one man as hostage, we can control millions?"

"What else did you think we should do when we came here?" Cortés asked him.

Oh, he has planned this from the beginning, Benítez thought with horror. This was always his plan, probably even as early as Vera Cruz. "You said we had come here not to fight but to trade," Benítez said. "To talk."

"Benítez," Cortés said with a smile. "You are such an innocent."

They all looked at Cortés, then at one another, each of them brought face-to-face with his own greed. Cortés was right, Benítez realized. Had they really been so naive? They had followed him to this point hoping that by some subterfuge they might walk away from the valley of the Mexica with their pockets full. They had allowed themselves to be mesmerized, led by the glimmer of gold to this terrible confrontation.

This terrible *hidalgo* who leads us is utterly mad, Benítez thought. But we are lost without him.

"Is there any other suggestion?" Cortés asked.

No one spoke. He was right, of course; taking Motecuhzoma as their hostage was their only hope. From the moment in San Juan de Ulúa when they had voted Cortés his colony and his position as *caudillo,* the die was cast.

"Then it seems you are decided, gentlemen," Cortés said. "Let us all make our peace tonight with God. Tomorrow we shall visit Motecuhzoma."

✳ ✳

Benítez, Rain Flower, and Norte sat around the low table, picking at the food the Mexica slave girls had brought for them: some bits of roasted meat that Norte identified as iguana, sweet potatoes, maize cakes, beans in a chilied sauce. Rain Flower was animated during their dinner, seemed to have finally broken free of the melancholy that had gripped her since Cholula. She put endless questions to him through Norte.

"*Where were you born?*"

"*Do you have a wife?*"

"*How old are you?*"

Benítez answered her questions as best he could, but his mind was elsewhere. He had no appetite for his dinner and pushed his plate away, his food hardly touched.

"Rain Flower wants to know what is wrong," Norte said.

"Nothing. Nothing is wrong."

"She thinks she has done something to displease you."

"It is nothing she has done." He stared moodily at a frieze of warriors and monsters captured in perpetual battle on the wall in paints of vermilion and ocher. "I think, Norte, that you may have been right all along."

The renegade looked up, surprised.

"I now doubt that what we do here in this city is godly."

Norte chewed slowly, without pleasure, as if the food in his mouth were sawdust. "Your doubts will not save the Mexica...or us."

Benítez lapsed into troubled silence. Rain Flower leaned forward and whispered something to Norte.

"What did she say?" Benítez asked.

"It is difficult to translate. I do not know the word."

"You can make an attempt at it."

Norte shrugged. "She is unhappy because you look sad. She wants you to know she thinks kindly of you."

"That she loves me?" Benítez was surprised at how much pleasure the thought gave him.

Norte avoided his eyes. "The word is not quite the same in their language."

Benítez sighed. What should it matter what she thought of him? He remembered how he had once nursed thoughts of returning to Cuba with gold in his pocket and living out the rest of his life in ease with this beautiful little Indian. What a stupid dream.

Tomorrow they were all going to die in this infernal place.

"Tell her she is free to do as she pleases tonight," Benítez said, suddenly.

Norte looked startled. "My captain?"

"We are going to die tomorrow, so it doesn't matter anymore. So you may tell her that she may sleep tonight wherever she chooses. She has fulfilled her obligations to me. Don't stare at me like that, Norte, just do as I say."

He thinks I am soft in the head, Benítez thought. Perhaps he is right. But when all your mortal fancies are gone, it is easy to be just and generous.

Norte smiled and whispered to Rain Flower. Her eyes went wide.

Let them do as they wish. I shall find a jar of Cuban wine somewhere to see me through this last, cold night.

Rain Flower whispered something to Norte, who sucked in his breath as if he had been stabbed. Then he got to his feet and rushed out of the room. The tiny silver bells on the curtain across the doorway jangled and shook.

Benítez looked at Rain Flower. She smiled, moved closer, picked up his hand.

"God in heaven," Benítez murmured.

Who would have believed it?

※ ※

Malinali lay asleep on her back, her arms above her head. The blanket had slipped below her waist. Cortés watched her in the candlelight, her long black hair fanned across the sleeping mat, the brown aureoles of her nipples ripe as fruit, her lips open and pursed in the shape of a heart. The murmur of the beast in his heart, the growling of shame.

He started to strip off his clothes.

He pulled back the blanket, placed a hand between her legs. These Mexica had little hair down there. Not like Catalina. She had a pelt like a bear. This Indian's smoothness excited him in ways he did not fully understand. She reminded him of the marble statues in the cathedral in Sevilla, the smooth mounds of the golden angels in the frescoes...

Yes, his angel, his copper-skinned and ministering angel. God was with him, and Malinali had been sent as his helpmate and guide.

Tomorrow he would confess again his adulteries, his weaknesses of flesh, and he would go out again to fight and vanquish for the Lord, cleanse his soul once more.

But here, in the dark, the Beast ruled him.

MALINALI

I AM ASLEEP when Cortés returns from his final counsels with Alvarado and Sandoval. He wakes me roughly and mounts, strident in his demands. He holds my shoulders, thrusting deep inside, more savage than loving.

It is always like this when there is danger, before the great battles at Tlaxcala, before Cholula. The anticipation of death excites him. It is the restless god in him.

Tonight something takes place in my mind as well as in my body, for I see his seed rushing into me, hot and sticky, taking root in my belly. And afterward, as he kneels by the window saying his final prayers to the goddess Virgin, I think I feel the moment when it begins, when the seed of a god becomes a part of my own mortal body.

✳ ✳

My lord arrives at the palace accompanied by his captains—Alvarado, Sandoval, León, and Benítez—as well as a number of his soldiers under the command of Bernal de Díaz. They are all wearing their steel armor, and they march proudly past the bodyguards in Revered Speaker's apartments.

I can feel the panic that our unannounced arrival has created. We have taken a stick and stirred the nest, and there is frenzied but pointless activity around us. An usher directs us hurriedly to a private quarter of the royal apartments where

Motecuhzoma is amusing himself with his birds: black, glossy grackles in silver cages.

If he is alarmed by our unexpected visit, he does not show it. He takes his ease on a carved wooden *ypcalli* and gestures for my lord to join him.

My lord indicates that it is his desire to remain standing. I pass this sentiment on to Revered Speaker, and finally he perceives the threat. He attempts to disarm us by indicating the two lavishly costumed young women who sit demurely in the corner, their eyes on the ground.

"Motecuhzoma says these women are his daughters," I say. "He would like to offer them to you as your wives." The children of such a marriage would be offspring of both himself and the gods. With such an alliance of blood, Motecuhzoma hopes to avert any confrontation in the traditional Mexican manner.

My lord examines these new offerings. He raises his eyebrows appreciatively, and I cannot help but feel a stab of pain.

"That is most kind of him," my lord says. But there is no kindness in his voice and only steel in his gray eyes. "But please tell him I cannot take another wife because I already have one."

I bite my lip. Who is this woman who exercises such great control over my lord's life? Or is this just an excuse? Perhaps the woman he finds irreplaceable in his life is me.

"Tell him that I have not come here to discuss his daughters."

"My lord thanks you for your kind offer," I tell Revered Speaker, "but he wishes to talk to you of other things."

Motecuhzoma looks truly frightened now.

"Ask him if he still has the head of Juan de Argüello," my lord says.

At the mention of a decapitated head, Motecuhzoma turns the color of cold ash in a fire. "Tell Lord Malinche I do not know what he means."

My lord holds up his hand. "You do not need to translate that," he says to me. "I see he knows of whom I speak."

My eyes meet with his, and they lock together. I revel in

such moments of conspiracy between us. This morning we spoke at length of this encounter, and he has tutored me well. I have never felt so powerful, or so proud. I only wish that my father, his spirit wandering miserably in the Land of the Dead, could see me.

"Ask him to explain the unprovoked attack on my men at Vera Cruz."

I think Motecuhzoma will faint when I put this question to him.

"I know nothing of this," he answers, and breaks into a high-pitched giggle.

"He thinks this is a jest?" Alvarado snarls, and takes a step forward.

My lord puts a hand on his arm to still him, then returns to his inquisition of the emperor. "Nine of my men were killed by his warriors," he goes on, without waiting to hear Motecuhzoma's further protestations. "Tell him that my captains wish to take revenge immediately. I am all that keeps them from burning down his capital and its temples."

I repeat this ridiculous claim, and I am surprised that Motecuhzoma takes it seriously.

"You must tell Lord Malinche that it is not I who is at fault but the governor of that district, Smoking Eagle. I will send for him at once to answer your questions."

"He blames the governor of the district. As you said he would."

My lord nods his head. "Tell him what we require of him."

I turn to Motecuhzoma. "My lord is very disappointed. Thus far he has shown you nothing but friendship, but now he believes you have treated him falsely. However, he says he will forgive you if you accompany him, without fuss, to his palace, and remain there with him until this matter is settled."

Motecuhzoma stares at me, as if these were the ravings of a madwoman. I cannot say I blame him, for even I do not think my lord's plan can work.

"I have . . . I have explained I had nothing to do . . . with this," he stammers, finally. "I cannot be given such an order. Whoever . . . whoever heard of this?"

"He refuses, my lord."

"Explain to him that if it were up to me, I would certainly never ask such a thing, but that my captains are insistent. There is no other way to solve this problem."

Motecuhzoma continues to twitch and stutter, unable to comprehend what is going on around him. "This is a most grievous affront . . . affront to the dignity of the Mexica. My chiefs and priests could never consent . . . to such an arrangement."

"Explain to him," my lord says, all gentility and patience now, "that there is no affront here. After all, the palace where he will abide once belonged to his own father. He will be treated with every respect accorded a great king."

"My people would never allow this to happen!" Motecuhzoma shouts, over my lord's words. "There would be uproar!"

"Tell them your gods have asked it of you," I tell him, shouting louder, "and that you are going of your own free will!"

"I cannot do such a thing! It is impossible!"

And so it goes on. The Thunder Lords become uneasy as the arguments rage back and forth, going nowhere. I see their eyes stray nervously to the guards now ringed around the room.

León is the first to break. His hand goes to his sword. "Let us just drag him out of here with a knife at his throat," he hisses. "We do not have time to waste on more of this!"

My lord's head snaps around. "Silence!"

"We have already spent too long arguing with this dog!" Jaramillo joins in, for fear has made even him bold.

Motecuhzoma watches this angry exchange in terror and bewilderment. Something must be done to break the stalemate. I move closer to the throne. "They want to kill you," I whisper to him.

"Kill me?" His voice is suddenly shrill, like a girl's.

"It is only the lord Malinche holding them back. They want to kill you and put the Great Temple to the torch."

"They would not dare!"

"Look at them, my lord. These men are afraid of nothing. I know: I have been with them since the very beginning."

"Tell Lord Malinche he may take my daughters, my son as well, if he wishes. Will that not satisfy his warriors?"

I relay this offer to Cortés, who is, of course, contemptuous.

"This is taking too long!" Jaramillo shouts, the panic betrayed in his voice. "Let's just grab him now!"

"No one makes a move against the emperor unless I give the order!"

Meanwhile, Motecuhzoma pleads privately with me. *Oh, Father, if you could only see him now, how he sweats and grovels!*

"There is only one way you can avert the disaster we all dread," I tell him. "My lord is very angry with you and with all the Culhua-Mexica. You must do as he asks and go with him. Nothing else will pacify him."

I am certain Motecuhzoma will defy us. If he does, of course, he will die on the end of León's sword, and we must certainly die soon after at the hands of the palace guards. But while Motecuhzoma believes that my lord is Feathered Serpent, there is uncertainty as to what he will do.

We wait.

Suddenly it is as if the burden of his situation overwhelms him. He places his head on his chest and begins to weep.

 **68**

MOTECUHZOMA WAS BORNE from the palace in a plain litter that his chamberlain used for visiting the Tlatelolco markets. He wore only a plain white cotton robe, the same robe he used to visit the temple. As he passed through the cavernous halls, he shouted to his startled servants and courtiers that he was going with the Thunder Lords of his own accord, that he simply wanted to know and understand the strangers better, that he had consulted Hummingbird and he had endorsed his decision. He gave orders for his court, his entertainers, and concubines to be transferred to his father's palace at once.

Then there was silence, except for the tramp of the Castilians' boots in the cavernous halls. They escorted him, swords drawn, eyes staring straight ahead. The whole palace simply stopped and ogled at this extraordinary, unthinkable sight.

Finally one of his bodyguards called out to him, asking him if he wanted them to fight the Spaniards.

"No," he answered. "These strangers are my friends. I am in no danger at all."

And all the while he wept.

✳   ✳

The palace of the Face of the Water Lord was no more than a hundred paces away, on the other side of the plaza. News traveled quickly, and Motecuhzoma saw that a small crowd had gathered in the court to watch this unlikely procession, every face etched with horror.

What else can I do? Motecuhzoma asked himself, breathless with the humiliation of what was happening to him. At all costs I must avoid a confrontation between the gods that will ruin the Culhua-Mexica forever. Perhaps when Smoking Eagle has been punished for his infraction, they will release me. Lord Malinche will marry my daughters, and this terrible moment can be forgotten.

I may outwit this Feathered Serpent yet.

MALINALI

"HE REFUSES TO answer your questions."

My lord sits on his throne of beaten gold, Motecuhzoma

seated at his left side. I stand at his right. The Thunder Lords are arrayed behind him in open court. The fifteen Mexica chiefs who have accompanied Smoking Eagle from the coast are on their knees in front of us, not out of obeisance to my lord but in deference to Motecuhzoma.

My lord regards his prisoners for a long while. "If he will not answer to me," he says finally, "perhaps my lord Motecuhzoma would care to ask this Smoking Eagle why my men were attacked."

Motecuhzoma, his head buried in his chest, does as he asks, his voice so soft, it is barely audible.

Smoking Eagle speaks once more, at length, his remarks again addressed to Motecuhzoma.

"What is he saying?" my lord ask me.

"It seems Smoking Eagle was sent to collect tribute from the Totonacs. Motecuhzoma had ordered him to punish them for giving us assistance. He was not just to take a portion of their annual produce in levy but to take everything they have, as well as all the young boys and girls in the town for sacrifice. *Gordo* defied him, saying that you yourself had excused him from all further taxes to the Mexica. *Gordo* then sought help from your soldiers. Smoking Eagle says that to run away from this fight would have been unthinkable. Not only would it have been contrary to the orders from Motecuhzoma, it would have disgraced the Mexica nation and his own manhood."

"You think he is telling the truth?"

"Motecuhzoma says he is lying, but the emperor is afraid for himself. Yes, I believe this Smoking Eagle is telling the truth."

My lord gives this evidence long consideration, then says this to me: "The law states that any man who commits murder must himself die. I therefore have no choice but to sentence Smoking Eagle and his chieftains to be burned alive in the plaza in front of this palace in full view of the population. The execution will take place immediately."

I cannot believe my ears. Was this why we have risked so much, to slaughter a few innocent Mexica warriors? If anyone is guilty of the murder of these Thunder Lords, it is Motecuhzoma.

I catch Benítez's eye for a moment, and I know he is thinking the same thing.

"But my lord, this is not just. Motecuhzoma—"

"I did not ask you to contend with me. You overreach yourself. You are my translator—translate. Tell them what I have said. That is all."

But now Benítez also steps forward. "This is not justice, my lord, this is murder."

The blue vein in my lord's temple bulges, knotted, against his white skin. "Do not dare to question me! Be silent or I shall give you cause to repent it! I have made my decision in accordance with the law! These men must die!"

69

THE PYRE WAS built with the wood from arrow shafts and *atlatl* spear throwers plundered from the palace armory. In the midst of it, Smoking Eagle and his fellow warrior chiefs were bound hand and foot to stout poles.

Cortés watched the preparations from the palace walls. He turned to Alvarado and asked for two more sets of chains. When they were brought, he held them toward Motecuhzoma. "Mali," he said, "tell the emperor he must hold out his hands to me."

Motecuhzoma did as he was ordered, and Cortés placed the irons on his wrists and snapped them shut. Then he knelt and placed the other set of fetters around Motecuhzoma's ankles.

With this simple act, he breaks him, Benítez realized, both in the eyes of the crowd watching below and, as important, in the emperor's own mind. It would have been kinder to have killed him.

The Revered Speaker of the Mexica was crying like a woman.

Below in the courtyard, Jaramillo threw a flaming torch into the wood at Smoking Eagle's feet.

Through the drifting smoke, the Mexica chief did in death something he would not have dared to do in life. He raised his head and looked up into the face of Motecuhzoma. From the terrace above, Benítez could see the bewilderment and hatred in his eyes.

He turned to the *caudillo*. "My lord, why do we murder a brave man?"

"Nine of our own brave men died at Vera Cruz at his hand. Or have you forgotten?"

"That man down there was merely following orders." Benítez pointed at Motecuhzoma. "That is the wretch who killed them."

"If we murder him, we forfeit our own lives. Meanwhile, by this simple act, we teach the rest of the people what to expect if they ever again lay their filthy hands on a Spaniard."

Motecuhzoma's chest heaved, his face creased and wet with his tears. What spell did Cortés put on you? Benítez wondered. Or is it some private madness of your own that imprisons you? One word from you, and your people would fall on us, crush us like insects.

The crowd in the plaza watched the execution in silence. Only the Spaniards seemed to enjoy the spectacle. Benítez heard Jaramillo call up to Alvarado: "Now the Eagle is really smoking!"

And Alvarado laughed.

✳   ✳

When it was over, the stench of charred flesh hung in the plaza like a pall.

Cortés bent to remove Motecuhzoma's chains.

"Mali, tell him that I am sorry for what has taken place here today. Tell him also that even though I know that it was he who was the guilty one and that he deserved to die along with Smoking

Eagle, I would not harm him for all the world, as he is my friend. Tell him I will help to spread his fame far and wide and give him even more lands for his empire. From this day on, should he look for salvation, he should look to me."

Mother of God, Benítez thought. The man is a monster. How did we not see it?

PART III

THE BRINGER OF DARKNESS

The Pope must have been drunk.

—Reaction of the Cenu Indians when told Pope
Alexander VI had divided the world between the
Spanish and the Portuguese

 **70**

The Year of Our Lord 1520,
Two Flint on the Ancient Aztec Calendar

THE CENTER OF the world had shifted its focus to the palace of Face of the Water Lord.

Motecuhzoma's favorite tapestries and dwarves and wives had been abruptly transferred to the new court. Scribes now hurried across the plaza between the palaces with codices and tribute records, and the great princes of the empire gathered in the reception halls of the Castilians to visit their emperor in apartments his own guests now guarded.

But many did not come: Cuitláhuac, Lord Maize Cobs, Falling Eagle—all refused to obey his summons to present themselves. They withdrew to Texcoco and Iztapalapa and brooded there.

An uneasy peace returned to the city, although the political wrangling between Motecuhzoma and Cortés continued behind the palace walls. As a further concession to Cortés, Motecuhzoma's daughter and niece were initiated into the Christian faith by Father Olmedo and baptized Doña Ana and Doña Elvira.

Meanwhile, in Vera Cruz, Juan Escalante died of the wounds he had received in the battle with the unfortunate Smoking Eagle's army and was replaced by Gonzalo de Sandoval.

The soldiers settled into a routine: playing cards and dice, observing the life of the city from the isolation of the palace walls, looking to the mountains for sign of the reinforcements they believed that Puertocarrero would soon bring. They stared at the swelling belly of the Lady Marina and muttered among themselves.

Benítez noticed a change in the behavior of his own squadron, and one member in particular: Gonzalo Norte. Since Tlaxcala the soldiers had stopped mocking him, and as the slow months in the capital passed, he was even accepted into their pastimes and their ribald talk. He stopped shaving his beard and no longer bathed every day, like an Indian. He spent much of his time gambling with Flores and Guzmán, his former tormentors.

In fact, Benítez decided, he is well on his way to becoming a Spaniard once again. I should be pleased for him.

MALINALI

"YOU MUST TELL my lord Motecuhzoma there is a matter I need urgently to discuss with him. A religious matter."

The laughter freezes on Motecuhzoma's face. He has aged these last few months, and today he looks like a frail old man. His captors treat him with patronizing forbearance, as one would an enfeebled uncle. He has lost pride in himself.

With Alvarado and Jaramillo, he is busy at *patolli*, a favorite game of the Culhua-Mexica played with marked white beans. Players move six pebble counters around a board according to the fall of the beans. Since his confinement, his only passion is gambling on the results of these games, though whenever he wins, it is his pleasure to give all his winnings to his guards.

"What is it he wishes to say to me?" Motecuhzoma asks me, turning from his game. He has about him the sulky expression of a child about to be scolded.

I translate my lord's words and wait, stiffly, at his side. These last weeks he marches the corridors of the palace with a retinue of servants following him everywhere, puffed up as an emperor. The god in him has been pampered by ease and power. I have seen the way he looks at Motecuhzoma's daughters. Now he is past the mountains and inside the kingdom's heart, he no longer needs me.

"Tell him it is about the future of the *Templo Mayor*," my

lord says. "For months Fray Olmedo and Brother Aguilar have been instructing him in the ways of Christianity, and I also have explained to him at length about his false gods. Tell him the time has now come to pull down the idols in the temple and erect in their place an image of the blessed Virgin. Tell him if he does not agree to this, we shall do it by force and kill any priests who try to stop us."

A familiar look of dread settles itself on the *Tlatoani*'s face when I tell him this. What did he expect? Cortés cannot be stayed forever.

"Tell the lord Malinche he must do not do this," Motecuhzoma whispers to me. "Should he attempt it, our gods will surely strike him down, and my people will rise up in revolt. It is a very delicate matter. I need more time to handle this my own way."

When he hears this, my lord's expression becomes kinder. "You may tell Motecuhzoma that if it were up to me, I would leave the matter entirely in his hands. But my captains press me every day. Perhaps, though, if I could give them something to occupy their minds…"

What game are you playing now?

"If he can tell us where his jewelers obtain all their gold, it might perhaps relieve the sickness in my captains' hearts and make them more amenable."

It is like a blow to the stomach. Just gold, my lord? Is that all you ever wanted?

"My lord says that it is not he, but his captains, who press for the destruction of your temples. He thinks he can buy them off with your gold mines. He wants to know where they are."

A flicker of a smile, but a sad one. What is he really thinking? Does he still believe my lord is Feathered Serpent? Does he not realize that the world can never return to the way it was, that he can never again be emperor? He must know the Thunder Lords will never leave, that the only way the Mexica can be free again is for Motecuhzoma to give them the order to fight, and if he does, they will kill him. Perhaps he still hopes to rule by ingratiating himself with them. Or does he think this waiting game will lead to something else, some last maneuver he has conjured in his own mind?

"Tell him that most of our gold is obtained by panning," Motecuhzoma is saying. "There is Zacatula, in the south, which belongs to our vassals, the Mixtec. There is another near Malinaltepec—"

"Wait," Cortés says, and holds up his hand and calls Cáceres to come forward. The majordomo is holding quill and parchment. "We must write these names down, together with precise locations, so that we can send expeditions to these places. Now, this Zacatula, how many days is it from Tenochtitlán...?"

✺   ✺

When the inventory is finished, the Thunder Lords quit the room, and I am left alone with Motecuhzoma. He broods silently, staring at the corner of the room, where there is a yellow parrot in a silver cage. "Now I know how that little bird feels," he murmurs.

He takes the cage down from the wall, walks over to the terrace, and opens the cage. The bird hesitates for a moment, surprised, unsure, then launches itself from its prison and flaps away over the roofs of the palace.

He hurls the empty cage across the terrace. "The strangers have the gold sickness again, then?"

"It seems."

He watches the bird until it is no more than a speck. "I wonder what is so valuable about gold. Silver is harder to work, jade and quetzal feathers rarer and more beautiful to look at." I am surprised to see that he has a smile on his face. "Why do you do his bidding?"

"Why do you, my lord?"

"I have no choice." He studies me intently. "Do you trust this Lord Malinche?"

I am silent. How am I supposed to answer such a question?

"I have noticed your waist has thickened. Are you growing stout on *tamales,* or is his child swelling in your belly?"

I place a hand on my womb. "The future ruler of Mexico."

He shakes his head. "He will betray you. Your son will never rule Tenochtitlán."

For a moment I cannot get my breath. The words echo in the room; fragile clay dreams shatter on the marble floors. *He would not betray me.*

"Your son will never rule Tenochtitlán," he repeats.

"Nor will yours," I answer, and hurry away.

✳ ✳

I wake in the final watch of the night to find him already dressed in his quilted armor, staring out of the window, waiting impatiently for the dawn. There have been many nights like this one since we arrived in Tenochtitlán. These days he seems hardly to sleep at all.

"My lord."

"I did not mean to wake you."

"Come back to bed." He hesitates, then crawls under the blanket fully clothed. I mold my body around his; my head nestles into the crook of his arm. It is harder now, with my belly stretching to accommodate his son.

"What were you doing?"

"Thinking."

"About what?"

"About that morning at Merchant's Meeting... How did you know that the lord they sent to us was not Motecuhzoma?"

"It was the way the others behaved toward him."

"That was all?"

"How a man holds himself, how others hold themselves when they are with him... How else do you tell if a man is a king or a peasant?"

He kisses my forehead. "And how do I hold myself, my lady? Am I a king?"

"More than a king, my lord."

"More than a king..." It is growing light. I can make out the lines and hollows of his face. There is something wrong.

"What is it, my lord?"

He shakes his head.

"I would do anything for you. Anything."

He enfolds me in his arms. I wish I could always have his arms around me. I have cut myself loose from the ties of my ancestors and my people, but here at least I am safe. Yet since reaching Tenochtitlán, he has become a stranger to me. What can I do? I am helpless in his thrall.

He will betray you. Your son will never rule Tenochtitlán.

I hold him tighter. He will never betray me. I have his child in my belly. He is my destiny. Without him there is no meaning to my life.

❋   ❋

They are all here gathered in one of the great halls of audience, all of Motecuhzoma's elite: his brother Cuitláhuac, his nephew Lord Maize Cobs, all of his most favored noblemen, including the lords of Taluca and Tacuba. They are seated on mats with their wrists in manacles. The Thunder Lords ring the walls.

Motecuhzoma sits on a throne beside Cortés on the dais, his head bowed onto his chest. I myself stand at my lord's right shoulder.

He turns to me now, his eyes hard as flint. "My lord Motecuhzoma knows what he must say. Be sure that he does not stray from the speech he has been given."

I look at the emperor. He appears shrunken, as if his vitals have been hollowed out of his chest. His noblemen stare up at him, none of them afraid now to look openly on their god-king.

Motecuhzoma begins, his voice shrill, like a small bird caught in a trap. "Lords, you all know the legend of Feathered Serpent, who ruled this land many bundles of years before we, the Mexica, were led here by Hummingbird. You all know that on the day he left, he promised to return and end human sacrifice and reclaim his seat here in our kingdom. I believe that day has come. I have prayed to Hummingbird ... for enlightenment on this question, and ... and he has ... has advised me ..."

Motecuhzoma's voice breaks, and he cannot finish.

My lord raises an eyebrow. "Remind my lord that this is not a time for weeping but for celebration."

I do this, but it has little effect on the emperor's ill humor. He is making tiny mewing noises, like a baby in its crib. I am afraid he does not share my lord's view of the circumstances.

"Tell my lord Motecuhzoma we need to complete our business here!"

I nudge our whining lord. "Lord Malinche grows impatient," I tell him.

Motecuhzoma makes an effort to compose himself. "Feathered Serpent . . . wishes us . . . to hand over the throne . . . as is his right . . . and agree to pay him . . . yearly tribute . . . in gold."

"This is not Feathered Serpent," Cuitláhuac shouts. "You have allowed a thief into our house, and now he wants to take everything we have!"

"We should have attacked him before he reached our city," Lord Maize Cobs says, "as we planned to do at Chalco. By your cowardice and indecision, you have shamed the name of the Mexica!"

"I will never agree to this," Cuitláhuac says. "I would rather die!"

Motecuhzoma's face is wet with his tears. "We have no choice!"

Why is he doing this? I wonder. Does he still fear the gods, or is it, as Lord Maize Cobs says, just cowardice?

"What are they saying?" my lord asks me.

"They cannot agree among themselves."

"They have to obey their emperor. To do otherwise is treasonous."

"They say they would rather die."

"I can oblige them in their wish. By my conscience, they are an intractable people!" A pulse pounds in his temple. "Very well. We do not require their sanction at this point." He turns to one of his moles, who is scribbling on a piece of parchment. "Let it be known that I asked of Motecuhzoma, the emperor, if he agreed to become a vassal of the king of Spain and pay regular tribute, in gold, to the king and his agents, of a sum yet to be determined."

This is my cue; I turn to Motecuhzoma. "He wishes you to

formally declare your vassalage and accord him tribute in gold each year."

Motecuhzoma cannot speak. Instead, there is an almost imperceptible nod of the head.

"He accepts your terms."

"Very well. Let the royal notary record that Motecuhzoma is from today under the protection of his most Catholic majesty, the king of Spain, according to the bequest of the Holy Church." He glares at the gathering of rebel noblemen before him. "As for these others, keep them here, under guard, so they can do no mischief. Doña Marina, will you kindly ask my lord Motecuhzoma to rise."

The emperor, fearing further humiliation, gets slowly to his feet, aided by his own courtiers. My lord rises also. Unexpectedly he embraces him.

"Thank my lord Motecuhzoma for his help in this. Tell him he has nothing more to fear. I will care for him as if he were my own brother."

He leaves the room. Motecuhzoma stares blankly at the wall, his body stiff, startled by this final humiliation, this violation of his person.

"My lord conveys his thanks," I tell him, "and tells you not to fear. From now on he will treat you as his own brother." And then, in a whisper, I add through some mischief of my own: "But I do not think you should believe him."

 71

CORTÉS STRODE FROM the room, jubilant. He had within his grasp that treasure he had glimpsed from the first; he would hand to his king a new kingdom, fully made, fully realized, the most beautiful city ever made, together with unheard-of riches in gold. He would scrub the temples clean of their accursed idols, and the pyramids would become shrines to the Virgin. He would not only have served his king but fulfilled the destiny shaped for him by God. He would bring light to this darkness and save millions of lost souls for God. His deeds would bring him fame and honor such as no Spaniard since the Cid had achieved.

When it was done, he would ask the king's permission to be grandee of this land, to rule as absolute governor. How could any king refuse such a request?

He was just one small step from achieving his goal. There was just one more risk to take for God.

✳ ✳

The allotment of the treasure took place in the courtyard, in the presence of the royal notary. Cortés climbed on one of the carts that had been used to transport the artillery. A hush fell over the assembled soldiers. This was the moment they had been waiting for, when they would know how much of the fabulous wealth they had seen would be theirs. Each of them nursed a dream of what he would do with his share when he returned home, to the Indies or to Extremadura or to Castile.

The treasure-room had been unsealed and the trove melted down, to make for easier accounting: the gold figurines, the gold scabbards and gold collars with their pieces of jade and turquoise, the head-dresses and masks bossed with gold—all had been stripped and smelted into bars, stamped with the royal seal. No value had been placed on workmanship; it was only weight of metal and cut of stone that would buy land and power and women.

"I am aware that you all have been eagerly awaiting reward for your efforts," Cortés began. "You have fought long and hard and showed great loyalty and endurance, and I commend you for it."

A ripple of eagerness passed through the crowd. Yes, they had fought hard, and if sufferings were diamonds, they would all be grandees.

Their captain-general brought out a scroll of parchment and began to read.

"We have weighed that treasure we found in the hidden chamber, as well as those gifts so far presented to us by Motecuhzoma. We estimate them at a value of three hundred thousand crowns."

A gasp of excitement. Three hundred thousand crowns! A fortune!

"From this we must deduct the *quinto real,* the royal fifth of the king, and also a further fifth part, for the captain-general of the army, as was agreed by you all at Vera Cruz."

Somewhere in the crowd, Benítez folded his arms, impressed. So, Cortés has voted himself sixty thousand crowns. Not a bad sum.

Cortés went on: "This leaves us with a sum of one hundred and eighty thousand crowns. From this must be deducted my further expenses to fit the expedition in Cuba, and we have put aside a further sum to give as compensation to the governor in Cuba, to ensure that he causes none of you further trouble. There must also be a share for the Holy Church and an extra bonus for those men who brought with them their horses, which have proved such a decisive factor in our victories at the Tabasco River and at Tlaxcala. There should also be special consideration for those men who went to Spain to plead our case for us in the court at Toledo."

Well, Benítez thought. That means all the officers and captains, except perhaps for Ordaz and Mejía, will receive handsome commissions. That should ensure their loyalty.

"That leaves us with a sum of sixty-four thousand crowns."

There was a murmur of apprehension through the waiting soldiers.

"We have put aside ten thousand crowns for the families of those who have been called to heaven since the commencement of our expedition. We have split the remainder among the rest of you here, granting that we must also include the one hundred still remaining at the fort in Vera Cruz and granting also a double share for those with harquebuses and crossbows." Cortés consulted the figure on the scroll. "That will leave each man with around one hundred crowns."

Uproar.

The men shouted and waved their fists at Cortés. Long minutes passed before order was finally restored.

"Must you cause so much trouble over so little?" Cortés shouted. "This meager treasure is nothing to what we shall gain in the future!

There are hundreds of rich cities in this land and as many gold mines!"

"And when you allot the shares, we will again receive a dribble in the flood!" It was Norte, of all people.

"Be silent!" Cortés hissed. "Mind what you say or I will have you punished!"

"One hundred pesos will not buy me a new sword!" someone shouted.

"The allotment has been done in accordance with the law!" Cortés shouted. "May you all repent of your greed!" He jumped from the cart and stamped away, the men shouting their insults at his back.

Norte caught Benítez's eye. "One hundred pesos! Is this reward for all we have been through for him?"

"I did not think the gold concerned you."

"I am just a dirty Indian, of course, but what about the others? Flores lost an eye, Guzmán a part of his hand at Tlaxcala. They followed him to hell for one hundred pesos?"

"I will put your case to him, Norte. But it will do no good. Do you think I am happy about this?"

"You are a captain. He will take care of you!"

"I will see you have your proper reward. Even if it comes from my own purse."

"I want nothing from you, Benítez."

"Then what do you want?"

"I want . . . I want . . ." He shook his head. "I don't know. I don't know what I want anymore."

MALINALI

MY LORD TAKES breakfast with the emperor accompanied by Alvarado and Fray Olmedo. They sit down to a table piled with maize cakes sweetened with honey and a selection of meats: venison, dog, turkey, and wild fowl. When they are finished eating, they are brought sweet drinks of *chocolatl* in painted gourds. Then the women who have brought them their food wash their hands with soap-tree roots and anoint their feet with copal incense. My lord plays the emperor now: we have replaced a smooth-faced *Tlatoani* with a bearded one. I have placed him above me, and each day I feel more slave than helpmate.

When the servants have left, my lord beckons me over to translate for him.

"Mali, I want you to speak to Motecuhzoma for me. Ask him if he has made progress on the rededication of the Great Temple."

"I need a little more time," Motecuhzoma tells me, when I relay the question. "This is not something that may be quickly achieved."

For weeks now he has been stalling on this, and for weeks my lord has not pressed him. I wonder when the explosion will finally come.

"My captains grow insistent," my lord says. "I cannot stay them longer. Something must be done now."

Motecuhzoma gives me a shy smile. He still exercises power here. He relishes my lord's discomfort. He thinks the Thunder Lords still will not act against his priests without his approval. I think he underestimates them.

"Tell Lord Malinche it is in his best interests to wait," Motecuhzoma says.

I am losing heart for this. I believe my lord cares more for the gold now. He allows Motecuhzoma to manipulate him. Greed has the better of the god in him.

And yet I notice with some excitement the telltale pallor of his face, the angry blue pulse of that extraordinary vein at his temple. "Soon after I invited Motecuhzoma here to our palace, he promised me that the human sacrifices would stop. I have been patient. But the time for waiting has passed."

Perhaps this is the moment at last. I turn triumphantly on

Motecuhzoma. "My lord is very angry now. He has had enough of waiting."

Motecuhzoma does not see the danger; he has become complacent. He bestows on me an unctuous smile. "The decision is not mine. You cannot commit sacrilege in our temple. The gods would be very angry. They may not stop at taking all our lives."

How long they have been doing this, tossing responsibility for the gods between each other, like a hot coal taken from a brazier?

I pass on what Motecuhzoma has said, perhaps layer it with a little more arrogance than was intended.

"He toys with me, Mali," my lord murmurs.

"Yes, my lord."

Here it is again, the calm ferocity I remember from Cempoala and Cholula. Fray Olmedo leans forward, hoping to forestall the storm. "We must not act rashly," he whispers. "Day by day we make progress with my lord Motecuhzoma. Through the Lady Marina we have taught him the creed in his own tongue, even the Lord's Prayer."

My lord gives him a look of utter disdain.

Now it is Alvarado's turn. "*Caudillo*, you know how I deplore their devilish religion, but now is not the time to press the question of the temple. The treasury is bursting with gold; we must not risk its loss! Puertocarrero must soon return from Spain with reinforcements. Then we may be in a better position to force our demands!"

"We cannot stay our hand any longer and leave our honor unstained. We have done enough for ourselves. Now we must do something for the Lord." He gets to his feet and strides from the chamber. Fray Olmedo and Alvarado stare after him. I see fear on their faces, and at last I am glad. Now we hurry to the brink.

72

Whatever else they may say about us when the histories are written, Benítez thought, today we are magnificent.

He went ahead, Cortés close behind him, in full armor, sword drawn. The *caudillo* looked exultant, in the grip of some great emotion that had transformed his gray eyes into burning coals. Like Benítez, he took the steps two at a time, a picture of the Virgin and Babe under his left arm. Behind him came Alvarado, León, Jaramillo, Malinali, a dozen infantrymen with pikes and swords. Straggling far below, Father Olmedo holding the great cross, Aguilar with him.

As Benítez reached the top, one of the temple priests came at him with a flint knife. The razor-sharp blade of the Spaniard's sword sliced through the black robe, and the priest fell to his knees screaming and clutching at his entrails as they spilled from his wound.

Another came at him, but he brushed him aside with the hilt this time. He ran inside the temple and used the good Toledo steel to tear aside the curtain that led to the shrine.

He was prepared for the stench, but still it made him gag. Obsidian eyes gleamed from the darkness; into the lair of Satan now.

Another creature came at him from the gloom, but by now Alvarado and three of his infantry were there, and they wrestled the apparition onto the blood-caked floor and pinioned his arms and legs. The other priests shrieked like grackles; the great snakeskin drum boomed as others sounded the alarm. The noise was deafening.

The blood on the walls was like black paste, and thick as plaster. Something black and shriveled sizzled in a brazier of copal incense. Painted monsters glared at them from the shadows, stone serpents and skulls.

Cortés sheathed his sword and held out his right hand. Aguilar put the iron bar he had been carrying into the *caudillo*'s fist.

"Today we strike a blow for the Lord!" Cortés shouted, and leaped into the air, at the same time bringing the bar down in a broad, swinging arc into the face of the idol. The obsidian eye shattered, and the golden mask crashed to the stone floor.

The priests howled. Alvarado and his men kept them at bay.

Cortés reverently placed his picture of the Virgin in a niche in the wall, then fell to one knee and made the sign of the cross. He turned and pointed a trembling finger at the priests. "Tell them should they dare lay a finger on the blessed image of the Madonna, they shall answer for it!"

Malinali quickly shouted a translation of what he had said.

They howled again but retreated as he strode among them. "Doña Marina! Tell these ghouls to remove their devils and whitewash these walls or we shall do it for them!"

He strode back down the steps.

Benítez would have died for him at that moment. Such a calculating bastard, he thought, yet today he acts on a moment of passion. And not one of us here who would not follow him to hell when he is like this. I believe he truly thinks he can conquer the Mexica and their gods by the force of his will alone.

Today he understood why men loved Cortés. The *caudillo* had made him part of something that was both magnificent and just, a deed he could never have achieved if left to his own ambitions. Today this cheat, this schemer, this thief, has made me more than I am, and I will always be grateful.

✳　✳

Three days later several hundred priests ascended the *Templo Mayor* and, with elaborate care, laid Hummingbird and Smoking Mirror and Rain Bringer on mats of maguey fiber. Using ropes and greased planks, they lowered them from the temple to the court below, where they placed them on litters and carried them out of the city. All of this was done in absolute silence.

The walls and floors of the shrine were scrubbed and whitewashed, and Cortés's carpenters built a cross and an altar there. The next day almost the entire Spanish army marched into the temple precinct and ascended the steps for a special thanksgiving mass.

Cortés had achieved his dream. He was lord of Tenochtitlán now.

73

IT WAS A different Motecuhzoma today. What has happened? Cortés wondered. He seemed confident, even tranquil. He reclined on his *ypcalli* watching his dwarves and hunchbacks tumble and clown for him. They scattered when the Spaniards entered the room.

Motecuhzoma invited his overlords to sit and ordered that foaming cups of *chocolatl* be brought. Malinali took her place beside Cortés and relayed the emperor's pleasantries as he inquired after the well-being of his daughter and his niece. Cortés answered pleasantly, wondering privately what had brought on the emperor's change of mood but determined not to allow Motecuhzoma to see his unease.

He waited for the emperor to reveal his hand.

"There is something he wishes to discuss," Malinali said. "He says this is difficult for him, but he wants you to know he has always regarded you as his friend."

He thinks to use my own diplomatic words against me, Cortés thought. "Tell him I have always valued his friendship. He is like a brother to me."

Motecuhzoma launched into a long monologue. Cortés watched for Malinali's reaction. She appeared startled. He also noticed that the habitual wheedling tone in Motecuhzoma's voice was gone, an ominous sign.

Finally the soliloquy ended, and Malinali began a halting translation. "Motecuhzoma says that you are in great danger. He says that he, personally, does not wish to see you come to harm but that his gods are very angry with you. They have watched as you removed him by force from his palace, burned several of his chieftains in the plaza, stole his gold, and now insult the gods in their own temples. His priests tell him that Hummingbird and Smoking Mirror cannot remain in Mexico while you and your followers are here. Rather than have the gods desert them, his people must fall on you and kill you all, because they love their gods very much, as Motecuhzoma himself has tried to explain to you many times. The people wait only for Motecuhzoma's word. But he hopes that such bloodshed can be avoided. He is giving you the chance to leave peaceably."

"By my conscience, does he intend to dictate to me?"

"Let us see if he is so arrogant with my sword in his guts," Alvarado hissed.

"He has sworn allegiance to the king of Spain and his Holy Church," Aguilar said. "What he says is treasonous."

Cortés put up a hand to end their protests. How many times had they warned him against recklessness, and now they themselves wished to attack without knowing how their enemy was armed. "Mali, tell him we thank him for his concern," he said, his voice sweetly reasonable.

Alvarado gave a snort of outrage. "By Satan's spiny cock, why are we toadying to this—"

Cortés silenced him with a look.

"We thank him for his concern, . . . and we are sorry we have brought him so much trouble. Tell him we shall leave immediately . . . immediately we have ships to carry us back to our own lands. If he would permit us to fell wood in his forest and allow us some of his own carpenters, we shall set to work on the construction of these craft straightaway."

Motecuhzoma beamed. Cortés knew what he was thinking: the end of the nightmare was in sight.

"*Caudillo,*" Alvarado hissed, "they will never let us go! As soon as we release Motecuhzoma—"

"I understand that, but we must play for time!" He turned back to Malinali. "Tell Motecuhzoma we make this concession not out of fear for ourselves but because we wish to save this city from the complete destruction that would surely follow any battle. We would do this through concern for his own safety, as he, too, would surely perish in any conflict."

Motecuhzoma's smile vanished when he heard this. The threat was plain.

Cortés rose to leave without waiting for the emperor to formally end the audience. Something had shifted the delicate balance. He had to know what it was.

MALINALI

As soon as we reach our quarters, my lord removes his sword and buckler and flings it to a corner of the room. He upturns his writing desk with a booted foot, then hurls the throne Motecuhzoma has given him against the wall, loosening several of the studded gemstones and sending them spilling across the floor.

His moles and captains watch in terror.

Now he rounds on me. "What is going on?" he shouts.

"He no longer fears you, my lord."

"That much is obvious."

"It may have something to do with the changing of the season. The rains have stopped."

He stares at me, mystified. Perhaps he thinks I mock him. "Have you gone mad?"

"It is a new year on our calendar, my lord."

"What witchery and superstition are we talking of now?"

"My lord, we have reached the Stopping of the Rains, the first month of the new year. Last year was One Reed, Feathered Serpent's year, and a bad year for kings. It is now Two Flint, a more promising time. Perhaps Motecuhzoma feels he has outwaited you . . . perhaps even outwitted you. By delaying his destruction this long, he may feel he has nothing more to fear from challenging you. The calendar is in his favor."

"And do you believe this also?"

How can I tell him? If he truly were Feathered Serpent, he would understand. Our time has come and gone. The stars have moved in the sky; we reached for the golden moment, and our hands have come back empty. One Reed was his year, and my year, and now it is gone.

But my lord seems only amused by the inexorable turning of life. He smiles and kisses me gently on the forehead.

Why am I so pathetically grateful for these small crumbs of his affection? He comes to me now only when I am needed, and I lap up his small and graceless attentions as if they were mountains of jade.

He pulls away from me as Cáceres ushers Martín López into his apartments. López is one of the tallest of these Thunder Lords, a lean man with a sparse beard and the most enormous hands I have ever seen.

"López."

"You wanted to see me, *caudillo*."

"Indeed." Cortés ignores the wreckage he has left around the room. Cáceres meanwhile hurries to right the upturned throne, and Cortés settles himself upon it as if nothing had happened. López glances curiously at the table lying on its side in the corner and the spilled ink and parchment on the floor but wisely does not remark on it.

"You signed on to our expedition as a soldier," Cortés is saying, "but Alvarado tells me that in Cuba you earned your living as a carpenter and shipwright."

"Yes, my lord. I had some experience in the shipyards in Cádiz."

"Good. Do you think you could build a brigantine?"

López stares at my lord in astonishment but quickly recovers his wits. "With the right equipment, perhaps. I would need carpenters—"

"At Vera Cruz there are anchor chains, sails, rigging, and pitch from the fleet we were forced to scuttle at San Juan de Ulúa. If you had your choice of timber from the local forests and you were given skilled Indian carpenters, would that suit your needs?"

"I think so, my lord. How long do I have?"

"I do not wish you to hurry the task. Work slowly but contrive to look busy so that the Mexica believe you are in earnest. Can you do that?"

"As you command."

"You shall begin straightaway. You may take a dozen of our own carpenters with you. That will be all."

López bows and leaves, stunned at his sudden advancement.

There is a long silence in the room.

"Are we to leave here, then?" I ask.

Cortés laughs. "No, this is my capital, my seat. I shall never leave here until I am master. Any day Alonso will return from Spain with reinforcements. Then we shall instead dictate our terms to the Mexica."

"And should he fail to return?" one of the Thunder Lords asks.

"I shall not flee because my lord Motecuhzoma has the temerity to rattle his saber. If López gives me two brigantines, I shall use one to remove the gold, the other to send for more horses, men, and arms from Santo Domingo. Either way, I shall not leave the vale of Mexico."

I pay scant attention to this explanation. How many times have I heard my lord say he will do one thing when I know that he plans to do the opposite? A thought strikes me: What if he does decide to leave and sail back to the Cloud Lands? What will happen to me?

Without him I lose my value and my power. I have spoken with generals and emperors and even gods as equals, but without him I must return—at best—to loom and hearth. But that is unlikely because the Mexica cannot now let me live. Without the protection of the Thunder Lords, I will end my days stretched on a stone.

My lord must have divined what I was thinking, for he comes toward me and takes me in his arms. "Do not fret," he whispers. "I will never leave you, whatever happens."

I cling to him. When he holds me like this, the world is beautiful and safe. How could he leave me now? He is tied to me with bonds of blood. I have his son in my womb. Like Serpent Mother, the future gods of Mexico will come through me.

74

THE GIANT WITH the red beard watched, hands on his hips, as the culverin was maneuvered to the beach between two lighters. He had with him fourteen hundred men, eighty horses, more than a hundred crossbowmen, and almost as many musketeers. The litter of this great army spilled along the beach; men sweated up the dunes loaded with armor and weapons and crates of provisions; the cries of the sergeants at arms mixed with the hollow drum of horses' hooves on the hard sand and the frantic barking of lurchers.

This Cortés had overreached himself. His commission had been to make a few forays on the beaches, scout the ground. When he did not return, it was thought the expedition was lost. But then, a few months ago, a *nao* from his original fleet had called at one of the islands, and some sailors on board had boasted that Cortés had founded his own colony! Unfortunately this news had not reached Santiago de Cuba in time to intercept the *nao* on its way to Spain.

Well, if the story was true, he, Pánfilo de Narváez, would soon bring a halt to the nonsense. The sailors had also talked about a distant city of fantastic wealth. It would be a pleasure to do his duty and fill his pockets with gold at the same time.

But first he would deal with Cortés. There should be enough rope in the hold to do that.

※　※

"He seems sprightly this morning," Olid said. Cristobal Olid was captain of the guard at Motecuhzoma's apartments. Over the past months, he had come to know the emperor's moods very well, and this information, Cortés decided, was yet more bad news. *I much prefer him when he is bowed and depressed.*

Cortés, Alvarado beside him, went through to the apartments and discovered that, as Olid had said, Motecuhzoma was not only sprightly but positively animated. He was pacing the room when Cortés entered, talking to his caged birds, apparently eager for the audience to begin. He offered the two men a cup of *chocolatl*, which Cortés politely declined. Motecuhzoma then settled himself

on a mat, and the *caudillo* and his lieutenant took up their custom-
ary positions beside him.

"He asks how the building of the boats progresses," Malinali
said.

"Tell him progress is certain but a little slow. Our great war
canoes are not as simple to construct as one of the pirogues his
people use on the lake."

She conveyed this news to Motecuhzoma, but he did not
appear to be listening. He interrupted Malinali's translation to
clap his hands. A servant appeared carrying a great sheet of folded
bark paper, which he laid reverently in front of the emperor.
Motecuhzoma showed this codex to Cortés.

"His messengers brought this from the coast," Malinali said. "He
says that more of your companions have arrived from the Cloud
Lands in war canoes. Now you no longer have to wait here in
Tenochtitlán. The boats you require are already at the coast."

Cortés felt a surge of relief. At last! Puertocarrero with reinforcements and a commission from the king!

He bent over to study the codex and felt the blood drain from
his face. The glyphs and pictures showed thirteen Spanish *naos* and
brigantines at anchor above the palm trees. In the foreground there
were drawings of bearded soldiers, warhorses, and cannons camped
in the sand. The central figure was a fat man with a great red beard,
obviously the leader. It was quite evidently not Puertocarrero.

"Narváez!" he murmured.

✳ ✳

Cortés stamped out into the courtyard, where Ordaz was drilling
his harquebusiers. "Ordaz! Tell all the men that reinforcements
have arrived at the coast! Fire the muskets into the air! Make as
much noise as you can!"

He turned and walked away. All the men within earshot of this
exchange started cheering. Ordaz did as he had been ordered, shouting to his men to load their muskets with powder.

But Benítez saw the look on Cortés's face and realized that the
celebrations were premature. He ran after him. "*Caudillo,* is it true?
Has Puertocarrero returned from Spain?"

"It's not Puertocarrero," Cortés hissed. "It's Velázquez's toady, Pánfilo de Narváez, and the rest of those gold-hungry bastards from Cuba!"

"Narváez?"

"Keep your voice down! We have to keep this from the men until we decide what to do. We must allow the Mexica to think we are pleased with this news. One hint of dissent and they will fall on us like wolves!"

✲　✲

Night fell over the city. The Spaniards continued to celebrate. The last of the jars of Cuban wine were consumed, and the sounds of revelry echoed around the courtyards. Alone in his apartments, Cortés tried to ignore the shouting and singing as he wrestled with the dilemma he now faced. He paced the room while hot grease from the candle leaked onto the table and spread like a stain.

Elsewhere in the palace, other dramas were played out. The torches that lit the way along the passages still left long pools of darkness where a man might hide. And hide he did, for hours, waiting. It was as Rain Flower made her way back to Benítez's apartments around the Third Watch that he took her.

A hand clapped across her mouth, and he dragged her into an alcove. She could smell the sweat and drink on him. At first she thought it must be one of the Spanish soldiers, intoxicated from too much Cuban wine or Mexican *pulque*. She bit and kicked.

"Don't be frightened," a voice said to her in Chontal Maya. Norte. *Norte!*

She stopped struggling, and he took his hand away from her mouth.

"Are you mad?" she hissed. "Benítez will hang you if he finds out!"

"Only if he discovers us," he said, and pulled her hard against him. She could feel the heat and hardness of his penis.

She turned around and put her arms around his neck. She felt his tongue explore her mouth, his hands greedily squeezing her breasts. She bit down hard on his bottom lip, tasted the saltiness of his blood.

Norte cupped his hands to his face, making tiny animal screams. "You whore," he swore in Castilian. "Demon cunt! Mongrel bitch!"

"Don't ever touch me again. Love is a gift to be given, not stolen."

"I'm bleeding." Norte slumped to his haunches, sobbing. "Why did you do that? I'm bleeding."

Now that she had tamed him, she felt bad about what she had done. She knelt beside him. "I'm sorry," she said.

"What's the matter with you?"

"You frightened me. Is it bad?"

She tried to touch him, but he pushed her away. "You don't look at me anymore," he whimpered.

"Because you're not a Person anymore. You came here a devil. For a while you were a Person. Now you're a devil again."

"Why not? What is there for me as a Person? You spend all your time with Benítez."

"I was given to him."

"That never mattered to you at San Juan de Ulúa."

"That was yesterday. This is today. Besides, I have grown fond of him."

"And me?"

"I have grown less fond of you." She got slowly to her feet.

"I want you," he mumbled.

"I know what you want," she said. She slipped away, down the torch-lit hall, her bare feet silent on the stone, back to Benítez, her lover, her hairy lord, her Spaniard.

MALINALI

I WAKE TO the sound of weeping. I sit up, startled. It is coming from somewhere close by. I feel the small hairs rise on the back of my neck. There is an unearthly nature to it; perhaps a ghost.

I get up and throw a cloak about my shoulders. I hear my lord talking in the next room. Can he not hear it? I pick up the candle and push aside the belled curtain. Unwise for a pregnant woman to walk abroad in the night: the spirits of the dead can infect my baby, bring him bad luck. But I cannot ignore it.

The guard turns around, surprised.

"Can you hear that noise?" I ask him.

He shakes his head. "No, my lady."

Perhaps it is just my imagination. I gather the cloak tighter about my shoulders and go up to the roof. A breath of wind extinguishes the candle flame, but by the light of the new moon, I can now make out a figure hunched against the parapet. I move closer.

Rain Flower.

"Little Sister?" I kneel beside her. "What's wrong? Tell me. What are you doing up here? Is it Benítez? Has he beaten you?"

"It's not Benítez."

I put my arms around her. She is as stiff as wood. "What is it?"

"I'm frightened."

"There is nothing to be frightened of. We are safe here while we have Motecuhzoma."

"It's not the Mexica I am afraid of. I am frightened of your lord Cortés."

I feel myself stiffen. I do not want to hear any more calumny against him. Sometimes it seems to me that the whole world is against him.

"You have to stop him before it is too late."

"Stop him from doing what? Stop him freeing us from the Mexica?"

"These Thunder Lords are worse than the Mexica. They want to bring down all our gods, take all our gold and quetzal plumes, everything we have. They are as divine as coyotes with a corpse."

"You're just a baby. What do you know of these things?"

"You have seen how pitiless he can be. He pretends to be kind. He is a monster."

I slap her face. Rain Flower gapes at me.

"Stop it. I won't listen to any more. Go to bed."

"You're wrong, Little Mother." She gets to her feet and hurries away.

After she has gone, I sit alone on the roof for a long time, watching Sister Moon climb over Sleeping Woman, her silver turning the temple pyramids as white as bone. I try to think about what Rain Flower has said, but my mind is just a stew of panic and despair. I have come too far to believe that Rain Flower may be right.

 # 75

CORTÉS WAS WRITING a letter to the king of Spain by the light of a candle. When Cáceres ushered Benítez into the chamber, he laid the quill aside and invited him to sit in the ancient chair his Cuban servants had carried all the way from the coast. He himself now preferred the gilt throne Motecuhzoma had given him.

"Well, Benítez," he sighed, "these are worrying times, are they not?"

Benítez said nothing. What are you up to now, you old fox?

"A courier has just arrived from Vera Cruz with a letter from Sandoval. Five of Narváez's men came to the fortress and demanded his immediate surrender."

"What did he do about that?"

"What any self-respecting commander would do. He had them beaten and hog-tied. Indian porters are at this moment bringing them to Tenochtitlán roped together on poles. They should arrive here late tonight."

Typical of Sandoval to end an argument in such a decisive manner.

"I trust I can count on your loyalty in this crisis," Cortés said.

You bastard, Benítez thought. I admired you when you took on the priests in the *Templo Mayor*, but how I loathe you at all other times. "My loyalty has been sorely tested by recent events, my lord."

Cortés raised his eyebrows. "In what manner?"

"In the manner of the division of our treasure."

Cortés gave him a soft and golden smile, both knowing and contemptuous. He reached into the drawer of his writing desk and produced a gold bracelet, studded with large emeralds. He slid it across the table. "Will this make up for any ingratitude you perceive on my part?"

Benítez looked at the bracelet with some interest but did not touch it. "I was not concerned on my own account."

Cortés looked genuinely surprised. "Then what?"

"You have not dealt fairly with the men, *caudillo*. What you did was not just."

"The men?" He sounded incredulous.

"They fought hard at Tabasco and at Tlaxcala and endured much during the crossing of the *sierra*. One hundred pesos was not reward commensurate with their sufferings and valor."

Cortés leaned forward. "Is that the price of your loyalty, Benítez?"

"My loyalty does not have a price. It follows justice as naturally as water flows downhill."

"A very elegant speech," Cortés said, replacing the bracelet in the drawer. "You are a strange man, Benítez. I do not think I understand you completely."

"At least I sleep well."

"We have enough of sleeping when we die. But very well, if that is what you want, you can have it, though I think you will receive little gratitude for your greatness of heart. I shall give the men a greater share of our profits. There, you have my word on it. It may have to come from my own share, but never mind. In return I wish you to do something for me."

"My lord?"

"When Narváez's messengers arrive, we will need to impress them with what we have achieved here, show them that they have more to gain by joining with us than fighting against us. More flies are trapped with honey than with salt, are they not?"

"So what is it you wish me to do?"

MALINALI

HER SCREAMS WAKE me, and I know at once that it is Rain Flower. When I reach Benítez's quarters, the sentries are standing helplessly in the doorway, horror etched on their faces. Mendez, the doctor, is there, too, but he looks as frankly terrified as the two soldiers.

Rain Flower lies writhing on the floor, foam flecked on her lips. There is blood on her face and in her hair.

"What is wrong with her?" Mendez shouts.

I push my way past him into the room. A gourd lies upended in the corner. I pick it up, sniff at the contents. Rain Flower has been eating the flesh of the gods, sacred mushrooms.

"Where is Benítez?"

"He's with the captain-general, Cortés," one of the guards answers.

"Tenochtitlán is burning!" Rain Flower laughs, in Chontal Maya.

"What is she saying?" Mendez asks me.

"It is just a fever. I have seen it before. I will look after her."

He is relieved to pass over the responsibility for her. "All right. If you need to bleed her, let me know." He turns and leaves the room. I push the guards out of the door after him.

My Little Sister, my Rain Flower. Blood is leaking from the corner of her mouth. She has bitten her tongue. "They have set their dogs on all of us!"

I kneel down and bind her hands and feet with leather thongs to stop her injuring herself further. There is a large cut on her forehead. She must have hit her head on the floor when she fell. Fortunately the wound is not deep.

"God in heaven!"

Benítez stands in the doorway, his face gray. "What has happened here?"

"Mushrooms. There is nothing anyone can do. If she has eaten too many, she will die."

He kneels down beside her, tries to cradle her in his arms, but her body bucks and twists in the grip of her phantoms. "Lord Malinche is going to kill us all!"

I think about last night, how I slapped her. Did my indifference drive her to this? The sacred mushrooms are meant only for those about to die a flowery death on the sacrificial stone or the owl men when they wish to glimpse behind the curtains of the future. But such visions sometimes kill even the adepts. What is it that Rain Flower is seeking out, I wonder, the future or oblivion itself?

"Tenochtitlán is burning! The whole city is burning!"

Benítez drops to his knees and makes the sign of the cross. Here is something he does not understand, something beyond the veil. And in truth, I do not understand it either.

 **76**

RAIN FLOWER OPENED her eyes, found Benítez lying beside her, snoring, his head resting in the crook of his arm. She leaned over and kissed him gently on the forehead.

She sensed another presence in the room. She looked around, saw Malinali, her face shadowed by candlelight. She was kneeling on a reed mat, a cloth and a bowl of cool water between her knees.

"Little Sister," Malinali whispered.

"Little Mother."

Malinali stroked her hair. "It is passed."

"Was it very bad?"

"We did not know how much you had eaten."

"Just a spoonful. Then I lost my courage. And you, have you been here all night?"

She nodded. "With your hairy lord."

Rain Flower reached out a hand. My Mali, you have been both mother and sister to me. And best friend. But I have lost you to

Cortés, and soon you will learn to hate me for what I have to do. "I will be all right now. Should you not return to your lord's bed-chamber?"

"He does not need me these days." She patted her swelling belly. "I think my new shape displeases him." She leaned closer. "Did the dreams roll back the curtain for you, Little Sister? Did you see the future?"

"I saw many things," she whispered. "I hope what I saw was not the future."

MALINALI

JAGUAR KNIGHTS LOOM on coyote-colored walls; the silhouettes of the sentries dance in the long shadows of the torches. It is the final watch of the night, the time when wounded men rush to meet the shadow and infants come into the world still-born.

I hurry along the passageway to our apartments, longing for the warmth of my lord's body. This evening's events have exhausted me. I grow tired so quickly these days from the merest exertion. I do not know where Jaramillo comes from, where he has been hiding; but suddenly he is there beside me in the darkness. I gasp aloud. His pockmarked face seems even more grotesque in the torchlight.

"Pardon me, my lady. I did not mean to alarm you."

"What do you want?"

"A late hour to be walking the palace."

I do not like the way he looks at me. He is drunk; I can smell the stale Cuban wine on his breath.

He keeps pace beside me. "A pretty creature like yourself, you should not be out here. You should be in your captain's bed."

I keep walking.

"The *caudillo* is a lucky man to have two beautiful women to while away his nights."

I stop and stare at him.

"But of course, you know about Doña Ana?" A crooked smile. "You didn't? I beg your pardon. Well, good night, Doña Marina." He bows and walks away, his mischief done.

I run up the stairs to our apartment, past the guards, through the belled curtains.

The only light is the faint glimmer of a candle in a silver cup. Two bodies are sprawled on the sleeping mat. I stare at the sleek and copper-colored spine of the princess, her long black hair fanned across his chest, an arm entangled with his thigh.

I think I am going to be sick.

Be still, Malinali. It is in the nature of kings to have large appetites and many concubines. There is nothing you can do about this. Your petty jealousies have no place in the great scheme of his life. If you wake him now, to play the harping wife, it will win you nothing. You must be clever and wait your time.

It is because I am swollen and ugly with our baby that he no longer wants me. This will change. I have the son of Mexico in my belly, and nothing can change that.

I find a sleeping mat in another of the rooms and lie in the darkness, watching the dawn creep silently as a thief into the room. I will not weep. Although I love him, I have always known I was not born to happiness, not in that way. Why waste tears on what could never be?

But the tears do come, hot and blinding, a flood I cannot contain, for all my reason and knowledge. It is the curse of being a woman.

77

"You SHALL PAY for this," Father Ruíz de Guevarra shouted. "When Narváez discovers what you have done, he will have you and all your officers hanged for sedition!"

The priest had arrived during the Fourth Watch, with four others, all emissaries of Narváez. Their once-white shirts were now filthy rags, and there was blood in their beards where Sandoval and his men had been a little less than courteous. They had spent the last three nights laced tightly into hammocks, and their humor was not good.

"You are a fool, a braggart, and an ungrateful dog!"

Cortés smiled as if Guevarra had paid him a great compliment. He took him by the shoulder in comradely fashion and led him toward a low table in the corner of the room. It was piled with steaming plates of roasted rabbit, venison, beans, and maize cakes.

"How can I ever apologize to you for all that has happened?" Cortés said. "It is the fault of one of my junior officers. He will be most severely punished, but I fear his greatest fault is his overzealous nature. Please, take your ease here. You must be hungry."

Father Guevarra and his companions stared at Cortés in complete astonishment. After their treatment at the hands of Sandoval, an apology and fulsome hospitality were quite unexpected. They stared ravenously at the food.

"Please," Cortés urged them. "Eat."

Sandoval, at Cortés's instructions, had deprived them of everything but water for the three days of the journey, and they now fell on the food without further encouragement. As they ate, Cáceres placed gold bars at their elbows. They had been smelted and pressed by Cortés's own goldsmiths.

"What is this?" Guevarra asked, his mouth full.

"I would like to redress in some small measure all that has happened to you. Take the gold with my blessing. It is only a fraction of what my men have already received from me for their services. Around here we use gold to shoe our horses."

Benítez wondered what Norte with his one hundred pesos would think of that outrageous claim. Guevarra just stared at Cortés in bewilderment while continuing to shovel food in.

Cortés watched him eat with an expression of benign forbearance. "So, you were sent by my friend and comrade Narváez. What matters bring him here to New Spain?"

Guevarra had never heard the expression "New Spain." It was a term Cortés had only recently coined for Motecuhzoma's kingdom. It took him some moments to realize what Cortés meant.

"Narváez was sent here at Governor Velázquez's express command," Guevarra said, less sure of himself now. "He has named you a traitor, for you deliberately disobeyed his orders on this expedition. He wishes you brought back to Cuba in irons."

Cortés received this news with equanimity. "How is Narváez? He treats you well?"

Guevarra looked at his fellows. Narváez's niggardly ways were legend in Cuba. "Passably."

"I am most happy to hear this. As you are all aware, a generous commander is as rare as he is welcome." Alvarado and Benítez came to join them at the table, each with a gold medallion at his throat. The eyes of the newcomers were inevitably drawn to the jewelery. "Is that not so, Pedro?" Cortés said.

"Indeed, my lord," Alvarado said.

"Of course," Guevarra said, "generosity is not one of Narváez's greatest gifts."

Cortés contrived to look surprised.

"Our men would be disappointed to hear that," Alvarado said, "for we have all done well under our own captain-general."

Guevarra and the others stared at the gold bars.

"I hope the governor has not acted peremptorily," Cortés said. "He must recall that I am trained in law, indeed that he himself appointed me his justice of the peace in Santiago de Cuba. What we have done here is quite proper. We have established a colony in accordance with all statutes of law, which makes us answerable for our actions only to the king himself. Any day my courier will return with official endorsement. Should Velázquez act unjustly toward me, he—and his agents—will find themselves answerable to the Crown."

That perspective will not aid their digestion, Benítez thought.

Cortés leaned forward. "If the Mexica see that we are in disharmony with one another, all that we have gained here will be lost. At present we have the emperor of this great land under lock and key and have found here riches beyond comparison with anything discovered so far in the New World. Should Velázquez and his creature Narváez put all this at risk, I fear the king will be most displeased and there may be dire consequences."

Guevarra again studied the slab of gold.

Cortés smiled. "Does it not seem to you gentlemen that a great misunderstanding has taken place? If so, perhaps you might like to tell us how many men Narváez has brought with him and what his plans are?"

✳   ✳

Rain Flower made love to him with a ferocity he did not understand, kissed him as if he were life's breath itself, and when it was over, she wept. He rocked her in his arms, bewildered.

"What is wrong?" he said over and over, in his own Castilian, even though she could not understand. "What is wrong?"

"Forgive me," she whispered back, in Chontal Maya. "I don't know what is going to happen to us or what you will think of me at the next sunset. I only hope you will not hate me too much when it is done."

Of course, he did not understand what she was trying to tell him, and so he crooned to her and stroked her hair, utterly bewildered, utterly helpless.

✳   ✳

Torches crackled around the great hall. The Spaniards crowded in, shoulder-to-shoulder, only a handful left to patrol the walls. Cortés climbed onto a table to address them. On the floor in front of him was a pile of gold bars, gleaming dully in the torchlight.

"Gentlemen," Cortés said, and the hall fell silent.

They expected him to make a formal announcement of Puertocarrero's return, but the sight of so much gold unsettled them all.

"Gentlemen, many of you complained to me and my officers about the shares you received when the profits of the expedition thus far were divided. Now although I believe the division was done fairly, and in accordance with the provisions laid down at the start of our campaign, I have decided that because you have all served our cause so faithfully, and with such courage, I shall forgo a part of my own share of gold in order to reward you better. At the end of the meeting, therefore, you will all receive a further sum of gold from Alvarado, and I trust you will be satisfied."

He paused. Norte, standing at the back of the hall, thought: That was the honey, now here are the bees.

"This may be the last occasion you receive such a bonus, for Diego Velázquez, the governor of Cuba, intends you to have a new commander."

Silence.

"Two days ago you were told that our comrade, Alonso Puertocarrero, had returned from Spain. Unfortunately this is not the case. The ships that were sighted along the coast in fact belong to Governor Velázquez."

Norte looked around, saw the shock on the other men's faces.

"The man he has sent to relieve me is none other than his close friend Pánfilo de Narváez."

Hoots of derision.

"That fat goatfucker!"

"Now we have won the kingdom, the governor intends for Narváez to claim it for himself. Those of you who would like to throw yourselves at the mercy of his legendary generosity may go to join him. For myself I believe we have lawfully established our colony here, and I intend to resist this invasion of our territory."

Now some of the men were cheering. Oh, you idiots, Norte thought. Can you not see that he has just bought you off?

"Will you stand with me?" Cortés shouted.

The men were already baying for blood. Cortés once again had them in his palm. Their *caudillo* might be a cheat and a liar, but he was *their* cheat and liar. With Cortés they might at least get out with their lives and a little extra gold. With Narváez they were all dead and poor.

MALINALI

I LIE AWAKE in the darkness. The infant lord in my belly is restless and will not let me sleep. I go over and over in my mind what Rain Flower said to me that night on the roof. I cannot believe my father's prophecies will go unfulfilled. For me the future is already etched in stone on the great wheel.

The cry of a screech owl. A shadow moves against the wall; a silhouette appears for a moment against the window. I glimpse Little Sister's face, painted like a Mayan warrior.

The creak of timber, the flash of an obsidian knife unsheathed in the moonlight. A whisper of breath, and the candle dies.

I do not think; I have only time to react with my heart. I throw myself across his body, wait for the shock of the blow and the pain. My sudden movement wakes him, and he jerks upright. I hear the knife clatter to the floor.

He pushes me away, scrambling for his sword. He shouts for the guards. They rush in, one of them holding a flaming pine torch above his head.

The knife lies on the timber floor, its handle shaped as an eagle warrior and inlaid with turquoise and mother-of-pearl.

My lord looks at me. There is fear in his face, also astonishment. "You saved my life."

I am too shocked to speak.

"Did you see who it was?"

I remember Rain Flower's face, striped with paints of red and white, glimpsed just before the candle was extinguished. "I only saw a shadow," I whisper.

The next morning my lord Benítez looks for Rain Flower, but she is gone. He searches the palace for her everywhere, but there is no trace.

I wonder what made little Rain Flower do this terrible thing. When she was in the grip of the future, did she see something to persuade her to sharpen her knife on her return?

I do not want to believe it, for it will mean my own future is tainted by it.

I am convinced of my destiny; my father still whispers to me to look for the ledge as I fall. But Rain Flower is the nagging doubt, the thorn pressed into the sandal, the mosquito whining in the darkness, disallowing all rest.

 **78**

Cofre de Perote

THE COLD BREATH of the Nombre de Dios set Benítez shivering inside his cloak. His mare turned her head to the wind and stumbled on.

He felt numb. It surprised him; he had expected to feel something. But what? Rage perhaps, that she had betrayed him; shame that he had harbored an assassin in his own bed; grief that he had lost her. Should he also feel like a fool because he had never suspected? Or just pain, because he missed her smile, her gentleness, her caresses?

He cursed himself for his stubbornness and slowness at learning her language. Had she been trying to warn him that last night together? He remembered only falling asleep in her arms and waking to the shouts of the guards spreading the alarm through the palace.

He had reached out for her, and she was gone.

Doña Marina had sworn to Cortés that the assassin had been a Mexica warrior, and they had mostly believed her. That next morning Benítez rode out of Tenochtitlán with Cortés, and Rain Flower's absence was overlooked in the haste of their preparations. Those left behind would think she had gone with Benítez; those with the expedition would think she had stayed in the city.

He shivered again inside his quilted armor.

She was his enemy now. But oh, how he missed her.

Cempoala

León had always been popular, always knew how to stir a crowd. Narváez watched him now, surrounded by the younger officers, loud, laughing, dangerous. Around his neck was a large gold chain with two returns.

Damn him.

"León!" Narváez shouted. "Cousin!" He embraced him. "You look none the worse for your adventures! Have you come to join us?"

"I have come hoping to avert a catastrophe."

"A catastrophe? Whatever can you mean by that? How can the crushing of a traitor be called a catastrophe?"

The smile left León's face. "I do not think of Cortés as a traitor. Quite the contrary. He is a loyal and valorous subject of the king, and I will not abide such talk in my presence."

The men around fell silent; all laughter stopped. "So why have you come?"

"I hoped we could talk of peace and avert an ignominious defeat for you."

You insolent son of a whore! Narváez thought. I have at least three times as many soldiers and horses. I can crush Cortés's tiny army anytime I wish. How dare you speak to me this way!

"Let me deal with him," Salvatierra hissed in his ear. "Let us see how proud he is when we have him in chains!"

Fray Guevarra rushed forward. "My lord," he whispered, "when my comrades and I were taken prisoner by that dog Sandoval, Cortés proved himself to be a reasonable man. Surely he would not have released us had he desired only war? Let us talk with Señor León and see what he has to say."

Parleying with a man like Cortés went against all Narváez's instincts. But Guevarra was a priest, and his opinion could not easily be discounted. And León's own popularity must be taken into account. It will not sit well with my officers if I throw him in chains. Better see if I can win León over; then I will have a friend and a spy in the enemy camp.

"Now is not the time to talk about such matters," he said. "You must be fatigued from your journey. We can discuss this later, after food and some good Cuban wine."

It pained him to be pleasant. Smiling savagely, he turned and went back to his tent.

Tenochtitlán

"Give him a taste," Alvarado said.

The man writhed and twisted on the table, his ribs heaving as he screamed. There was the smell of burning fat. Alvarado wrinkled his nose in distaste, as if the taint in the air were the fault of his victim.

The priest had been tied, spread-eagled, to the table. His long and matted hair spilled over the edge, almost to the floor. The smell of him, even without the additional complications provided by Alvarado, made them all choke. Even Jaramillo looked pained.

But there was little sympathy for their victim here. An Indian was less deserving of compassion, of course, but the fact that he was a priest made their duty a pleasure. His tattered ears and blood-caked hair made him an unappetizing creature, a demon come to life. Alvarado wondered how many living hearts this particular devil had excised in the name of his gods.

They waited while Fray Díaz went outside to vomit. They could not proceed without a witness from the religious. Alvarado was disgusted. He thought a churchman, of all people, would have a stronger stomach.

When Fray Díaz came back into the room, he was pale and sweating.

"You are unwell?" Alvarado asked.

"I find the odors unpleasant."

"You have our sympathies. May we continue now?"

He nodded.

Alvarado turned to Aguilar, who was acting as interpreter for the interrogation. "Would you ask this creature if it is true that the Mexica plan to attack us and when this assault will take place."

Aguilar put the question to Laughs at Women, who relayed the words in *Náhuatl* to the man on the table. The priest groaned an answer.

Aguilar turned to Alvarado. "He claims to know nothing of this."

"He's lying," Alvarado said. He looked at Jaramillo. "Persuade him to search deeper for the truth."

Jaramillo removed a smoldering green oak log from the brazier with a pair of metal pincers and placed it on the priest's stomach. The man's eyes started from his head, and he bucked and rolled on the table. After a while his shrieking gave Alvarado a headache.

He signaled for the log to be removed. The priest was making a curious whooping noise. The devils coming out of him, Alvarado suspected. He examined the man's torso. It was black and blistered and weeping a straw-colored fluid.

"Brother Aguilar, will you please ask the prisoner again when the Mexica plan to attack us?"

Another long exchange.

"He asks what it is you want him to say."

"All we want is the truth."

Laughs at Women conferred once more with the unfortunate priest.

Finally Aguilar nodded, satisfied, and turned to his fellow Spaniards. "Laughs at Women has told him that we know the Mexica were planning to attack us. He has confessed our suspicions are correct. He does not know when it will take place, but it will be soon. Probably before the end of the festival."

"You are witness to his answer," Alvarado said to Fray Díaz. "This is our proof."

He turned toward the door.

"What shall we do with this one?" Jaramillo asked, indicating the groaning man on the table.

"Kill him," Alvarado said.

 **79**

Cempoala

"Look at him," Salvatierra said. "I have sailed from Spain on smaller ships."

They watched as *Gordo*'s servants maneuvered him up the steep, stepped terrace of the pyramid. There were eight of them, muscles straining, faces slick with sweat.

"It would be easier to drag a culverin up to the tower of the cathedral in Sevilla," Narváez said, and his officers laughed.

When *Gordo* was finally at the summit, Narváez beckoned to his interpreter, Francisco, a *Náhuatl*-speaking Indian captured by Grijalva. The four-way exchange was time-consuming, but it at least made possible some communication between his expedition and the *naturales*. Narváez indicated the picture of the Virgin that his men had found inside the shrine and the cache of gold objects, feather work, and cloaks.

"Ask him why he keeps all his gold in a Christian church," Narváez said.

He waited while his question was translated to *Gordo*, and the fat *cacique* formulated a reply.

"He says the gold does not belong to him, my lord. It belongs to Lord Malinche."

"Malinche? Who is this Malinche?"

It was explained to Narváez that Lord Malinche was a white god with a beard who had come from the Cloud Lands in a great war canoe, as Narváez had done. "He also says... I think... he says this Malinche is some sort of god."

Narváez stared at the fat chief in amazement. When he finally realized *Gordo* was referring to Cortés, he threw back his head and roared with laughter.

"He thinks Cortés has supernatural powers!" he shouted.

Salvatierra and the rest of his officers liked that. A knee-slapper.

Narváez wiped his eyes. For all their gold and fine architecture, these Indians were as credulous as the savages on Cuba. "Tell him the gold does not belong to Cortés; it is the property of the king of Spain. As we are his agents in this part of the New World, we will take care of it for him."

When *Gordo* heard this, he started to tremble and sweat.

"What's the matter with him?" Narváez snapped.

"He keeps saying that Lord Malinche will return and punish him for losing his gold," Francisco said.

"Tell him not to worry about it. I will deal with *Cortesillo!*" Narváez said. By Satan's ass! If these *naturales* could be intimidated by a ninny like Cortés, then he, Narváez, would have the whole country licking his boots in a week!

Tenochtitlán

The Feast of *Toxcatl,* the Waiting for the Rains.

Below them in the plaza, Hummingbird's chief priest, his face striped with charcoal, supervised the placing of a series of tall poles. Torches were suspended from them. These would illuminate the Dance of the Young Men the following night.

All that day the sounds of drums and flutes and chanting wore at the nerves. Young girls danced, their arms and thighs decorated with red feathers, feet raising clouds of dust from the dry red earth. A huge crowd assembled to watch.

The sun reached its zenith, a boiling yellow ball, casting no shadows. The great snakeskin drum in the *Templo Mayor* joined the frenzy, and the festival statue of Smoking Mirror, *Tezcatlipoca,* appeared at the edge of the plaza.

It was eighteen feet high, a hideous devil molded, so Malinali said, from a dough made from amaranth seeds and sacrificial blood. It was encrusted with jewels, huge earrings of turquoise, and a nose of beaten gold. It bore a headdress made from painted tree branches. Severed heads and human bones had been sewn to the cloak that draped this giant demon. An obsidian leg flashed in the sun.

Alvarado watched the procession from the parapet of the Face of the Water Lord palace, angry and afraid. The Tlaxcalans said the feast would culminate in the sacrifice of a young man dressed to impersonate one of their devilish idols. There was talk that the *naturales* would go ahead with this part of the barbaric ceremony in defiance of Cortés's orders to the contrary.

Aguilar stood beside him. He had his prayer book clutched to his breast as if it were a casket of precious jewels. "This is Satan's work," he murmured. "If Cortés were here, they would not dare flaunt their demons at us in this manner."

"He gave permission for this festival before he left," Alvarado said, bridling at this implied criticism. The *caudillo* had departed for the coast a few days before, intending to intercept Narváez's army. He had left Alvarado with just eighty soldiers to hold Tenochtitlán. And the Tlaxcalans, of course. They had refused to fight against other white gods, and Cortés had not pressed the point. Perhaps better that they did not teach their allies how to kill a Spaniard.

"He expressly forbade the practice of human sacrifice," Aguilar said.

Alvarado said nothing. He resented comparisons being drawn between his leadership and that of Cortés.

"I have spoken with one of the Tlaxcalan chiefs, Laughs at Women," Aguilar went on. "He speaks a little Chontal Maya, and we can understand each other passably well. He told me that after the sacrifice, the Mexica plan to restore their god *Huitzilopochtli* to the temple and burn our image of the blessed Virgin. He says he has seen the ropes and pulleys lying ready in the temple court."

"They would not dare."

Sweat on Aguilar's high forehead glistened in the sun. "He told me also that the stakes you see before you are used for human sacrifice. One of the Mexica boasted to him that they were going to eat us all. But first they would spice us with onions, to disguise the pestilential smell."

Alvarado's right hand closed to a fist on the palace wall.

"It would seem they intend to attack us after Narváez has defeated Cortés. The big stake is for *Tonatiuh*. I suppose they meant you."

"That is just Indian talk!" Alvarado turned away, trembling with fury born of terror. He did not want to imagine falling prey to these savages or think about what they might do to him before he died. Aguilar could be right: this festival was deliberate provocation. Should he sit here and endure their insults, wait for them to slaughter him and his men like dogs?

He thought about what Cortés had done at Cholula, and suddenly he knew what a good commander would do.

 **80**

Cempoala

GORDO'S SERVANTS HAD prepared a feast for them; Cuban porters had brought chairs and tables from his ships on the coast so Narváez could dine in his tent in the same splendor he had enjoyed in his own house in Santiago de Cuba. They even brought his silver service.

He was master and host, but it was León who held court, and as he ate, he regaled the younger officers with his adventures over the last fifteen months. Narváez felt a prickle of irritation at how they hung on his words, lapping them up like kittens with warm milk.

"When we first arrived in New Spain," León was saying, "I was one of Cortés's loudest critics. It seemed to me we had left ourselves exposed to military disaster and had possibly even contravened the governor's orders. Even when I was persuaded that my brother officers were acting quite legally in establishing a colony—"

An eruption of coughing. Salvatierra almost choked on his wine. But Narváez said nothing. *I shall leave him enough rope to hang himself.*

"—Even when I was persuaded that my fellow officers were acting properly, I was still of the opinion that we courted disaster. We were so few, in a hostile land, against so many. But Cortés did not waver. And as our victories and our fortunes grew, day by day, I was persuaded that here was a man who could win us all untold fame and wealth."

The candlelight reflected in the gold collar at his throat, making his point for him.

"Indeed, we have already won for ourselves and our king a fortune in gold and precious jewels. We are masters of Tenochtitlán, which is the most wondrous city I have ever seen, and where Cortés is esteemed as a great lord. He has claimed these lands for Spain and brought many of the *naturales* for conversion to the one and holy faith."

"Perhaps he will do Spain one further service," Narváez said. "He can come and surrender peaceably to me, so he may answer the charges brought against him by the governor of Cuba."

"The governor's authority is not recognized here," León answered. "We are directly responsible to the Crown. Indeed, you are now entering the realm of my lord's friend, Motecuhzoma, who is a sworn vassal of the king and under his protection. By such an action you risk having your army destroyed and your lives held forfeit."

Narváez stared at him, speechless with rage and astonishment.

"You dare to threaten us?" Salvatierra snarled.

"Gentlemen," Fray Guevarra said quickly, "I am sure there is an amicable way to solve our differences. Is there not, Señor León?"

"My lord Cortés feels your arrival here is opportune. He is willing to allow you to explore the coast between Vera Cruz and the Grijalva River. In fact, he would consider it a great service. So would His Majesty Charles, as it would consolidate this kingdom for the Crown."

"I will see your *Cortesillo* in hell!" Salvatierra shouted.

"I am sure that is where you will one day find yourself. But I doubt you will see my lord Cortés there, though someday he may gaze down at you from above."

Salvatierra jumped to his feet, hand on his sword. Narváez restrained him. If it came to a duel, León would fillet him into thin strips.

Narváez looked around the room. Some of his officers seemed amused by León's posturing. Narváez decided it was time to play his ace. "I think you are wrong in saying that this Motecuhzoma is friend only to your lord. He has also sent tribute to us, much of it in gold. You seem surprised. Do you still believe *Cortesillo* has a mortgage on the emperor's friendship?"

For the first time, León was off balance. Narváez pressed his advantage.

"I intend to make your Cortés answerable for what he has done. At the same time, I shall free the emperor from his illegal imprisonment, in return for a great deal more gold."

León stood up. "In that case, I must tell you that my lord Cortés will not be answerable for your safety."

"My safety! I have an army of fifteen hundred men and thirty cannon. Do you suppose for one moment your little band frightens me?"

"We have beaten greater armies than yours these last twelve months."

"Your attitude disappoints me, León. I thought you had more sense. I was even about to offer you a senior position in my command."

"I could not betray someone who has done so much to further the fortunes of his country and his church."

Astounding, Narváez thought. When did little *Cortesillo* come to command so much loyalty?

"Tell him I will roast his ears and eat them," Salvatierra said.

"A fine attitude for a cannibal, but not for a Spaniard."

"I think you should leave us now," Narváez said, "before you impose too far on my patience and generosity."

"I should not dream of staying a moment longer in such company."

He walked out. Narváez felt the eyes of his junior officers on him. This had not gone well.

Later, when they were alone, he told Salvatierra he did not want León to leave the camp. "Wait till everyone is asleep, then put him in chains." Salvatierra beamed. He hurried away to issue the order. His men conducted a thorough search, but they found no sign of León. Someone must have warned him.

❈　❈

León rode slowly west, guided by a full moon. Cortés was right, the morale in Narváez's camp was low, the officers suspicious of their commander and of each other. The twenty thousand *castellanos* he had offered to each captain who would join them had found their way into many purses. Fray Guevarra had told everyone what he had seen in Tenochtitlán, how Cortés's troops roamed the fortress with their pockets bulging with gold.

Cortés would be less pleased to hear of Motecuhzoma's perfidy. León himself worried about what was happening in Tenochtitlán; he hoped Alvarado knew how to play the king as well as their *caudillo*.

Tenochtitlán

As the sun dropped down the sky, the drums beat faster, quickening the rhythm of ten thousand hearts. The statue of Smoking Mirror was dragged to the steps of the great pyramid and the Mexica gathered there for the Dance of the Young Men. There were six hundred dancers in the plaza, the cream of the noble families, their finest sons. People from all over the city crowded into *Templo Mayor* to watch.

Ta-tam, ta-tam, ta-tam . . .

The drummer stood, legs astride, at a snakeskin *huehuetl* drum, his hands a blur of movement, quickening the pace.

The men danced around him. They wore spectacular costumes, cloaks woven with brightly colored feathers, and on their legs, greaves of ocelot skin sewn with golden bells that jangled as they danced. Their shaven skulls were brilliant with paint and quetzal plumes. They all wore nose plugs and labrets of jade or shell.

The hammer of drums, the pulse of blood.

Ta-tam, ta-tam, ta-tam . . .

They danced faster and faster.

At the Eagle Gate, the Gate of the Reed, and the Gate of the Obsidian Serpent, armed Spaniards arrived unannounced, slipping through the crowd, taking up position in the narrow doorways. . . .

✳ ✳

As he danced, Falling Eagle saw Spaniards moving among the crowd. They were wearing swords, steel armor, and helmets. A thought occurred to him: here are thousands of our best warriors, trapped

and unarmed in this court. Surely no enemy could be so treacherous, so cowardly, as to attack us when we have no means to defend
ourselves?

He saw *Tonatiuh* standing on the steps of the Great Pyramid, the
setting sun reflected on his breastplate, watching. Another of the
Thunder Lords, the one they called Jaramillo, was grinning crazily,
as if he had drunk too much *pulque.*

The dancers leaped and spun.

Ta-tam, ta-tam, ta-tam . . .

More soldiers, holding firesticks, were climbing the steps of the
temple, crouching to load.

Alvarado was reaching for his sword.

No.

No!

✳ ✳

"*¡Mueran!*" Alvarado shouted. "Kill them!"

The harquebuses cracked, the smell of cordite drifted across the
plaza. Screams, panic; everyone rushed toward the gates. A Spaniard
was hacking at the drummer with his sword. He struck his arms,
then his head.

Falling Eagle stood quite still, searching for escape.

The Spaniards were everywhere, slashing with their swords. He
turned and ran toward the Gate of the Reed. A Spaniard loomed in
front of him and he veered away, felt the breath of his sword as it
arced down. He veered again, dodging and twisting. He saw a
Spaniard with a brown curly beard tearing the jewels from the body
of the bloodied Mexica warrior at his feet.

Falling Eagle reached the gate but there was no way through.
The Spaniards were gathered there shoulder to shoulder, slicing at
anyone who came near with their swords. He found strength in his
terror. He picked up one of the bodies at his feet, lifted it over his
head, and tossed it at one of the soldiers. The man lost his balance
and fell. Falling Eagle vaulted over him and ran through the gate.

81

Cempoala

RAIN.

Gray sheets of it, flooding the river, throwing a pall over the flat horizon. Cortés's small army, bolstered by reinforcements from Sandoval, struggled on through the mud. The sound of their approach was muffled by the rain; a scouting party surprised two of Narváez's sentries and took them prisoner. The battle had been joined.

※ ※

You upstart, Carrasco thought.

I heard of you in Cuba. I remember the scandal when you refused to marry Catalina Suárez, whose father was so friendly with the governor. Escudero arrested you on charges of sedition, and the governor had to force you to act honorably.

I've even seen you carousing in Santiago de Cuba in your fine clothes, you and your *hidalgo* friends, always talking and laughing too loud, acting as if you were grandees because you owned a little bit of dirt on some godforsaken heathen island. Now look at you. Because a few *naturales* have run away from you, you think you are a king.

The torches crackled and smoked in the rain, the rain dripping down through the branches of the great ceiba tree. Carrasco struggled back to his feet, his boots slipping in the slick mud. He was encumbered by the ropes that held his wrists behind his back.

"What is your name?" a voice said. He looked up. Cortés.

"Juan Carrasco," he said.

Sandoval pushed him back into the mud and kicked him in the ribs. "Show some respect."

"Juan Carrasco . . . my lord."

"Do you know who I am, Juan Carrasco?"

"You are Hernán Cortés." He grunted at the pain in his ribs. "You own a gold mine and an *encomienda* on Cuba."

Cortés crouched down so that his face was inches away from his prisoner's. "No, I am not that Hernán Cortés. I am the Hernán Cortés who is the master of this whole kingdom. You would do well to remember that."

Fool! Carrasco thought.

"I want to know," Cortés went on, "how Narváez has deployed his forces." He held out a purse, emptied its contents into his palm. A few jade and turquoise stones glittered in the dull light of the torch. "These are yours if you tell me."

The rain slapped on the leaves above their head.

"I'm waiting," Cortés said, and Carrasco felt the first thrill of fear.

Suddenly Cortés was on top of him, his fingers clawing at his throat. Carrasco kicked helplessly. He couldn't breathe, couldn't breathe...

"You are not going to stand in the way of my *entrada*, you little peasant! Do you understand me? This is New Spain, my kingdom!"

Saliva spilled from Cortés's mouth onto Carrasco's cheek.

"I will make you talk, even if I have to cut off your toes and ears and force them down your throat!"

Couldn't breathe.

"Talk to me!"

He tried to nod his head, desperate to surrender, but the fingers were clamped too tightly around his throat. He lost control of his bowels. He saw someone struggling with Cortés, trying to drag him away, and then black spots appeared in front of his eyes, and he passed out.

✳   ✳

He might have killed him, Benítez thought. If I had not intervened he might have killed him. My lord Cortés is terrifying when he is angered.

A helmet of river water thrown in Carrasco's face and he had recovered quickly enough. He had then told them all they wanted to know: Narváez had made his headquarters in the temple where a year ago Cortés held a knife to *Gordo's* throat. The artillery had been drawn up in front, the cavalry divided, so that forty *jinetas* were now isolated on the road to the west. There were no patrols, Carrasco said, as Salvatierra had told them Cortés would not dare attack at night.

The *caudillo*'s brutal methods were justified with quick results, Benítez supposed. But he could not forget the look on Cortés's face when he had his fingers around Carrasco's throat.

The man was mad.

But then perhaps only a madman would have dared so much; only a madman would dare what he proposed to do now.

MALINALI

RAIN DRIPS FROM helmets, soaks into quilted armor, leaks down tunics, and marches down the spines of shivering men. My lord's soldiers are cold and hungry, exhausted from the long march from Tenochtitlán.

My lord turns his horse to face them, resplendent even on this cold and black night in breastplate and plumed burgonet. One of his moles, Cáceres, stands beside his horse holding a pine torch. It sizzles in the rain.

And he starts to talk, to mesmerize: "Tonight, gentlemen, you carve your names in the histories. You can choose to die here or go on to make your fortunes here in this land of New Spain."

The steady patter of rain on the soft earth and ripe leaves.

"You will recall that it was the governor himself who made me commander of this expedition, with orders to explore and barter along this coast. This I attempted to do. But you will also remember that while we were at San Juan de Ulúa, it was demanded of me that we establish our own colony there. I wished all that time to return to Cuba, but at your insistence we stayed on here, and time has proved you all wise in pressing that decision.

"You did me the honor of voting me captain-general of your colony until His Majesty's pleasure was known to us. How often in this past year did we succeed when all odds were against us? How much suffering and death have we known in carrying Christ's banner into these heathen lands?

"Now the governor's lackey, Narváez, lands on these shores and declares war on you, wishing to take away all you have so gloriously won. Shall we meekly stand aside and let him march in? Not if we are men, not if we are Spaniards! This usurper will not rob us of the riches and the glory that are rightfully ours!

"They are greater in number, yes, but when has that deterred us? We battled thousands on the Tabasco River, *tens* of thousands on the plains of Tlaxcala. We are hardened in battle these many months, and they are not. Furthermore, our comrade León tells me there is great discontent in their camp. Many are sick with the fevers of the coast, and others recognize the justness of our cause and have no stomach for the fight.

"The storm has made them incautious. We will launch a surprise attack against their cannons while Sandoval takes a squadron of men to capture Narváez himself. When he is taken, the rest will put down their arms, for they will have no heart to continue the battle without him.

"So let us gird ourselves. Rather we die here today, if that is God's will, than let these scoundrels take from us what is rightfully ours!"

His soldiers cheer. His eyes seem to glow in the darkness, the only light in this whole black valley. How can we not believe, when he talks to us this way? Outnumbered, tired, and hungry, his moles and soldiers are spoiling for a fight. He drags us all along in his wake. Feathered Serpent is returned, and there is no standing against him.

82

SHOUTS OF ALARM, men running for their weapons, the moon hidden by ink-black clouds. Narváez stared into the darkness. All around him he saw lighted matches as Cortés's harquebusiers prepared to fire their muskets. The rain must have masked the sounds of their approach. Cortés had surrounded them. But it was impossible. How had he mustered such a force?

The captain of the artillery shouted at his men to load the cannons. A panicked voice screamed back that the cannons had been spiked, the firing holes had been plugged with wax.

A volley of musket fire, the whine of arrows, men screaming in pain in the darkness.

Salvatierra tugged at his sleeve. "We must withdraw!"

A single cannon fired, then fell abruptly silent. Narváez heard infantry charging across the court. He ran after Salvatierra, up the steps toward his sanctuary atop the pyramid.

※　※

I am going to die, Benítez thought.

He had charged the steps at the head of Sandoval's pikemen. The moon appeared for a moment from behind the clouds, silhouetting their opponents against a smattering of stars. At that moment a giant came at him, perhaps Narváez himself, wielding a great two-handed broadsword, the *montante*. He tried to ward off the blow; there was a sparking clash of steel, and he felt his sword wrenched from his grasp. He fell sideways onto the steps, Narváez standing over him, the massive sword raised above his head a second time.

I am going to die.

He was not sure how it happened. Perhaps Narváez slipped on the rain-slick stone; somehow the fatal blow was delayed. Benítez took advantage of this reprieve to search desperately in the darkness for a weapon. His fingers closed around a fallen pikestaff. He thrust it desperately toward his assailant, heard Narváez scream.

"Holy Mary protect me! They have killed me and destroyed my eye!"

"Victory for Cortés!" someone shouted. "Narváez has fallen!"

Benítez clambered to his feet, saw Martín López, the tallest man in their force, rush forward with a lighted brand and set fire to the thatched roof of the temple. The sky glowed red. Narváez's soldiers streamed out of the smoke, throwing down their weapons and screaming for mercy.

The luck of Cortés has won out again, Benítez thought. And today a little of it even rubbed off on me.

MALINALI

NARVÁEZ LIES ON the surgeon's table, a blood-soaked cloth bound over his left eye. His face and beard are caked with blood, and his wrists are chained in front of him.

My lord enters, pushing aside the canvas tent flap. His hair is matted with rain and sweat; his chest heaves from his exertions. Rain glistens on his armor like dew on a cactus leaf, and he holds his sword, unsheathed, in his right fist. He stands in the entrance, staring at his adversary.

Narváez opens his one good eye. "You intend to murder me?" he asks, as if the matter is of no concern to him.

"You are my prisoner. You have nothing to fear. I have placed you under my protection."

Narváez appears relieved. He does not understand that my lord's protection does not extend further than his next whim. León appears for a moment from the darkness outside the tent. He is here to report on the outcome of our latest battle: "We have lost two dead, against fifteen of theirs. There are perhaps another one hundred and fifty wounded, mostly theirs."

My lord is angry that so many useful men have been hurt when we will surely need them all when we return to Tenochtitlán. "You see what you have done?" he says to Narváez.

Narváez appears unconcerned by his losses, or ours. He is more troubled by the wound to his pride. "It has been a great feat, your defeat of me," he says.

"Indeed? I regard it as the least of my achievements in New Spain."

Narváez scowls, does not want to believe it. He notices my presence in the tent for the first time. "Who is this? Is this your whore?"

"Go sit on the devil's cock. I am no one's whore."

Is there the suspicion of a smile on my lord's lips? Hard to tell. Narváez is gaping at me as if he had just been rebuked by an animal or a bird of the forest. Does he think a Person cannot learn such a simple language as his? "She speaks Spanish like you or I, Narváez," my lord tells him, and there is a proprietorial pride in his voice that I do not dislike, "and several other tongues besides. You would do well not to cross swords with her. I shall leave you to her tender mercies, for now."

He stalks out.

The storm has eased, just a drizzle of rain on the canvas now. Narváez lies there for a long time without speaking. "Do you know who that man is?" he asks me suddenly, and I am startled, for I had thought he had passed out from the pain of his wound.

I think he is trying to trick me on some religious matter and say nothing.

"In Cuba we called him *Cortesillo,* little Cortés. He has an *encomienda* with a few cattle leases. He studied some law at Salamanca University and thought himself a lawyer. So Governor Velázquez, fool that he is, made him a magistrate in Santiago de Cuba. He made a little money mining gold on the Duabán River, and you would have thought he was the grandee of Valladolid. Then that idiot Velázquez—I warned him about this—puts him in command of a small expedition to the coast, and now look, he thinks himself a great general and explorer."

"He has done wonderful things here, heroic things."

"Then we must be talking about a different Cortés."

"Or perhaps between this Cloud Land you talk of and here, a god came and entered him. For he has behaved like a god."

Narváez grunted at the pain in his eye. "Where is that damn doctor?" He took a deep breath and held it for a long time. He released it slowly, battling against the pain. "This 'god' of yours betrayed his own lord in Cuba. He was sent here to explore the coast; instead, he tries to invade with five hundred men and take all the gold for himself. You see? He is a traitor and a braggart and a thief."

I do not understand a word he is saying, and I shall not stand here to listen to calumnies against my lord Cortés. I leave Narváez there to suffer and go in search of my lord.

✷ ✷

He stands alone, a cloak wrapped around his shoulders, watching the sun rise over the jungle. The debris of the battle lies around the temple courtyard: abandoned weapons, a few bloodied rags. The smell of smoke hangs heavy in the air.

"What did Narváez say to you about me?"

"He says you are just a man."

"Well, he is right in that."

The jungle is waking. The cry of birds, the rattle of insects. "I think not."

"Why do you persist in making me more than I am? He is right. I am the son of a poor *hidalgo*. You see the way your own poor farmers live, fertilizing their fields with human manure, wearing only loincloths, eating maize cakes and gruel? Yet the humblest of them has a more contented life than mine once was. I was born in the poorest part of Spain: flat dust to the horizon in summer, frozen mud in the winter. My family had its own coat of arms, yet our greatest luxury was to eat ham and eggs on a Sunday. While I was at university, I had patches in my breeches, and my friends laughed at me behind my back.

"I was rich in dreams is all. I dreamed my way through my poverty. I always knew I was more than what I seemed to be.

That knowledge was set in my heart like a precious stone, and until now it has brought me no peace.

"You see, Mali, I always believed that with strength and determination, a man might change his circumstance. And here, in Mexico, I have remade myself, become more than I was before. Here I am no longer *Cortesillo,* the womanizer, the braggart, the gambler, the petty landowner and law student. Here I am Lord Malinche. Here, tonight, this Lord Malinche has defeated proud men who would not have deigned speak to me on the street in Salamanca or Toledo. Here . . . here I really am a king."

I stand closer, and he wraps his cloak around my shoulders. His body burns like a furnace. Much of this I already knew, or had guessed. It is the story of a man chosen and inspired by gods.

Poor Rain Flower. Did she realize what she had almost done?

I wonder where you are now, Little Sister. If you had not run away, I might still have protected you. No one would have suspected that a *Mexicatl* woman would dare such a thing. I would not have whispered your name under the most terrible of tortures. Why did you do it? If only you had not eaten the flesh of the gods. It made you mad.

I wonder where you are now . . .

 **83**

CORTÉS SAT ON a stone bench, steam rising from the cloak about his shoulders. Narváez's officers and men waited in line to pay him their respects and pledge him their future loyalty. In return Cortés had promised that they would have their horses and their weapons returned to them. Only Narváez and Salvatierra were exempt from the amnesty. They were to be kept in chains in the fort at Vera Cruz.

It had indeed been a great victory. The Virgin had watched over him once again. The fireflies that had swarmed in the rain had been mistaken by Narváez's men for hundreds of musketeers lighting matches to their weapons. The rain had also made Narváez's gunpowder too damp to use.

He had also bought his own luck with the gold *castellanos* that León had distributed in Narváez's camp a few days ago. It had persuaded certain officers to put wax in the firing pins of the larger artillery pieces.

Narváez's arrival was not the end but a new beginning. Cortés now commanded an army of thirteen hundred men and a hundred cavalry—enough, surely, to secure their future in New Spain.

After he had received pledges from each of his new recruits, he climbed onto a plinth to thank them all for their support and assure them of a triumphant welcome when they reached Tenochtitlán. "You will all be showered with gifts," he shouted over their excited laughter. "There are crowds to cheer us wherever we go, and all Mexico bows at my feet!

"You cannot imagine the glory that awaits you!"

84

Tenochtitlán

UTTER SILENCE.

It was as though there were not a soul alive in the whole valley. Even the Xolo dogs were silent. There were no canoes on the lake, not one farmer in the *chinampas* or on the causeway to watch them enter. As they drew closer to the city, they were relieved to hear the sound of trumpets from the walls of the Face of the Water Lord palace. A single cannon shot welcomed them, the only sign that the city was not entirely deserted.

Cortés felt his face burning with humiliation. He heard one of

Narváez's officers shout to a comrade: "Hey, Gonzalo! If the people get too close to your horse, force them back with your lance!"

Several men laughed.

"Oh, but these garlands of flowers are heavy about my neck!" the one called Gonzalo shouted back.

"I have never seen such crowds."

More laughter.

"It is like the marketplace in Sevilla."

"At midnight!"

Cortés spurred his horse on, away from these idiots. He looked back only once to confirm his worst suspicions. They were no longer alone. In the distance he could see Mexica warriors gathering behind them on the causeway.

He could almost hear the trap slam shut behind him.

✹ ✹

"How could this have happened?"

"My lord, they were plotting against us, just as they did at Cholula," Alvarado pleaded. "One of the priests we brought here confessed in the presence of witnesses—"

"Tenochtitlán is not the same as Cholula! They were planning a festival, no more. Now you have turned the whole capital against us!"

"They have just thrown a few stones and lances," Alvarado protested, his voice sulky.

"They were waiting for us to return! So they would have us all trapped here in their prison!"

"We will have Motecuhzoma talk to the people. Perhaps you can pretend to be angry at me to placate him."

Pretend. Alvarado truly does not understand the nature of the blunder he has made. Perhaps that is my own fault. Alvarado is a loyal and good soldier, but I entrusted him with too much responsibility, elevated him beyond his intelligence.

Malinali entered the room from Motecuhzoma's apartments. Olid, the captain of Motecuhzoma's guard, accompanied her.

"My lord, Motecuhzoma wishes urgently to speak with you," she said.

"I would rather talk to my dog."

It was Olid who interjected on the emperor's behalf. "But my lord, he is weeping most piteously and is greatly distraught. Perhaps we could—"

"By my conscience! Who is your commander, me or Mote-cuhzoma?" The rebuke silenced him. In truth, the emperor's guards have spent too long with him. They treat him as if he were their favorite uncle. "Our great friend Motecuhzoma has had secret relations with Narváez. I have always treated him as I would my own brother, and now he has betrayed me!"

I came so close! Cortés thought. I could have presented to His Majesty this great city intact, without fighting, but because of Velázquez's greed and Narváez's foolishness, I was lured away from my city at the moment of greatest crisis. Motecuhzoma has to shoulder some of this blame also, dealing with Narváez while he still called me friend. Between them they have ruined my grand design through their stupidity and treachery!

But there was hope. Alvarado was reckless, but he was also very thorough. Every noble family had lost at least one family member in the recent massacre, and so many of the important generals and senators had been murdered that it must surely have created a vacuum of power. Perhaps even the Mexica might not recover from such a loss. He might yet be able to conjure victory from this disaster.

 **85**

BENÍTEZ WATCHED FROM the roof as Ordaz led his men through the gates of the palace. An eerie silence hung over the streets and canals. Only the skeins of smoke that drifted from the temple shrines proved that the Mexica had not utterly abandoned the city.

Ordaz had four hundred infantry with him. In the next few minutes, they would discover the Mexica's intentions.

"Where is she?" a voice said.

Benítez looked around, startled. It was Norte.

"What?"

"Rain Flower. Where is she?"

Benítez returned his attention to the column of nervous troops below, arrows nocked in crossbows, firearms loaded, swords drawn. "I don't know."

"Why did she not accompany us when we rode against Narváez?"

"Is it your intention to interrogate me, Norte? You forget yourself."

"I am concerned for her safety."

"She is no concern of yours." Look at him, he does not even try to hide from me how badly he still wants her. I should have hanged him: it was within my power. Instead, I feel an unnatural kinship with him, due, it seems, to our shared concern for a copper-skinned savage.

Below him the line of infantry snaked through the streets and across the plaza. Still no sign of an attack. Perhaps they would have the miracle they had all prayed for.

"Cortés does not suspect?" Norte asked.

He knows, Benítez realized. Somehow he knows what she did. The thought would have alarmed him more except that at that moment bedlam broke out in the streets of Tenochtitlán. It started with a shower of arrows and stones from the roofs, a murderous rain on the heads of Ordaz's soldiers. Moments later the attack started in earnest, the *naturales* coming from all directions, their bodies painted, feather plumes dancing as they ran, their terrible ululations freezing the blood. The emperor's Eagle Knights, in their beaked helmets and feathered suits, led the assault.

Many Castilians fell under the weight of that first attack. The bugler sounded the retreat.

The plaza, empty a few moments ago, was suddenly filled with Mexica warriors. Jaguar Knights rushed the walls with ladders; others tried to fire the gates with their torches. They were answered with volleys of musketry and crossbows.

Cortés and Alvarado shouted the alarms from the parapets. Benítez drew his sword. I never wanted to be a soldier, he thought. I wanted to have a farm and a little *hacienda* of my own. Look where my greed and ambition have led me.

86

I KNOW THAT head, Benítez thought. It belonged to a soldier named Guzmán. Now here it is patrolling the distant parapet with the aid of a severed foot. Silver moonlight is reflected in his empty eyes.

Fray Guevarra turned from the window, pale and trembling. "The Devil's work!" he cursed.

Not the Devil, but a clever tactic nevertheless. The Mexica had many tricks like that. The severed head had had a particularly telling effect on Narváez's men, who were new to the country and not hardened to the ways of the *naturales*.

Ordaz's venture into the streets had proved disastrous. His force had fought their way back to the palace only with the greatest difficulty, with the loss of twenty-three men killed or captured. Guzmán and Flores were among those missing. Of those who survived, nearly all had been injured; Ordaz himself carried three wounds.

That evening they had counted another forty-six of their comrades wounded; a dozen of those had since died from their wounds.

The attacks had continued, day after day. The Mexica hurled rocks and blazing pitch at the walls while their Eagle Knights led further charges against the gates. The once-peaceful courtyards and patios and fountains were carpeted with arrows and stones.

The great drum on the summit of the temple beat continuously, night and day, part of the war on their nerves.

"We are low on food and water," Alvarado said. "The Mexica do not need to defeat us in battle. They can starve us out if they wish. I say we run for the coast. Our position here is intolerable."

"How will we do that?" León asked him. "You saw what happened to Ordaz. They will massacre us before we go a hundred yards."

"The Mexica do not fight at night," Benítez offered. "If we leave under cover of darkness, we might slip past them."

"What about the bridges? They have cut the causeways in several places."

"We can make portable bridges," Benítez answered. "There is enough wood in the palace that we can use. Martín López has already told me that he can build us what we need."

"Even if we escape, our troubles are not over," Sandoval said. "What about the Tlaxcalans? Will they help us, or will they turn on us to regain favor with the Mexica?"

Fray Guevarra put his head in his hands. "I should never have followed you, Cortés! See where you have led us!"

Cortés took no part in their deliberations. He stared out of the window, his hands crossed behind his back. Below him in the plaza, torches flitted like giant fireflies, Mexica women searching for their sons and brothers and fathers among the piles of rotting dead. Their attackers continued to shout their defiance from the surrounding buildings, and occasionally an arrow would clatter harmlessly onto the roof.

"The Lord will save us," Aguilar said. "He has stood with us from Vera Cruz, and he will not abandon us now."

"I rather think we have all tempted the Lord's patience a little far with our adventures," Fray Olmedo said.

"What about the gold?" León said. "If we run, what about the gold? We risk losing everything we have fought for!"

And so it went on. Benítez glanced over at Cortés. Any moment now.

✳ ✳

"No!" Cortés shouted, turning from the window and striding to the head of the table. A circle of frightened faces stared back at him. Most men are like dust, he thought with disgust. They are just blown about with the wind.

"Enough of this! Do none of you see? If we run from Tenochtitlán, we lose more than the gold. We lose a kingdom! This is our prize, and we shall not give it up. Never!

"What manner of men are you? Did we endure so much to win this city only to give it up so easily?"

Silence. None of them could meet his eyes.

"Perhaps Motecuhzoma can speak for us with the people," Fray Olmedo mumbled, finally.

"That dog! I will not request anything of him."

"But, my lord—"

"No! By my conscience, I want nothing of him!"

"There may perhaps be one other way."

He turned around; Malinali had come to stand quietly behind his chair.

"My lord, the tactic of war among the Mexica is to capture the enemy's town and burn his temple. This desecration of his gods is tantamount to defeat. Should we do the same with the temple here, they may believe their gods have deserted them and give us their surrender."

"But if we leave these gates," Ordaz protested, "we face slaughter. My men were hard-pressed to return to the palace that first day."

"Out there we have no protection against their missiles and darts," Benítez said.

Alvarado nodded. "If only we could put our fort on wheels, as we do our cannons."

Cortés stared at him. "Perhaps we can. Get me Martín López. Now that he is excused his commission of building ships, I have other work for him."

 87

THE FOUR WOODEN towers—*tortugas*—that Martín López had built for them were ready. Each was roofed over with timbers and mounted on wooden wheels, so that it could be physically propelled by the soldiers inside. There were loopholes for as many as two dozen crossbowmen and harquebusiers.

Well, the moment has come, Benítez thought. Fear had left him dry-mouthed, and his bowels felt loose. He wanted to be on with this work. The worst time was always before the battle. When it was begun, there was no time to be afraid.

The main gate creaked open, and he shouted to his men to put their backs to their work. The great wheeled fortress groaned and began to roll.

Holy Mary, Mother of God...

Baking hot in here, smelling of wood sap and sweat. Someone had pissed himself in fear, and the acrid reek of the urine made him shudder. As they rolled out of the gate, he heard the whoops and screams of the Mexica, then the sharp crack of the muskets as the harquebusiers fired their first volleys. He threw his own weight against the rollers. Rocks thudded against the wooden walls, followed by the hiss and shudder of arrows.

The temple was less than a hundred paces from the palace of the Face of the Water Lord. It might as well have been a hundred miles.

✳ ✳

Benítez ran after Cortés. Behind him he heard the splintering of timber as the last of the *tortugas* toppled and fell, destroyed by the incessant barrage of stones from the roofs. No time to wonder how they would get back across the plaza to their sanctuary in the palace. He must follow Cortés, burn the temple, do his duty. If this was his day to die, then so be it.

The priests were hurling burning logs down the steps. One of the logs hit the man beside him, sent him screaming down the steep stone terrace. Benítez struggled on.

Cortés was already at the summit. By the time Benítez reached him, two of the priests already lay dead at his feet. Stragglers from Ordaz's infantry helped them pitch the great stone idols over the sides of the pyramid and down into the plaza.

Benítez ran inside the Hummingbird shrine with a torch.

※ ※

The faces of the five Spaniards taken the day of Ordaz's first sally hung on the walls like bearded masks. The Mexica had tanned the skins expertly, painting them with great cunning so that they appeared to be living, except that pieces of jade had been inserted where the eyes had once been.

Benítez recognized two of the heads. They belonged to Flores and Guzmán.

Xipe Totec, the Flayed One, God of Harvests, watched him from beyond the open pit where they delivered his sacrifices, the stinking grave where Flores and Guzmán now moldered.

The sounds of the battle outside seemed to fade away. He suddenly felt quite calm.

"This is where all greed and ambition end," Flores whispered. *"This is the filling of every appetite. This is the last chapter of the flesh."*

"You can dream of riches and fine wines and women and jewels," Guzmán said, *"but this is where the road leads us all."*

※ ※

He heard someone behind him. It was Norte, blood in his hair and blood on his sword, breathing hard, his eyes wild.

"Your friends," Benítez said.

Norte tore the skins from the poles and flung them into the pit below. It was black and empty. No coming back from there.

Cortés ran in, snatched a flaming torch from the walls, held the fire to the dry thatch of the roof. "Get out of here!" he shouted at them. "We must withdraw to the palace!"

The thatch caught readily; there was an angry roar as the flames took hold, and the shrine filled quickly with black smoke. In moments the Hummingbird shrine was engulfed by fire; that of Rain Bringer, too.

Perhaps now the Mexica would relent.

MALINALI

"It will make no difference," Motecuhzoma tells me.

The smell of smoke is strong. From the window I watch the adobe walls of the Yopico shrine shiver in the heat of the fire and collapse.

It is evening. Below us in the courtyard, the Thunder Lords are preparing to bury their dead; others silently repair the breaches in the walls. I hear the groans of the wounded and the keening cries of the Tlaxcalans as they mourn their losses.

"If you think this will break the spirit of the Mexica, you are wrong. The Flayed One will be angry, but Smoking Mirror and Hummingbird are safe in the forest."

I do not answer.

"I can still save you, Malinali Tenepal."

"How?"

He takes off his ring, extracts the turquoise seal, and hands it to me. "This will guarantee your safe passage with the Mexica generals outside these walls. You can organize a parley, lure Lord Malinche out of the gates. Once he is taken, his soldiers will weep like women and will soon be vanquished. Do this for me and I will save your life."

"What life? Making *tamales*? Weaving yarn?"

"You forget, you are just a woman. You hope for too much."

I put a hand on my belly, where my lord's dynasty is nourished and grows.

"What I hope for is to be my lord's wife and the mother of the next Toltec Empire."

"The revered speakers of the Mexica come through me. You are nothing. Your Lord Malinche is not a god but an impostor! If you defy me, you will die with him here. I will take out your heart myself and fling it in the face of Smoking Mirror."

"You are wrong. He does have a god in him, a god more powerful than any you or I have dreamed of. He will perform his miracle."

I want to escape this room, but he calls me back.

"Tell me one thing."

"My lord?"

"Why do you do this? We have the same ancestors, the same language, the same gods. These invaders do not threaten only me, they threaten us all."

"Us? Who is this *us,* my lord? My mother was *Mexicatl,* like you. She stole my birthright and gave me to slavery. Lord Malinche is my *us.*"

He has no answer for that. I leave him to watch the smoke from the burning temple stain the darkening sky, a funeral pyre for the Hummingbird people.

88

"WE ARE GOING to die," Fray Guevarra shouted. "Because of you, Cortés! I should never have listened to your lies!"

"By my conscience, you will keep quiet, sir, or you will repent it!"

They had become accustomed now to the rituals of the siege: the acrid and pervading smoke, the booming of the falconets, the crack of muskets, the ululation of the Mexica warriors, the infernal hammering of the drum in the *Templo Mayor*.

"We have to do something," Alvarado said.

"I will not give up this city."

"Caudillo," Sandoval said quietly. "Alvarado is right. We cannot hold them forever. The walls are breached in many places, and our water is fetid. We are short of gunpowder, and our stock of balls for the cannons is running low."

"Then we will make more out of our gold! I have promised Tenochtitlán for my king and my god!"

Benítez looked at Malinali. She read the desperation in their eyes.

"Doña Marina," Alvarado whispered. "Please. Talk to him."

Even Alvarado knows we need her now, Benítez thought.

She took Cortés by the arm, led him away from the others. There was a long, whispered exchange. Cortés's shoulders slumped in defeat. He nodded to Cristobal Olid, captain of the guard.

"Fetch Motecuhzoma," he said.

MALINALI

MOTECUHZOMA LOOKS LIKE a wizened old man. But as he peers around the room, when he sees the fear on the faces of these Thunder Lords, hears Fray Olmedo's whispered incantations of prayer, a golden smile comes to his lips.

His eyes turn to me. "Why have you brought me here? It is weeks now since Lord Malinche has come to visit me. Now suddenly I am ushered into his presence without time to prepare. What does he want of me?"

"He needs your help, my lord."

"I cannot help him."

"You must."

"Why should I listen to him? See what a fate he has brought me to!"

"What does he say?" my lord asks me.

"Just whines and cries, nothing of consequence."

"Tell him that the city is in rebellion. So far I have been patient, but unless the attacks cease, I will be forced to kill them all and burn Tenochtitlán. If he wishes to prevent this catastrophe for the Mexica, he must go out and talk to the people."

An empty boast. Perhaps it worked once, against those ignorant dogs of Tlaxcala, but Motecuhzoma knows better. So instead I tell him, "Lord Malinche wants you to talk to the people. You must stop the rebellion."

Another smile. "If only I could."

I take a step closer to him. How thin he is, how much more gray there is in his hair! But the greatest change is in his eyes. They are like obsidian mirrors, black and empty.

But today he has regained power over them. He starts to laugh, a high-pitched giggle that infuriates the Thunder Lords.

"Doña Marina," Cristobal Olid shouts, "remind him that we are his friends. Have we not treated him kindly these last months? Will he see us all killed?"

"My lord Motecuhzoma, you can see by that one's face how he now pleads for his life. Now look at my lord Malinche. Which one are you most inclined to assist?"

"There is nothing I can do for either of them."

"For our sakes," Olid shouted again, "will he not help us?"

"Hold your tongue!" my lord shouts. He takes me aside. "What does Motecuhzoma say?"

"He says he is powerless to help us."

"I told you we should not have asked anything of this treacherous dog!" A muscle ripples in his jaw. "Will you kindly remind him that he agreed, in front of witnesses, to accept vassalage to the king of Spain. If he does not help us now, I shall construe it as an act of rebellion against His Majesty and have him executed for treason. Tell him that and let us see how powerless he is!"

Now it is my turn to smile.

"Revered Speaker, if you do not help him, my lord Malinche says he will ensure he does not perish alone. Before he dies, he intends to tie you to a stake and burn you over a slow fire. Do you remember Smoking Eagle and how he suffered?"

"He would not dare!"

"My lord Malinche will dare anything, you know that. Look around the room at the faces of these other Thunder Lords. Do you see mercy anywhere here, O Angry Lord?"

Motecuhzoma hangs his head. How sweet this is. If only my father could see it!

The Thunder Lords look on. They do not even try to put

words in my mouth now. They have no choice but to trust me, anyway.

"I learned from this Narváez," Motecuhzoma said, "that Cortés is no god. He does not even have the authority of his own king. He is a mercenary and a traitor. A nomad. Narváez was sent here to arrest him."

"And for this nomad and mercenary, you forfeited your throne!"

"Do not taunt me!"

"What a fool you have been! Even the gods curse you."

Spittle spills from his lower lip.

"What does he say now, the old fool?" Cortés hisses.

"More whimpering and pity for himself, my lord. It is good you do not have the elegant speech, and you are spared this whining."

"Repeat to him that I will have him hanged for treason should he continue with his rebellion."

"My lord says that all he wants now is to depart in peace. He will even leave you all your treasures. All you have to do is tell your people to desist, so that he can march away from here with his life. You have his word on that."

"His word! When has he ever kept his word to me?"

"Everything can be again as it once was."

Motecuhzoma shakes his head. "I cannot betray my people."

"Then I shall tell them to prepare a fire for you. It will be a slow death, much slower than Smoking Eagle's. They will roast you one limb at a time."

I watch him struggle with himself. He wants to defy them. Perhaps a few months ago, he would still have had the strength.

I know I have won. "You are thinking the Jaguar Knights will storm the gates in time to save you. Suppose that should happen. What fate befalls the former king? Will they fall to their knees before the *Tlatoani* who allowed the thieves beyond their gate to burn the temple and murder their sons? No, my lord, this is your one chance to reassert your authority as emperor. If you can make them obey you, then tomorrow we will march away from here, and your rule will be restored. You may rebuild the *Templo Mayor* to a greater glory than before, do penance before your gods, redeem your spirit. But if we die, you will die with us, and on your shoulders will lie the blame for all this. There will not even be jade in your mouth to pay the Yellow Beast, just pain and ashes."

He raises his head, just a little. "If I do, this . . . Malinche . . . and all of you . . . will leave this city?"

"Call off your warriors. We only want our lives."

Motecuhzoma looks at Cortés. "And I thought him divine!"

"As I once thought you."

I know—I had always somehow known—that though he wants to obey his gods, he wants the throne above all. A captive to his religion, he is enslaved also to his greed for the life to which he was born. He has nowhere to turn.

He takes a deep breath. "I will do what I can."

89

A TRUMPET BLAST heralded the emperor's appearance on the roof. He was marched onto the parapet protected from the rain of stones and arrows by Spanish shields. Falling Eagle saw one of the Castilian priests with him, the one called Aguilar.

A murmur passed through the ranks of warriors, like a wave. A slow and shuffling silence fell over the plaza.

Even now a few still lowered their eyes, afraid to look directly upon Revered Speaker. But Falling Eagle did not avert his eyes. He stared, appalled at how ill the emperor looked, how shabby his clothes appeared. He wore a makeshift headdress of yellow bark paper and a poor robe of white maguey fiber. The Spaniards had stolen his gold and silver jewelery, even his cotton mantles. Falling Eagle felt overcome with shame.

Motecuhzoma started to speak.

"My people! You of the Aztlan! Of the Eagle and the Cactus! I command you all to desist from this war! I have spoken with Lord Malinche and his followers, and I have told them they are no longer welcome in our capital. They are sorry they have caused so much dissension among us, and they are now ready to leave immediately. They wish only that you withdraw and allow them to return to the East Lands in peace."

Falling Eagle listened to this speech with growing incredulity. *Motecuhzoma still believes he has authority over us, after all that has happened, after all the humiliation and disgrace he has brought us. We have all seen him grovel at the feet of these thieves and murderers. Does he still believe that we revere him as our* Tlatoani?

He looked at the young warriors around him in the plaza. *Motecuhzoma could hold sway here,* he realized with plunging dismay. *Some of these young men might yet obey him, those who were not from noble families and had been brought up to believe the emperor divine.*

Something must be done to break the spell.

Falling Eagle took a deep breath. "Who is this boy?" he shouted. "Who is this disgusting wife of a Spaniard? We will not listen to you, Motecuhzoma! You are no longer our king! You have disgraced us before our gods! We will not shame ourselves further! Cuitláhuac is our king now, and we will fight on until all the foreigners are dead!"

He picked up a stone lying at his feet and tossed it at the walls, saw it fall harmlessly on the patio at Motecuhzoma's feet. But his stone had its desired effect, for now others were shouting, too; more rocks, even several arrows, arced toward the walls. One arrow slammed into Motecuhzoma's shoulder, and he gasped and fell back. He was struck by several small stones before the Castilians threw up their shields and dragged him away.

✳　✳

"We have to get away from here!" Alvarado shouted, as he dragged Motecuhzoma from the terrace.

Sandoval raised his voice, trying to make himself heard above

366 ※ Colin Falconer

the din from the plaza. "He is right, *caudillo,* our situation is hopeless. The decision must be made!"

They all looked at Cortés. His face betrayed bewilderment. He could not believe he had been beaten.

Motecuhzoma had fainted. There was blood matted in his hair where the stone had struck him, and an arrow lodged in the muscle of his shoulder. He lay on his back, his eyes rolling in his head. Mendez bent down to minister to him. Motecuhzoma cried out as the doctor pulled the arrow shaft from the wound.

"What shall we do with him, my lord?" Benítez said.

"Well, he is no further use to us."

"I disagree, my lord," Malinali said.

"My lady?"

She took him aside. "When an emperor dies, tradition demands that he be taken outside the city, to a place called Copulco, and there cremated with all due honor. His priests, dwarves, hunchbacks, and concubines all must be properly sacrificed, so that they may serve him in the next world. Cremation and mourning can last perhaps eighty days, time enough for us to leave the capital, return to Tlaxcala, even reach the coast. Motecuhzoma can serve us better from the spirit world than he ever did in life."

"His wounds are not mortal."

"Not yet."

A grim smile, a bitter smile. If he could not have Tenochtitlán, neither would Motecuhzoma. "I will have Alvarado do it. Or Jaramillo. They enjoy that sort of thing."

"No, my lord."

"No?"

"Let me have your knife."

He raised an eyebrow in surprise. He hesitated for a moment before sliding the dirk from his belt and placing it in her palm. She concealed it beneath her cloak.

MALINALI

AND SO WE are left alone.

I put my lips close by his ear. "My lord, I wish you to open your eyes."

Motecuhzoma is in great pain. The doctor has bandaged his forehead, and there is another bloodied cloth wrapped around the muscle of his right shoulder, where the arrow shaft has done terrible damage.

His eyes flutter open. "You . . . you still . . . wish . . . to bargain?"

"Lord, my lord, my great lord. What a pitiful wretch you have become."

"The prophecies were . . . true. There was . . . nothing . . . I could . . . do."

I hold an obsidian mirror close to his face so that he might see his own reflection. "What do you see here?"

"Take it away!"

I grab a handful of hair, forcing his head back, make him look. "Do you not see a murderer and a butcher? Do you not hear countless widows and daughters weeping?"

"Leave me——"

"Do you remember my father?"

A flicker of fear in his eyes. "I did . . . not know . . . your father . . ."

"No, you did not know him, but you ordered his execution anyway. Because he could read the stars and the winds, because he spoke against all the human sacrifices you demanded, because he prophesied the end of the Mexica. It was a long time ago, and I am sure you have forgotten giving the command that ended his life. But I have not forgotten." I show him the dagger beneath my cloak.

His eyes are open now.

"I served my . . . gods . . . faithfully. They . . . did not . . . serve me."

"Your gods curse you. As do I." I hold the knife to the light. "This is for my father."

90

A TORCH-LIT COURTYARD, rain slapping on the cobbles, a cold wind. They were to leave that night, head for the shortest causeway, the one leading west to Tlacopán.

Preparations were taking place in silence all over the palace, but nowhere were they more circumspect than in this quiet court. Eight wounded horses had been mustered, their hooves muffled with cloth, and a hundred Tlaxcalans assigned to guard them. Wooden boxes had been strapped to the horses' backs. Benítez opened one and examined its contents.

Alvarado watched him, hands on hips. "When we leave, you will be assigned one hundred and fifty men, Narváez's best infantrymen. You are to guard the treasure in these bags with your life. It belongs to the king."

"If the king wants his gold, he can come here and stand over it himself."

"A treasonous point of view."

"If you think me treasonous, *you* can guard the gold."

Benítez watched the heavy ingots being loaded. If this was the *quinto real*, the king's fifth, they had won much more than had been declared. Cortés had claimed the worth of the gold at three hundred thousand crowns. Unless half of these boxes were filled with stones, the bullion here amounted to almost double that. Benítez suspected that what he saw here was not the king's fifth but Cortés's hidden profits. Small wonder the *caudillo* had not wished to leave.

"There is more here than the sixty thousand crowns that Cortés claimed."

"You would do well to keep your silence, Benítez. You will get your reward."

"Yes, a Mexican spear in the back before the night is out."

"Cortés always remembers his friends."

"He always swears *by his conscience*. He has no more conscience than a dog."

Benítez pulled his cloak tighter around his shoulders. Another sodden night, like the night they attacked Narváez. Then it had been their friend, had cloaked their movements. He hoped the weather would serve them as well tonight.

He found himself thinking, unexpectedly, of Rain Flower. He wondered where she was, what had become of her. Another of his weaknesses, he supposed: he had allowed himself to feel an unnatural love for an Indian concubine. He wondered, not for the first time, what would have happened to him if he had been in Norte's position, shipwrecked and alone in Yucatán, and had been given as husband to a woman like Rain Flower. He had to allow that in certain circumstances it might be all too easy to forget about Spain and the Christian world.

Perhaps he and Norte were not so different, after all.

As for Rain Flower, he supposed she had run to the Mexica. He hoped they had not harmed her. He tried to push from his mind the image of her spread-eagled on the sacrificial stone at the Tlatelolco temple.

How he wished she were with him now.

He wondered what would happen should he survive this night. Back to Cuba, he supposed, an impoverished *hidalgo* with a petty landholding, without courtly looks or manners or connections, sweating in the sun, fearing disease and an early, wine-sodden, and anonymous death on his *encomienda* . . .

Better to die tonight, if that was what God intended.

MALINALI

"HAVE YOU SEEN Cortés?"

Cáceres's face is pale with strain. "I think he is in the chapel, my lady. He offers up his prayers for this night."

I hurry down the passageway. The room next to Cortés's apartments has been converted into a shrine for the goddess Virgin. Inside, Martín López has erected a wooden cross. The chapel is bright with candles: halos of light shine on the cedar-wood altars and in the niches in the wall where the Mexica's gods once stood.

The shrine is empty except for Aguilar, on his knees in front of the cross, his ancient book clutched to his chest.

I hurry on to the next apartment.

The quarters given to Motecuhzoma's daughter, Doña Ana, adjoined the emperor's former apartments. I ignore the protests of the guards and push through the bell-hung curtain over the door.

Doña Ana is on her knees, bent over the low bed, and my lord has both his hands on her shoulders to keep her there. He has mounted her from the rear, so I am face-to-face with them both as I enter the room. My lord's forehead shines with sweat, his face fierce with tension; below him the girl's monkey-brown face is screwed up in pain at my lord's rough taking of her.

She really has nothing to recommend her, except her birthright.

My lord does not stop. He continues thrusting until he has finished. I wait, my hands crossed on my swollen belly. I feel my small son kick and struggle.

When the act is completed, I watch a bead of perspiration make its uncertain way along his temple to his beard, listen to the sawing of his breathing in his chest. Doña Ana has covered her face with her hands.

My lord wants a child with the emperor's blood, thinks it will make his claim to the throne legitimate in the eyes of the

Mexica. He still has not given up his attempt to conquer them, by any means at his disposal.

"Doña Marina. You should not be here. You should be resting, in your condition."

"Does my condition make me repulsive to you, my lord?"

"It is not for the ladies of the household to question a king on his appetites."

"Your last moments should be with me."

"Who knows who will survive tonight? I must do all I can to ensure that my seed secures the throne of Mexico. It is my right. I have earned it."

I caress my swollen stomach. "The throne of Mexico is here, my lord."

My lord reaches around, cups Doña Ana's plump brown stomach in the palms of his hands. "And here also."

Well.

We will see about that.

91

"What's going on here?" Benítez asked.

"Cortés gave orders," Sandoval said. "Everything that cannot be loaded onto the packhorses is to be piled here in the courtyard, and the men are to help themselves."

Benítez stared. The ingots had been made to Cortés's precise specifications: flat bars two inches broad and half an inch thick, the perfect size to fit under Spanish armor. A mountain of them lay on the flagstones in front of the main gates, along with the discarded jewelery and feather work and cotton capes. An emperor's bequest left in the rain, shimmering in the dim light of smoky torches.

Benítez was reminded of pigs feeding at a trough, a frenzy of squealing and shoving as men fought one another to get at the gold, pushing bars into their tunics and their armor, filling their pockets with silver medals and gemstones, cramming rings and beads into their mouths.

"And you, Gonzalo, are you going to stuff your pockets?"

Sandoval reached into his purse, spilled a few pearls and opals into his palm. "Do as I did. A few large stones, enough to buy you some ease should we ever see Cuba again. Not too heavy to slow you down if there is fighting."

The icy needles of rain slanted down.

Benítez saw a familiar figure in the crowd: Norte, in there with the others, scrabbling for the best pieces, his eyes burning with that particular hunger that had so disgusted the Mexica on the beach at San Juan de Ulúa.

I believe I liked you better as an Indian.

 **92**

THE NIGHT WAS dark, no moon, no stars, freezing rain. Sheet lightning flickered over the mountain cols. The three priests—Díaz, Olmedo, Guevarra—were kept busy hearing confessions. At midnight Fray Olmedo spoke a last benediction, and the gates were thrown open. Cortés was leaving the city of his dreams.

They filed in silence down the road to Tlacopán, the falling rain masking their departure. The streets were slick underfoot, no lights burned anywhere, and only the gentle lapping of the lake and the murmur of the rain cleaved the silence.

An army of wraiths, bandaged and hobbling, melting into the mist.

Martín López had constructed a portable bridge from cedar beams plundered from the ceilings in the palace. Four hundred Tlaxcalan porters had been assigned to carry it, under the command of one of the officers, Francisco Magariño.

Benítez had prepared himself for sudden death in the street. But they reached the causeway without alarm and went safely across the first breach. Benítez felt drunk with relief. It was going to work.

Cortés's luck had held again. The Mexica had broken the siege to mourn their dead emperor, as Malinali had promised they would.

Cortés had his miracle.

✳ ✳

An old woman, drawing water from the lake, gave a shrill scream of alarm, which was taken up somewhere in the mist by two Mexica sentries. A crossbowman silenced the woman's screams, but it was too late. From the summit of the *Templo Mayor* came the mournful boom of the *huehuetl* drum. It echoed across the lake and through the valley, summoning the warriors of Hummingbird.

✳ ✳

Panic.

Cortés was shouting for the bridge to be brought forward. Benítez twisted in the saddle. What was happening? Where was Magariño? Without the pontoon, they were trapped here in the open and helpless.

"Where is the bridge?" Benítez screamed.

It had stuck fast. The rain that had muffled their exodus had betrayed them now, softening the banks of the lake and jamming the bridge supports into the mud at the first divide. As Magariño and his men desperately tried to raise it, they saw torches speed toward them from all over the lake as the war canoes descended, like thousands of fireflies. Their column was utterly at the mercy of the *naturales*, like a huge caterpillar being swarmed by ants.

Benítez's horse stamped its hooves, sensing fear. He could hear the splashing of paddles, saw the white cotton tunics of the Mexica warriors through the fog and rain. They made good targets for the crossbowmen and the harquebusiers, but there were so many of them . . .

Cortés shouted again for the bridge, but his voice was lost amid the ululations of the Mexica and the cacophony of horns and whistles. The first volley of stones and arrows rained down from a pitch-black sky.

Suddenly the column surged forward, pushing on toward the second breach. Benítez went with them, a cork on the tide,

angry, frightened, bellowing defiance, his last thoughts of Rain
Flower.

MALINALI

I SCRAMBLE DOWN the muddy banks into the water, slipping
on the musket balls and Venetian glass beads that have spilled
from overturned chests. The breach in the canal is already
filled with dead horses and overturned carts. Soldiers are trying to scramble across, but many of them are so weighed down
with gold ingots, they immediately disappear under the water.
Others cannot run because of the gold they carry under their
armor and are overtaken by the Mexica and dragged away
screaming, captives for Hummingbird.

All the time more canoes are speeding across the lake to
join the battle.

I swim to the far bank. The mud has been so churned up
by hooves that it is impossible to clamber out again. My fingers hook desperately around a stone flag, and I drag myself
out of the water. I dare a glance behind me, clasping my
swollen belly. I hear myself sobbing. I am more frightened for
him than for me. My lord's destiny, perhaps yet my father's
prophecy, are entrusted here with me in my womb.

I look up. A scene of utter chaos, screams, and death, all lit
by fire. The breach is almost filled now with Mexica war
canoes. I see Doña Ana wade from the water, hands and feet
scrambling for purchase in the slick mud. She sees me and
reaches out her hand.

I wonder if she has my lord's seed in her.

Our fingers lock, I pull her toward me. When she is close
enough, I place my foot in her stomach—about the place of
her womb—and push hard. Doña Ana screams and falls back

into the canal. I see her head bob once in the darkness, then disappear.

I scramble to my feet and start to run.

93

BENÍTEZ STAGGERED ACROSS the gravel beach and fell to his knees. He wore only doublet and breeches, had been forced to abandon his steel breastplate and helmet in order to swim the last two cuts in the canal. His horse was gone, the king's fifth also. It was out there somewhere, sinking into the mud of the canals. If the king wants it badly enough, he thought, he can come back and get it.

He raised his face to the black sky, mouth open, gulping in air. Around him the remnants of Ordaz's squadron lay sprawled on the beach, exhausted.

Benítez felt hooves drumming on the sand. A horseman approaching.

"Who's there?" someone shouted.

He recognized Cortés's voice. "It is Benítez, my lord."

"Captain!" Ordaz shouted, somewhere close by. "Captain, you must lead us back. We have to help the others."

"There is nothing we can do, Ordaz. You are fortunate to have survived. We all are."

The sounds of fighting were muted now; the Indians were already celebrating their victory. It was quiet here on the beach, almost peaceful. Benítez wanted to sleep. Sleep: a little death, like running away.

More stragglers were staggering up the beach, a handful of Tlaxcalans, covered in blood; one immediately fell dead from his wounds. Then Alvarado, on foot and alone.

"Caudillo!"

"Pedro?"

Alvarado's hair was plastered to his skull with mud and rain. He was hollow-eyed, and there were black bloodstains on his tunic. When he saw them, he fell to his knees and started to weep. Benítez and Ordaz rushed to help him.

"Where are the others?" Cortés barked from the saddle.

"Dead," Alvarado said.

"Not all of them, surely," Ordaz said.

"We must save ourselves now," Alvarado sobbed. "There is nothing else we can do."

The last straggler from the water was El Romo, Benítez's stallion, a dark sheen of blood on both flanks. He collapsed in the shallows.

"Well," Cortés growled, "at least we will have some meat for dinner."

MALINALI

ONLY SANDOVAL AND his vanguard reach the village of Popotla unscathed. The rest of our army has been routed on the causeway. Now Cortés sits under a great cypress tree, his shoulders hunched, weeping. None of the Thunder Lords will approach him; even I am frightened of this.

I sit a little distance away, my limbs still shaking uncontrollably. My stomach is hurting, and I feel wetness leaking down the inside of my thighs. Blood. *The baby*.

"Why do they not come after us?"

It is Benítez. He has lost his helmet in the fight, and blood and mud are plastered in his hair and his beard.

"They will not attack us tonight." I am surprised by the sound of my own voice, strong and clear.

"Why? We are at their mercy. They could finish us."

"They have many captives to offer Hummingbird. The warriors who took prisoners must attend the ritual fasting and lead them to the stone for sacrifice. The Mexica know that if

Hummingbird is not properly honored tonight, it does not matter how well they fight tomorrow, they cannot possibly win. But if they give their god his sacrifice, they will defeat us no matter what we do or how fast we run. That is what they believe."

I look at Cortés. He is on his knees in the mud, shivering with cold, fingering his sacred beads as he stumbles through a prayer to the goddess Virgin. I cannot bear to look at my god so destroyed.

He is just a man now, just clay like myself, like these poor others.

I take shelter under the branches of an ancient ceiba tree. I rest my back against the trunk, put my head on my knees, and fall into a black sleep.

※ ※

Dawn.

We reach the pyramid at Tototepec, the Hill of the Turkey Hen, and take refuge in the temple there. It is a natural fortress, with an uninterrupted view of the surrounding plain. The rain has stopped, and the earth steams under a weak, yellow sun. Men move about like ghosts, eyes redrimmed and empty, sodden rags wrapped around their wounds. Others throw themselves on the cobbles of the temple court and lie there, not moving, utterly spent.

"Where is López?" a voice is shouting over and over.

I look around. It is Feathered Serpent, reborn with the morning, his spirit reawakened by the cries of the ocelots and the bewitching light of Morning Star. He sits astride his horse, in full armor, moving slowly among the knots of groaning, exhausted men.

"Is López here?"

His eyes are black points in a ghost-pale and chiseled face. He rides straight in the saddle, arrogant and impatient beneath the plumed burgonet.

Alvarado hobbles toward him, limping, pale, and bloody. "Who is it you require, *caudillo?*"

"Have you seen Martín López?"

"The carpenter? He is here somewhere. He was wounded in the fighting, but he survived."

Cortés slams his fist onto his wooden saddle and laughs. "Then we have lost nothing!"

"My lord?"

"We have our shipbuilder! You see?"

Alvarado shakes his head. He does not see. I do not see. None of us sees.

"I have been thinking on this during the night," Feathered Serpent shouts, "and it now occurs to me that when we return, we may use their greatest defense against them."

Alvarado's face is quite blank. He sways on his feet, faint from loss of blood. "Return?"

"The lake, Pedro! We will build brigantines and encircle them in their own city! We will send for more cannons from Santo Domingo and lay siege using their very own lake!"

Alvarado stares up at him, slack-jawed.

"Because of one setback, you do not abandon a whole campaign. We shall return with brigantines and quell this rebellion for our king!"

Even in the gray chill of the morning, I feel a warmth spread through my whole body. I love him now, more than I have ever believed I could love anything. He is defeated but cannot be destroyed. While the moles around him huddle, shivering and beaten, the god in him strides ahead of the dawn, clothed in the man. Everything else he has ever done is forgiven now.

He is, after all, Malinche, my *Malintzin*, Malinali's lord.

 94

He's mad, Benítez thought.

We shall return with brigantines and quell this rebellion for our king. Quite mad.

We lost six hundred men tonight—not counting two thousand of our Tlaxcalan allies—as well as some of our finest officers, including León. All our cannons are gone, disappeared under the mud on the causeway, and we have barely two dozen horses left, most of them lame. Many of us who survive have grievous wounds. We number a few hundred, and we are surrounded by the Mexica in their millions.

But all that concerns him is whether López is injured.

Madness.

Benítez stumbled away and slept, eyes open, his back against a skull rack, though he was not aware of it. His dreams were of Mexica warriors: he was trying to run from them, but his legs were stuck in thick mud and he could not move. When he woke—minutes or hours later, he could not tell from the gray overcast of the sky—he heard the blast of conch shells as the priests on the summit of the Tlatelolco temple heralded the victory. The great drum that had sounded the alarm a few hours before reverberated around the valley, announcing that Hummingbird would now take his pleasure of the captives.

Benítez thought about Norte. He hoped he had died quickly, drowned in the canal with his pockets weighted with gold, like Fray Guevarra. He hoped the conches did not sound for him this gray morning.

✳   ✳

The priests waited, their faces smeared with soot, black robes stained with fresh, bright blood. They had done brisk commerce that morning.

The fresh heart throbbing in the brazier belonged to León.

Norte's legs would not support him. He fell and was dragged the rest of the way to the summit by the warrior who had claimed him as his captive. How many times had he seen this happen to some other poor wretch?

The sun appeared for a moment through a lead-gray sky.

A headdress was forced onto his head, plumed fans thrust in his hands. The priests forced him to dance in time with the drums, prodding at his feet and legs with spears and flaming torches. Hummingbird watched hungrily from the darkness, eyes glowing in the light of the braziers, body lustrous with jade and pearls.

Four of the priests grabbed him, forced him backward over the stone, each grasping a limb. Another slammed a wooden yoke across his throat. He stared at the sun with unblinking eyes and said a brief prayer to the god of his baptism.

※ ※

The high priest sawed open his chest with a stone knife. His movements were mercifully quick. In moments he had ripped out the palpitating heart with his hands. He showed it to the Spaniard as the light dimmed in his staring eyes. Then he offered the steam to the sun before flinging the organ into the face of Hummingbird on the Left.

He kicked Norte's body down the steps of the pyramid and called for the next captive to be brought forward.

MALINALI

OUR ONE HOPE lies in Tlaxcala. None of us can be sure if Old Ring of the Wasp will receive us now we are broken and defeated, but we know we cannot survive a long march to the coast without his help. There is no choice.

We are attacked intermittently at the temple fortress, harassment rather than a concerted assault. The Mexica are busy with the sacrificial rites demanded by their gods. It is the respite that my lord had hoped for; indeed, that he had counted on.

We march out soon after dark, leave the fires burning in the temple court to persuade the Mexica that we are still inside.

Such a pitiful retreat after our glorious arrival. Most horses carry two riders, at least one of them sorely wounded; other soldiers support themselves on stout sticks or drag themselves behind the horses, hanging grimly to tails or strappings. The most grievously wounded are thrown across the croups of horses considered too lame to fight.

Benítez is given a piebald mare whose rider died of his wounds during the night. Along with other Thunder Lords still fit to ride, he tries to chase away the Mexican raiding parties who torment our long retreat with stones and arrows.

The surviving Tlaxcalans guide us to the northeast, around Lake Texcoco. The next day we reach a town called Tepotzotlán, three leagues to the north. The population has fled before us, and we are overjoyed to find stocks of maize and vegetables in the dry stores, as well as flocks of turkeys crowded into pens. We eat well that morning and sleep for a few hours on the floors of the *cacique*'s palace, lords and ladies, gods and moles side by side.

That afternoon we set off once more, pass through Citlatepecon on the most northern point of the great lake, then strike east. Again we pass the night in a temple, this one dedicated to Feathered Serpent. An omen perhaps. Again the population has fled, but this time they have taken all their food with them, and now we must deal with our hunger as well as exhaustion.

All day the Mexica nipped at our heels, like yellow dogs. Our progress is painfully slow. By day some part of the column is always under attack, and each night more of the wounded give up their spirit. My lord now commands just three hundred soldiers and twenty-seven *jinetas*. Everyone, even the horses, is wounded in some way. Of our Tlaxcalan allies, less than a thousand are left.

As we climb into the high passes, we are reduced to eating the grass.

My belly still cramps with pain, though the bleeding has stopped. I cling to Tollán and the dream of the Toltecs as tenaciously as Feathered Serpent clings to his dreams of Tenochtitlán.

95

A ROCK HURLED from the tree line had struck Cortés just above the eye. He had not been wearing his helmet, and the missile had opened a gaping wound in his forehead. Now, in the dying light of the day, Malinali sat him down beside the campfire and prepared to stitch it closed. She had a maguey thorn to use as needle and had plucked out a long black hair from her own head to use as suture.

Cortés grunted as she probed with the sharp thorn. There was nothing to numb the pain. He concentrated his mind on other things: on his plans for the siege of Tenochtitlán, for instance.

"I will work as swiftly as I can, my lord," Malinali promised.

He felt the maguey spine pierce the skin above his eye. "Any pain is preferable to death."

"Not all men think so."

"They should. Death comes soon enough." He glanced up at her. Her pretty brown face was creased with concentration, her swollen belly just inches from his face. *There beats the heart of my son.* "Are you afraid?" he said.

"Not when I am with you."

He smiled. Ah, Malinali, my dark and carnal angel, where would I be without you? You are no Christian gentlewoman, for all Fray Olmedo's ceremony and sprinkling of water, but you are brave as any Spaniard, and you have the cunning of a Moor. I could not even have stepped off the beach if it were not for you. What a pity you are not the daughter of a Spanish duke.

"Will you weep for Doña Ana?" she whispered.

"She was the dalliance of a single night."

The thorn bit into his flesh. He clenched his teeth against the pain.

"And you, my lord? Are you afraid?"

"No, I am not afraid. I am at an age where a man must succeed or die. Let us be done with it, whatever it is. Fate will decide."

No, he was not afraid. Instead of fear, there was only this black and vicious anger—anger so deep it set his limbs to trembling and his heart to palpitating. These Mexica, these dogs, these heathens, had brought him to the point of defeat and despair, and he would never forgive them for that. They had taken away his dreams.

Well, he would make them repent, every last one. It was now his burden to make them see that he had God on his side.

✳ ✳

They marched day and night for five days, a stumbling column of ghosts. They climbed to the top of the pass, above a town called Otumba, and glimpsed the mountains of Tlaxcala, a little more than ten leagues distant. Below them lay the richly cultivated plain of Apam. They also saw, spread upon the plain and waiting for them, the entire Mexican army.

MALINALI

A FIELD OF plumes in jade and crimson, a sea of banners and shields, an army too huge to count. At the head of each squadron of painted warriors stands a commander: an Eagle Knight peering from beneath his beaked helmet, talons clinging to the sleeves of his silver-gray armor; a Jaguar Knight in black-spotted fur and snarling helm.

Even from a distance I can make out the generals, their rank denoted by nose plugs, labrets of jade and crystal, ornate cloaks. The battle standards are strapped to their backs, feather work and reeds worked into regimental insignia and stretched over wicker frames, the rallying points of their armies.

The valley echoes to the thunder of drums, the blast of conches and whistles. Our tiny army stares in dismay and despair. Our Thunder Lords believe they have suffered for nothing. This is where it must end, for all of us.

✳ ✳

Feathered Serpent orders his soldiers and moles into a tight square, Thunder Lords to the outside on their beasts of war, wounded in the center and protected. Without the iron serpents and thunder sticks, we lay no claim to a killing field. We must simply stand and fight until we are all dead.

Only my lord still believes. I can see it in his eyes and in the set of his shoulders. He is quite magnificent, my lord, my great lord, my Feathered Serpent. I love him now as I have never loved him before.

He turns his mount, walks her slowly around until he faces his tiny command. He holds in his right hand the ragged blue banner the Thunder Lords brought with them all the way from the coast.

"Gentlemen," he says, "before you, behold the armies of the Mexica."

He does not speak for long minutes, holds us all with his eyes. The whistles and ululations are deafening. When he speaks again, we must strain to hear him.

"They come here hoping to destroy us. We are, once more, greatly outnumbered. And yet..."

And yet, my lord? And yet?

"And yet, how many times in these past months have we thought ourselves beaten and prevailed? Did we not fight side by side at the Tabasco River against a great army such as this? Did we not claim victory then? And what of the great hordes of Tlaxcala and the cannons and cavalry that Narváez brought against us at Cempoala?

"Always we prevailed because you and I, we are not ordinary men nor ordinary soldiers. From this day you may, with my permission, tell the world that you were with Cortés the day of his great victory over the Mexica. In years to come, ballads will be written of your exploits, for it is not only your great valor and your skill at arms that separate you from mortal men. No, more than this, you are each of you chosen by God himself to march under the protection of his banner." He holds aloft the ragged blue-and-white pennon he clutches in his fist. "Under this cross, I promise you, we will prevail!

"Now I say this to each of you: remember that while you have strength in your arm, you still hold the advantage, even today. These Mexica want only to take you captive for their loathsome rites, and because of that, they will leave themselves open to your killing strokes. You fight not a battle today but a series of duels, and I believe God will give you strength to face this test. Do not slash wildly but thrust with your swords, so they may not get inside your guard to lay hands on you or use their clubs."

He paused, allowed his words to take effect on them.

"In the centuries to come, when men write the history of the world, you will be the shining chapter! People will talk of this day until the end of the world, and you will each be remembered as heroes.

"So, gentlemen, guard yourselves and turn to the enemy. When I give the word, we shall attack, and by my word, we shall prevail!"

✹ ✹

I hold the strappings of his great chestnut beast. "My lord."

He leans down from the saddle. "How is the future emperor of Mexico?"

I put a hand to my belly. The bleeding was heavy that night on the causeway, but now it has stopped. Just now he heard his father's speech to his soldiers, and I thought I felt him move. "He is well, my lord."

He removes the leather gauntlet from his hand, touches my cheek. "Stay inside the square of our defense. All will be well."

"Do not let them harm you."

"We will sit together in the palace of Tenochtitlán. I swear it." And then, a sweet kiss. "My love." He smiles and spurs his horse forward. The rest of his Thunder Lords follow; the brass trappings jangle, the great beasts snorting and stamping, sensing the fear and excitement in the air around them.

We will never sit in the palace. Even gods may die, and today the odds against us are too heavy. You will die on this field of flowers, and I will die with you. We have tested the gods too far with our pride and arrogance.

But I will never regret it. For I have found my Feathered Serpent and followed my destiny, and if I were given my time over, I would do it all the same.

My father's prophecies will not be fulfilled, but I have at least avenged him, and I can hold my head high when I join him in the place of the spirits.

 **96**

BENÍTEZ FORCED HIMSELF into the saddle. Every muscle in his body ached. He had received a slash with a lance the night of the retreat—the *noche triste,* the sad night, as Cortés now called it—which had opened his cheek to the bone, and now his face felt as if it were on fire; two days before an arrow had lodged in his calf, and he could barely move his right leg. He had not eaten for days, and he feared he might faint from his horse. But he was determined that the Indians would not take him alive, would not stretch him over their infernal stones. He would fight to the end.

"We will charge in squadrons of five," Cortés shouted. "Keep your lances high, aim for the eyes, and return at a gallop. Ignore the common warriors; aim only for the officers, the ones with head-dresses in the form of birds of prey or of tigers. Better even than these, kill those with plumes and nose jewels and wicker standards, for they are the generals."

And then he said to his officers what he had not dared say to his men: "If we are to die, better to die proudly. May God be with you all."

✳   ✳

The battle went on, hand to hand, for hours. Young Mexica warriors with obsidian-bladed clubs, intent on glory and capture, were thrown against squadrons of well-drilled Spanish pikemen who fought as units and slaughtered them in their thousands. The Spaniards' lurchers and mastiffs, already demented with hunger, took a terrible toll of the Indians. Hundreds of Mexica died for every Spaniard.

But gradually the weight of numbers began to tell, and by the middle of the day, the Castilians, weak from their wounds and from starvation, were at the point of exhaustion.

Their lines began to waver. The Mexica pressed on.

MALINALI

"Here. Take this dirk." Jaramillo reaches into the scabbard at his waist and presses a dagger into my hand. He was pierced through the thigh with a lance during the *noche triste* and now lies with the other wounded inside the defensive square. The Mexica howl and whistle as they throw themselves against the thin line of pikemen, all that lies now between them and us.

"My lord?"

"I do not wish them to take me alive. I am not having my blood spilled in their bestial temples!" His hands are shaking. "I have seen your dexterity with this weapon. I just ask that you make the end a little cleaner and a little quicker than it was for my lord Motecuhzoma."

I hold the knife, bewildered. A man should not fear the flowery death on the battlefield or on the stone. But to die at the hands of a woman?

Jaramillo lifts his shirt, grasps the hilt of the dagger, and pulls it toward him, so that the point rests against the skin above his heart. "Do it!"

I shake my head.

"Why do you wait?"

"No!" Strong fingers close around my wrist and try to wrest the knife away from me. It is Aguilar. "You must not! He will burn forever in the fires of hell!"

"Only if I die by my own hand!" Jaramillo shouts.

"The intention is the same." Aguilar seems calm. A gold cross hangs about his neck now—my lord had forced the Mixtec jewelers of Tenochtitlán to produce these for him from smelted gold, at Fray Olmedo's request—and he clutches it now in the same manner that he once held his book of prayers. He falls to his knees. "Let us pray to God to give you strength for the end."

Jaramillo pushes him away. "I don't want your prayers!" He turns back to me. "Do it now! Do it now, you demon cunt! Let me die quickly!" His voice is shrill, like a woman's.

Aguilar again tries to snatch the knife away. "He will lose his mortal soul!"

Oh, these men are not worthy of Feathered Serpent. How did he come so far with such cowards and fools?

The battle is all around us now, the screams of men as they meet the flowery death, the din of whistling and drums. I bring the knife down. The blade pierces the earth to the hilt, a few inches from Jaramillo's head.

He starts to cry.

"You have saved his soul," Aguilar tells me.

"No, Aguilar. I just do not believe my lord will lose."

 **97**

I AM DEFEATED, Cortés thought.

Even as he broke his charge, he knew he had disobeyed his own instruction, had ridden too far from his own lines. Fatigue had blurred his concentration. The Mexica had run from his charge, but now, as he wheeled his horse, they ran back to encircle him. They could have killed him easily with their clubs and lances, but none of them dared spill his blood because Lord Malinche belonged to Hummingbird.

He slashed wildly with his sword, chopping at the hands that tried to hold him, cutting the nooses of the snarers. But there were too many of them, and he was dragged from the saddle. He hit the ground hard, and the breath went out of him.

He heard the thunder of hooves, saw Benítez and Sandoval charging through the Indian ranks. Three others joined them: Olid, Alvarado, and Juan de Salamanca. Cortés jumped back to his feet and regained his mount.

I cannot die, Cortés thought. God has chosen me for a destiny. He has kept me alive, even now, for a purpose.

It was then he saw her, in the clouds above the hill. Her smile was serene, her face pale, yet shimmering with some inner luminescence. She stretched out her hand toward him, and the east wind whipped the folds of her purple robe.

Nuestra Señora de los Remedios.

Below her, on a grassy knoll, he saw the royal litter, shaded by a golden canopy, and reclining on it a great lord with an elaborate wicker standard strapped to his back by a shoulder harness. The towering basketwork emblem was worked with rich feathers into the insignia of the Woman Snake and decorated with gemstones and gold. The lord who carried it wore a great headdress of quetzal plumes, and his ears and nose and arms flashed with gold ornaments.

It was their chief general. Cortés realized his rash charge had brought him to within a hundred yards, with just a handful of Mexican warriors between them. He remembered the first battle with the Tlaxcalans and what Malinali had told him then: *When they lose their commander, they lose heart.*

"We must move back before they encircle us again!" Benítez shouted.

"No! We go there!" He pointed toward the knoll. "The Virgin points the way! Kill their chiefs and we are victors!"

He spurred his horse up the slope, slashing a path through the ragged lines of Mexica. The Virgin beckoned, the promise of victory in her mother's outstretched arms.

✳ ✳

Cortés galloped toward the golden canopy. He was just a hundred paces away when the generals saw his intention, and he read the confusion and dismay in their faces. There was nothing they could do to stop him. He rode straight at Woman Snake, struck him with his horse, the elaborate wicker standard smashing under the hooves of his mare. Cortés wheeled around, saw the general stagger to his feet, bleeding and dragging his leg. Juan de Salamanca, charging in behind, drove his lance through his chest, driving him off his feet. Benítez, Olid, Sandoval, and Alvarado scattered the rest of his captains and advisers with their swords.

Cortés reached down from his horse and picked up the shattered wicker standard. He held it aloft in his fist. At once there was a bedlam of whistles and drums.

He watched in amazement as the Mexica began to withdraw, melting away across the plains, a tide turning from his feet, as if he had commanded the very ocean to retreat. A miracle. Our Lady had brought him a miracle.

Cortés let his sword hang limp at his side.

It was over. He had won.

PART IV

SPIRITUS SANCTUS

If there's Spaniards in Heaven,

I don't want to go there.

—RESPONSE OF HATUEY, CHIEF OF THE CUBAN
INDIANS, ON BEING OFFERED THE LAST RITES
BEFORE BEING BURNED AT THE STAKE

MALINALI

Tenochtitlán, August 1521

"I NEVER WANTED this."

A tent with a crimson canopy has been erected on the rooftop of a Tlatelolco palace. It overlooks the last enclave of the Mexica. *Tonatiuh*'s men are making a final sweep of the city. Still the defenders hold out, although now their only means of resistance is to hurl stones on the Castilians from the roofs of the few remaining houses.

The city lies in ruins now. The soldiers have destroyed everything, toppled statues, smashed down the adobe walls of the palaces, torching thatch, burning temples.

My lord's orders.

Feathered Serpent's victory has a bitter taste: *If I cannot have the city as it was, then I shall destroy every last stone of it*. Tenochtitlán was the most beautiful city I have ever seen. Soon it will be gone.

"I never wanted this," he whispers again, as if he is trying to convince himself.

Only a genius or a madman, Benítez had said, would dream of building a navy in a landlocked valley. But Martín López, once he had recovered from his wounds, had set about this very task, at my lord's urging. He salvaged iron and sheet from San Juan de Ulúa and shaped twelve great canoes from freshly cut timber. Eight thousand porters carried my lord's navy, in pieces, across the *sierra* to the shores of Lake Texcoco.

And such ships they were, each of them the length of twenty ordinary canoes. They captured the Serpent's wind in canvas cloaks, and each had a single iron serpent at its prow. With these great canoes, and the soldiers who joined us from the Cloud Lands, we laid siege to Tenochtitlán, exactly as my lord had said that we would. Tens of thousands of warriors from surrounding provinces rushed to join us, eager to participate in the destruction of the Mexica.

Inside the city another weapon did its work: the Thunder Lords called it "smallpox," a terrible magic that left thousands of black bodies rotting in the streets. It was Feathered Serpent's revenge on the Mexica.

"I had no other choice. To save this city, I had to destroy it. Do you understand?"

What can I say to him? From my vantage point here on the roof, I can see *Tonatiuh's* men enter the Tlatelolco quarter, his soldiers like ants swarming up the temple pyramid. My head aches from the dust-stench of falling masonry and the acrid stink of smoke from the burning buildings. The air crackles to the sound of the thunder sticks; I can hear the shrill screams of those trapped under buildings, the whistles and drums of these last defiant Mexica. These are the hymns of Motecuhzoma's city as it dies.

"You know my heart, Malinali. I never wanted this."

I cannot answer him.

"These Mexica are determined to die. But how else can we establish our authority here? I did not want to destroy them, I did not want to destroy this city. I had no choice."

My father was right. I have found my destiny in destruction, and I have brought chaos and the end of the fifth sun. I wonder I do not feel more proud.

One of the new Thunder Lords, his clothes covered in dust, appears on the roof, panting for breath. "Good news, *caudillo*," he gasps. "We have captured Falling Eagle."

✳   ✳

My lord is seated in a chair on the terrace of the Face of the Water Lord palace, or what remains of it. He wears a suit of black velvet and a cap with green plumes, to imitate the quetzal feathers of the Mexica emperors, who wore them as symbols of divine rule. Falling Eagle stands in front of us, his wrists and ankles in chains. He wears the helmet of an Eagle Knight, with silver-gray feathered leggings and cloak. García Holquin, his captor, stands behind him, two Tlaxcalan warriors as guard.

I wonder about this Falling Eagle. Here is the man who taunted Motecuhzoma for being unable to die. Perhaps he himself found it was not so easy.

I am struck by the silence. For ninety-three days we have lived with the sounds of battle: the screams, the whistles, the drumming of the *teponaztli* from the pyramids, the crash of falling masonry. The very moment of Falling Eagle's capture, it had ceased. Now the silence almost hurts my ears.

Falling Eagle murmurs something so softly I can hardly hear him.

"What does he say?" my lord asks me.

"He asks if he may have your knife."

"My knife?"

"He wishes to kill himself. He says he has fought you as hard as he can, and now he has failed, he wishes only for death."

"You must tell him, my lady, that he must not blame himself, for he has acquitted himself with great valor." He smiles, but I know his heart in this, and it is not the same as his words. In truth he would like to rip out Falling Eagle's vitals for not surrendering Tenochtitlán to him intact. "Tell him I am his friend, and from this time on, I shall treat him as I would my own brother. I will personally guarantee his safety."

I relay this to Falling Eagle, but I know he does not believe it either.

"Now I would like you to ask him what happened to the gold that was left on the causeway during the *noche triste*."

I put this question to Falling Eagle, who stares back at me down his beak of a nose. "Tell Lord Malinche it is all gone. It vanished in the mud of the lake or disappeared under the rubble when his band of thieves burned our city. All that is left of our treasure was in my canoe when they took me captive."

"He will never believe that."

"I do not care what he chooses to believe. You are a prostitute, and he is a thief and a murderer. Why should I answer to you?"

I pass on his answer but omit these final insults. Despite his contempt for me—perhaps because of it—I find that I somehow admire him.

My lord's fingers are claws around the arms of his chair. "What we found in his canoe was some gold helmets and a few armbands. That cannot be all."

"It is all his thieves left us when they departed Tenochtitlán," Falling Eagle answers.

I see the familiar knot of a vein at his temple. "Ask him where he hid my treasure!"

"He is very angry," I tell Falling Eagle. "He demands to know where you have hidden his gold."

"*His* gold?" Falling Eagle shakes his head. "All *our* treasure disappeared beneath the mud of the lake the night you fled like dogs from our city."

I lean close to my lord's ear. "My lord, he insists it was lost during the *noche triste*."

He smiles, and this is unexpected. He gets slowly to his feet, takes two steps toward Falling Eagle, and embraces him. "Tell him we shall not worry over such matters now. Everything that has passed between us formerly must be forgotten. The dark hour is gone. I want him to think of me from this moment on as his friend."

His friendship falls upon Falling Eagle like a curse. I shudder for him.

 98

BENÍTEZ TIED A cloth around his mouth and nose and tried not to breathe too deeply or look too hard at the bodies lying in the streets or floating in the canals. Some were victims not of Spanish or Tlaxcalan lances but of hunger or disease and had been there a very long time. He could not imagine their sufferings. The ground had been broken up where the starving Mexicans had tried to find roots to eat. Even the bark was missing from the trees.

Those still living were huddled on the ground with the dead. Mexica warriors, their wounds rotting, lay silently waiting for death, and none of them cried out for mercy. They appeared indifferent to the killing blows that ended their torments. As in Cholula, their Tlaxcalan allies took revenge on the women and the children and the old.

The great city of towers and palaces was a smoldering ruin, reeking of blood and corpse fires. Rain hissed on burning timbers; smoke trailed into a limp gray sky.

A line of wraiths filed along the causeways, mostly women and children, the few who had escaped the massacres, sacks of bones in ragged loincloths.

He felt a tightness in his belly, appalled at himself, at his fellows. *What have we done? We came here to serve God and serve ourselves. How far did we take that commission? Here was a city, greater than Sevilla, greater perhaps than Rome or Constantinople, and we have laid it to waste. Norte was right. Who, truly, are the heathens in this land?*

He watched a group of soldiers pull a woman from the line of refugees. A rumor had been circulating in the Spanish camp that the Mexican women were hiding gold in their most private places. The *conquistadores* had taken it upon themselves to search for it when and wherever they fancied.

There were three of them, officers, and they were all drunk. Two of them were men who had arrived only recently from the coast. Benítez recognized only one of them: Jaramillo.

"There's more than one place to hide gold," Jaramillo shouted, laughing, and threw the woman to the ground. He started to tear at her tunic. "Let's see what she has in her vault."

For the sacred pity of God, Benítez thought. *She is no more than a pile of bones. How can you desire such a creature? What pleasure could you get from tormenting her further?* Rage overtook him.

"Leave her," he shouted. "Leave her!" The rasp of steel as he drew his sword from its scabbard was unmistakable warning, and Jaramillo looked up, alarmed.

"Benítez?"

"Leave her alone!"

The officers with him stopped grinning and put their hands on their swords.

Jaramillo seemed to relax. "Stop carping, Benítez. I am sure her vault is large enough to accommodate us all."

"I want none of it. Find your sport somewhere else."

He tilted the blade in front of Jaramillo's face. He watched his former comrade make his calculation, looking first at Benítez and then at his companions. Benítez knew what he was thinking.

"If you wish to try your luck against a former planter, you may," Benítez said. "But I remind you that I have a little more experience with a sword than I once did. Thanks to Cortés, I am accustomed to fighting against the odds. I do not know how good your friends are at swordplay, but let me tell you this: you will see your guts on the ground, regardless of what follows."

Jaramillo shook his head. "You are a fool, Benítez. Little wonder you lost the favor of the *caudillo*." But he decided against a fight, as Benítez knew he would. He nodded to his companions, who moved their hands away from their swords. He stood up, gave Benítez a last contemptuous glance, and walked away. *Plenty more Mexica women to toy with, and Benítez cannot follow us all day.*

Benítez sheathed his sword, wondering what he had achieved. He looked down at the ragged pile of skin and bones at his feet: matted hair, haunted eyes, a terrible stink coming from her. Poor wretch.

Then he realized with shock that he knew her.

A soft groan escaped his lips. He bent down, felt as if he had been stabbed in the chest.

"Rain Flower," he murmured, in the *Náhuatl* that Malinali had taught him in Tlaxcala.

He lifted her easily and carried her back along the causeway. He saw soldiers grinning at him. *An easy way to secure a bride for the night,* they were thinking.

They don't understand, Benítez thought. I am not like them; I never was like them. It is why I mourn the death of this wondrous city and the end of our proud and savage enemy. What I hold in my arms is not a bride for tonight but a bride for life if my God and hers wills that she lives. In the end what they see here is not a Spaniard and a Christian gentleman, like themselves, but a renegade—a renegade like Gonzalo Norte.

MALINALI

Coyoacán, the Place of the Wolf

THEY HAVE TIED Falling Eagle to a rack and basted his feet in oil. When they bring the white-hot brands close, I can hear the skin crackle and burn. The stench of burning flesh makes me sick to my stomach. Yet he makes no sound.

The only solace is that my lord has not ordered or approved this. At least he tried to keep his word.

But oh, God, the smell of charred meat.

The one called Alderete strokes his beard. He has a long and narrow face, as solemn as a priest's. He has requested my presence should Falling Eagle break and wish to reveal where the gold is hidden. He nods to the torturer, who applies a little more oil to his victim's feet and retrieves the brand from the glowing coals.

"Ask him again if he has clearer recollection of what happened to the gold that was lost on the *noche triste*," Alderete says.

A tiny blue flame licks along the poor man's soles as the oil ignites. Sweat beads down his face, and his chest heaves. His eyes roll back in his head, and his muscles twist like whipcord against the pain. He makes a sound deep in his chest, a sound I have heard many times since that day at Ceutla, the kind of sound a man makes as he gives up the spirit and swallows the earth. But he is not yet ready to meet the shadow. Death is not that kind.

I repeat Alderete's question, and Falling Eagle turns his face toward me, his eyes burning with pain and hate. "Tell him...may his wife grow teeth in her place of pleasure...and may all his children drown in dog shit."

"What did he say?" Alderete asks me.

"He swears his innocence and calls on the Virgin to intercede on his behalf."

Cristóbal de Ojeda, the doctor, examines the wounds. Blackened skin hangs in strips, like bark, revealing glistening white bone. Ojeda looks at Alderete and shakes his head. The king's treasurer bites his lip. I believe it is of small consequence to him if Falling Eagle never walks again, but he is, after all, under my lord's protection.

Falling Eagle is staring at me. "You betrayed...your own people."

"You are not my people."

"They have made you...a Spaniard, then? Will they claim you...as one of theirs?"

"What is he saying?"

"He repeats that everything left of our treasure was found that day in the royal barge. The rest lies in the mud of Texcoco. He asks why you persist in torturing him when he has answered all your questions as best he can."

"I am not without compassion. If men would only give up the truth more freely, there would be no need for this."

I turn my eyes away so I do not have to watch as Alderete continues his lonely quest for veracity. The pine torches throw terrible shadows on the stone walls of the cell. I wish Falling Eagle would tell them what they want to know. After all, what does it matter now?

This is not the world I imagined Feathered Serpent would bring, not the magical kingdom of Tollán I dreamed of as a child.

✻ ✻

What has happened to us since Otumba? I wonder as I hurry across the plaza. If that day had ended differently, I would not be wearing this fine dress of black lace, with a mantilla covering my face, a fan of mother-of-pearl in my right hand; I would not be the consort of the most powerful man in New Spain. I would also not be required to listen to the screams of tortured men or watch my dreams crumble to dust before my eyes.

The white adobe walls of the palace at Coyoacán loom ahead. They have proved an excellent surface for the messages of the graffitists. Someone has scrawled across one of the walls, in black paint:

MORE WERE CONQUERED BY CORTÉS THAN BY MEXICO.

Even the heroes of Otumba are in revolt over the profits from their sacred expedition. When they did not find their pockets bulging with gold, they blamed the treasurer, Mejía, who in turn had blamed my lord Cortés. Rumors spread that he had taken out a second *quinto* for himself, that he had retained many pieces of worked gold his men thought had been forwarded under their names to the king.

For his own part, my lord claimed that it was the fault of Falling Eagle, that he had hidden much of the gold from them. He protested that all had been done in accordance with the law, that he had behaved properly at all times. But he lives in a palace and eats his food from golden plates and has a retinue of servants to attend him. They have won for themselves no more than the price of a new sword. Why should they not wonder at the justice of it?

As for Tenochtitlán, the carrion birds were still gathering overhead when the rebuilding got under way. Falling Eagle was forced to order his people back to the capital to bury the dead and start work on the new shrine to the god *Cristo* rising over the site of the *Templo Mayor*. My lord built himself a new palace on the site of Motecuhzoma's former seat, using thousands of felled cedars from the surrounding forests. Even the canals were filled with stone salvaged from the ruins, so that no other conqueror could isolate the capital as we had done. The Mexica are bent at their work every daylight hour, carrying stones and earth under the lashes of the Thunder Lords, and many are dying of starvation and disease.

The priests have ordered that all the Mexica's codices and statuary be burned or broken with hammers. Brother Aguilar has been especially active in these endeavors.

If Feathered Serpent were to return to the valley, I do not think he would recognize it.

※ ※

My lord sits at his desk, quill in hand. He wears a suit of black silk trimmed with white lace, there is a thick rope of gold at his throat, and an emerald flashes on his finger. His attendants are gathered about him, and armed soldiers guard the doors. Mexican servants await his pleasure. His moles go with him everywhere, and when he passes in the street, all *naturales* must prostrate ourselves on the ground, as once we did for Motecuhzoma.

I am ushered into the room, and my lord dismisses his retinue with a nod. I recognize only Benítez; he is accompanied by a fine Christian gentlewoman in a black mantilla veil. This woman has an Indian's eyes, and our glances meet and secretly caress. It is Rain Flower, saved from the holocaust. Her Spaniard is here to obtain my lord's permission for the marriage. There are many such marriages now, for there is a shortage of delicate Spanish brides in the new colony. I do not think Benítez wants her for the sake of convenience, though. After the city fell, he sat by her bedside day and night for two weeks, feeding her back to health by his own hand. I know it is true, for I was there, and I watched him do it.

As she leaves the room, our fingers touch lightly for a moment. But then the door closes, and my lord and I are left alone, only the servants standing mute against the walls.

"I take it, as you are here, that Alderete has finished his interrogation."

"Indeed, my lord. They are bandaging Falling Eagle's feet as we speak."

"Did he answer the *señor's* questions to his satisfaction?"

"He gave him the same answer he gave you, my lord."

A frown. "I told him it was useless. He would not listen to me. Well, so be it. I am tired of distracting them from their greed. Let them wallow in it if they must. God will decide the justice of it."

"You gave your word to Falling Eagle. You told him he was under your protection."

He looks up, his eyebrows sharply raised. "My lady?"

"As I was leaving, I heard one of the guards say that it was you who ordered the torture, not Alderete."

"Do you think to interrogate me on this matter?"

"I ask you only to give me the truth."

"I gave you the truth. It was Alderete's decision, not mine. Let us leave the matter there."

"But you gave your word to Falling Eagle!"

He lays his quill aside and stands up. He puts his hands behind his back and walks to the window. "We all have bright and shining dreams, Mali. Those who are blessed by God never see their dreams come true. Somehow they lose their luster in the living of them."

I put my hand to my belly, feel the babe kick. Our first son, the gift I had so wanted to give him, had died stillborn in Tlaxcala. I wonder what throne will be prepared for this new son. "I have loved you, my lord, more than it is possible for a woman to love a man."

He turns to me, and I wonder what moves behind his eyes, for today they are as gray and cold as winter. His presence is forbidding, even here, when he stands at ease and unarmed. It is hot in the room, and from outside I hear the ring of a stone-mason's hammer, building a new Spain. "I know you have, Mali. I know you have."

We stare at each other, naked in our ambitions and weakness, and this is how I will remember him best. He has made me a lady of New Spain; I have made him the conqueror of Mexico. I do not see the end in his eyes, but I do see the beginning of it. We have traveled together to the top of the high mountain, elevated ourselves for our own sakes. But now the pinnacle is attained, and although we shall talk often about our journey in the days to come, I can see it in his face, in that moment, in that room, the end of our travails together.

He was not Feathered Serpent after all. The future my father saw in the stars was skewed in the sky's terrible mirror; the chaos and destruction he foretold were intended not for the Mexica alone. I have fulfilled my destiny, and it will haunt me now for all eternity.

The god in him has departed, leaving behind the man. I should hate him for what he has brought me to, but I love him too much.

✹　✹

And so tonight I walk the streets, dressed in the rags of an Indian, crying for my lost children: the dirty streets, the ancient streets, the streets of the homeless and the dispossessed.

The city of Motecuhzoma chokes now on its own dust and fumes; the *chinampas* are buried, the temples are just a few ancient and crumbling stones, the centuries have buried Hummingbird on the Left forever. Time has even buried the Spanish.

Feathered Serpent now guards the metro station at Piño Suárez, and the Mexica warriors in the plaza dance only for the tourists' copper coins.

Not far from here is the Church of Jesús Nazareño, and I wander inside, to sit there in the quiet, another weeping woman, praying for myself, praying for my family, praying for Mexico. He is buried here, my lord, my great lord, fifty years left in peace now, though you would have to look hard to see where they put him, just a few scratchings up on the wall by the altar there. That's how much the priests think of him now.

He crumbles to dust in the place where he first met Motecuhzoma, for the church is built on the causeway, or at least where the causeway once stood. Outside, the city dies in its own sulfurous haze; you will not find much beauty there now. I stay here until the priest will no longer tolerate this crazy woman and the church is shut up for the night. I leave my lord there to molder and return to my weeping streets, my tormented city, my Mexico.

Like a comet in the black sky, my life flared and soared, dragging portent and disaster across the firmament. Now I fall through the vacuum of these endless cold and silent days, cursed and cursing wherever I go.

EPILOGUE

MALINALI TENEPAL WAS only one of a large number of women living under Cortés's roof when his wife arrived in July of 1522. Doña Catalina de Cortés, however, fared much worse than the others. Four months later she was found dead in her bedroom. The doctor attributed the death to natural causes, but no one was allowed to see the body, and the lid of the coffin was nailed down before it was buried.

Cortés rewarded Malinali for her service to him by giving her in marriage to one of his officers, Juan Jaramillo.

He continued to serve as governor of the land he called New Spain, waiting for the king's official elevation of his position to viceroy. He became extremely wealthy, the Crown granting him gold and silver mines, cotton and sugar plantations, mills and grazing lands. He built a turreted palace in Cuernavaca and was given the title of marquis. It was his pleasure to be called Don Hernando.

But in 1526 the king's commissar arrived from Spain to examine accusations of misconduct during his *entrada* five years before, including charges of murder and defrauding the Crown. Cortés was never convicted on any of these charges, but the proceedings damaged his reputation beyond repair. Consequently he never did receive the imprimatur from the king for which he so longed. The administration of the country was instead turned over to bureaucrats from the court in Toledo.

Despite the opprobrium that surrounded Cortés, his fame brought him a marriage to Juana de Zuñiga, a relative of the Duke of Bejar, one of the most powerful men in Spain. Juana brought with her a substantial dowry, which gave Cortés for a short time the respectability and the courtly connections of which he had always dreamed.

But the scandals of the past dogged the rest of his career.

Restless and tormented, he spent the remainder of his life searching for another Mexico, another Motecuhzoma. He squandered much of his wife's dowry in a futile quest for the legendary Amazons and passed his last years in Spain trying to solicit an audience with the king. He became an embarrassment, an old man buttonholing minor functionaries with petitions regarding the wrongs, real and imagined, that had been done him. Finally, realizing he would never receive the regal blessing for which he so longed, he decided to return to his beloved Mexico. He fell ill just days before he had planned to sail and died suddenly, an embittered and lonely man. He was sixty-two years old.

In a footnote of history, his son by Malinali Tenepal, Martín, was implicated in New Spain in 1565 in a conspiracy against the Crown. Accused of treason, he was subjected to torture and then exiled from Mexico.

The gold lost on the *noche triste* was never found; it may still lie somewhere under the streets of Mexico City.

No one will ever know.

> *It is not true, it is not true*
> *that we come on this earth to live*
> *we come only to sleep, only to dream*

—ANCIENT AZTEC POEM,
BASED ON A SPANISH TRANSLATION
BY MIGUEL LEÓN-PORTILLA

 *Glossary*

adobe	sun-dried brick made of clay
alcalde	Spanish term for mayor
burgonet	helmet with a low collar at the back to protect the neck
cacique	village chieftain
camarada	servant-concubine
Castile	one of the two great kingdoms of what is now Spain
caudillo	captain
chacmool	stone figure representing a messenger between men and the gods
Chontal Maya	language spoken by the Mayan Indians
culverin	large bronze cannon capable of firing a ball of between eighteen and thirty pounds
encomienda	grant of land
entrada	invasion of a previously unexplored land
Extremadura	province of Castile, in southwest Spain
falconet	wrought-iron cannon, smaller than a culverin, capable of firing balls of two to three pounds
grandee	lord
harquebus	musket steadied on a supporting metal rod for firing
hidalgo	landed gentleman of Castile
huehuetl	drum made from a hollowed log, often bearing carvings of eagles and jaguars
jinetas	Spanish horsemen riding *a la jineta,* with stirrups very high
labret	ornament inserted into a hole pierced in the lip

maguey	species of cactus plant
maquauhuitl	war club; also means "penis" in *Náhuatl* slang
maravedí	unit of currency; in 1519, 450 *maravedíes* equaled 1 crown or peso
Náhuatl	the "elegant speech" of the Mexica
nao	large Spanish galleon
naturales	Castilian term for indigenous peoples
noche triste	literally "sad night"; term Cortés used for the night on which he and his party retreated from Tenochtitlán
peyotl	white trufflelike cactus, which causes hallucinations when taken powdered in water
pulque	alcoholic liquor distilled from a cactus plant
puta	prostitute
quetzal	indigenous bird with startlingly green plumage, highly valued among the Mexica
teponaztli	snakeskin drum
teules	gods
Toltecs	race of people, once preeminent, that lived in the valley of Mexico some five hundred years before Cortés arrived at Yucatán
ypcalli	low wooden throne

FEATHERED
SERPENT

Colin Falconer

READER'S GUIDE

For Discussion

1. When we first meet Norte, he's considered by his companions "a plague carrier, incubus of a contagion worse than any
black-blistered pestilence known. . ." What is this contagion? In
what ways do the Spaniards' attitudes toward him change in
the course of the novel? Does Norte himself evolve, and if so,
is it for better or worse? Why does he bother to carefully
explain Indian battle tactics to the Spaniards who have treated
him so poorly?

2. Malinali's father described Feathered Serpent like this: "He
was very wise and so gentle he would not kill any living creature or even pick a flower from the ground. He taught his people the art of healing and how to watch the stars move around
the sky." Yet Malinali is most enthralled with Cortés whenever
he is enraged or on the brink of violent warfare. How is it that
she believes this vicious warrior is her gentle god?

3. Benítez and Norte constantly clash over the notion of bar-
barism. Benítez finds cannibalism and human sacrifice utterly
intolerable, while Norte argues that warfare in the name of the
Christian god is equally barbaric—and perhaps more so, since
it seems inextricably linked to the quest for gold. Do you think
Falconer is promoting a political opinion here? If so, is it one
that can be translated into a modern setting?

4. When Malinali asks herself, "And if a god may find his way
inside a man, could the divine not also find a warm place inside
the heart of a living woman?" is she musing about the Virgin

Mary, to whom Cortés has just dedicated a shrine, or is she referring to herself? Do you think Malinali is motivated by a desire for personal glory or does she truly see herself as Cortés's servant?

5. Cortés is a master of manipulation who gets people to do his will by removing all other options. Where can you find examples of this tactic?

6. Who is Smoking Mirror? Why is Motecuhzoma convinced that Cortés is Smoking Mirror? Why is Malinali convinced that Aguilar is Smoking Mirror? If we define Smoking Mirror as any powerful force of confusion and obscurity, could you argue that Malinali's father is perhaps the real Smoking Mirror in the novel?

7. Of Cortés, Malinali, Benítez, and Norte, whom do you consider the most tragic? The most misguided? The most victimized? The most righteous? With whom do you identify the most?

8. Why does Malinali call Rain Flower "the nagging doubt, the thorn pressed into the sandal, the mosquito whining in the darkness, disallowing all rest"?

9. Motecuhzoma forecasts that Cortés will betray Malinali. Why does she listen to him, when she considers him both a pathetic fool and her enemy? What do Motecuhzoma and Malinali have in common?

10. Benítez is a smart man, a peace-lover, and the classic good guy trying to act tough in a war situation he finds terrifying. He recognizes Cortés's weaknesses and his corrupt nature, yet he can't help celebrating Cortés the mighty conqueror: "Today this cheat, this schemer, this thief, has made me more than I am, and I will always be grateful." How do you explain

this dichotomy? When does Benítez prove to Norte that he (Benítez) is a just man?

11. Throughout the novel, Malinali skews the translations between the Spaniards and the natives, both to make culturally incomprehensible ideas palatable to each side, and to further her own agenda. Discuss the use of skewed translation as a primary theme of *Feathered Serpent*, particularly in the areas of religion and history.

12. When Malinali single-handedly instigates the massacre of the Cholulans, she feels for the first time the "burden of the dead" as a "crushing weight" on her chest. It's only after this that she admits to herself, "Without his protection, I am a heart roasting in a brazier; without the means to realize my father's promise, I have nothing to live for." What frightens her more: her ability to cause mayhem, or the possibility that she'll end up tending a hearth like a common woman? How has she survived this long without realizing the human cost inherent in her plan?

13. What do you make of the provocative quotes at the beginning of sections three and four: "The Pope must have been drunk" and "If there's Spaniards in heaven, I don't want to go there"?

14. Of sleeping with Cortés, Malinali says, "I entwine with my god, my destiny won." It seems significant that she uses the word "won" rather than "fulfilled"; throughout the book, she struggles to forcibly shape her destiny or to "win" it through hard work. How does this attitude toward destiny differ from the typical one?

About the Author

COLIN FALCONER is the author of *When We Were Gods* and three other historical novels, which have been published in many languages throughout the world. A former journalist and native of London, he now lives with his family in western Australia.

Also by Colin Falconer

COLIN FALCONER takes us inside the walls of ancient Alexandria's great palaces and into Cleopatra's very heart, creating a vivid portrait of an unforgettable woman who thrived and triumphed in a world ruled by men.

"Spectacular historical fiction blazing with intrigue, romance, and dramatic action. The author interweaves the fast-paced narrative with authentic period details that vivify the exotic splendor of ancient Egypt. . . . An enthralling fictional portrait of one of the most powerful and beguiling women of all ages."
—BOOKLIST

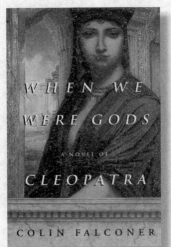

0-609-80889-3
$12.95 paperback (Canada: $19.95)

THREE RIVERS PRESS
NEW YORK

WHEREVER BOOKS ARE SOLD
WWW.CROWNPUBLISHING.COM